Libertas Americana

THE AMERICAN AMARANTH ANTHOLOGY

J. R. ORTIZ

ISBN: 0615645216
ISBN 13: 9780615645216

Library of Congress Control Number: 2012909153
J. R.\Ortiz, Miami, Florida

For My Sons

Contents

Maps provided through the courtesy of public domain maps at
the University of Texas Libraries

Medal photographed by my brother, Rafael G. Ortiz MD

Maps

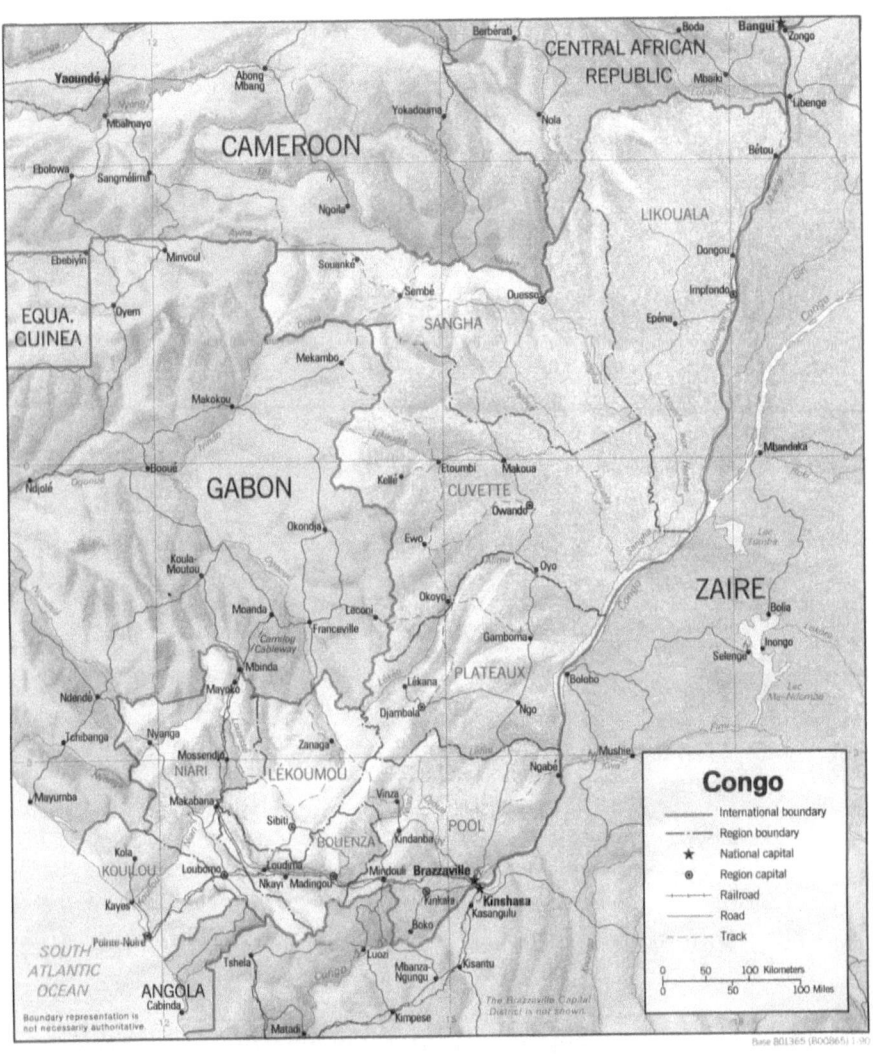

Congo Lands

Commonwealth of Independent States - European States

Black Sea, the Ukraine, and the Crimea

Central Balkan Region

Central Balkans

Central Europe

Central Europe

Germany

Libertas Americana Medal

Obverse

Reverse
Medal photographed by my brother, Rafael G. Ortiz MD

Preface

Of all the complex creatures in the animal kingdom living on planet Earth, human beings are the only ones with a conscious mind. When mature, the human mind realizes its own mortality. We must all eventually accept that one day, we die.

In undertaking many of life's duties, people are sometimes asked to risk their lives in the process of attaining a specific critical social goal. Courage comes from proceeding with these tasks, knowing fully well that one may expire in the process. As Aristotle once said, "Courage is the greatest quality of the mind next to honor."

In Homer's classic Greek epic poetry, the heroes were dramatically idealized to the extreme with respect to their courage. However, they remained mortal. Courage in an individual or character is not perceived if the subject is not mortal. A champion's courage is measured by his actions when knowing, and still accepting thoroughly, their dangerous potential consequences to life. A hero is what he is only when he perceives his own mortality.

Human history is composed from the acts of courageous valor and honorable sacrifice which have been required in man's eternal struggle for freedom. The instinctual need and drive to live free has literally written the "Epic of Man". However, a steady state equilibrium in the freedom of man has never been attained in the several thousand year history of "civilized" mankind. It appears that freedom, like life itself, is fleeting and not eternal. Nevertheless, human beings continue to strive and die for it.

In the early decades of the twenty-first century, America experienced the horrors of the 9/11 terror attacks and the subsequent "Global War on Terrorism". Years of fighting in Afghanistan and Iraq had bled America dry - economically, politically, and socially. The "Great Economic Collapse" of 2008 and the subsequent European Union meltdown led to the instability and fall of governments around the world. Numerous trade and shooting wars evolved from the chaos. Arab revolutions in North Africa and the Middle East eventuated in the final cultural poisoning of relations with the United States. The rise of nuclear terror regimes in Iran and North Korea, and their support from the People's Republic of China, concluded in global war against the United States and her allies. America's victory in the world war spurred the spread of democracy throughout the Middle East, Asia, and Latin America.

Unfortunately, these years also saw the resurgence of Fascism in Central and Eastern Europe. Radical ultra-nationalist right-wing extremist movements spread like a wildfire throughout the region. Fascist ideology consumed the political process in Russia and Germany, and led these nations to form a "Friendship Alliance" against the interests of the United States. In conjunction with similar movements in other European nations, an anti-American, anti-Globalist bloc was formed to rid the continent of American influence. A complex plan of Terror against America was formulated by fascist militants and put into action.

In *Libertas Americana*, Book Two of the American Amaranth Anthology, brothers Julius and Michael Stansfield are brought together by CIA Director Joseph Mitrano in a mission to Europe to stop a terror plot destined for the American homeland. Assisted by other CIA and

US Naval Intelligence officers - and agents from France, Switzerland, Poland, and the Ukraine - the Stansfields take the reader on a high-risk odyssey along the Danube, Main, and Rhine rivers in a classic tale of "Good versus Evil".

As in Homer's idealized epic heroes - the mortal fears, strengths, and weaknesses of a diverse cast of champions are studied philosophically. The villain antagonists are also morally investigated in detail. The virtues espoused in *American Amaranth* are seen in the actions of the various individual proponents of liberty throughout the novel.

Each chapter in *Libertas Americana* is introduced by the "*Ghost of Wisdom*". The thoughts expressed are both delicate and provoking. They are made to cause the reader to sense both calm spirituality and brutal fear, distrust, and apprehension. The "*Ghost*" takes the reader to the extremes of human emotion. It is in these extremes of contemplation where you, like the characters in the novel, are torn between what should be and what often is. The thoughts reflect life's realities, whether we accept them or not. Perhaps, the "*Ghost*" is someone you knew and loved. We all have a "*Ghost of Wisdom*" inside of us.

The journey, on which you are about to embark, follows a cast of freedom fighters as they risk their lives to stop a human calamity. Their thoughts and emotions are dissected to better understand the concepts of honor, courage, hope, love, justice, and the spiritual need for liberty. It explores the human mind and all its complexities in the eternal struggle for freedom. While you course through the story, I pray the reader comes to better understand the virtues which made America in the past - the greatest land on the face of the Earth. I sincerely hope you enjoy this journey into self-discovery.

CHAPTER 1

Born in America

How would one best describe America to an unknowing first time visitor? Would the beauty of our natural wonders such as the Pacific coastline, majestic mountain ranges, and national parks capture our essence? Certainly, the awe inspired by Yosemite, Yellowstone, the Grand Canyon, and Niagara Falls would take a visitor's breath away. Or perhaps, our grand man-built structures such as the Golden Gate Bridge, Hoover Dam, national highway systems, and city skyscrapers would emotionally move the visitant. Maybe America's farmlands and abundant agricultural bounty would provide a clear description for our guest. If not these symbols of America, then possibly our great national monuments could explain the story of Lady Liberty to our visitor. Surely, our memorials of remembrance along the National Mall in Washington would arouse the affect of our guest.....

No..... Our foreigner would need to spend time living in America's small towns and communities, attend little league baseball games and Fourth of July picnics, observe religious ceremonies in our many houses of worship, participate in our electoral process, and finally, sing our National Anthem on a Memorial Day. Our visitor would quickly appreciate that America was truly "The land of the free and the home of the brave".....

America's freedoms and special characteristics have evolved over the centuries. They have been earned and reconfirmed many times since America's inception. Liberty, in all its forms, is essential to our existence as a nation.....

How could anyone want to destroy our "American Amaranth"? And how could anyone believe Americans would allow it?.....

From the deepest recesses of the opaque and obscure land of darkness flowed an effluvium of terror and doubt. A black and mysterious discharge carried evil our way.

The impenetrable rainforest of the Congo lands was shrouded by the pall and shadow of its wickedness. A diabolical secret emanated from the banks of the Ubangi. The jungles of the Congo had once again become a domain of doom. Our sense of reality was about to change; and as always, the first casualty of war would be the 'truth'.....

From the despair of hopelessness would be born a more vigorous faith in righteous freedom and justice. From the terror of evil, courage and honor would rise. From the depths of sorrowful loss, we would have a resurrection of the 'American Spirit'. We would see a rebirth of love and a stronger freedom to love. We would have again – a 'virtu-ous life'.....

But if we failed in our mission and allowed the better natures of mankind to be vanquished, the uniqueness of humanity would be washed away from our souls. We, as creative singular beings on the canvas of the earth, would lose everything. And in the extinction of our compassion and spiritual totality, we would lose ourselves for an eternity.....

"Steady, Bruno. Steady," whispered Jimmy Calhoun to the Frenchman. "Wait for the fog to finish rolling by. Be ready to shoot on my order. We may have only a few seconds to act, Bruno. You must be on target."

The Ubangi River flows lazily through the Congo rainforest. It meanders its way down from Bangui - the capital of the Central African Republic - to its confluence with the Congo River, straddling the two Congo nations. Halfway to the Congo, the Ubangi turns acutely to the east and then quickly to the south again. A basin pool at the bend of the river provides still water for human settlement. It was here that James Calhoun and Bruno Bonnet stalked their prey.

The second largest rainforest in the world, behind only the Amazon, the Likouala Swamps of the Congo basin are a mysterious land of mythical giant beasts and snakes, plagues, and cannibals. The Congo River is the largest in Africa, and has the third largest flow in the world. The Ubangi River is the Congo's largest right-bank tributary.

Huge African evergreens form a thick canopy over the tropical jungle. Red cedar, mahogany, and umbrella trees - some with trunks wider than ten feet - rise high into the equatorial sky. Little sunshine filters through to the under-story and forest floor below.

More than half the animal species of Africa live in the Congo jungle's million square miles. Hippopotamus, antelope, buffalo, elephant, and okapi live in or near the countless river tributaries and watering holes. Bush pigs and hogs fill the forest. Gorillas, chimps, and bonobos are the leading non-human primates. Giant snakes and spiders, many of them venomous, control the underbrush. The African leopard preys on all the fauna inhabitants of the Congo rainforest.

The Aka nomadic Pygmy people of the Likouala Swamps are also mythical. They live in small settlements, using a hunter-gatherer lifestyle to survive in this desperate place. Their small size allows them to move through the rainforest more efficiently and compete with all the other predators of the jungle.

The Congo basin is historically a land of ethnic violence and tribal massacres. Since the days of the Arab slave trade and the ivory conflicts, to the African civil wars of the recent past, the Congo lands have been inhospitable to modern man. In this bio-diverse tropical jungle, there is much evil and darkness. In the Congo, Darwin's theories are being played out in overdrive.

"River Raider One to River Raider Two, the fog should roll by you, Jimmy, in less than five minutes. Do you copy?" asked Tom Garfield from his hidden position on the same bank of the Ubangi, five hundred meters down-river.

"I acknowledge," said Calhoun into his radio. "Our crossfire must be accurate, Tom. None of these sons-of-bitches can get away. Don't acquire the dominant targets. Let Bruno acquire those. Stick to the peripherals if there are any left, Tom, and shoot to kill. I have no one beyond you on the southern perimeter. I'm counting on you to keep it clean."

Bruno Bonnet was lying on his belly along the upland edge of a sandy beach, south of the Ubangi's bend. The shade of the tropical canopy hid his presence. He looked through the telescopic sight of his French bolt-action sniper rifle. He steadied his gun atop a large root at the base of a cedar tree.

An apocalyptic white smoke like mist rose slowly up from the river as the springtime morning equatorial sun began to bake the region. A thicker fog rolled from the south, gradually fading into the calm blue sky to the north. Exotic birds and wild monkeys in trees screamed out their calls. The scene was alive with the struggle for survival. The evolution of combat was self-evident.

The flora competed vigorously for the rays of the sun. Each tree or strand of vine tried to strangle its neighbor as they extended themselves toward the life-giving light. The fauna - big and small - lurked behind every shadow and blade of grass, waiting to pounce on the unsuspecting. Every creature wanted to win. Losers expired and were absorbed by the earth.

"This is River Raider Three to River Raider Two. We are in position, just north of Ibutu," said Thomas Egan from the rainforest on the opposite bank of the Ubangi. "Our targets are beginning their escape from the village. They're streaming through the jungle towards their boat on the river."

"Stay where you are, Egan," ordered Calhoun. "Prepare into haz-mat and don't move until the firefight is complete. On my order, get into Ibutu quickly and get confirmation material."

The visual and auditory imageries of the Likouala Swamps were primitive and pre-historic. The smells of the jungle were organic and ancient in origins. Calhoun and Bonnet would not have been surprised if a long-necked sauropod suddenly stretched its small head out of the dark waters of the Ubangi. This was a land forgotten by time. It was dark and sinister in every aspect.

The humidity was stifling as the wind had died minutes before. Beads of sweat fell from Bonnet's face onto the cool, dark ground beneath him and his rifle. He blinked away a small bug which had crawled across his right brow and upper eyelid.

The fog had thinned out considerably. Bruno Bonnet centered a large green lizard on the far bank of the Ubangi as a target in the reticle of his scope. He took a deep breath, exhaled slowly, and emptied his lungs. He waited between heartbeats to minimize barrel motion, and pretended to pull back the trigger with the ball of his right index finger.

"*Bang. Vous etes mort,*" he whispered to himself.

"Okay, Bruno! We're in action," Calhoun said suddenly to Bonnet next to him.

The American looked intensely through his binoculars. "Pick them up from the edge of the forest, Bruno. Follow them down to the river. Count them off to me."

"One, two, three, four," quickly counted the Frenchman.

"Four of them are returning to the boat, Jimmy. We're still missing Colonel Asinus and Draker," murmured Bonnet in a French-accented English.

"No..... I don't see either of them," responded the American.

James Calhoun, kneeling down next to Bonnet, peered through his field glasses at the boat across the river. The strong metal riverboat had beached on the western bank of the Ubangi, just south of the river's bend - a half mile away. A herd of hippo frolicked in the water between the two banks.

"We have to wait for Asinus and Draker," whispered Calhoun. "We don't move until we spot them."

Calhoun spoke into his two-way radio. "Egan, get ready. We got four pricks in the boat. We're still waiting for the other two. We haven't seen Asinus and Draker. They must be back in the Aka village. As soon as we verify those two, we move on the target. Wait for my orders, Egan."

Thomas Egan and his support team of seven heavily armed CIA troopers hid in the jungle, north of the Ubangi's bend. Egan perspired into his Level A hazmat suit and waited for Calhoun's call.

The misty fog on the Ubangi continued to dissipate, clearing the way for Bonnet's right eye. He checked his rangefinder and accounted for vectors of gravity, windage, and elevation. The terrain on both banks was flat. The wind had remained asleep. Only eight hundred meters away, his targets would be sitting ducks for Bonnet's 7.62 mm sniper rounds.

"Don't move, Bruno," said Calhoun as he swung his machete around and lopped off the head of a venomous Congo Water Cobra which had slithered along the side of Bruno Bonnet.

"He was about to bite you in the ass, Bruno," laughed Calhoun.

More sweat beaded off from Bonnet as he smiled nervously. "Was it male or female?" he asked Calhoun.

"How the fuck would I know? Does it really matter with you Frenchmen, anyways?" laughed the American CIA specialist.

"A bite in the ass is a bite in the ass. Although this one would have been your last, Bruno," smiled Calhoun.

"Finally! Asinus and Draker have shown their pretty heads," said Jimmy Calhoun, looking through his spotting binoculars. "They're walking to the boat from the edge of the jungle, Bruno. Do you see them?"

Bonnet centered his scope over the Russian, Asinus. The German, Draker, walked next to him.

"Don't kill those two, Bruno. Leave them for Egan's men. We want them alive. Take out the four in the boat, now.

"Listen out, Garfield!" alerted Calhoun on the radio. "Let Bruno take out the dudes on the boat. If any escape down-river, they're yours. There can't be any escapees to shout out what happened here. Do you understand?"

"Affirmative, Jimmy," replied Garfield.

Bruno Bonnet aimed first at the enemy agent behind the boat's wheel. One second later, the target's head exploded like a watermelon, scattering its fragments into the Ubangi.

The next three enemy targets were shot in the chest. Two fell into the Ubangi and were quickly devoured by crocodiles. The third slumped over the boat's edge with his left hand near the water.

Bonnet and Calhoun watched a twelve foot reptile leap up and grab its prey at the shoulder. The animal returned with its catch to the water for breakfast.

Colonel Asinus and Draker began running back towards the Congo jungle. The soft sand by the Ubangi slowed them down.

"Shoot Asinus and Draker in the back of the kneecaps," said Calhoun to Bonnet. "Let them wait on the beach to either be taken by crocodiles or be 'saved' by Egan. Let them choose their fates."

James Calhoun talked into his radio. "You can move into Ibutu, Egan. Have your men take Asinus and Draker into custody. I'm calling in helicopter transport back to Bangui. Move quickly and get the information we need."

The CIA mission, led by Jimmy Calhoun to one of the remotest locations on Earth, would uncover an important 'final' clue to what was coming America's way. The mysterious Congo rainforest would reveal an unimaginable evil. An evil so profound it could lead to an end of days for the human race.

This story was neither beginning nor ending in the jungles of Central Africa. Like with most narratives of evil, it is impossible to detail its actual beginnings or define a conclusive 'final' end. Like the twilight of dawn and dusk are difficult to differentiate, so too are the commencement and demise of evil. There lies the fear of evil. It has no terminus, as it has no birth.....

Months earlier, on a cold and blustery evening in Cambridge, England - fifty miles north of London - Nasrin and Michael Stansfield waited for Christmas. Several inches of snow had fallen during the day, creating a white landscape around the university.

Nasrin and Michael arrived at the King's College Chapel for a Christmas Eve choral celebration. Being a professor at Cambridge University, Nasrin had attended many of these events in the past as a university dignitary. However, this time was different. She was grateful to be alive and with the company of the man she loved. She was also six months pregnant with Michael's son, conceived in Chalus, Iran, as they battled with Iranian freedom fighters against Iranian Revolutionary Guards.

They had survived the ordeal of the Allied invasion of Iran and had married in Baku, Azerbaijan, while Michael recovered from wounds at the US Army Hospital. Both Nasrin and Michael were well aware of their great fortune in finding love in such terrible times. Their child would be further affirmation of this love.

On this night, they would pray for world peace and the continued safety of their loved ones. Although organized hostilities against China and North Korea had ended by August 1, large scale US combat operations in Iran and Pakistan had lasted into late September. On Christmas Eve, the world was still a very dangerous and unstable place.

After Michael's discharge from the hospital in Baku, Nasrin had traveled with him to Washington. She had met his brothers, Julius and Mark, and his gifted sister, Rebecca.

Captain Julius Stansfield, a US Pacific Fleet submarine commander, had performed heroically in the South China Sea campaign and the Battle of Taiwan. US Marine, Mark Stansfield, had fought bravely in Pakistan and was to be awarded a Congressional Medal of Honor in a White House ceremony, the following January. Mark would receive his award in a wheelchair after suffering a gunshot wound to his spine at Shishkat Bridge.

Nasrin had also met Michael's beloved father, Admiral Julian Stansfield, and had quickly grown close to him. Although unspoken, their spiritual connection had been born from their deep mutual love for Michael. The evening of their meeting, the admiral had seemed particularly interested in her life. He had shown her great affection and exhibited obvious satisfaction with her love for his son.

Only a few hours after the Stansfield family reunion in Washington, the admiral had unexpectedly succumbed to a heart attack. The loss of his father had left both Michael and Nasrin deeply saddened. It had been decisive in Michael's urging of Nasrin to return to Cambridge for the fall semester term.

While Nasrin would leave every morning to teach nuclear physics to her graduate students, Michael would attend the morning services at King's Chapel. He'd pray for the souls of his mother and father, and all those lost and crippled in the recent war.

With these thoughts in their minds, Nasrin and Michael took their seats in the King's College Chapel and waited for the choral ensemble to begin the night's celebration. The chapel, emblematic of Cambridge University, was one of the world's great examples of late Gothic English architecture. Characterized by its accented vertical lines, it was an expansive and breathtaking structure. The world's largest fan vault reached over 80 feet in height. The chapel's many windows contained the finest medieval stained glass. Rubens' painting, *The Adoration of The Magi*, sat above the altar.

The chapel's construction began under the reign of Henry VI in 1446, and was finally completed nearly one hundred years later by Henry VIII in 1544. The King's Chapel was defined by its splendid acoustics and its world famous Chapel Choir.

Nasrin held Michael's hand throughout the entire program. They both listened silently as John Rutter's "There Is A Flower" finished the night's presentation. The song's words were particularly moving to both of them and personally reflective of the Stansfield family belief in "American

Amaranth". The new year would hopefully be a more joy-ous one for the extended Stansfield family.

With their baby due in mid-March, Nasrin took a leave of absence from Cambridge for the winter and spring terms. She wished for Michael's son to be born in the United States. Symbolically, she felt all Stansfields should be born in America.

Nasrin and Michael left England on January 15 to attend Mark's award ceremony at the White House. By January 20, they had arrived at the Sierra-Stansfield family home on Key Biscayne, Florida.

While Michael recovered from his injuries in famil-iar surroundings, he requested to leave the CIA Special Activities Division at Langley and be assigned to European Planning and Logistics at the Agency's office in London upon his return in September. His appetite for dangerous clandestine work had lessened since his wife's pregnancy. Nasrin's hopes had been realized without her having to urge Michael into the decision.

Alexander Stansfield was born on March 13. For the next two months, Nasrin, Michael, and their baby lived an idyllic life on their tropical compound near Cape Florida.

Tomas and Manuela, an elderly married couple in their mid-sixties who had worked for Raul Sierra since 1978, still helped maintain the house. The look of the home had not changed.

Raul Sierra's orchid house by the beach appeared as he had left it with his abrupt death in 1983. Raul's famous Panama hat, with "FREEDOM" embroidered on the front, still hung on a rusty nail on the interior door.

In late May, Julius and his wife and children came to spend a week with Michael's family on Key Biscayne.

On the morning of May 23, Michael and Julius jogged to the island's marina and took out their father's sailboat, *American Amaranth*, onto Biscayne Bay.

Admiral Stansfield had taught all his boys to sail on this boat. Before the age of ten, all three boys could captain this ship all the way to the Florida Keys.

The Stansfields in their youth would spend July and August at the Florida home. The boys had the time of their lives sailing on Biscayne Bay in the summer. On this day, like in old days, they sailed south towards Key Largo.

It was a warm and humid South Florida morning. A strong southerly wind filled the sails of the sloop as it raced across the eastern edge of the bay past Elliot Key. Julius manned the wheel while Michael played the sails.

"They have approved my transfer to Naval Intelligence at the Pentagon," said Julius as he turned the ship in a southwesterly direction.

"They've offered me Dad's old office. Admiral Culligan was adamant about it. He said it would have been Father's wish. I suspect he's right. Dad was a traditionalist and a romantic. He wouldn't have wanted it any other way," added Julius.

"Culligan said the office has been left as Father last saw it, before leaving for Taiwan. I don't think I'll be able to go in there and change things around much. How could I?

"I'll never forget his face, Michael, when he visited me at Subic Bay. He struggled with what he knew would come my way in the slot between Taiwan and the Chinese mainland. He knew how it would be. He needed to see me before the battle of all battles, just in case," paused Julius.

"I guess after almost fifteen years in the submarine service, I'm looking forward to staying on dry ground for a while. It'll be nice not having to evade Chinese sub killers. I think I'll sleep better at night," murmured Julius. "Sandra and the girls are happy. I suspect it may take a while to get accustomed to Pentagon work."

Julius smiled at Michael after a spray of seawater hit him squarely in the face. "You never get to feel that on a submarine," laughed Julius as Michael spit out a mouthfull of salty bay water.

"You're going to tell me, Julius, you won't miss the action and adrenaline rush of giving orders on a submarine in combat patrol? Give me a break!" shouted Michael while he took off his seawater soaked Annapolis t-shirt.

"That high is addictive. When you don't have it, you have withdrawals. How do you cut it out of your DNA?" asked Michael, without expecting a response.

"What are your plans, Michael?"

"I've asked for a transfer to our offices in London," answered Michael with a sheepish grin.

"I've suddenly become more respectful of dangerous situations since meeting Nasrin. I suppose I've finally begun to consider my own mortality. I've become chicken shit like you, Big Brother!" laughed Michael....

"Nasrin's love is too good for me to leave behind.... I guess America can use me just as easily from behind a desk," said Michael in a low voice, motioning to his brother to change places.

"It's all a question of which addiction is stronger - the girl or the job?" smiled Julius while flipping a cold beer to Michael.

"Things may be dying down a bit with China and Iran, Michael, but the world doesn't seem to be getting any safer. With the horrible economic conditions in Europe and Russia, ultra-nationalist extremist movements have begun to take political power. Russia, Germany, Spain, Italy, Austria, the Ukraine, Croatia, Serbia, and Greece - the whole of Europe is losing its mind. Even France's situation is getting tentative. It's an insecure crazy planet. Maybe these desk jobs are not so bad after all," smirked Julius.

"It's Russia and Germany we need to watch, Brother!" shouted Michael at Julius. "They're evolving another one of their crazy relationships. It's all about geo-political positioning and pipelines."

"What do you mean?"

"We negotiated Russia out of the war. We made some fair arrangements for them to provide energy to Europe. They also got preferential rig rights in the Arctic," answered Michael.

"As usual, they began exploiting the privileges. They increased the prices of their oil and gas to Europe, and began putting down rigs in the Arctic where they had no rights. The Canadians and Scandinavians have protested but to no avail.

"In response, American oil companies have opened up the Trans-Caucasus pipelines through Azerbaijan and Georgia. The new Qatari-Saudi lines through Jordan and Syria have also increased flow to Europe. Next month, the Israeli-Cypriot lines open up. All this oil and gas will flood into Europe, pricing out the Russians and worsening their economic situation. My friends at Langley tell me the Russians are pissed off like never before. Their posturing is getting more aggressive. Langley expects trouble. We'll see what happens," said Michael.

"Yeah..... We'll see what happens," agreed Julius.

In Key Largo, the brothers had lunch at a marina fish shop and talked of old times. They played billiards with the locals. They enjoyed mojitos with friends. In the afternoon, they started back for Cape Florida.

Nearly home, Michael and Julius anchored their boat over the spot in southern Biscayne Bay where they had scattered their mother Olivia's ashes, and later - their father's. Olivia and Julian had needed to be together in death as they had been in life. In these waters, they had fallen in love; and here, they would stay together forever.

As the brothers had done most recently for their father, Julius recited aloud from memory Olivia's "American Amaranth" poem. The men prayed silently for several minutes.

Michael and Julius reached Key Biscayne before sundown. They dined with their wives and children on the pool terrace behind their home, facing the Atlantic Ocean. They talked deep into the night at the candle-lit table, sitting adjacent to Raul Sierra's old orchid house. The same place where Julian had asked permission to marry Olivia in 1976.

Two nights later, Rebecca arrived in Key Biscayne after a one month piano concert tour through Italy and Austria. Mark and his family arrived from Washington the same evening.

After greeting everyone, Rebecca ran to the Steinway in the sun-room by the Atlantic surf. She played Chopin. She had first learned to play the piano here, with instruction and endless encouragement from her mother.

Rebecca made the piano sing like no one else anywhere in the world. She was the best at stirring emotions with its keys. Her sounds on recordings were known to stop conversations in public places where music was played. Like all great artists, she created silence in her audience. The Sierra-Stansfield family home was no different. The reunited family could only congregate around her in silence and enjoy the beauty of her art. Chopin would have been proud, just as her mother and father had been.

The next morning, the brothers helped prepare breakfast in the outdoor kitchen by the swimming pool. The women stayed indoors out of the sun and readied sourdough bread, orange juice, and coffee. Julius' two daughters played in the pool with Mark's two sons.

"You look well, Mark," commented Julius as he began to fry a dozen eggs and bacon on an oversized skillet.

Mark sat quietly in his wheelchair, close to his other brother. Michael patted him on the back before beginning to prepare pancake batter.

"How's your new job at the Pentagon?" asked Michael.

"They have me parading around in my wheelchair, wearing my Medal of Honor to social functions I don't understand. I think it's pathetic," complained Mark.

Julius and Michael remained silent for a moment. Mark sensed their consternation and added, "I'm fine guys. Don't worry about me. It's taken me longer than I expected to get out of this wheelchair. It's been just over a year since my injury. I can't seem to get enough strength back into my legs. I'm making progress, but not at the speed and consistency I'd like. Eventually, I'll get out of this goddam chair."

"We know you will," said Michael encouragingly.

"Did you finally find Callanan's sons, Martin and Gilbert?" asked Julius.

"The Navy Department helped place them with Marcus' brother in Colorado," said Mark, looking down.

"The Navy flew me to Boulder, and we drove sixty miles to the small town where they live. I gave them both a big hug and returned their father's pakol head cap to them. It was a very emotional day for all of us," Mark said quietly.

Julius placed the fried eggs and bacon on the outdoor buffet stand, while Michael finished cooking the pancakes. The Stansfields collected for their feast.

Nasrin sat between Michael and Mark. "The network news is reporting a civil war has started in China," Nasrin told Michael alarmingly.

"It's expected," said Michael, hushing her with his eyes and quickly turning the conversation to Rebecca's recent concert tour in Europe.

The Stansfield brothers never discussed sensitive geopolitical issues outside of their working environments. The men simply knew too much to risk making a comment which could potentially affect the safety of Americans in complicated situations.

Julius, Michael, and Mark understood from private discussions with their father in the past that if war came to China, and they were defeated on the field, domestic chaos would ensue. Civil war would erupt. Economic and social inequality in their bureaucratic culture of endemic corruption would lead to growing public demonstrations and likely violent reprisals from the People's Liberation Army. Strong separatist movements in Xinjiang, energized and recently freed Tibetan political action groups, emerging violent terrorist networks across China, and several strong provincial leaders would help galvanize a national movement against the weakened communist central government. The large number of unmarried young men without jobs, older citizens with lost pensions, and a more computer literate young population who used the internet to communicate their dissatisfaction with the central leadership, would all eventually combine to cause a fragmentation of China along traditional regional lines. It had happened many times in their history. CIA analysts were expecting the creation of four weaker competing nations out of one large powerful China.

The Stansfield men knew America's intelligence services were actively engaged in this difficult and dangerous process. They remained quiet on the subject while the family ate their breakfast, surrounded by beautiful lush vegetation and the roar of the Atlantic surf.

"How was Europe, Rebecca?" asked Michael.

"Horrible! There were public strikes throughout Italy and Austria. My last concert in Milan was canceled due to street demonstrations. After two shows in Vienna, I decided not to proceed to Innsbruck and returned home.

"There's economic misery throughout Europe. People are acting strangely. The governments are reacting more aggressively than ever before. It's not safe to walk the streets. Sightseeing is out of the question.

"I would stay in my hotel room most of the day and travel with an escort to the concert venues in the early evening. I'd return to the hotel immediately after the show and order room service. The hotels are severely understaffed due to the economy. The fine hotels of the past are now shoe-stringing services to their few guests. I felt like I was in a prison.

"I'm going to spend the rest of the year in the Americas and see how the austerity programs in Europe work themselves out," said Rebecca.

"It's expected," commented Julius as he looked at Michael.

"How is it expected?" asked Sarah, Mark's wife.

"For God's sake, Sarah, the sky fell in 2008," said Mark. "It's been years, and most of America hasn't recovered yet. Interest rates have shot up all over the world. Money isn't worth the paper it's printed on. No one qualifies for a loan from a bank because the banks are empty, and so are the consumer's pockets. US unemployment is up again, and our government doesn't know what to do. Europe is ten times worse. They'll be eating each other in a short time. It's ugly and it's going to get uglier."

"That's pretty gloomy, Mark," said Rebecca.

"I know it is. But from my world, it's easy to see. People just need to open their eyes before the truck hits them. What's happening in Europe will directly impact the stability of America. This debacle has become like an infectious disease without an anti-microbial cure. It spreads to everybody without mercy. It's a pandemic. If it doesn't get you the first time around, it'll kick you in the ass on the second time.

"We should all worry for our country. An angry European mind is capable of great horrors. The past is full of examples. We're going to re-live them," responded Mark.

The Stansfield family finished breakfast and withdrew to the glass enclosed sun-room. Rebecca returned to the Steinway and played Beethoven's "Fur Elise" with her usual magical excellence. The mood improved. The rest of the day was spent at the beach, enjoying each other's company.

By Memorial Day, Nasrin and Michael were alone again at the villa. Rebecca flew to New York City. Julius and Mark returned to Washington and their new jobs at the Pentagon.

Before going to bed that evening, Nasrin urged Michael to get ice cream from her favorite local parlor. Like always, Michael obliged.

The ice cream shop was empty when Michael arrived and requested the usual pistachio mint chocolate chip in the largest container. While Michael waited at the counter, a young Arab-looking gentleman in a dark blue suit walked up next to him.

"They tell me the ice cream here is outstanding," said the man in Arabic-accented English to Michael. "I've heard it was President Nixon's favorite. He'd get it shipped up to the White House on a weekly basis."

"Yeah..... This parlor is famous around here," laughed Michael. "President Nixon lived just around the corner. I guess he loved it just like everyone else. Though I can't imagine he liked it more than my wife."

"This ice cream sure attracts a lot of patriots," smiled the man.

Michael Stansfield found the comment unusual and didn't respond. With his peripheral vision, he could see another dark-skinned man in a suit standing outside the door. He prepared himself for confrontation.

Stansfield was given his ice cream. He began to walk out when the gentleman next to him said, "Michael, the Director would like to speak to you."

To Stansfield, this could mean only one thing. His friends were in town. He wouldn't need to knock out anybody's teeth.

The men walked out to a black Cadillac sedan in the parking lot. The back door on the left side opened, and

Stansfield peered in to find Joseph Mitrano - the lanky CIA Director and old friend of his father - sitting in the backseat.

"Come in, Michael, and get comfortable," said Mitrano. "You can eat your ice cream as we talk."

"It's for my wife," corrected Stansfield. "She's expecting it shortly."

"Well then, pass it on to Abdul and allow him to eat it. We'll get you some more in a little while so it's cold when it gets home to Nasrin."

"Alright. I hope you enjoy it, Abdul," grinned Stansfield.

"Where are you from?" asked Michael as he passed the ice cream to Abdul in the front passenger seat.

"I was born in southern Iraq, Sir. I'm a Shia Arab. My parents were killed by Saddam in 1991. My people weren't much liked by neither Saddam nor the Persians. My two brothers and I were accepted by the American government as small children. I was raised in Michigan on a farm by a beautiful German-American family. I've been with the Agency for the past four years."

"Only four years and you're working for the Director. That's very impressive, Abdul. It's a sign of confidence from the very top. Keep up the good work and enjoy my ice cream.

"By the way, Abdul, what are your brothers' professions in life?" asked Stansfield.

"My older brother is a Constitutional Law professor at Harvard. He was a teacher of mine when I was there. And my younger brother is an accomplished Grand Prix race-car driver."

"You're a Harvard-educated lawyer, Abdul?" questioned Michael.

"Yes, Sir. I went straight from law school into the Agency."

"Quite an American family, Abdul," smiled Michael. "Perhaps you'll be sitting back here one day calling the shots."

"I certainly wouldn't doubt that," said Joseph Mitrano.

The director motioned to his driver to get on the move. Two more security vehicles followed them out of the parking area and onto Cape Florida Drive.

"Have you recovered fully from your injuries, Michael?" asked Mitrano.

"Yes, I believe so. I still get a little pain jogging on the beach in the mornings. But I'm moving well."

"That's very good, Michael. Your injuries in Iran were considerable. I was worried for you. Nasrin must be an excellent nurse.....

"I understand you're considering a transfer out of Special Activities to a desk job in London. Is that Nasrin's doing also?"

"I suppose you could say it is, in a way. She hasn't mentioned anything to me, Director, but I felt it was time to make the move. I never thought I'd leave the field..... Love has a way of changing minds, I guess."

"Isn't that the truth," said Mitrano. "Love is a drug. It's hard to be on the field when your brain is medicated with it. You see things differently. Self-preservation takes over and you become hesitant. Perhaps, it's a good idea to move on."

"I still have the next two months to make a final decision, Director. In the event you need my services, I'm available on your orders at any time....."

In his mind, Michael castigated himself for having volunteered his services to Mitrano. He was speaking against his true wishes. He desired to leave the field and go to the desk. He couldn't imagine leaving Nasrin alone to raise his son without him. The idea of dying in duty was now always in his thoughts. It had never been before. Michael did not want a tragedy for Nasrin.

"Congratulations, Michael, on becoming a father. The admiral would have been very happy for you. He loved you dearly. We all miss him very much," said Mitrano as the car drove down the dimly lit, palm tree-lined avenue towards the Cape Florida Lighthouse.

"Let me cut to the chase, Michael, so you can get back to your beautiful wife as soon as possible.

"You're my best agent out on the field. Regardless of the dangers, you have always completed your mission and gotten the information that America desperately needed. You obviously have also avoided becoming another star on our wall. You have incomparable survival instincts and always seem to know what to do in the most difficult circumstances. I would not be here if these things were not true. Likewise, I would not be here on Memorial Day if America did not urgently need your services once again.

"We have quite a catastrophe in development coming out of Europe. When Russia withdrew from the Strategic Arms Reduction Treaty three years ago, she began to build a powerful new ICBM network which they believe can outduel our missile defenses in Eastern Europe. Our shield stations in Poland, the Czech Republic, Romania, and Bulgaria have suddenly become vulnerable. The civilian populations in these countries are becoming anxious and have begun to show some displeasure in our presence there. Strategically, we can not afford to get out.

"An ultra-nationalist movement has developed inside of Russia over the past several years. The miserable economic realities have greatly increased their profile and given them a wide based support in the general population. These are bad people, Michael. They are intent on regaining Russia's old empire in Europe, the Caucasus, and Central Asia.

"Recently, this right wing nationalist movement has formed a loose alliance with rapidly rising similar movements in Germany, Austria, Hungary, Italy, Spain, Greece, Croatia, Serbia, and the Ukraine. The militant factions of the Russian and German movements have infiltrated and poisoned the workings of government in most of the Eastern and Central European countries. The political leaders of these groups are winning trumped up elections and taking seats in their respective national governments. They are gaining the support of the people.

"There is a rising tide of anti-American and anti-Globalist sentiment among the populace in these nations. England, Poland, the Czechs, Romania, and Bulgaria are still extremely supportive of US policy. Leaders in these countries still remember the oppression of the Russian bear. They fear the bear is hungry again and intent on satiating himself on Eastern Europe.

"France has become more difficult in its positions because of the recent election of several right winged nationalist radicals. However, the French intelligence services and military are still with us."

Director Mitrano ordered his driver to go back. He turned in his seat towards Stansfield and looked him in the eyes.

"Recently, our agents in Russia and Eastern Europe have discovered that a group of right wing radical Russian fanatics, with assistance from similar elements in the Russian federal government and national military, have acquired a significant allotment of highly dangerous bio-terror material from the VECTOR Institute in south-central Russia. These men have transported the material into the Ukraine. Although we don't have specifics, we know it is a new bio-engineered virological weapon with extremely dangerous biological characteristics.

"They have split the shipment into two cargoes. One of these will arrive in the Crimea in the next several days. Unfortunately, our agents have lost the second cargo. We suspect it is somewhere in western Ukraine.

"We also know the Crimean cargo at Sevastopol will be transported on June 8 by a small freighter across the Black Sea to the Danube Delta in Romania. They will rendezvous in Austria or southern Germany with the second lost cargo, and together continue through the Europa Canal in Bavaria into the Main and Rhine rivers all the way to Rotterdam on the North Sea. There, the shipment will be placed on a trans-Atlantic ship to America where they hope to use their weapon to kill millions of Americans.

"They are establishing a false electronic trail back to a radical anti-American anarchist group based in France and Germany. The Russians hope the US government will lay blame on this anarchist group, and on the French and German governments for allowing the incident to happen. The Russians believe this will drive a wedge between the Americans, and the Germans and French. Russia wishes to capitalize on this division and bring at least the Germans into their sphere of influence. They think this may allow them to regain lost territories in Eastern Europe and force the Americans out of Poland, Romania, and Bulgaria.

"The recently signed 'Russian-German Friendship Pact' would be strengthened into a formidable alliance against the United States. This would be an ultra-fascist alliance with severe repercussions to the rest of Europe and America. France would have little choice but to acquiesce to their demands in Eastern Europe. The US would be forced to close their bases in Eastern and Central Europe or involve themselves in another costly war with high risks of nuclear escalation. I don't believe America is emotionally prepared at present for the consequences of this geopolitical nightmare.

"Needless to say, the French and Polish intelligence services have been notified of this plot at the director level only - to decrease the risk of leaks. They are also very concerned.

"Michael, I need you to lead a team of highly trained specialists up the Danube behind the Russian freighter. After it takes on the second cargo in Central Europe and passes further into Germany, sink it into the deepest part of the Rhine.

"America is coming out of a very costly war. We have lost thousands of patriots. The economic conditions of the world are becoming progressively more chaotic. We don't want a war with Russia at this time. Find that cargo and kill the men planning to hurt more Americans."

The director's car pulled back into the parlor parking lot. Several agents screened off the area.

"Your wife must be worried by now, Michael. Abdul will get you another ice cream so that you can hurry home. We want only the best for Nasrin and your family.

"Think about what I've said. Don't give me your answer right now. If you decide to take on this operation, present yourself at 8 AM tomorrow morning at the Regal Biscayne Hotel - down the road from your home. Knock five times on room number 427. Our agent there will go over all the specifics of the mission. You will recognize him. He is very familiar to you.

"If you don't show, I'll immediately approve your transfer request to the desk job in London.

"Michael, you've already done more for America than my next ten best operatives. America is eternally grateful to you and the rest of the Stansfield family," concluded Mitrano.

Michael Stansfield slowly exited the car and was given fresh pistachio mint chocolate to take home to Nasrin. He returned to the beach home and handed Nasrin her ice cream.

"What happened, Michael? You've been gone two hours," said Nasrin with hesitation. She felt something extraordinary had happened. She could see it in Michael's eyes.

Without saying a word, Michael walked into the study and closed the door. He stared at all the family photographs on the walls and desk. Photos of his father as a young boy on Lake Michigan sailing with Michael's grandfather, Dr. Robert Stansfield. Pictures of Raul Sierra fishing for blue marlin with Ernest Hemingway off the north coast of Cuba. A photo of his mother, Olivia, learning to swim in Trinidad, Cuba, with her father, Jorge. Many photos of Julian and Olivia on their sailboat in Biscayne Bay.

Finally, Michael looked at the largest frame in the room. It contained Olivia's poem, written in her hand shortly before she died. Rebecca found it neatly folded in their father's left breast jacket pocket - next to his still heart, the night of his passing. Julian had carried the poem with him since Olivia's death.....

**Do not cry for me,
I will not fade, I will not die.**

**Like the words of the Prophet,
I am immortal.**

**Like scientific discovery,
I am illuminating.**

**Like the mighty old oak,
I am enduring.**

**Like the energy of the Universe,
I am eternal.**

**Like the march of Time,
I am irrepressible.**

**Like passion,
I am invigorating.**

**Like true love,
I am everlasting.**

**I am in everything that stands for justice
and the natural rights of free men everywhere.**

I am American Amaranth.

Michael quietly left the study and walked into the dark living room where Nasrin was feeding their son. He sat next to them and gently whispered in her ear, "Nasrin, I love you....."

CHAPTER 2

Operation Europa

We as Americans, fighting for the salvation of humanity, had become obstructed once again. The impediments had become larger and more difficult to overcome with each successive challenge. A great fatigue had developed, and necrosis was evolving.

At times, we were like patients with an expressive aphasia after a brain affliction. We could see, hear, and understand what was in front of us; but we had almost insurmountable hardship in saying or doing anything about it. Changing the future for better had become more complicated than ever before. Danger flowed from our frustration like a fountain.....

Michael Stansfield walked towards the end of the hall where the morning Caribbean sunshine radiated through a large plate glass window. The window looked out over the Regal Biscayne's enormous coconut palm tree-lined swimming pool. Beyond the pool area, a white sandy beach stretched for miles in both directions and the blue-green waters of the Atlantic shimmered in the sunlight. When he reached the last door on the left, he turned and knocked five times. It was exactly 8 AM on May 30.

"You giant son-of-a-bitch!" laughed Michael.

"Cuba! My boy, Mikey, it's good to see ya'!"

Stansfield was surprised to see his old friend, James "Hickory" Calhoun, standing before him with a welcoming smile. Jimmy, who had been born and raised in Hickory, North Carolina, had been Stansfield's classmate at Annapolis and also a teammate on the Naval Judo squad.

After graduation, Hickory had served on surface vessels in the Mediterranean and the Middle East before transferring to Naval Intelligence in 2009. After being recruited into the CIA in 2011, he had served as a case officer at the US Embassy in Berlin. He had been transferred only recently to CIA Analysis at Langley, Virginia.

Calhoun was considered an expert in the radical right wing fascist movements which had sprung up throughout Europe in the past eight years. He was particularly knowledgeable of the groups in Russia, Germany, Austria, and Serbia.

Standing tall at 6'4" - with a hard and heavy muscular frame reflecting his nickname - Hickory had a tooth-gapped boyish grin with short red hair, freckles, and deep blue eyes. His phenotype contrasted with Stansfield's long and lean body, dark hair and eyes.

After a warm and affectionate greeting at the door, the men sat at a table facing the ocean and the white powdery sand four stories below. They spoke a few minutes about old times.

"I was saddened to hear of your father's death last year, Mikey. It was a shock to me. He meant much to all of us."

"Thank you, Hick. I appreciate your kind words. My family and I miss him greatly. I believe his Navy family does as well."

"Your brothers are heroes, I hear," said Hickory proudly. "Julius kicked ass in the Pacific, and Mark came home with a Medal of Honor. They're both the talk of the Academy," smiled Calhoun.

"Yeah..... They're both tough guys, Jimmy..... But Mark also came home disabled. He's in a chair, I think, for the rest of his life. We're hoping for more recovery. It's been hard on him and his wife. I believe they're both planning for the worse, as Julius and I are. It's unfortunate, but it's reality."

"I heard you got hitched in Azerbaijan. And in the hospital of all places, Mikey!" laughed Jimmy. "What happened? Did the doctors have you knocked out with pain meds? Did you think you were going to die?"

"Well, I did think I was going to die, but that didn't cause me to marry Nasrin. She's the most wonderful girl I've ever known. She's different from all the others. I just asked myself, if I was to live, could I live without her? The answer was easy, so I married her."

"A lot of girls' hearts were broken with that decision, Michael. You've always had them lined up like race cars at Indianapolis, revved up and ready to go!" Hickory Calhoun laughed loudly.

"Yeah, perhaps. But Nasrin was worth breaking their hearts, Hick."

"Tell me about her, Mikey."

"I'd rather not. I don't want anybody else falling in love with her," smiled Michael. "She's for me only to know."

Calhoun smiled and nodded his head. "I understand, Mikey. Keep her for yourself."

"How are your wife and sons, Hick?"

"They're all fine, back in North Carolina. I don't see them as much as I wish, but it's been crazy lately. My three boys are growing up without me, it seems. Hopefully soon, I'll have an opportunity to make up time. At least that's what I keep promising Vitoria," said Jimmy.

"Crazy lately!" said Stansfield. "Now there's an understatement of fact."

"There's a lot going on, Michael. Some things are known to the American public, yet much more has been hidden from their view. For national security, we believe it is better to keep our populace cloistered from some of these issues.

"Everyone's heard China is in civil war and likely millions will die. And that Africa and the Middle East remain sociological disasters.

"We're all aware of the piss-poor world economy that continues to struggle with massive debt and inflation. The dollar has regained world reserve status, but many countries are fighting to prevent the collapse of their currencies. Every nation is hoarding gold.

"Our US Treasury debt to problematic unfriendly governments won't be paid back. We're talking trillions of dollars,

Mikey. We've ticked off a lot of people. They should have been on our side from the beginning. Let them kiss our asses now.

"We know of the on-going disintegration of world culture, and the breakdown of trust in authority. After the war last year, things began to brighten a bit. A wave of freedom rolled over the planet. But it didn't last long. Corruption and poverty led to a resurgence of chaos. The world understands that Islamic Fundamentalism and terrorism haven't died out. We all know these things, Mikey.

"But there's more the world doesn't know. Perhaps, they shouldn't know. That question is up for debate, depending on who you ask. I personally feel there are secrets best kept quiet. I suspect you feel the same."

Michael Stansfield nodded his head in agreement. "My father would often tell me, there were few individuals who were singly 'bad'. But as humans in groups, the mob could be ugly. Sometimes, uncomfortable information can create a mob mentality which spreads quickly. We don't want that in America."

"Our main job, Michael, is to keep the peace in the United States. Over the past few years, it hasn't been easy. This struggle we've had between 'Left' and 'Right' has come close to anarchy several times. The recent global war unified us for a while, but the rift has opened again. We can't afford to have a destabilizing event in our country at this time.....

"We have a very dangerous situation evolving from Europe, Michael. I've been working on this case for months. I've knocked my head against the wall over it many times. There are things about it that I still don't understand. Langley is very hush-hush about the case.

In reality, I believe information has been kept from me. However, I know enough to feel very uncomfortable with it. The stakes are high, Michael. It could be more dangerous than even the recent world war."

Calhoun opened his computer and showed Stansfield a grotesque digital image.

"What I am about to show you, Michael, is 'Top-Secret'. Only a handful of men have full knowledge of our mission. Your presence here now makes you a full participant. The further conduct of this operation requires that details be kept to a minimum. We are to know only what we need to know.

"Have you ever been to Central Africa, Michael?"

"No, Hick, I haven't."

"Trust me, Mikey. You never want to go," murmured Calhoun.

"I like adventure as much as you do, Michael. But this place is beyond adventure. In the jungles of the Congo, danger lurks everywhere. You go back in time to the origins of life on the planet. Not only are there animals that can eat you, but plants as well. If they don't get you, the cannibals will.

"The heat and humidity suffocate the life out of you. The rains drown you. And the terrain is impenetrable. The location makes your work almost unendurable.

"Add bad guys to the cocktail, and you get the picture, Mikey. The Congo jungle is one fucking horrible place.

"But considering all I've said, none of these things were as horrific as what I saw coming from there to America. This final fearful fact doesn't just shake the world, it shatters it completely.

"This is Ibutu in the Likouala Swamps of the Republic of the Congo in Central Africa. It was a small settlement of the Aka Pygmy people along the Ubangi River.

"It was a 'Jurassic moment' for me when I visited the Congo basin six weeks ago. The Likouala is a very creepy place. It's from another epoch. The swamps are definitely 'early Earth'. I don't want a return ticket, Mikey.

"I took many photographs of what I saw there. This one is an aerial shot from a helicopter. You see only part of the village in the grassy clearing near the river. It extends beneath the heavy tropical canopy of trees. Approximately 150 Aka inhabitants lived there.

"The boat visible on the beach was enemy. We neutralized the agents on it. Their bodies were taken by the crocodiles.

"The next photograph was taken by Dr. Thomas Egan, a virologist. He and several others accompanied me into the Congo rainforest. As you can see, there are several dozen bodies of all ages scattered throughout the village. There were no live villagers found by the expedition.

"Two weeks before, our team had passed through Ibutu without finding any irregularities. The Pygmy people were friendly and offered us bushmeat in return for cigarettes. Monkey brains and kidneys, antelope steaks, and raw snake meat were not my preference. I did enjoy the bush hog very much.

"This next image shows a makeshift hospital with several dozen dead bodies piled like cordwood in the corner and several others on small wooden cots. You can clearly see the open bloody sores on their corpses, and signs of prior extensive bleeding from their mouth and rectum. They all had diffuse subconjunctival hemorrhages.

"Egan's formalin-fixed post-mortem skin specimens from several victims were sent to a CIA laboratory in Nairobi, Kenya, where immunohistochemical tests confirmed his intuitions that the villagers had died of an Ebola viral hemorrhagic fever. Further testing at the CDC in Atlanta and Fort Detrick in Maryland agreed it was Zaire Ebola virus. However, there was an additional alarming revelation which validated the CIA's mission into the jungle. The virus had been bio-engineered into an airborne form, more easily transmissible through aerosolized nasopharyngeal secretions."

Calhoun walked over to the kitchenette.

"Do you want a cup of coffee, Michael?" he asked.

Stansfield nodded, yes.

"In February, our agents in Russia were passed information that the militant terror arm of the Russian Galichina Party for National Revival (GPNR) had paid a large amount of gold to three senior scientific researchers at the VECTOR Institute in south central Russia. In return, the GPNR was given a quantity of a top-secret Russian virological terror weapon which had been developed there in 2012. Our specialists at Fort Detrick suspected it may be Airborne Zaire Ebola Virus (AZEV).

"The CIA subsequently tracked the militants in the Crimea and followed a group down into the jungles of Central Africa. That's where Egan and I were called in.

"The Aka people of the Congo have perhaps the highest Ebola seropositivity in the world. However, they have no significant defenses against this new virus strain. No human being could have.

"Our team tracked the GPNR fascist militants down the Ubangi River. We followed them past the Ubangi's confluence with the Congo River. We got as far south as Brazzaville, when the bad guys doubled back to the north again. Returning by Ibutu, we sensed a break in the GPNR's routine. Why had they stopped at the Aka village?

"The terrorists had released the virus in the village several days before without our knowledge. They returned to the scene of the crime to check for result. We struck them at the bend in the Ubangi and saw the result as well.

"The catastrophe at Ibutu was simply a trial run for the radicals. They proved to themselves that the bio-agent was thoroughly lethal. The GPNR virologically executed an entire village of Africans to confirm the potential of their new weapon.

"Now these mother-fuckers want to release the bug on America, Michael. We have strong evidence indicating they plan to unleash AZEV in the United States and kill millions of Americans. This is where the situation gets geopolitically complicated."

Calhoun returned to the table with the coffee and closed his computer.

"I couldn't make this shit up, Mikey. It all seems like a spy-novel for Hollywood. In the movies, it'd be a case for super-action heroes. It sounds like big-time entertainment, but it's real life. And Langley wants us to stop it cold."

"With what you know, Hick, do you think we can stop it?"

"I don't want to answer that question just yet, Michael. Let me give you some background information first, and then I'll let you decide the issue.

"The GPNR is named after the Galichina SS Division of Ukrainian nationalist volunteers who took an oath to Hitler and Germany in World War II. It is an extremely anti-Globalist, anti-American, ultra-nationalist fascist movement in Russia which has gained tremendous power in the federal government over the past five years. They are supported by a significant segment of the Russian people. This is a very aggressive and belligerent movement. The GPNR is intent on soon dominating the political machine in Russia. They want to regain the lost territories of the old Soviet Empire in Eastern Europe, the Caucasus, and Central Asia - even if it leads to war with the United States.

"The GPNR has formed an alliance with the surging Feuhrer's Nest Nationalist Party (FNNP) in Germany and similar groups in Austria, Hungary, Spain, Italy, Croatia, Serbia, and the Ukraine. These groups have millions of members who are radical followers of the GPNR's fascist ideology. The fanatics have formed a multinational coalition against the United States. United, they want to project their power across Europe and the world.

"Needless to say, England, France, Poland, the Czech Republic, Romania, and Bulgaria are very anxious about this ideology. They feel it's reminiscent of the 1930s."

Calhoun nervously pushed himself away from the table and began to pace. Stansfield noted his agitation with concern.

"Recently, Mikey, the CIA received information that the leadership of the Russian GPNR, in coordination with the leaders of the German FNNP and the Fascist Ukrainian Party (FUP), were supporting a militant terror operation on the United States using the AZEV provided to them by the VECTOR Institute. They have established a fraudulent paper trail back to the Victoria Movement (VM), a combined French and German militant anarchy group which has gained popular support in Western Europe since the Euro collapse, a few years ago.

"In essence, the Fascists want to kill millions of Americans with a horrific bio-terror weapon and blame it on the uninvolved Victoria Movement. They expect the US government will also put blame on the French and German governments for their perceived lackadaisical attitude in preventing the attack, leading to a breakdown in relations in these terrible economic times. The GPNR believes this will drive France and Germany into Russia's sphere of influence, and subsequently make it easier for Russia to regain her lost territories in Eastern Europe. The Russian Fascists are determined to force the Americans out of the region. We are certain the German FNNP radicals have designs on Eastern Europe as well. This may be a point of friction between these groups in the evolving situation," added Calhoun.

Calhoun stepped up to the window facing the sea, and after a short pause, continued his project discourse.

"The GPNR and the Russian intelligence services think America is suffering from war exhaustion. They feel the US is unlikely to entangle herself in another major war in Eastern Europe for the foreseeable future. They are also under the impression that most of America's intelligence assets are preoccupied in the developing civil war in China, and the post-war turbulence in Iran and the Levant region of the Middle East. Although a logical presumption on their part, it is inaccurate. America has over 600 intelligence agents involved in the developing crisis in Europe. Most of these agents are either CIA or US Naval Intelligence officers."

Calhoun sat down again after getting another cup of coffee. He stared into Stansfield.

"The AZEV was divided into two parcels shortly after leaving the VECTOR Institute. One shipment of AZEV in tissue culture was transported to Sevastopol in the Crimea and placed on a small freighter with a secure refrigerated compartment. The other allotment was transported into the Ukraine, and its trail was subsequently lost by our agents somewhere near Kiev.

"The freighter in the Crimea, the *Katarina*, will leave Sevastopol on June 8 with a crew of 47 militants. It will sail west across the Black Sea to Sulina, Romania, and enter the Danube Delta. They are expected to go north into the Upper Danube, and somewhere in Austria, or further north in Bavaria, take on the second 'lost' allotment. They plan to traverse the Europa Canal in Bavaria and enter the Main River, going west to the Rhine and then north to Rotterdam on the North Sea. On the Dutch coast, the militants will transfer the full cargo of AZEV to a trans-Atlantic freighter destined for America. We do not know their plans beyond that point," added Calhoun.

Stansfield asked, "Why don't we sink the freighter in the Atlantic?"

Calhoun nodded. "The United States wants the shipment sunk into the Rhine to shake up the German government, and make them realize the impending disaster that awaits the German people if they allow the FNNP to gain control of the Bundestag. This decision was made at the highest level of our government. The CIA is simply following orders.

"In addition, Michael, the *Katarina* must not be sunk until it has received the second 'lost' shipment. Under no circumstances are we to attack the *Katarina* before the two parcels of AZEV have been confirmed to be on board by our 'inside man'. If the second shipment stays 'lost', we're in a heap of trouble. We'll have to redevelop leads to track it down before it's used in an alternative plan. We do not know their secondary plans. We can not afford this. Limbo land is not an option here.

"Our operation has been code-named *EUROPA*. It's a combined CIA/Naval Intelligence mission. Coordination will come from Langley and the Pentagon. You will lead a team of seven specialists up the Danube River and pursue the *Katarina* at a safe distance, maintaining communications with our agents on land and ahead in the river system to approximate the *Katarina's* rendezvous point with the 'lost' shipment. The CIA expects the rendezvous somewhere in Bavaria."

Stansfield looked out at the sea as he listened to Calhoun. A tropical storm was coming. The marine blue sky had turned a sullen pewter color. Thready streaks of white and black cloud entwined like aggressive lovers locked in an embrace. Their moisture swirled to the forces of nature. The brightness and shine of the good earth had vanished, replaced by mercurial turbulence and insecurity. Michael's lightness of being had died like the sun, and darkness would stay.

"Mikey! Are you listening?" asked Jimmy Calhoun. "You seem lost in a daydream."

"I'm with you, Hick. I've heard every word you've said."

"Your team, Michael, will include Dr. Thomas Egan, a 44 year old microbiologist. He joined the CIA three years ago as a field agent, after spending several years working at the Centers for Disease Control (CDC) and the US Army Medical Research Institute of Infectious Diseases (USAMRIID) at Fort Detrick, Maryland. He is an outstanding agent with tremendous powers of intuition and deduction.

"Also joining you is Bruno Bonnet, a 37 year old agent in the French General Directorate for External Security (DGSE). Bonnet is a highly trained sniper. He was on the CIA team in the Congo and saw the horror of Ibutu.

"Jakub Krol is a 32 year old agent in the Agencja Wywiadu (AW), the Polish foreign intelligence service. He is experienced in Eastern European espionage. Krol is also a martial arts expert, and is probably the only man I know who could kick your ass, Michael," smiled Calhoun.

"Peter Reynolds, 30, and Tom Garfield, 32, are Navy SEAL specialists in river combat tactics. They have fought on the Euphrates, the Nile, the Indus, and the Amazon. Both men are tough crackers who don't like to lose scrimmages. In their eyes, they're undefeated and they want to remain so. Tom was with me in the Congo.

"Basha Ludwik, a female Polish agent, has been spying counter espionage against the Russian GPNR for the past three years. She knows all the characters involved. I have worked with her before. She's a lovely girl with great skills.

"We also have a man inside on the *Katarina*. His identity is known only by me."

Calhoun paused and then added, "I'll be going along with you too, Mikey. I know the enemy as well as Basha. You'll need me."

The old friends smiled at each other, looking forward to their adventure together.

"You'll fly out of Miami to Madrid tomorrow and pick up your first alias, Dr. Rodrigo Busto, Professor of History at the University of Madrid," said Calhoun. "You go onto Istanbul and then Sevastopol to do 'research' for a book you're writing on the history of the Crimean War.

"In Sevastopol, you'll meet with your 'travel guide' to see the battlefields between Sevastopol and Balaclava. The travel guide is a middle-aged Ukrainian woman who has worked for the CIA over the past twelve years. She will show you around the wharf in Sevastopol and point out the *Katarina* as it sits in the harbor. Make a mental imprint of the characters you see around the freighter. They'll be our targets for the remainder of the operation.

"You will then drive southeast to the harbor at Balaclava on the south Crimean coast. A fishing trawler will take you on June 5, the 200 miles west to Sulina, Romania, where you will meet the remainder of our team on a specially designed Italian sport yacht. Our ship has a shallow draft, enabling it to maneuver through the European river system. I'll go over its special features when you're on board.

"We will sit in Sulina's port until we pick up the *Katarina*'s GPS location trackers. Our 'inside man' has secretly placed them on the bio-cargo itself and in the wheelhouse of the ship. After the *Katarina* sails by, we will begin our pursuit up the Danube. I expect her arrival in Sulina on the morning of June 9."

Calhoun asked Stansfield if he had any questions. Stansfield motioned with his right hand for Hickory to continue his presentation.

"Now let's talk about the bad guys," said Calhoun. "Of the 47 terror militia members on the *Katarina*, 27 of them are GPNR.

"Their leader is 42 year-old Aleksei Batkin. Born in St. Petersburg, he attended St. Petersburg State University where he studied European History. He later entered the military and participated in the Second Chechen War in 1999 as an enlisted man. After graduating as an officer from the Russian Combined Arms Academy in Moscow, he led a company of 200 Russian infantrymen in the 2008 Russo-Georgian War. He went rogue in 2010, and became the leader of the military arm of the GPNR in 2013. He is personally responsible for the assassination of multiple political leaders in Russia and Eastern Europe. He has close ties to several active high ranking Russian Army officers who keep him informed of any movements against the GPNR. He is a despotic, ego-maniacal individual who commands total control over the *Katarina's* mission and holds himself personally responsible for delivering the AZEV shipment to Rotterdam."

Calhoun showed Stansfield a digital image of Batkin with a hero's scar over his left cheek from an injury suffered in Chechnya.

"The GPNR's scientific advisor is Feodor Dashkov, a 44 year old graduate of Moscow State University with a doctorate in virology. He worked as a basic researcher at the VECTOR Institute until 2011, when he departed for the private pharmaceutical company ZaftraPharm in Moscow. Dashkov disappeared three years ago and had not been heard of again until he recently sprung up in our surveillance activities in the Ukraine. We believe he was instrumental in acquiring the AZEV from his close acquaintances at the VECTOR Institute."

Calhoun showed Stansfield a photograph of the tall, blond haired Dashkov.

"Fifteen of the *Katarina's* crew are FNNP members. They are led by Andreas Fuchs, a 38 year old physician from Munich who became an active member of the fascist movement in 2010. He is the youngest brother of Leopold Fuchs, the German foreign minister, and Manfred Fuchs, a member of the German Bundestag. The CIA believes there may be meaningful contact between Andreas and his political brothers, and we are keeping our minds open to that probability. Over 15% of the Bundestag are members of the FNNP's political arm, either overtly or covertly."

Calhoun showed an image to Stansfield of the diminutive, bespectacled Fuchs. The elfish German stood in front of a red flag emblazoned with a reversed image black swastika, the symbol of the FNNP.

"Vying with Fuchs for FNNP leadership on the *Katarina* is 40 year-old Captain Konrad Wagner, a veteran of the German Army Special Forces in Afghanistan, and once highly regarded in the rapidly developing German military. He's been rogue since 2012. This crazy Kraut has tremendous power in the militia arm of the FNNP. He is a racist, fascist ideologue.

"Wagner's grandfather was a colonel in the 12th SS Panzer Division, *Hitlerjugand*, which fought the Americans at Caen - near the Normandy invasion beaches, and at the Battle of the Bulge. After fighting the Red Army outside of Budapest in 1945, the colonel surrendered to the US Army in Enns, Austria. He spent 17 years in an Allied prison for war crimes committed in Normandy."

Calhoun showed Stansfield a photo of the tall, blond-haired, blue-eyed Wagner holding a *Sturmgewehr MP44* - the world's first modern assault rifle, made famous by the German Army in World War Two. Wagner leaned forward in assault position, aiming the gun at a large wall poster of 'Uncle Sam'.

"The remaining five members of the *Katarina* crew are radical troops of the Fascist Ukrainian Party (FUP). They take their orders directly from the GPNR's Batkin.

"Together, the militants form a formidable group with brains and brawn. They have all sworn allegiance to the fascist ideology and are intent on getting the AZEV to Rotterdam. They want it used against the 'suffocating imperial power' of the United States. Their communications, as picked up by CIA interceptors, are full of references to the 'oppressive' intentions of America in Europe. They see their fight against America's presence in Central and Eastern Europe as a crusade. These Fascists appear as dedicated as the jihadists of the Muslim world.

"*Operation EUROPA* must be successful, Michael. Secrecy is critical. If the enemy gets onto our plans, and they take their cargo off-line into the German countryside, capturing the AZEV intact will become difficult. If even a small portion of the bio-weapon reaches America, we will not be able to prevent their next move. They will likely be successful in killing millions of innocent US civilians. We do not have an effective therapy against AZEV in a mass casualty situation.

"In turn, the geopolitical fallout from a catastrophic loss of American lives in a terror attack will lead to the breakdown of relations between the US and Russia, and the commencement of major war operations by the United States in Eastern Europe. Blame will also be put on the German government for their inability to control these radical fanatic nationalists inside their own country. The Fascists are intent on destroying Germany's alliance with America. They represent a movement to direct the future course of Europe away from the principles of democracy."

Calhoun finished his presentation by showing Stansfield digital satellite images of Russian troops moving into the northern Caucasus region, Belarus, and the western Ukraine. Major troop concentrations could be seen near the borders with Georgia in the Caucasus, and the Baltic States, Poland, Hungary, and Romania in Eastern Europe.

"The Russian government appears to be aware of the *Katarina's* mission. High ranking officials must know of her intentions. They are already preparing for the military consequences. We must snuff out their hopes," exhorted Calhoun.

"Hickory, I'd like more information on the scientific characteristics of the AZEV," said Stansfield. "I want to understand how this bug works."

"Egan will meet with you in Sulina and explain the biological data. It's complicated. I'm only a wood craftsman from North Carolina. I'll let the scientist do the teaching," nervously laughed Calhoun.....

"So what do you think, Michael? Do you feel we have a chance to terminate these bastards?"

"Killing the enemy is not the challenge of the mission, Hick. We seem to have the assets to kill them all a million times over..... The crux of the operation is to take the bug off the field of play. The AZEV is the real terrorist. We'll never know exactly where the bug is until we confiscate it. Getting all of it is the vital point..... If I were these bastards, I wouldn't unify the package. I'd split it up even further. I'd force America to track and chase all the pieces around Europe. Dividing the weapon safely would put much more pressure on us..... The fact that they want to carry one package tells me their lines of communication are insecure. They don't trust the AZEV going in ten different directions. Their support system is likely not strong enough to safeguard and control a multi-path approach..... I think that's good news for us. It's easier to hunt one fox than ten, Jimmy. It allows us to concentrate our assets.

"In the end, it's always the brightest guys and gals in the room who decide the outcome of a mission. My money will always be on us, Hick."

Jimmy Calhoun escorted Michael to the door and wished him luck on his road to Sevastopol. The old friends embraced.

"I'll see you in Romania when we start our European vacation," laughed Calhoun.

Michael retorted, "I'd rather go nude bathing with Nasrin in the Aegean, but your company, Hick, on a Danube river cruise would be my next wish."

Michael walked home along the sandy shore. The same shore his mother and father had walked long ago, after meeting at a Christmas party in 1975. Michael thought of the dangers of his mission and the always present possibility that he wouldn't return home to his family.

His beloved Nasrin and Alexander needed him. If he didn't return, Alexander would never remember his father. Michael would never share in his son's life. He was intent on surviving and coming home. For the first time, Michael Stansfield truly understood a father's love.

CHAPTER 3

Offshoots

In the life of a family, we learn immensely from loved ones who came before us. They have much to teach us, if only we listen to their whispers.

Likewise in the struggle for freedom, a worthy nation can strengthen her cause and effort by appreciating the trials and tribulations of other cultures, past and present, which have faced similar challenges. It is in the understanding of the cohesive human experience driving for liberty that benefits are derived for all.....

A pensive Michael Stansfield stopped along the beach. He had taken off his shirt and shoes. He stared out at the black sea. A tempestuous charcoal sky rose above the dark waters like a violent curtain. Storm winds drove a heavy rain onto the shore. Stinging forceful drops of fresh and salt water hit his face and body like tridents from Poseidon. Booms of thunder and dazzling electrical flashes played above him. Nature had become angry all of a sudden. The gods were awake and quarreling.

Michael took his time to come off the beach. He loved the energy of a Caribbean storm. Even as a child, he'd hesitate coming in from one.

He stepped onto the thick grassy plain behind the Sierra home. The green Bermuda grass was well maintained by Tomas. Michael's sandy feet sank into the wet grass comfortably as he walked up the slow natural incline to the pool terrace.

On the southeast corner of the grassy area stood Raul Sierra's orchid house. Michael found the door to the glass structure open and walked inside.

Raul Sierra, his maternal great-grandfather, died before Michael was old enough to think. Michael had no memories of the man. Yet, he did remember as a child helping his mother tirelessly maintain the orchids like Raul had left them. Tomas would also help care for the hundreds of unique plants inside the large enclosure.

Michael remembered the silence of the space. It was a deep solemn silence, interrupted only by the soft tick-tock sounds of an old pendulum clock in the corner of the room. His mother would nurse the orchids quietly and almost never speak to him inside of the structure. He'd stand next to her and wait for her to finish. Mostly, he'd observe the rhythmic swinging motion of the long pendulum. The back and forth movements drove the hands around the face of the clock. Occasionally, his mother would pull a chain to rewind it. The look and sounds of the clock intrigued Michael. It was fascinating to him how the machine kept time. The swinging pendulum mesmerized him as a child. In Michael's young mind, the measurement of time in the company of his mother sanctified the orchid place.

In his past, Michael had not paid attention to Raul's flowers. Today remarkably, something besides the orchids' beautiful exotic forms and tropical colors seemed to attract him into the shelter. He had always sensed the flowers, like the pendulum clock, held secrets known only to Raul. They had a story to tell, he had presumed. But as with most young boys, Michael had left the orchid rituals to his mother. He had never inquired about them. Mainly, Michael had left the memories of the clock and the orchids behind him. He had never again paid much interest to their probably meaningful personal significance.

Michael closed the door of the orchid house, shutting out the stormy winds and rain outside. A lightning bolt struck the beach nearby, shaking the ground and the strong weather-resistant glass walls of the enclosure. The electrical show flickered around the flowers like a strobe light. All motion was slowed down.

On the inside of the old unvarnished wooden door, hanging on a rusty nail, Michael found Raul's Panama hat with "FREEDOM" embroidered in faded red letters on the front. He delicately took hold of the hat and instinctively brought it close to his nose to smell its age. Although old, it still seemed ready to wear. Tomas had taken care of the hat as much as he had the orchids.

Michael placed the hat on his head and walked through the structure. He took his time to appreciate the beauty of the flowers and breathe in their light fragrant scent. Tomas had done a wonderful job of keeping the orchids healthy since his mother's death, two years earlier.

Michael stepped up to the old pendulum clock. Through the thunder, he could not hear its sounds. He closed his eyes and placed his hands on the glass of the time-keeper. He felt the vibrations of the swinging rod on his fingertips. They hummed into him mystically. With each swing, a second of his life expired away.

The storm continued to rage outside. The sky was dark as night. The black sea foamed in anger.

While Michael slowly paced the aisles, Tomas entered the orchid house to perform his morning ritual of pruning and cutting. He and Manuela had escaped Cuba by small boat in 1978 and had settled in South Florida. Married and in their early twenties at the time, the couple and their young son, Gabriel, were invited to come live on the Sierra estate by the sympathetic Raul. Manuela would manage the domestic chores while Tomas would landscape and do handy-man work around the estate. Raul Sierra's 'Last Will and Testament' left a significant amount of money to keep their positions paid indefinitely after Raul's death in 1983. The gracious Raul also provided appropriations for Gabriel's education through college.

"Good morning, Tomas," said Michael.

"Good morning to you, *Muchacho!*" greeted Tomas.

"It is unusual to see you here, Michael," said the old man as he put on work gloves.

"I was caught in the storm while walking the beach. This orchid house provides shelter but still allows you to view the beauty outside," answered Michael.

"You always loved a storm, Michael. Your mother would send me to find you all the times in the summers. I'd always know where to look, *Muchacho*. You'd be sitting on the shore looking at the sea. Surprisingly, you never seemed afraid of the thunder and lightning. I'd throw you over my back and carry you inside. You would kick and scream the whole way. Your mother would change your clothes, and you'd return to the window as fast as you could to continue viewing the tempest. You were attracted to the light and darkness of it all."

"I remember that, Tomas," smiled Michael.

"You were always a brave boy, *Muchacho*. I guess things never change!" laughed the old man.

"It's a little late for you to work with the orchids, Tomas. I typically see you coming in here early at sunrise."

"You're right, Michael. I've already worked with the flowers earlier this morning. But something drew me back. It happens sometimes. Senor Raul's orchids call me when they need me. I respond accordingly."

"You do a fine job of keeping these flowers alive and healthy. They all seem vigorously fresh and full of life. How many of these are originally Raul's plants?" asked Michael.

"Before I answer you, let me say you wear the hat well, Michael. Not many could wear that hat with conviction. But you can. I can plainly see it with my eyes. You should keep it. Raul would have wished it so, I am certain of it. Consider it a legacy passed to you from a wise man. There were none wiser than Raul, *Muchacho*," smiled Tomas.

"I feel Mr. Sierra's absence, *Muchacho*. It is apparent to me in so many ways. He was a good friend. My wife and I miss his quick incisive wit and wisdom for all things," sighed Tomas.

"He had much taken from him, Michael. His country, his son, and his wife were all taken too early. He had money and position, but those things were not of significance for him. He'd often say to me that only 'things of the heart' were worth living and fighting for. Without love, there was no warm blood in your veins, he'd say. To live, you had to love.

"He left everything he had to Olivia. This home and these flowers were given to her and your father. He loved your father very much. He could sense Julian's devotion for Olivia. That was important to him.

"After Raul became ill, he was comforted by Olivia's happiness. He knew Julian would take good care of her. He no longer felt necessary to anyone.

"He chose to die as he had chosen to live - strongly. He left this world on his terms, and his terms only. He was quite a man, and my wife, Manuela, and I loved him dearly.

"You remind me much of him, *Muchacho*. You have that same aura of invincibility, of chivalrous honor, and of courage, which is rare in today's world. You also have the mischievous spark in your eye, as he had. Use it always to your advantage," smiled Tomas.

"Yes..... You wear Raul's hat well, *Muchacho*. It seems made for you. Wear it proudly, as Raul did....

"Now getting back to your question, Michael - none of these plants are original. One must continuously divide, cut, and replant fresh young offshoots so that your flower lines thrive and keep reproducing healthily into the future.

"Mr. Sierra believed strongly in continuous maintenance of his garden. He always said his orchids were simply a metaphor to symbolize his family, and that the young off-shoots would need nurturing until they grew and became independent on their own. The young plants helped to propagate the beauty of his garden. He said his orchid house was much like America. It depended greatly on the vigor and strength of its young offshoots. I consider it an honor to keep Mr. Raul's flowers vigorous. It's the least I can do to honor his memory.

"This orchid house is very symbolic for me, *Muchacho*. The flowers here are a part of my soul, as they were for Mr. Raul.

"Mr. Raul was a very emotional and deep thinking man. He loved his family and greatly admired the United States of America...."

"What about the clock, Tomas? What was its significance to Raul?"

"Time, Michael! Time..... With the passage of time went one's life. You needed to make your life significant in this world of ours. Every person was in a race against time to contribute something worthy and good to society. There were only a few hundred thousand hours in a lifespan. You needed to make each one count. In a sense, the pendulum clock symbolized death to Raul. It stood as a constant reminder of his place in the cosmos. It reminded him of his end, just as the orchids reflected his beginnings. The flowers were life, Michael, and the swing of the pendulum was death."

The storm had ceased. Rays of sunshine broke through the gray clouds. The sea became blue again. The thunder passed. Michael could hear the tick-tock of Raul's clock.

The elderly Tomas tended to his gardening. Michael gently placed Raul's hat back on its rusty nail support. He would come back for it when he could.

The old orchid house had now taken on a much more sentimental place in Michael's heart. In just a few minutes of speaking with Tomas, he had gained insight into what made Raul Sierra the man he was. He had also seen a little of Raul Sierra in himself.

Early the next morning before daybreak, Michael walked into Alexander's nursery. He held his young son in his arms. Looking out at the Atlantic Ocean through the room's large window, Michael held his son until he began to see the sun's rim rise above the horizon at a distance.

Michael placed the still sleeping Alexander back into his crib and lightly kissed his cheek. He gazed out again at the rising sun and quietly stepped out of the room.

As Michael and Nasrin walked out to the front yard, both could physically sense the danger approaching them. Having lived through danger in the past did not make it any easier on either of them. With love came the natural aversion to danger.

Chalus had bonded their love but also taught them how easily life could be lost. They both understood the unpredictability of one's fate. Loving someone deeply, and hoping and praying for their safety, did not necessarily secure their good fortune. It was not as easy as that. There were factors beyond anyone's control.

Like before, they would have to wait out their destiny. However this time, Nasrin and Michael would be apart while they anticipated his homecoming. Their separation would make the suffering much more difficult to tolerate.

Michael gently kissed Nasrin's lips and whispered in her ear how deeply he loved her. He promised he would return to her soon. He got into the waiting taxi cab and drove off to the airport.

Another adventure was beginning, but this time his heart longed to stay. As Michael rode further away from Nasrin and Alexander, he realized he would need to muster greater courage this time than on any other mission in the past. He could not be weak. America was depending on his performance. He would need to be sharp in his decisions and actions at all times. This mission and his family legacy would demand perfect execution.

Stansfield arrived in Madrid in the early evening. After retrieving a key out of a pay locker at the airport, he drove to an apartment near central Madrid, three blocks from the Museo Nacional del Prado. He was accustomed to the routine drill.

In the apartment, he found all the necessary materials to assume his new temporary identity, Dr. Rodrigo Busto, Professor of History at the University of Madrid. Present were his identification papers and the materials to change his physical appearance to a man twenty years older. Also in the apartment was a box containing information on Sevastopol and the Crimea, the Black Sea, and the long 2200 mile trans-European transportation corridor from Sulina, Romania, to Rotterdam in the Netherlands, along the rivers Danube, Main, and Rhine. Stansfield spent the rest of the evening reviewing the information, and after eating dinner at a small restaurant across the street, he went to sleep until the next morning.

The next day after breakfast, Stansfield walked to the Prado Museum to pass time before his afternoon flight to Istanbul, Turkey. He spent much of his visit sitting in front of the 1814 Francisco Goya painting, *The Third of May 1808*, commemorating Spanish resistance to Napoleon's occupying armies. The work of art was a favorite of Michael's mother. She considered it one of history's greatest examples of resistance against oppression.

The classic painting depicts the execution by firing squad of several Spanish villagers. The central figure of the painting is a Spaniard with his arms outstretched in defiance. To Olivia, the central figure was her father, Jorge Sierra.

Stansfield sat in front of Goya's masterpiece for more than an hour. He thought of what drove unarmed people to defy the cruel and unjust burden of tyrannical power and despotism. There was a fine invisible line dividing hopeless acceptance of a people's fate and the courageous rejection of a controlled imposition of tyranny. Some individuals would lay down and not rebel. Others would fight to the death with their minds, fists, and military arms if accessible. What made people choose the latter against the overwhelming force of a strong occupier?

At the basic core of the combatant mentality was the acceptance of one's own death. All people were destined to die anyway, thought Stansfield. Sooner or later, people expired. In the scope of history, whether one lived thirty or sixty years was really immaterial. One could choose, perhaps, to live longer under oppression and keep your mouth shut. Or rebel with all your might in order to control your own destiny, regardless of the risks to life. To many, living longer under the boot of another was a fate worse than death. It was unacceptable to toil for others on their order. The rebel was compelled to fight and change his destiny for the better. The combatant spirit wanted to live and win the day, but he was also willing to die in the process of the achievement. The history-makers were guided by justice and the irrepressible desire to live free. They could all hear the tick-tock of the pendulum clock of history.

Michael Stansfield stared at the Goya. He could sense the brave spirit of those about to die for their noble cause. Spiritual defiance was a weapon difficult for the enemy to eliminate. Even if your life was taken, the vestiges of your spirit remained for those left behind. The memory of your defiance would invigorate others to keep fighting. Critical mass would eventually be achieved. Victory would finally be born from it.

In the face of the Spaniard, Michael could recognize himself and many others of his family. Injustice and enslavement were incongruent with his DNA. The decision to fight was a natural one for him. Whether it be with stone and stick, or gun and knife, he would rebel against unjust dictation until the end. Until the last breath left his lungs and the final beat of his heart, he would fight against oppression. Until his eyes saw the last light of day, he would struggle for liberty. It was his code of life, his 'American Amaranth'.

The Goya depiction of courage under fire was a battery-charger for Stansfield. The simple passive act of art appreciation had helped enliven the silver knight and white horse in him. He was suddenly ready again for any confrontation which could come his way. He left the Prado Museum feeling stronger than when he had arrived.

After connecting a flight from Istanbul to the Simferopol International Airport in the Crimea, Stansfield drove the few miles to Sevastopol on the southwestern tip of the peninsula. That evening he checked into the Tsarina Hotel, several blocks from the harbor and wharf where the crew of the *Katarina* was preparing for their mission to Europe.

The following morning he came down to the hotel's restaurant to have breakfast and wait for his CIA contact, Veronika Boroshkova. With her assistance, he planned to spend the next two days studying the *Katarina* and the men coming and going around her. Later, he would drive a few miles southeast to the "Valley of Death" and the infamous battlefields of Balaclava from the Crimean War. From Balaclava Harbor, he would board a fishing trawler which would take him to Romania across the Black Sea.

Sevastopol, formed from the classical ruins of the ancient 5th century BC Greek city of Chersonesus and its subsequent ancient Roman and Byzantine cultural additions, was a coastal city of 350,000 inhabitants on the southwestern tip of the Ukrainian peninsula of Crimea on the Black Sea. Because of its numerous well situated bays and finger inlets, it was considered one of the world's most strategic naval points. After its official founding by Russia's Catherine the Great in 1783, the city quickly became an important naval citadel. Sevastopol had survived two massive sieges in its history, and twice rose from the ashes.

The Crimean War siege of 1854-1855 by naval and land forces of Great Britain, France, Sardinia, and Turkey lasted 11 months, and was one of the deciding battles of the war won by the Allies. Sevastopol fell to the Germans in July 1942, during the "Great Patriotic War". It was subsequently liberated by the Red Army in May 1944, and awarded the title of "Hero City" by Josef Stalin a year later.

Its surrounding waters were filled with the sunken remains of warships from all the great powers which had fought for its control throughout history. Most famous of these underwater graves lied at the mouth of Sevastopol Bay where the entire Russian Black Sea fleet was scuttled during the Crimean War siege of the city. The shores of its 30 bays and inlets were covered by over 1000 monuments to Russia's fallen heroes of the Crimean War and World War Two.

Both the Ukrainian Navy and the Russian Black Sea Fleet had their main naval bases situated at Sevastopol. Because of its significant military importance, Sevastopol was a bee-hive of espionage activity. Intelligence services from all the great powers had agents working in the city. The major players worked for the Russian and Ukrainian federal governments, the GPNR, the FUP, and the CIA.

Stansfield sat in the Empress Room Restaurant of the Tsarina Hotel early in the morning of June 2, having a Russian breakfast of blini pancakes with sour cream, milk, and tea. He had requested to sit by the large window facing St. Vladimir Cathedral across the street.

The cathedral was a neo-Byzantine church built to the Russian heroes of the Crimean War. Three famous admirals - Kornilov, Istomin, and Nakhimov - were buried there, and the names of thousands of war dead were inscribed on the marbled walls of it interior.

Stansfield waited to see Veronika Boroshkova's arrival at the entrance of the cathedral. The attractive red-haired Ukrainian was to wear a red blouse with blue pants.

Shortly past 8:30 AM, Stansfield spotted his contact. He quickly paid his bill and left the four storied Venetian arched Tsarina Hotel. He crossed the busy intersection, walked up behind Veronika, and smoothly placed his right hand on her back. He continued to move north in the same motion.

Veronika Boroshkova was a 42 year-old linguist from the historically cultural western Ukrainian city of Lviv. She had worked in the CIA for many years. Lviv, like all of the Ukraine, had been under the rule of several masters over the past thousand years. The kingdoms of Poland, Austria-Hungary, Nazi Germany, and the Soviet Union had taken turns controlling the workings of government in the Ukraine. With the fall of the USSR in 1991, the Ukraine had finally gained their long sought independence.

Veronika's ancestral family had been almost wiped out by the "Great Famine" of 1932-1933. Induced by the agricultural collectivization programs of Josef Stalin, the famine claimed ten million Ukrainian lives. World War Two claimed many millions more. Both the Soviets and the Nazis had been responsible for the slaughter.

Since 1991, independent Ukraine had been manipulated by Russia in an attempt to keep her out of the NATO alliance. In the past several years since the economic debacle of 2008 and the subsequent Euro collapse, the Fascist Ukrainian Party (FUP) had gained tremendous political power inside the country.

Veronika Boroshkova, who had learned five languages under the guise of her work as a travel guide, supported democratic government in the Ukraine. She was adamantly against both Russian influence and right wing fascist domination of her freely elected government. Veronika had gone to work for the CIA in the hopes that America could help her country stay free and prevent another national calamity. She was willing to die for her cause.

Speaking only Russian, Stansfield and Boroshkova walked the several blocks to Nakhimov Square. The walk to the Southern Bay waterfront down the chestnut tree-lined Lenin Street was easy in the dry 72-degree weather. They passed the two rows of Doric columns of the white colonnade entrance to the Grafskaya Wharf and moved down the granite steps to the sea.

Wearing sunglasses in the bright sunlight, Stansfield immediately saw the 240 foot long *Katarina* sitting along the second pier off the wharf. He could see tremendous activity around the ship as he approached her from the south. Large crates and barrels were being carried onto the *Katarina* by a number of men who Stansfield presumed were crew. Standing at the stern of the ship was Aleksei Batkin with his characteristic scar over his left cheek. As expected, he was loudly ordering the men to work more quickly.

Michael and Veronika changed their conversational speech to Spanish. They walked arm in arm slowly past the freighter and sat at a nearby resting area along the waterfront promenade.

Stansfield analyzed the *Katarina's* bulky reinforced exterior structure. He concluded large amounts of powerful ordnance material would be required to put a hole in her side. Well placed torpedoes would certainly do the job. He was sure the CIA would not send him on a mission of such importance without providing him with the destructive firepower to sink his target.

The supplies being loaded onto the enemy ship were certain to be arms and munitions to help defend it from such an attack. The assault on the *Katarina* would not be easy.

While Stansfield sat speaking to Veronika about their sight-seeing plans, he continued to assess the activity around him. He looked for signs that interested parties had been made aware of his true intentions in Sevastopol.

He observed the tall Feodor Dashkov arrive at the wharf, escorted by a Russian naval officer in full uniform. Stansfield had expected elements of the Russian Navy would likely be assisting the *Katarina* in the preparations for her mission. However, the officer with Dashkov appeared to be a senior member. He was also likely only a middle liaison connector. There would be even higher level officers involved in the scheme.

Stansfield also recognized Andreas Fuchs walking on the deck of the ship. His tiny 5'2" frame was unmistakable.

Michael and Veronika returned the way they had come, past the freighter and back up the granite steps of the wharf. Near the statue of Admiral Nakhimov, the two said goodbye and went their separate ways. Stansfield caught a taxi back to the Tsarina Hotel.

He had learned much in a few minutes. Sinking the *Katarina* would require a well calculated and coordinated effort by the CIA. If the *Katarina* carried as much firepower as he expected, there would be quite a show on the Rhine in the next twenty days.

After spending days assessing the *Katarina* and her crew, Stansfield was ready to be extracted from the Crimea. A Greek fishing trawler with a covert CIA crew of Greek and Bulgarian nationals was waiting for him in Balaclava Harbor on the southern Crimean coast, only a few miles southeast of Sevastopol.

On the morning of June 5, Boroshkova drove Stansfield south through the dry rocky valley towards Balaclava. The Crimean War battlefields in the area included the infamous "Valley of Death", where Britain's "Charge of the Light Brigade" had occurred against heavily fortified Russian positions during the Battle of Balaclava on October 25, 1854. The ill-fated cavalry charge, led by Lord Cardigan, had been ordered on a miscommunication and led to the annihilation of the brigade made famous by Alfred, Lord Tennyson's famous poem.

Michael Stansfield, a student of military history, asked Veronika to stop a few moments at the site of the "Charge". While Stansfield sat on the edge of a hill above the valley, he noticed a car racing towards them along the road to the northwest. Its long trailing cloud of dry sand along the hill road revealed its high speed.

"Would you say they're coming faster than the 'Charge of the Light Brigade', Veronika?" amusingly asked Stansfield. "I don't think we should wait for their arrival."

He returned to their car and removed a suitcase from its trunk. Stansfield got into the backseat and told Veronika to drive as fast as she could.

With the car behind them gaining ground, Stansfield opened the suitcase which had been delivered to his hotel room the night of his arrival in Sevastopol. He laid its contents out in front of him in the backseat. At his disposal was an arsenal consisting of a .45 pistol with several ten-round magazines, four M67 fragmentation grenades, and an M60 machine gun with ample supplies of armor-piercing rounds.

The trailing car began to fire at them. Stansfield busted out his car's back window with the butt of the M60. He calmly turned and said to Veronika, "Put the pedal to the metal and get our asses out of here, dear girl. I don't presume any English chap will be writing poems about us if we end up buried in this godforsaken valley."

Stansfield smiled at Veronika politely through the rear view mirror and turned his attention back on the enemy.

He shot three well aimed bursts at the trailer, causing its engine block to explode and light the car on fire. A second fiery explosion caused the car to veer off the road and tumble down the hill. Stansfield ordered the anxious Boroshkova to keep driving and not look back.

They arrived at Balaclava only a few minutes later. Stansfield and Boroshkova drove down the hilly road to the harbor entrance where the fishing trawler waited for him. Balaclava's harbor was surrounded by several 400 foot tall rocky hills which decreased visibility of everything above the town.

Stansfield stood at the docks for a moment, looking up at the top of the hills. He thought of his options.

"You won't be able to return the way we came, Veronika. There may be more of them up top. For the mission, I can't allow you to fall into their hands. There's too much at stake. You'll have to come with us to Romania."

He told the trawler's captain that he was going to have an additional guest. Stansfield rushed Veronika onto the deck of the ship and instructed the skipper to shove off.

As Stansfield's boat left the rocky shore of the Crimea behind, he did not see unusual activity along the hilltops. Experience had taught him, however, he could expect unwelcome company on his race to Romania across the Black Sea.

Michael Stansfield would again have to prove his mettle in defense of his country. His courage would be tested more than ever before. As one of America's great young offshoots, he would listen to the pendulum clock of history tick away.

CHAPTER 4

Fishing Trip to Sulina

During the Cambrian Period of the Earth's development over 500 million years ago, there was an explosive evolution of multi-cellular animal life in the seas. The process was led by the formation of intricate and complex visual systems which allowed for more successful predation and procreation. Complicated visual apparatus required more advanced central nervous systems to process visual information.

Natural Selection over the eons of ever more complex nervous systems led eventually to the human brain and cognitive thought. Complex human social groups formed. Differentiation and separation of opinion and disposition evolved. Tribal organization and division led to martial conflict.

War is a natural extension of evolution. Human coexistence on Earth is a complicated socio-biological phenomenon.

The old fishing trawler, the *Spartan Prince*, motored slowly west towards the Balkans and the Danube Delta port of Sulina, Romania. Traveling at only 8 knots would take the ship nearly a day to reach her destination on the western edge of the Black Sea. The "Hostile Sea", as called by the ancient Greeks, lacked islands and was characterized by severe storms. However, this northwestern portion of the Black Sea near the Crimea was protected from the cold north winds of the Eurasian steppes by the peninsula's mountains and had a mild Mediterranean climate. It had been a busy waterway since ancient times, carrying the trade between Greece to the southwest and the Eurasian landmass to the north, the Caucasus and Central Asia to the east, and Asia Minor and Mesopotamia to the south. It had been sailed by the Athenians, Persians, Romans, Byzantines, the Goths and Huns, the Christian Crusaders, the Venetians, the Ottomans, and the Russians. In Greek Mythology, Jason and his Argonauts had sailed the "Hostile Sea" in search of the Golden Fleece. This was a storied body of water.

By mid-day, Stansfield had removed all semblance of his alias, Dr. Rodrigo Busto. Only his dyed gray hair and sideburns remained while he laid shirtless on the deck of the ship's bow getting sun. He relaxed for the time being. The Crimean sunshine was settling. He turned off his situational awareness and let his mind rest.

Leonidas, the *Spartan Prince*'s owner and captain for the past 40 years, navigated the ship in calm waters. From the wheelhouse, he remained constantly vigilant for

Russian patrol boats. Leonidas had made many runs for the CIA in these waters over the past decade. He was familiar with the patrol patterns of all the navies in the region. The navies were also familiar with him and his boat.

The old Greek worked with a small crew, consisting of his four sons, three nephews, and nine grandsons. He also had three Bulgarian fishermen who had joined him two decades earlier. The lean operation allowed Leonidas to control every facet of his clandestine work. All his sailors were loyal to him and his various causes. No one on the *Spartan Prince* could move without an order from the old Greek.

The captain enjoyed using his wits to stay alive in the "Hostile Sea", even more than fishing in the warm sun. He found the curious combination of danger and peace energizing. He desired to boil his blood occasionally. It kept his spirits young.

His CIA affiliation had been born from his native country's bankruptcy and subsequent fall into chaos with the Euro meltdown. He was strongly against the radical movements which had progressively taken over the political process in Greece since 2013. The captain didn't appreciate getting mandates from people who he felt were more interested in 'ruling' his people than fixing their upturned world. The Greek's secret work was his way of expressing rebellion against the ugly forces of oppression.

Leonidas had been born and raised a fisherman on the island of Leros in the southern Aegean Sea near the Turkish coastline. His birth had come one year before the island's reunification with Greece in 1948, after 700 years of rule by the Venetians, Ottomans, Italians, and British.

He had been taught by his father the importance of self-rule and the necessity of fighting for freedom if the situation demanded it. Leonidas was wise, self-reliant, and fiercely independent - all prerequisites for working closely with the CIA.

"Good morning, Captain," said Stansfield squinting, as Leonidas walked over to him under the bright sunshine.

"What is your *nom de guerre*, American?" lively asked the old Greek.

"Why do you say I'm American?" questioned Stansfield with a Spanish accent.

"Whether you're American by birth or not, I do not care!" grinned the captain. "You are working for them. So functionally, you are American-spirited. To me, it is the same thing. For the past few years, I have worked only for the United States. So that makes you an American package for me to deliver.

"What is your war name, American?" again asked the captain.

"Rodrigo!" laughed Stansfield.

"I am Leonidas - sailor, fisherman, adventurer, and occasional warrior as well," smiled the Greek.

"Hero-king of Sparta, defender of the Greeks at the Battle of Thermopylae. That is a strong name, Captain. I like it. It fits you well," said Stansfield.

"I like it also," grinned Leonidas.

"I will presume you know these waters, Captain, and the patrol patterns of the Russians," said Stansfield.

"Know these waters, American? I know them like you know your bathtub at home, Rodrigo! Every fish in this sea is my friend, and every Russian is my enemy. At least for now!" laughed Leonidas.

"I don't expect problems from them today," said Leonidas with certainty. "The commander of the Russian

Navy is inspecting the Black Sea Fleet in Sevastopol. Most of their ships will be in port or just off the coast where they are clearly visible to impress the admiral," grinned Leonidas widely as he sat down on a chair next to Stansfield.

"I don't understand how the Russian naval leadership could be impressed with vessels that are less sea-worthy than my old fishing boat. Most of their ships need tugs to get them across the Black Sea. Only their submarines, based at the caves in Crimea, are in fighting shape. If it wasn't for their nuclear arsenal, they would have been overrun a long time ago."

"The Russians still have some able ships, Captain," stated Stansfield. "They may not be the best and the brightest, but they're still capable of stopping us before we reach Sulina. I left a few dead men back there at Balaclava. We can expect the Russians to be upset about it. I am certain they'll come looking for us soon."

"Perhaps, Rodrigo. Perhaps your assessment is correct.... But we're not talking about the 'best and the brightest', as you call it. These Russian brains are pickled in vodka. The neurons don't fire when they're supposed to. These Slavic barbarians are more interested in feigning strength than they are in projecting it.

"Besides, the Russian patrol boats in this area know me for several years. I'm just an old anchovy fisherman who runs his rickety boat between the shallow bays and estuaries of the Romanian coast and the inlets of the Crimea. I'm simply looking to make a living for my family from the sea in the best way I can," smiled the sun-wrinkled captain, with his deep blue eyes challenging Stansfield at every step from beneath his soiled white cap.

"If I would have known that you were bringing a beautiful lady-friend on the trip, I would have bathed this week," murmured Leonidas. The Greek rubbed his dirty grizzled beard and stared at the shapely middle-aged Veronika Boroshkova standing nearby on the bow's port-side.

"She is a fine woman to have on a ship like mine. Possibly, I can work out a different payment from the CIA for my troubles. Do you think that would be possible, Rodrigo?"

"Her coming was not part of the plan. So, it's not part of the deal, Captain," affirmed Stansfield.

"You will be paid as you usually are, in gold coin and good will, Leonidas. Veronika can not be made as payment for your troubles. She is my responsibility and will remain so until we arrive in Romania.

"We had an unexpected incident near Balaclava which required me to bring her along. It was too dangerous to leave her behind. Otherwise, I would have preferred to leave her in the Crimea. I don't like extra baggage on my missions. It's difficult enough to stay alive when responsible only for oneself. Attractive women are distractions. The last time I dragged a woman with me on a job, I ended up marrying her," said Stansfield as he also looked with a trace of lust at the red-haired Ukrainian beauty.

"Well, if you don't want her to continue with you, American, if she's too much of a 'distraction', I'll be happy to escort her back home when it's safe. However long that may be....

"If she cooks as well as she looks, she could be a fine addition to my crew. This pussycat would not be considered 'extra baggage' on the *Spartan Prince*. She could have many useful chores to fulfill," laughed the sly old Leonidas.

"It seems like you have been doing this for a long time, Captain," commented Stansfield, trying to take the old man's mind off the woman.

"Do you mean, desiring beautiful women?" asked Leonidas. "Yes, for a very long time..... Sailing men don't have many opportunities to ingratiate themselves with women of that quality," said the captain, ogling Boroshkova's long sexy legs as she stood barefoot in tight summer shorts.

"I love her clean white skin and red hair. Who could not admire that hard backside? She carries it extremely well in her short pants. My old eyes can envision the naked beauty of those mounds. Their both soft and strong character sizzles the genitals. Enough of the buttocks' flesh is visible to arouse even the meekest imagination. A man could never be timid with such erotic stimuli. My face would fit between them snugly, I am certain...."

"Her breasts are fine also. They are very well displayed. I could entertain myself with those teats like a schoolboy," added the Greek, still in his stare. "I could finally have milk for breakfast! It would be a very just compensation, I think...."

"No!" said Stansfield. "You misunderstood my statement, Captain. I meant to imply that you have been running a fishing boat for a long time, Leonidas," interrupted Stansfield, trying to break the Greek's delirium.

"I didn't misunderstand you, Rodrigo! I simply prefer to talk about beautiful women than my life as a fisherman. I may be old, but I'm not dead. Isn't it also an obvious preference for a smart young red-blooded American like yourself? Just look at this woman! All of her features tantalize and arouse the boy organs. Anchovies, sea urchins, and tales of summer storms can not compete with the sensations she gives.

"Perhaps, you can have the sensuous beauty move away far enough so that her estrogens don't filter into me, Rodrigo. Only then will the blood return to my brain and allow me to talk man to man."

Michael Stansfield walked over to Veronika. He explained the situation. She turned, winked at Leonidas, and stepped away.

"Now we can talk like warriors before a battle, Leonidas!" laughed Stansfield.

"I'm a Greek sailor, Rodrigo. This sea belonged to us in ancient times. We colonized this savage place. If it wouldn't have been for Hellenization, this region would still be full of wild tribes living out of caves. All the major settlements along these coastlines were first established by the sea-faring Greek adventurers. If you emptied the Black Sea of its brackish water, you would find thousands of ancient Greek ships lost in storms over the centuries of glorious discovery.

"The Turks and Russians pushed back civilization a thousand years, American. How this region would have been if only Athenian democracy had survived. The Athenians, with all their history and rhetoric, eventually succumbed to greed like most human beings left to their own devices. They discovered that popular vote and the freedom to choose also allowed them to appropriate public funds as generous gifts to themselves.

"It is pitiful my country repeated this mistake recently, as did most of Europe.... It is unfortunate America also did not review her history. These mistakes of nations allow the unscrupulous opportunists to take over and destroy centuries of human achievement.

"It is pathetic that an old fisherman like me is forced to protect democracy by running warriors like you from one fire to another. What has happened to the great cultures of the world to allow the evolution of such mediocrity? Where have our value systems gone? Where has our sense of cultural responsibility disappeared to?

"The American nation scares me, Rodrigo. Your country is full of non-Americans, spiritually.

"At the lower end, you have people who migrated to the United States out of economic necessity, not a thirst for liberty or ideals of political freedom. There are also natural born Americans who don't understand the concept of civility and hard work. A criminal thug mentality shrouds them all. Many of these persons in your country want to live off of America, not work and contribute to her.

"At the upper end, white-collar criminals are allowed to destroy the ethical and moral base of your country. They impoverished your nation without much penalty. What happened to the rule of law? Capitalism run amok is not a healthy blueprint for the development of the American youth.

"These are not the American pioneer mentalities of old. America has changed greatly, Rodrigo.

"Many old and new Americans don't respect the history of your country. Many even despise it, wishing to re-write it with every opportunity. The 'Founding Fathers' are seen flawed and in need of revision. Their principles of freedom are made to seem 'outdated' and not applicable to the modern American society. A new American Constitution is called for. New liberal ideas of conduct have been forced down the throats of traditionalists who know better. The people are not being educated in the true history of their country and seem disinclined to learn it on their own.

"A general apathy for education in general exists. Everyone agrees that an education in mathematics and science is important for the future of the American nation, but few choose it because it is hard. Sometimes, not even an elementary knowledge in the sciences is learned. This will cripple the society in the future. Foreigners are now invited to enter America and fill science positions.

"I don't see much desire in the American people to adapt to the changing requirements of the modern world. This will cost them their security in the future. Jobs are lost and shipped to other countries, while the population stagnates with poor preparatory schooling and lives progressively more off the government. I find it a sad statement on the 'American Spirit' of old.

"Naturally, this general ambiance of intellectual depression spreads like a cancer. It eats the fiber of America slowly and provides the perfect substrate for future tyranny. Someone will eventually come along and take advantage of the idiots, Rodrigo. Historically, someone always does.

"There is a 'Fifth Column' developing in your country, American. They are preparing to take you over. I see it and I smell it. It is so rotten and putrid that the smell reaches us here in the 'Hostile Sea'.

"I may be an old Greek fisherman with a dirty beard and missing teeth, but I'm not an idiot. I have spent many thousands of lonely hours on this ship at night, reading the great works of literature, history, and science. I am proficient in the English language and have read all of Shakespeare's plays. I have read the great historians of the ancient and the modern worlds. I stay informed of all news from Europe and America. I taught myself algebra and geometry. I understand the natural and physical sciences. I can use the stars at night to navigate the seas. I can survive on my own in any environment, Rodrigo. The CIA would not have contracted me so many years ago if they felt I was not a capable man.

"No, Rodrigo! I am not an idiot. I have been to America many times. I have studied what I saw there. My business has allowed me privileges with your government which have opened my eyes. Believe me, Sir! There is a 'Fifth Column' assaulting your nation. It may come at you from the left or the right, from above or below, but it's coming. And with its silent attack comes tyranny with a capital 'T'. It will deceptively undermine the sensitivities and sensibilities of your country's liberty. It will make you question the realities of your traditions. Before you know it, the nation will drown in the confusion generated by it.

"Remember that nothing is absolute. Nothing is pure - not even freedom. Use your intuitions to see the 'Devil' in things. Beware of the 'Fifth Column' in America, Rodrigo, before it's too late. They will use the ignorance of the people as a weapon against them. These individuals only need an American national calamity to precipitate their entrance onto the stage. It will happen sooner rather than later, and they will come like the savior knight to 'save the day'. Like a 'Trojan Horse', they will come to disembowel America. Don't allow their appearance onto the national stage, Rodrigo. Once arrived, they won't leave without a catastrophic struggle. I'm just a simple Greek sailor, but I'm no idiot."

"You make a good case, Leonidas," said Stansfield.

"It is only an obvious observation, Rodrigo."

"How did you go from fishing to high-stakes espionage, Captain?"

"Many years ago, I fished for mantis shrimp off the west coast of Greece in the Ionian Sea. One night while reading a marine science magazine, I came across an article on these magnificent creatures. I learned things about them that I never knew.

"I was shocked to find their eyes are much more complex than humans. Each of their stalked eyes has more depth perception and color vision than both of ours together. These large crustaceans use their vision to differentiate passing prey in fractions of a second. They can also visualize the phases of the moon from the bottom of the sea for breeding purposes. The mantis shrimp are better killers and copulators than we are.

"With such an advanced visual apparatus, I reasoned they could have an advanced brain and nervous system to process all that visual information. As the world conditions began to spiral out of control a few years ago, I began to feel remorse over killing these fine creatures. Almost naturally, I turned my attention to dumber animals – humans.

"So yes, I have been doing this for a long time..... Running a fishing boat to catch fish as well as to defend democracy anywhere I can..... And yes, Rodrigo, I do enjoy looking at beautiful women. Although usually, I must admit, I enjoy them in photographic form only."

Stansfield realized he had more things in common with the old salty Leonidas than he had originally thought. He had appreciated the Greek's diverse but coherent monologue on America's shortcomings, the intelligent life of mantis shrimp, and beautiful women.

"I have more faith in America's ingenuity than you seem to have, Leonidas," said Michael Stansfield.

"Well, of course you do, Rodrigo! You are young and American. I am old and not. However, I am not 'un-American'. I am a freedom fighter just like you, Rodrigo. And in that sense, we both share an American bond. We both wish for a better world. To have the luxury of a better world, we need a freer world - one with just liberties for all. Thus, I am a strong supporter of a healthy and strong America. Because I live outside of your country, and have a brain predisposed to consider it, I see the greater risks which you may be blind to. I am only providing an old man's insight on the future of freedom in America and the world."

The Greek captain told Stansfield that he needed to return to his crew and review the ship's position. If everything went as expected, they would arrive at the Danube Delta in the early morning. As he passed the Ukrainian, Leonidas continued to admire her sensuous figure. He whistled and shook his head in wonderment.

In the late afternoon, Stansfield found Veronika Boroshkova at the stern of the ship. She was reading a novel borrowed from Captain Leonidas.

"What are you reading, Veronika?" asked Michael as he sat next to her.

"An old 19th century Russian love story," she answered. "The captain reads and speaks Russian fluently, as well as English, Spanish, French, and German. He showed me his library of books and recommended I read this one. His collection is quite impressive. He says he's read them all. There must be over a thousand books in that room."

"I agree. The old Greek has a sharp mind. The fisherman is more sophisticated than he appears," smiled Stansfield.

"Leonidas also claimed he was an energetic lover with a vast experience of exotic positions," quietly laughed Veronika.

"I think we better just trust him on that," also laughed Stansfield.

"He was colorful and descriptive in his claim," said an amused Veronika. "The captain went as far as physically showing me how flexible his body is. He did stretches on the floor and even stood on his head. It became comical. He may be intelligent and experienced in love-making, but he's not my type....."

"Tell me about yourself and your family," said Michael.

"I was born and raised in the Ukraine. I married an older man when I was still young and innocent. He was a professor of mine at the university in Kiev. He taught psychology. We had no children. The doctors said I was infertile.

"My husband enjoyed staying late at work with his female students. Sometimes, he wouldn't come home at all. He left me many years ago and moved to Odessa. We have spoken rarely since.

"My parents are both dead. I have a younger sister who also lives in Odessa, yet I haven't seen her in over ten years. She was my husband's student as well. He left me for her. They live together and have two children.

"I moved to Sevastopol after beginning to work with your government in 2005. The CIA arranged for this. They wanted information on the Black Sea Fleet and their operations in and out of Sevastopol Bay. They particularly needed information on the submarine division and their underwater tunnels into seaside caves near Balaclava.

"I consider myself a patriotic Ukrainian. My people have been fighting for independence for hundreds of years. We became officially independent in 1991, after the fall of the USSR. Nonetheless, we didn't truly acquire our freedom until 2004, when our government moved away from Russia's persistent influence and embraced true democracy. This did not last long, and it became apparent to me one year later that Russia was not going to leave us to our own designs. By 2009, the Ukraine's neck was again under the boot of Moscow.

"The recent power moves by the Fascist Ukrainian Party (FUP) within the government worry me. I see the region is turning towards radical ideology to deal with its chronic historical problem of bad governance. This can only lead to further calamity for my country.

"The collaboration between the Galichina Party in Russia, with the FUP in the Ukraine, and the FNNP in Germany is going to change the lives of millions of people in Europe. Nothing good can come from this alliance. A fascist Central and Eastern Europe, with the natural resources of Russia, will be a menace to the entire Free-World. They have taken the opportunity of the long economic debacle to move public sentiment against America and Capitalism in general. They also believe the United States has been weakened greatly by her war with China and Iran.

"The Fascists are on the move and they are not going back. I am determined to help stop them," said the shy Veronika with emphasis. "In my life, I have learned there are only three human responses to despotic tyranny. The people can quietly accept oppression and remain at the mercy of their ruler. They can peacefully defy the oppression and sacrifice their lives to the execution squads. Or, the people can patriotically combat tyranny with armed rebellion. For myself, I have chosen the latter."

Stansfield appreciated Boroshkova's strong beliefs in free constitutional republican government. He had learned these principles at an early age and had understood them more deeply with his actions in Iran during the recent war.

Still, Veronika had not signed up for this dangerous mission into the belly of fascist Europe. She should be free to choose her next move. Returning to the Ukraine was going to be a complicated decision for her. The intelligence services there knew of her involvement with the CIA. Enemy agents were killed at Balaclava. The powers in control would most certainly seek vengeance against her. Stansfield would offer her safety through the protective services of the CIA. Perhaps, she would want to live in America. Stansfield had decided to pass her on to the CIA in Romania. After the mission's completion, they would allow Boroshkova to freely choose her next step.

With the sun in the western horizon and the *Spartan Prince* sixty miles west of the Crimea, Captain Leonidas motioned to Stansfield and Boroshkova to come quickly up to him in the ship's wheelhouse.

The Greek gave Stansfield his binoculars and said, "My eyes are not so strong anymore, Rodrigo, except maybe for enjoying the sight of your attractive lady friend. But unless I am deluded, that ship in the distance coming from the northeast appears to be a Russian Navy vessel. It's coming our way at a fast rate of speed. I estimate it's moving at over 30 knots. It's probably a Mirage Fast Patrol Boat. They are quick and well-armed," warned the captain.

Stansfield peered through the binoculars and could make out the Russian Navy flag on the ship's mast. It was certainly a battle boat.

"That's a 30mm six-barrel artillery system on its front deck," said Stansfield. "It fires 1000 rounds per minute and can reach 3 miles out to sea. I can also see men stationed at her two machine guns ready for action. She is not going to let us pass," agreed Stansfield.

A few moments later, as Leonidas and Stansfield weighed their options, several bursts of 30mm cannon fire came over the trawler's starboard side and landed in the sea, a hundred meters to port. It was too close for a warning shot. The Russians intended to sink the *Spartan Prince* if it moved a foot further.

The captain shouted to his crew in English, "Come dead in the water! Stop this ship! Our only chance is to stop and let them board. I can talk my way out of this."

The Greek ordered Stansfield and Boroshkova to come down with him to the fish containment area. He had a plan for this contingency.

"You smell that?" asked Leonidas, after he opened the hatch and showed Stansfield his last catch of anchovies off the southern coast of the Crimea.

"You're a genius, Leonidas," laughed Stansfield.

"Time will tell, young American!" yelled the Greek. "Time will tell!"

The Greek captain had intentionally left his catch of the oily green fish from four days ago stay in the containment area and go bad. He thought he could use the catch to hide the CIA extractions if the need arose.

Stansfield pushed Boroshkova into the sick-smelling mass of dead fish and followed her in. Both immersed themselves into the brown mush, using black snorkels to breathe. The Greek believed no self-respecting Russian sailor could be asked to go into that mess and search for contraband.

The trawler came to a complete stop as the Russian patrol boat ran alongside of it. Eight heavily armed sailors and a junior officer boarded the *Spartan Prince*. Leonidas gave the ship's papers to the young lieutenant.

"Why did you not stop earlier, old man?" loudly questioned the Russian officer.

"I held my ship as soon as I realized your desire, Sir," meekly responded Leonidas.

"Your brain is old, fisherman! You almost had your rotten boat sunk and all your men killed. You should know better. These waters are commanded by the Russian Navy. If you see our guns taking aim, I suggest you heed our warning."

"I am sorry for my senility, Lieutenant. It won't happen again."

"Next time, old man, I'll split your ship in half!" loudly laughed the Russian.

"I am and always will be at your mercy, Lieutenant."

"The Russian Navy will not have mercy for demented and misplaced foreign sailors. I recommend you return your boat to its home port and leave the Black Sea to its proper ruler, old man. But first, we need to inspect your vessel," said the Russian while reviewing the Greek's papers.

"We're looking for an American and his woman associate. They are suspected of espionage against the Motherland and have killed three of our security agents in Balaclava. If we find them on this ship, we will kill each and every one of you. Pray, fisherman, that they're not aboard!" shouted the Russian before ordering his men to search the *Spartan Prince*.

The officer waited on deck with a pistol aimed at the Greek's head as his Russian sailors raced through the boat. Leonidas kept his hands raised in the air.

The Greek captain's facial muscles began to twitch. He opened and closed his eyes tightly several times. His mouth quivered.

"What is your problem, old man?" asked the angry lieutenant.

"I have a weak stomach, Sir. I am missing parts of my intestines. At times, the food I eat does not agree with me."

"I don't give a damn! Keep your ugly face still, or I'll blow it off with my pistol and relieve you of your discomfort forever."

"May I have permission to rub my belly, Lieutenant?"

"Go ahead, old man, settle your stomach!"

Leonidas gently massaged his abdomen with his right hand and continued to grimace.

"Did you not hear what I said, fisherman? Or are your ears as sick as your brain and stomach? Keep your face still! You are ugly enough with your face quiet....."

The Greek placed his left hand over his mouth and burped loudly. He then released a series of clamorous eruptive flatulent emissions into his baggy white boat pants. The stench almost matched the foul smell coming from the fish cargo hold.

"Please forgive the inability to reign in my gases, Lieutenant," said the Greek. "We've been eating our catch of the last two days. It hasn't agreed with me. The fish must be infected with something. I suspect it's a virus or parasite, because my men have also been suffering fever and diarrhea. I hope it's not the nuclear waste from your submarines in the Crimea that is sickening the fish we depend on for our livelihoods. Without these Black Sea fish, our families can not survive," added Leonidas after another loud and long-sustained barrage of gaseous emissions had sickened the Russian officer.

"You Greeks are a bunch of pigs!" screamed the Russian.

"Your insides are rotten. You must have shit in your pants, old man. I should kill you just to prevent the spread of your plague to the mainland. Step back away from me a few steps so that I am out of your range of contamination. You are one sick old man, Greek!" yelled the unsteady lieutenant.....

Twenty minutes later, the Russian sailors returned to the top deck where the Greek had struck up a conversation with the officer about Russian women. The lieutenant had casually lowered his weapon.

"Where did you get these photographs, Greek?" asked the Russian officer while he perused through a thick stack of card-sized pictures from Leonidas' wallet.

"Look at the asses of these women!" shouted the officer to his men, all standing around him.

"We could drown in these vaginas! These are 'real' Russian women!" screamed the sailors.

"They are the women of 'Petrov the Russian' in Odessa," said Leonidas. "He has the best harem on the Black Sea. He has them exercised and sweated before giving them to you. Your order is their command. These Russian women are young and limber. They are world class athletes with world class bodies. All the girls are trained to please, Gentlemen. I have had each and every one of those beautiful specimens.... If you have time, I can show you video," said the Greek.

"You have had these women?" asked the Russian officer incredulously, giving back the stack of photos. "You have contaminated them with your filth?" he asked.

"Yes. I have had them all many times. I have spent countless evenings with the best of them. I pay well. I am one of Petrov's best customers," added the Greek.

The lieutenant glanced at his men and tilted his head in disbelief. His eyes became small. Deep furrows formed on his forehead.

"How can that be?" he murmured slowly. "How can women like these open their legs to something like you? You are a dirty Greek pig! Unbathed and unshaven, the smell of fish and shit are all over you. It's a disgrace!"

"Well, perhaps, you shouldn't visit Petrov in Odessa," said Leonidas to the Russian. "I am perfectly fine not sharing the women with you. They are beneath the standard of a glorious Russian naval officer, I am sure. Let all the ladies wallow in misery with me....."

"The trawler is clean!" reported the last sailor, running up to the officer.

"The trawler is clean?" yelled the officer. "Nothing is clean on this ship! Nothing this old man touches could be clean!"

The Russian finally asked to see the Greek's fish cargo. He was taken by Leonidas to the containment area. The captain opened the hatch and let the Russian peek inside. The foul stench caused the officer to quickly retract from the opening with watery eyes.

"Black Sea anchovies are very oily and we do not have refrigeration," said the Greek, explaining away the horrible odor. "It's hard to believe people enjoy eating these things," commented Leonidas as he closed the hatch.

"It's difficult to believe many things on this ship," said the Russian officer. "But it is not my job to believe all this craziness. God help the world from these Greeks!"

Without saying another word, the Russians returned to their ship and rapidly cast away from the trawler. When the patrol boat had disappeared from view, the Greek captain opened the fish storage hatch and told Stansfield and Boroshkova to come out.

"I said I could talk them into believing anything. These Russians are overestimated by your people, Rodrigo," laughed Leonidas, before pointing west and shouting, "Next stop: Romania!"

CHAPTER 5

Achilles' Heel

Human beings have weaknesses. Some are physical deficiencies or malformations which diminish our abilities to fight. Others are mental cognitive limitations which lead to misjudgements in action. Only shortcomings and misdeeds lacking moral and ethical rectitude are unconquerable with one's own sense of spiritual honor and courage. Because in the performer of the immoral and unethical act, there can be no honor or courage to call upon. There lies the weakness in the doer of wrong, a lack of all things virtuous and commendable.

The Danube River forms in the Black Forest of southern Germany as rivulets and flows for more than 1700 miles southeastwardly, passing four Central and Eastern European capitals. It empties into the Black Sea via its mouth on the shores of Romania and the Ukraine. The Danube receives more than 30 smaller tributaries as it travels through ten countries towards its delta - the second largest in Europe, next to the Volga River in Russia. It stood as the northern border of the Roman Empire for centuries and has been a valuable conduit for trade since man civilized the European continent.

The Europa Canal in Bavaria, completed in 1992, is a 106 mile long channel connecting the Danube and Main Rivers between the German cities of Kelheim and Bamberg. Because the Main discharges into the Rhine River at Wiesbaden, a 2200 mile European transportation corridor exists between the Danube Delta and the Rhine's delta on the Dutch coast of the North Sea.

The greater part of the Danube Delta lies in Romania. As the river nears the Black Sea, it divides into three main branches. The Chilia borders the Ukraine, while the Sulina and St. George Channels lie in Romania further south. The Sulina Channel is the shortest and most navigable of the three. The small town of Sulina, the easternmost point of the old European Union, lies at the mouth of the Sulina Channel on the Black Sea coast.

The Danube Delta is a low alluvial plain, formed by the deposition of sediment brought down by the river from the European highlands over thousands of years. It is composed of wetlands and marshes, streamlets, ponds, and lakes, with interspersed sand dunes and floating reed islands. Stands of willow, white poplar, and oak trees lie scattered across the area. Hundreds of species of birds and mammals inhabit the delta, creating a natural wonderland.

The *Spartan Prince* neared the Romanian coast before dawn. Captain Leonidas sat on the ship's foredeck with

Michael Stansfield, talking old fisherman stories. Aside from the close call with the Russian patrol boat, the trip had been uneventful. The old fisherman had again earned his keep, promoting and facilitating freedom in his own personal way. The voices of the ancient Greek philosophers were still vibrantly alive in him. And he liked to share what he knew with those he deemed worthy.

The weather had cooperated with calm seas and a clear sky. While the men spoke, the still dark night had a bright star-filled glow. The white band of the Milky Way spread across the black heavens as if spread by a painter's quick brush. A pale alabaster interstellar gaseous haze filled the space between the individually shiny stars. The scene imparted both a sense of smallness and vastness at the same time. Looking up at the wonders of the cosmos put everything in perspective. The problems of man were insignificant, except naturally, for man himself.

"What do you see and feel when you look up there, Rodrigo?" asked the old Greek, motioning with his head towards the stars.

"Like with everything else, it's all in the eyes and mind of the beholder," answered Stansfield. "Some will see mathematics and rules of physics, others see the periodic table of elements and the ingredients for life. While many will see artistic creative intelligent design and hear the voice of God, or hear the tones of Beethoven or the strings of Mozart. Some may feel diminished by the grandness of the heavens, while others may feel the empowerment of being. It's all in the eyes and mind of the beholder, Leonidas. I see, hear, and feel all these things."

"Where do you think it all comes from, Rodrigo? Are we all a big accident? Is the universe just a puff of smoke or misfire of random energy? And if so, from where was the energy born? Where is the beginning to all this? Is there an intention to the creation?"

"You ask too many questions for a fisherman, Leonidas!" laughed Stansfield.

"Even a fisherman desires wisdom, Rodrigo," whispered the old Greek.....

"Do you think there will be wars a thousand years from now, Leonidas?" asked Michael.

"No, I don't," responded the fisherman in the quiet of the night. "Quarrels over misunderstood ancient holy scripture will have ended us by then. Disputes between nations and religions over books written long ago from the imaginations of 'wise' men will lead to the demise of the life experiment on Earth. Instead of the greatness we were truly capable of, man will choose to follow his hardened heart. He will allow the vices of pride and competition to control his destiny. Man's misinterpretations of religious doctrine will channel us all into the oblivion.... The reason and logic required to survive and prosper will have abandoned us long before a thousand years, Rodrigo. That is what I think."

"If you think this way, why do you do what you do?" asked Stansfield.

The old fisherman took his eyes off the stars and turned his gaze to Stansfield. He smiled kindly.

"Young American, I do not wish to be part of the problem. I prefer to be a spoke in the wheel of the solution. I do not want my soul, or my sons' and grandsons' souls, to be burdened by the yoke of irresponsibility. I wish absolution from the sins of man. I will not be guilty in destroying the potential magnificence of the human spirit. I will not be a party to the illogical and the insane. I desire to return to my Creator with a clean conscience. I will have done all that I could, all of my life. It is all rather simple. Either one chooses to heal, or one seeks to harm. The road taken reflects the essence of the person.

"There are no excuses for selecting to injure man's fragility. My function on this earth is to cure the ills created by others' misguided mistakes. My contribution may be small, Rodrigo, but it is all that I can offer. Besides, everything is small beneath the glory above us...."

Leonidas returned his gaze to the stars. Stansfield did as well. Both men, young and old, contemplated the future of mankind.... Time passed.

"That white flashing light to the southwest is the main lighthouse at Sulina, twenty miles away," said Leonidas.

Then pointing slightly to the northwest, the Greek added, "There is the navigation light from Leuke Island, home of Achilles. We are close now. I sense his power."

Stansfield was fascinated by Leonidas' comment. "What do you mean, Leonidas?" asked Michael.

"Achilles, the Greek hero of the Trojan War, is buried in his temple at the base of the lighthouse at Leuke Island. It is a place of prayer for all Greeks," said Leonidas emphatically. "If one stays quiet, you can still hear his heart beat from beneath the sacred soil of his tomb. For sailors, it is more of a beacon than the shine of the lighthouse. Follow the beating of the heart, and one will arrive home."

Achilles, the great warrior of Homer's *Iliad*, had been a favorite story of Stansfield since childhood. His mother would often read him excerpts from the classic tale as he prepared for bed.

Famous for his rage and fighting prowess, the events of the Trojan War had humanized Achilles and had exposed his only weakness - his heel. Not protected by his shield or armor, Achilles had fallen to a single arrow shot at his heel.

The irony of such an unexpected cause of terminal failure had always intrigued the young Stansfield. As a boy, he had always guarded against the unexpected, hoping never to have a weak point where he could be taken advantage of. This thinking had served him well throughout his career in the Navy and CIA.

"Like Achilles, all men have weaknesses which can be exposed, Rodrigo. The mind must be constantly thinking and analyzing potential soft spots where your enemy can attack. Even an old fisherman like me can defeat you by taking advantage of your vulnerabilities.

"We all have debilities, Rodrigo. Our mental and physical armor is rarely complete. Deficiencies may lie in physical prowess or in the abilities of the mind. Perhaps honor or courage are lacking. Maybe we lack a sense of self-sacrifice or the wisdom to realize it.

"If you can define your enemy's weak point and take advantage, the contest's result will always be in your favor. At times, however, the exhaustive obsessive ritual of analysis can be your downfall. Courage comes from quick action before analysis exhaustion can take place. There is no replacement for the value of a fast analytical mind," concluded the Greek captain.

The old Greek fisherman was a tough man to beat, thought Stansfield. He was a repository of wisdom. Leonidas used his reflections like currency, enriching everyone he felt deserved to be paid in full. The fishing trip to Sulina had been a valuable one. Michael felt much wealthier for it.

"It is time for you to continue the job at hand, young American. Continue your journey intelligently. Sometimes the balance of the world tilts on the seemingly least obvious event. Make every move like it's your last. Don't believe one can come back and correct errors of prior judgement. You rarely can. Fix things the first time through and live to fight the next battle. And there will be a next battle. There always is. I wish you good fortune. Aim your arrow high and it will find its mark. I have confidence in you, young American."

Leonidas slowly walked away with his grizzled beard and youthful spirit. He returned to the captain's station and ordered the ship to sail towards the Sulina lighthouse.....

As the sun began to rise behind them, the *Spartan Prince* entered the Sulina Channel at the mouth of the Danube. It traveled past the towering lighthouse towards the port town, five miles further inland.

The river's delta reminded Stansfield of the Florida Bay wetlands and mangrove islands at the southern entrance to the Everglades. He had sailed that area extensively through the years with his father and brothers. It briefly brought back good memories of anchoring their boat, *American Amaranth*, in the clear blue waters of Florida Bay and swimming as children with their parents while dolphins swam nearby.

The ship sailed past two more inactive lighthouses, relics from the old Ottoman Empire days of Romanian occupation. Sulina was still asleep while the *Spartan Prince* continued along the channel toward the port's North Pier.

Captain Leonidas parked his big old boat at the western end of the pier, behind the fresh and sleek Italian sports yacht - *Conqueror of Worlds*. Waiting for Stansfield at the stern of the yacht was Hickory Calhoun.

Stansfield assisted Veronika Boroshkova off the trawler. Before leaving, she kissed Leonidas on the cheek. Michael politely turned to the Greek and thanked him for his work.

"America is appreciative of your courage, Captain. Your insight has been invaluable. Your wit and intelligence are priceless," smiled Stansfield. "Thank you again for your bravery."

"Young lady, please accept my gift," said Leonidas as he handed the Russian romance novel to the Ukrainian beauty. "I could never imagine reading that book again without having you before my tired eyes. It's yours to keep. Finish it when you can and imagine me as the protagonist lover in the story. Bring to your mind and life my unfulfilled desires," smiled the old Greek.

"What a woman, Rodrigo," whispered Leonidas while Veronika walked away. "I wish America would have considered my request for a change in payment. No amount of gold on this earth could match the value of that woman for me. She is a treasure to behold. Well, maybe next time, Rodrigo," sighed the fisherman.

"And for you my friend, Rodrigo, I have nothing worthy to offer as a keepsake. I'd give you my captain's cap, but I have no other to protect me from the sun. I hope a hearty embrace is enough."

The Greek captain bear-hugged Stansfield before he stepped off the *Spartan Prince*. As Michael walked onto the *Conqueror*, Leonidas shouted at him.

"By the way, Rodrigo, at my age there is nothing brave! I have nothing to lose! Courage and bravery are for the young. They have everything to lose....

"Remember to protect your heel and aim your arrow at your enemy's vulnerabilities. Think quickly and live. It is much better than dying!"

Leonidas tipped his cap at Michael with a sparkle in his eyes. The old man had enjoyed his company.....

Stansfield and Boroshkova were welcomed onto the *Conqueror* by Calhoun, while the *Spartan Prince* departed port for yet another mission. There was a lot to talk about before beginning the next phase of the operation.

"Nice to see you arrive as scheduled, Michael," said Hickory. "Who's your friend?"

"Veronika Boroshkova was my contact in Sevastopol. I didn't feel it was safe for her to stay after some unexpected housecleaning. She's asked to come along, if Langley approves, of course. If not, we'll turn her over to CIA here in Sulina," said Stansfield, setting his suitcase on the aft deck.

"Let me sit Veronika down in the salon with Peter Reynolds while they pass her information to Langley," suggested Calhoun.

"Meanwhile, I'd like to introduce you to the rest of the team, Michael."

Boroshkova was escorted into the boat. Calhoun and Stansfield walked towards the bow.

"Peter is a Navy SEAL, recently returned from Guam after deployment in the South China Sea. He and Tom Garfield, another SEAL, are fully trained in the operation of all offensive weapon systems on board ship. Tom was with me in the Congo, after spending time in the Persian Gulf over the past two years," said Calhoun with Garfield standing watch near the bow's stem.

"Peter and Tom are also specialists in naval underwater demolitions using Composition H6 explosives," continued Calhoun.

Michael and Hickory walked into the ship's galley kitchen where the rest of the team had congregated for breakfast. Dr. Thomas Egan stood over the gas burners like a mad scientist in his laboratory, cooking scrambled eggs and ham. Basha Ludwik, Jakub Krol, and Bruno Bonnet sat at a table waiting to eat.

"Thomas is our resident scientist and cook," laughed Calhoun.

"Bruno works with French External Security and is a dead shot sniper. Give him a rifle and he'll pass a bullet through a keyhole at a mile away without breaking the lock.

"Jakub and Basha are AW, Polish Foreign Intelligence.

"Jakub could duel you in a bout of judo and make you forget you were NCAA champion. I've seen him in action. He's better than the Jap masters that invented it. Don't cross him, Michael, and you'll be fine." The men laughed.

"Basha has been assigned to anti-GPNR for the past three years and knows all that can be known about our characters on the *Katarina*. She may look beautiful and refined, but she can strike faster than a pit viper. At the very least, she's pleasing to the eye. When you feel down, just rub up against her and get your testosterone levels up!" smiled Calhoun.

Stansfield shook hands with all his teammates. He'd get to know them better later.

"Now, let me introduce you to our ship, Michael," said Calhoun before he led Stansfield up the stairwell to the flybridge above the pilothouse.

"What problems did you encounter in the Crimea, Mikey?"

"The Russians knew we were there. They tried to take me down outside of Balaclava, but I intervened and sent them all to meet *Perun*." Stansfield referred to the ancient Slavic god of lightning and thunder.

"The question is, how did they know?" commented Stansfield. "Who informed them of my arrival? My intuitions tell me it wasn't Boroshkova."

"You presume it was the Russians, Michael. Who the hell knows for sure? There are so many interests involved in this caper that not even a clairvoyant could see through the fog. It's uncertain who 'they' were and 'who' tipped them off. It could be anybody.

"I've never been involved in a case like this. Behind every dark shadow, there's someone holding a knife. You never know who that someone is and for whom they work. There are many competing interests involved, Michael. We can't presume anything. Even with verification, we should hold some healthy distrust."

"Are you implying we should distrust information from home headquarters?" asked Stansfield.

"No..... Not necessarily... I just think we should use our brains to discern the potential confusions which can arise on this particular mission. I've been on this case longer than you have. Trust me. It's a very unsettling set of circumstances that we're facing. I personally am beginning to doubt any piece of information which comes my way. A healthy degree of doubt may save lives down the line."

"Because I still don't have my hands wrapped around this case as you do, I'll agree to go for now with your recommendations, Hickory. But regarding Boroshkova, I'll let Langley make the call. They engaged me with her, and I'll allow them to disengage if they wish. If they assign her to us for the remainder of the operation, we'll continue to carefully study the issue together as we go further along.

"One thing for certain, though, I didn't tip the enemy off while in Sevastopol – regardless who that enemy may be. They found out about my presence only at the last minute. That's why they rushed me outside of Balaclava.

"If they would have known of my presence earlier, they would have shown themselves earlier. They would have likely prevented my three days of surveillance around the *Katarina*. The enemy would have never allowed me time to gain valuable information which could have jeopardized their mission from the start.

"I must presume the men who intercepted me at Balaclava wanted the *Katarina*'s mission to be successful. And they wanted to disturb our plans on the *Conqueror* to stop them. They felt I was a risk to their mission.

"Naturally, my presumption is based on the information that you have provided. I am assuming the *Katarina* is carrying deadly cargo, intended to kill Americans. This is what you have divulged to me. Is this a fact, Hickory?"

"Yes..... That is a fact. There is no doubt that the *Katarina*'s mission is to transport materials intended to kill millions of Americans on our homeland soil. The men on that ship have evil designs against the interests of the United States. Those nations and groups supporting the *Katarina*'s mission are enemies of America. These are not assumptions. They are facts, Michael.

"An assumption is that the men who intercepted you at Balaclava were trying to impede your progress against the *Katarina*'s mission. We can presume, I suppose, those men you killed were enemies of the United States. They were 'bad guys'. But I can't truly begin to presume for whom they worked. The list of America's enemies is long and getting longer every day."

"I'm sorry, Hick, but this sounds elementary. Unless you're keeping important critical data from me, it is obvious the men trying to kill me were enemies of the United States. I don't give a fuck who they were working for. The bottom line is they got tipped off at the last minute. Someone fed the bad guys the information as they surmised it. It was a late leak. Someone who wasn't supposed to know, suddenly knew. Therefore, Boroshkova is not a clear suspect. Anyone else could be. I'll let the analysts at Langley think about that for a while," said Stansfield.

Calhoun had information unknown to Stansfield. As leader of the operation, he was under orders to discuss data only when pertinent to the immediacy of conditions. Even so, not even Hickory had all the details and specifics. Only Mitrano knew these important minutiae. But the minute details were the giant pieces of information which connected all the dots. No one on the *Conqueror* would have the luxury of being able to connect all the dots. Only Mitrano could.

Calhoun had many questions concerning the mission. He understood that only the directors of French and Polish intelligence knew significant details of *Operation Europa*, outside of Langley and US Naval Intelligence at the Pentagon. His teammates had not known of Michael Stansfield's involvement until his arrival on the *Conqueror*.

Possibly, there was a mole somewhere in the intelligence chain in Washington, Paris, or Warsaw, thought Calhoun. Maybe the director's office of French or Polish security had been infiltrated by the GPNR or FNNP. Perhaps Langley had been compromised.

Both Stansfield and Calhoun understood the fatal implications if their mission was compromised at the highest level. Under those conditions, their deaths could come swiftly. They also couldn't help but wonder about the true allegiances of their teammates on board the *Conqueror of Worlds*.

There was serious discomfort in their minds. Stansfield and Calhoun couldn't reveal all their doubts to each other. By nature, espionage was a game of shadow and distrust. Not even friendship could be depended on, under certain circumstances. *Operation Europa* was one of these circumstances. The men were uneasy while they toured the spy-boat.

"This ship was designed and built for the CIA outside of Naples, Italy," said Calhoun. "It's fully automated and fortified to deal with any contingency. Although heavy for a 107 foot long cruiser, it has a top speed of 38 knots and a shallow draft to maneuver the European river system. It has two gas turbine engines with 5400 horsepower and two additional auxiliary diesels.

"We have twin MK46 30 mm gun weapon systems at the stern with armor-piercing and high explosive incendiary rounds. On the bow of the ship, we have twin surface vessel torpedo tubes with lightweight 12 inch torpedoes and remote homing for use against surface vessels at any distance within ten miles. These weapon systems are physically built into the structure of the ship and are completely concealed. They are equipped with laser range-finders and infrared sensors, and can be operated at the weapon systems locally or remotely at the operating console in the combat information center of the pilothouse.

"In addition, we have two high speed jet skis and enough Composition H6 to sink the *USS Ronald Reagan*. Inside the main body of the ship, our storehouse contains three M60 machine guns and four Javelin shoulder-fired missile launchers with automatic self-guidance and infrared seekers. We also have Stinger anti-aircraft missiles. Reynolds and Garfield brought their US Navy scuba gear with closed circuit oxygen systems and dry suits for shallow cold water operations.

"Electronically - radars, depth sounders, sonars, and GPS instruments will keep us informed of everything around us. They will keep us tuned to the position of the *Katarina* at all times. Advanced encryption programs will allow us to communicate with Langley, the Pentagon, and our field agents on land without risk of having messages intercepted by the enemy.

"This ship is a floating arsenal. It is capable of doing tremendous hurt on anyone or anything of our choosing," concluded Calhoun.

Calhoun and Stansfield spent the next three days reviewing their plan of action along the Danube, Main, and Rhine rivers. The locations of all safe houses in towns and cities along the way were studied.

There were more than 600 CIA and US Naval Intelligence agents assigned to this mission. Most of them were on dry land along the route designated, and further inland searching for the second 'lost shipment'. There were also friendly units on the waters upstream from them. Stansfield realized there were many enemy agents scattered along the same routes.

This was a dangerous mission for everyone involved. The men on the *Katarina* could possibly know details of the CIA operation to intercept them. It was of critical importance for the CIA's 'inside man' to pass on vital information regarding decisions being made on the *Katarina*. Hopefully, he could also uncover any moles within the CIA's network. Finding the 'lost shipment' of AZEV, and revealing any potential rendezvous points along the river route, were essential to the mission's success.

Michael Stansfield and Hickory Calhoun sat in the *Conqueror's* pilothouse in the early morning of June 9. They watched their satellite screens show the *Katarina's* position just outside the entrance to the Sulina Channel at the mouth of the Danube. Langley had relayed information from the 'inside man' that the enemy ship would refuel in Sulina before quickly continuing into Romania. The *Conqueror of Worlds* would follow the enemy upstream at a discreet distance to avoid detection.

Langley ordered Calhoun to take Veronika Boroshkova into his team. Everything was set for *Operation Europa*. Nine agents of the Free-World - a squad composed of Americans, Poles, a Frenchman, and a Ukrainian - would do their utmost to stop a ship intent on delivering deadly cargo. The contraband had the potential to kill millions of innocent Americans. The consequences of failure were unacceptable to all the patriots involved. A great adventure was about to begin.

CHAPTER 6

Merchants of Death

The ancient instinctive social drive to congregate in tribal groups had tremendous survival advantages for primitive man. Defense in numbers was important for acquiring the necessary safe lands, water and food sources, viable quality sexual contacts, and trade materials essential in developing cultures. As human groups grew in number and size, government hierarchies emerged. The evolution of distinct languages and different religious beliefs further divided the many human cultures from each other. From large tribes, nation states formed.

Although advancing science and technology improved civilization, progressive modernity also produced harsher and more deadly combat weapons. The weapons were needed to protect the successful tribes from envious competing adversaries. They were also essential to expand the resource base for accommodating larger populations.

As more nations formed, alliances between them became more common. States with similar philosophies and viewpoints joined to defend their common interests against other states with different approaches to the world around them. The alliances would fight and compete against each other for the same reasons as the ancient tribes of the past – survival resources.

Modern man is more intellectually and emotionally complex than his ancient ancestors. He has more advanced science and technology. He enjoys more sophisticated forms of arts and recreations. He has more complicated forms of government. But at his core, he is still in a Darwinian struggle to survive against his competitors. Modern man continues to fight for his resources because they are limited. However, his weapons can now destroy the planet in which he lives. Belligerent separation of tribe or culture can now lead to global wars with catastrophic results for every living thing on Earth.

Unless the bellicose separations between human cultures can be eliminated, the near future of mankind is bleak. Not much hope exists for continuing our experiment in the universe. A global human cultural fusion is a prerequisite for our survival into the distant future. We do not want to join prematurely the 99.9% of creatures and plants which have gone extinct. Wisdom is the only remedy for war.

Alliance treaties have been at the center of European diplomacy for centuries. In recent history, "Friendship Agreements" between European powers have been more responsible for conflict than wars prevented. Especially in our age of atomic deterrence, the potential for paranoid distrust between nations and crescendo belligerent rhetoric leading to war must be always kept in mind when conducting state affairs. Today's wars carry much more risk for catastrophic consequences. The survival of entire cultures can be in play. The military concept of "Total War" has become an existential issue. The art of diplomacy has never been more important. The last two centuries have shown us how devastating the repercussions of poor statesmanship can be for the survival of nations.

Six years after the French Revolution of 1789, Brigadier General Napoleon Bonaparte took command of the French Army in Italy. As he achieved successive victories, France's influence spread across the European continent and into North Africa. In 1799, Napoleon staged a coup d'etat against the French Directory and was proclaimed First Consul at the age of thirty. The French invaded Austria in 1800, and expanded their border to the Rhine River. After a short period of peace, Napoleon's aggressive foreign policy led to war with Britain in 1803, and a series of conflicts against all of France's European neighbors.

Napoleon crowned himself Emperor of France in 1804, and continued to achieve repeated victories over the next eight years. The extended campaigns of the Peninsular War in Spain and the 1812 invasion of Russia were critical turning points in Napoleon's aura of invincibility. His Grande Armee became badly depleted and never fully recovered its prior glory.

An alliance between Britain, Russia, Prussia, and Sweden formed in the Spring of 1813. The stronger coalition defeated Napoleon's army at Leipzig in October 1813, and subsequently invaded France in early 1814. After being forced to withdraw to southern France, Napoleon abdicated on April 1, 1814, and was exiled to the island of Elba near his birthplace of Corsica. Less than a year later, he returned to France and reclaimed the French crown on March 20, 1815.

A coalition of 600,000 troops from Britain, Prussia, Austria, and Russia, under the command of the Duke of Wellington, agreed to assemble in Belgium for an invasion of France to begin in early July. Hearing of the plan, Napoleon marched his army north to destroy the coalition before it could organize. The defeat of the French Army at Waterloo set the stage for the next two centuries of European history. France never recovered its greatness after Waterloo, and the great powers of Britain, Russia, and a subsequently unified Germany dominated the geopolitical landscape on the continent.

Prussian Minister-President Otto von Bismarck's unification of Germany in 1871, after Prussia's defeat of Denmark, Austria, and France in successive wars, created a powerful behemoth on mainland Europe. Bismarck spent the next twenty years of his life trying to keep France isolated and maintaining friendly constructive relations with Austria and Russia. He promoted French colonial expansion into Africa to keep her occupied out of Europe. He also simultaneously tried to prevent war between Austria and Russia over the Balkans, which could have potentially forced Germany's involvement on the side of Austria and possibly driven Russia to an alliance with France. Notwithstanding Bismarck's delicate diplomatic dance, the latter nineteenth century saw Germany's progressive alignment with Austria and increasing economic, political, and military cooperation between Russia and France. The stage had been set for World War One.

After relatively friendly relations between Germany and Russia in the nineteenth century, the Great War of 1914-1918 found them on opposite sides. The Bolshevik Russian Revolution in 1917 forced the Russian Army to withdraw from her campaigns against Germany in Eastern Europe. Germany's defeat by the allied armies of Britain, France, and the United States in the Great War led her down a dramatic slide to economic collapse and eventually into the hands of Adolf Hitler.

The totalitarian systems of the Soviet Union and Nazi Germany were ideologically antagonistic. The world was shocked when Russia and Germany signed the Ribbentrop-Molotov "Non-aggression Pact" on August 23, 1939. Hitler and Stalin had made a number of secret pro-tocols, agreeing to "spheres of influence" in Finland, the Baltic States, Romania, and Poland. They would invade these lands and share the spoils. The pact was broken with Hitler's invasion of the Soviet Union in June 1941.

The Soviet Union occupied East Germany after the Nazi defeat in World War Two. On November 9, 1989, the Berlin Wall fell and the Soviets withdrew from their bases in Eastern Europe. The Americans, however, continued to maintain over twenty military bases in Germany into the twenty-first century. The US bases gradually became a source of friction among the German people.

Germany and Russia had been both "friends" and enemies multiple times over the past two hundred years. Through the centuries, intricate games of diplomatic strategy had been played by the best statesmen of both countries in attempts to further the positions of their people. They had fought two major wars against each other in the twentieth century with the resultant death of millions. Since 2000, both countries had seen the rise of radical nationalist movements among their people. The severe economic problems of Europe since 2008, and the subsequent austerity measures implemented, caused progressive growth of nationalism and radical ideology throughout Europe. Governments in Russia and Germany particularly became more anti-American with time.

The United States was blamed for the collapse of the Euro and for actively participating in the breakup of the European Union. America was seen as "gaining" geopolitical and economic power at the expense of a weaker and divided German-dominated Europe. In the eyes of the radicals, American globalization had to be stopped.

The US-Allied victory against China, North Korea, and Iran in the first global war of the twenty-first century had only hastened the speed and intensity of the anti-American movements in Germany and Russia. Their federal governments had become infiltrated with progressively more aggressive radicals. Nationalist underground militias had united and formed an "alliance" to further their aim of controlling the European mainland. They wanted to push the Americans out of Central and Eastern Europe.

The men of the *Katarina* were loyal fascist soldiers in the anti-American movement. They were willing to die in the advancement of their cause. The fanatical ideology had become an obsession. They intended to destroy America's power with evil means and then establish authoritarian rule over all of "lesser" Europe. The last vestiges of American influence over the French and German governments had to be eliminated. These were the sentiments of the *Katarina's* men as they assembled in the ship's kitchen galley for dinner, 100 miles up the Lower Danube in southeastern Romania on the night of June 9.

The CIA man on the *Katarina* sat at the long galley table and ate his plate of fried fish, potato pancakes, and rye bread. He quietly watched while others filed into the room to have dinner. Several bottles of vodka and German Schnaps were placed on the table at regular intervals. The men poured tall drinking glasses full of their favored drink, before sitting to eat and argue with each other.

The night before in the western Black Sea, there had been two bloody fistfights during dinner. Arguments developed over regional pride and the selective physical attributes of German and Russian women.

The developing talk tonight was about the qualifying rounds for the *futbol* world championships. A German and a Ukrainian were vehemently discussing the strengths of their respective national teams, when suddenly the Ukrainian threw his glass of vodka at the German and attacked him with his dinner knife.

The fight quickly broke up when Aleksei Batkin entered the room and stared down the men. The drunken combatants returned to their seats.

"Fucking queers! You pig bastards can't sit and eat for a half-hour without trying to hump the cretin next to you! You cerebrate worse than you smell," laughed Batkin as he threw a fork at the Ukrainian.

"Surely, if you're going to stick someone's throat, you don't use a butter knife! You use this, imbecile!" shouted Batkin, while slamming his Soviet-era combat knife into the wooden table.

"This blade cuts right through flesh and bone. A real man uses a real knife to decapitate the enemy," murmured the Russian.

"Keep your asses in the seats, or I'll cut off your heads and shit down your necks!" screamed the angry GPNR militia leader.

"Pass me that bottle of vodka!" yelled Batkin, pointing across the table.

Instead of pouring a glass, the Russian simply bit the cork away and drank straight from the bottle. Batkin's anger further distorted his already disfigured face. The upper third of his left ear was missing. So was his left eyebrow. A thick purple scar ran across his left cheek from beneath his lower eyelid to the lateral creases of his upper lip. His scalp and face were clean shaven to better expose his battle scars from Chechnya. The Russian's light blue eyes were steely cold. He was tall and burly with square shoulders. His ham-sized hands seemed capable of breaking someone's neck with a quick snap of his thumbs.

"You stupid pricks make me sick! Who cares about a game? Your country can win a *futbol* match and then have their asses kicked on a battlefield. Who wins in the end? The country with the biggest balls and most bullets wins!

"You Germans had better *futbol* players than us Russians before the war. In 1945, we destroyed your cities, fucked your women, and set all the rules. We had bigger balls and more bullets," laughed Batkin as he swigged from the bottle.

"The scars you see on my face only begin to tell you the story of my life!" shouted Batkin. "I have killed more men in a day than any of you in a lifetime. Women and children too have fallen in great numbers. I haven't discriminated in the killing.

"War is my playground. On the battlefield, I make my own rules. The things I've done would make your worst nightmares feel tame.

"I fed my dogs - human body parts, after butchering them myself. I've raped young girls in front of their fathers and brothers before cutting all their throats. I've burned people alive in their homes. I've bayoneted babies in the Caucasus and used their guts to grease the treads of my tanks.....

"I certainly won't hesitate to cut your hearts out and eat them for dinner. It'd taste better than the shit I'm eating tonight. So don't cross me wrong, cretins. I am the only alpha male on the *Katarina*. Don't ever forget it!"

Feodor Dashkov and Andreas Fuchs entered the galley together and sat near Batkin. Dashkov - a virologist, and Fuchs - a physician, were the most educated men on the ship. Their comical and anemic general physical appearances betrayed their bloodthirsty dispositions.

The very tall and thin, blonde-haired creepy Dashkov wore wire-rimmed spectacles too small for his long face. He had deep set, tiny green eyes with a peculiar psychotic stare. He carried a red leather pouch with his own eating utensils, which he would personally clean after every meal. He was unusual in every aspect of his manner, including his deep voiced monotonic speech that sounded machine-generated.

Fuchs appeared like a midget, next to the giant Dashkov. Only a little taller than five feet, he weighed no more than 110 pounds. Sitting at the edge of the chair, his feet barely touched the ground. He wore round turtle shell-rimmed myopic glasses which made his dark eyes look small. His high pitched voice contrasted with Dashkov's bass.

Dashkov and Fuchs were characters fit for a comic book. They were circus freaks. Their unusual phenotypes and peculiar mannerisms were alarmingly strange.

Batkin, drinking more than eating, looked at Fuchs and grumbled, "Have you spoken to your brothers lately?

"You tell them that if they double-cross me, I'll kill them. I'll put their heads on pikes in front of the Brandenburg Gate and let their blood flow down to the Reichstag. I don't give second chances.

"We control the politicians. I expect them to come through as ordered. You may be a big guy in Germany, Fuchs, but to me you look like a gnome.... You better hope your country abides by our agreement," said Batkin, between swigs of the vodka.

Captain Konrad Wagner, leader of the FNNP militia, had been sitting next to the CIA man. He had listened quietly to Batkin's arrogant display. He had not been amused at all. Tall, muscular, blonde-haired with blue eyes, Wagner typified the German soldier prototype made infamous by the SS troops during World War Two.

Wagner, with the stub of a cigarette at the edge of his mouth, looked at Batkin and said loudly, "Cossack, our politicians listen to us. They don't give a damned shit what you think! You take care of your drunken Russian politicians and we'll manage ours.

"Although we have similar goals in this operation, I don't need to show you any love, Batkin. I don't need to tolerate your psychotic inclinations, *arschficker*! When you speak to my men, address them with respect or I'll cut your tongue out!"

Batkin stood up from his seat, knocking it down behind him. He slammed his fist into the table. "You insolent German bastard! I've broken men's necks for less vehement venom from their mouths. I will not accept your insults, bitch-trooper! Apologize or die!"

Wagner remained calmly seated. He laughed and poured himself a large shot glass of Shnaps, swallowing it in one gulp. The German stared down Batkin at the other end of the table.

"I will not excuse myself for stating the truth, Batkin. No! I will not apologize for stating the obvious facts. And no, you will not kill me! Particularly now, since I have a pistol in my right hand beneath the table, aimed at your testicles. Yes! I will blow away your balls and serve them to my men in nourishment. So sit down and relax yourself. I am certain you and I will have many opportunities on this trip to settle our differences. But tonight will not be one of them. Killing each other so early in our mission would not be advantageous to its success. Put ice in your vodka and cool your spirits."

There was significant competitive friction between Batkin and Wagner. Both were the leaders of their respective groups, and their strong, stubborn, and intolerant personalities would not allow either of them to back down from a fight.

Ivan Petrenko, the leader of the small Fascist Ukrainian Party (FUP) team, abruptly stood from his seat at the table and asked Batkin and Wagner to be recognized. Petrenko was a disciplined and ultraconservative 34 year-old engineer from Odessa who had joined the FUP shortly after its creation in 2004. The heavy set, mild mannered gentleman from the southern Ukraine was considered an intellectual and deep thinker, with a vast knowledge of history and political science. He was known to have some philosophical differences with the fascist groups in Russia and Germany, but generally agreed that America needed to be expulsed from Central and Eastern Europe.

"My grandfather was a young Ukrainian officer in the 14th Waffen Grenadier SS 'Galichina' Infantry Division. He was killed fighting the Red Army Communists in the Battle of Brody in July 1944. My father, Viktor Petrenko, while a professor of mathematics at Moscow State University, was the founder of the Russian Galichina Party for National Revival (GPNR) in 2000. He was assassinated in 2002. While a student at Odessa University, I sensed the Ukraine was being torn apart by Western and Russian interests. I joined the FUP in 2004 as a moral reaction to my perceptions that my birth country was again being manipulated by outsiders, like so many times in the past. I feel I have license to speak frankly.

"Russia's economic and political situation is a catastrophe. A country of nearly 150 million people - birthplace of great scientists such as Ivanovsky and Pavlov, writers of masterpieces such as Tolstoy, Solzhenitsyn, and Pasternak, life changing musicians such as Tchaikovsky and Rachmaninoff - has had dysfunctional government for centuries. It is pitiful. As a result of years of geopolitical squabbling with the West, Russia now finds itself surrounded by American missile systems. Mother Russia never knows when her people will tire of corrupt leaders and overthrow their government. The historically pathetic state of the Russian people continues," said Petrenko as he watched Batkin get progressively drunk.

Ivan Petrenko paused and turned towards Wagner. Their eyes met forcefully. The Ukrainian continued his diatribe.

"Germany is the state equivalent of a manic-depressive bipolar psychiatric patient. Like Russia, 'The Fatherland' has also had its great and accomplished individuals. Geniuses such as Bach, Beethoven and Brahms, Nietzsche, Helmholtz, Koch, Virchow, and Planck have been master contributors to human culture. They are all icons of Western civilization.

"However, extreme miscalculations of German leaders, Wilhelm II and Hitler, led to the ruin of your nation after two apocalyptic world wars. What wastage of human potential. How many brilliant young German minds were poisoned by sick rhetoric, Wagner? How many boys and girls were sacrificed uselessly because of the freakish fancies of deranged leaders? An entire nation was crippled, not once but twice! How much introspection did all this carnage cause in the German survivors of the apocalypse?"

Petrenko's assistant, Pavlo Mitnick, sensing the audience was becoming less charitable, tried to calm the angered FUP leader. He was stared down by Petrenko.

The Ukrainian added, "In essence, we here desire our nations to have conservative nationalist governments which cooperate with each other in order to liberate ourselves from American influence and manipulation.

"The Russians want to eliminate the US missiles pointed at them and drive American troops out of Poland, Bulgaria, and Romania. If this requires subjugation of the peoples of these nations, so be it.

"Germany, and the Fuehrer Nationalists specifically, want to expulse the American military from their country and then economically subjugate the rest of Europe as they feel entitled. Because of their 'presumed' superior intelligence, the German Fascists believe they are the rightful people to dominate the continent. The German people seem unknowing of the direction their leaders are taking them. Perhaps the third time around will be more favorable for the German leadership. I don't know and I don't particularly care.

"Russia and Germany's problems are not necessarily the Ukraine's problems. The Ukraine simply wants to be free. We also wish to regain lost land from our golden Middle Ages, north and west to the Vistula River. This land is historically ours, and we want it back.

"The Ukrainians are willing to cooperate with the Russians and Germans in creating a new Europe without the oversight of the US, Britain, and France. We are amenable to changing one overseer for another, but only if we can recover our lost lands.

"However, and let me be precise with my comments, we will not allow your nations to abuse and plunder our country as you have done in the past. We are determined to dictate our own future. We will rebel and fight against you if not given the opportunity to pursue our due course.

"The ship's mission is to secretly deliver a unique and dangerous cargo to Rotterdam. This material's use in America may later consequentially allow the Ukrainian people's ultimate goals - recovery of our nation and self-dictation. It is a radical and savage plan, I must admit; but centuries of servitude have created savages of the Ukrainian people.

"In order to complete our mission, we must not squabble with each other over women and *futbol*. We can not fail in our duties. If we don't succeed, we will have the Americans breathing down our neck for the next several centuries. We won't be able to pass gas without their approval. You all decide if you wish that to be your fate."

Petrenko sat back down and continued eating his meal. The room remained silent for several minutes. Batkin finished drinking the remainder of his bottle and fell out of his chair in a drunken stupor. Two of his men carried him out of the galley.

Wagner complained, "I am to believe this Batkin character is being supported by high-ranking officers of the Russian Army and Navy? Heaven help my government in dealing with these people. They may be worse than the mongrel mixed-race Americans."

Petrenko asked Dashkov, "Is it possible to tell me when we will receive the second shipment of AZEV?"

Dashkov turned his head to face Petrenko and in his slow-cadenced, deep monotone voice stated, "That information is known only to me, and it will remain that way. That cargo is the GPNR's responsibility, and I don't intend to give information of value to you."

Dashkov walked from the table to the sink nearby and obsessively washed his eating utensils. He carefully dried the cutlery with a clean white towel and held each piece to the light, inspecting for imperfections of uncleanliness. When satisfied, he placed each of them, one by one, into his smooth red leather pouch. He stepped out without making further eye contact with the others in the galley.

Tiny Fuchs laughed out loud as he jumped off his chair. He threw his unfinished meal into the garbage bin and squealed, "These Russians are psychotic!" He also left the kitchen.

The CIA's covert "man inside" perceived that the crewmen of the *Katarina*, these "merchants of death", were dysfunctional and mentally deranged. Yet, he could not decide whether the fact was beneficial for America or more dangerously unpredictable.

He exited the galley to smoke a cigarette out on the deck. He needed to ponder his next move. The CIA had ordered him to create suspicions among the different groups on the *Katarina*. He realized that creating doubt among these thugs would be the only easy part of his mission.

CHAPTER 7

Expect The Unexpected

Spend as much time as possible with the people you love. Learn all you can about them. Appreciate their special gifts and try to see the world through their eyes whenever you can. Empathy and sympathy will help you understand their souls more strongly. In our lives, these will be the moments that you remember and cherish. Their love will stay with you forever.

Captain Julius Stansfield arrived at his Pentagon office early on the morning of June 11. He found Lieutenant Commander William O'Brien, Admiral Thomas Culligan's aide, waiting for him inside. O'Brien had been ordered to personally escort Stansfield to the admiral's office immediately for a special emergency meeting. Stansfield had been at the Pentagon less than two weeks, serving in the

Department of Naval Intelligence and assigned to the Mediterranean and Black Sea regions of operations.

Admiral Culligan had been Vice-Chief of Naval Intelligence under Admiral Julian Stansfield. Culligan had cared deeply for the "Old Man" and reluctantly accepted the position of Director (DNI) after Julian's unfortunate passing.

A few weeks ago, Tom Culligan urged Julius to transfer to the Pentagon. His expertise was needed in analysis of Russia's recent surge in naval ship construction and deployment. New fast and stealthy Russian submarines patrolled European waters and the Atlantic. Silent and well-armed, their aggressive offensive posture was keeping US Navy Intel busy.

Julius was working in his father's old office. Admiral Julian Stansfield's space had remained exactly as he left it a year earlier, before Guam and the Battle of Taiwan. Julius had kept all of his father's photos, memorabilia, and books in the same places his father last saw them. The "old cot" still sat in the corner of the room, with its coffee-stained white pillow at one end.

Captain Stansfield set down his briefcase and officer's cap on his father's desk, and left with O'Brien. It was only a short walk down the hall to the DNI.

Julius was passed into Culligan's private office area, where he found the admiral in conversation with CIA Director Joseph Mitrano. Both men stood to greet the young officer.

"It's nice seeing you again, Julius," said Mitrano. "We weren't able to speak at your father's funeral, but my wife and I were with you in heart and spirit."

"Thank you, Director."

"It's been quite a while, Julius, at least five or six years. I think the last time we conversed was at a lunch at our farm in Maryland. You and your father came for some morning horse-back riding and fine southern cooking. You're an excellent rider, Julius. I was very impressed by your equestrian skills. Your old man wasn't so bad either," laughed Mitrano.

The three men sat in leather sofa chairs around a low table where a simple breakfast had been served.

"Have some coffee, Julius. It's not the high-octane black nectar that your mother was fond of making for us as young naval officers at the Pentagon, but it'll still wake you up a bit before sunrise," smiled Mitrano.

"Olivia's Cuban coffee was the tastiest and most powerful stuff I've ever had. Two cups of that and you could run through walls. No wonder Julian nearly conquered the world for Olivia. I am certain Alexander and his Macedonian Army had some stockpiled during their Persian adventures. It should be standard issue for the US military," loudly laughed the director.

"Tom tells me that you're quite a submarine commander," said Mitrano. "It doesn't surprise me one bit. Cool and collected is how they describe you, Julius. They say you are relentless in pursuit and very timely with your decisions. 'Invincible' is how Pacific Command defines you in their personnel files. These are all qualities of a great leader. I was good friends with your father for over forty years, and I would have described him similarly. So it definitely doesn't surprise me.

"I have always kept up with the exploits of Julian's brave sons. Your brother, Michael, is my best agent, Julius, and I was present at your brother's Mark Medal of Honor ceremony at the White House earlier this year. Your father was very proud of you all, as is America."

Director Mitrano looked over at Culligan. He drank his coffee while the admiral walked over behind his desk and flipped a switch by the bookshelf. A continuous, barely perceptible, high-pitched tone sounded in the room.

"I hope the music is not too uncomfortable on your ears, Julius," said Mitrano.

"You've been a frontline soldier your entire naval career, Julius. As a submarine commander in battle, information flowed to you unimpeded. Accurate data was supplied to you as rapidly as possible. You could count on the validity and timeliness of the information. Your command decisions, crucial to the lives of your men, were made with the aid of trusty facts.

"In my world, Julius, reliable solid data is hard to come by. Deception rules over all other things. You know only on a 'need to know' basis. Confusion and chaos reign in the intelligence environment. Intuitions are critical in achieving a successful outcome even more in my world than in yours.

"Now, I'd like you to imagine a scenario, Julius. Let's say you have been leading a company of men in a violent struggle. Your 200 soldiers have fought bravely with small arms for days to defend a dark, heavily wooded forest. Incessant attacks by the enemy have whittled down your force to less than fifty courageous warriors. There is a lull in the fighting. Night falls. You collect your dead and walk among the troops, preparing them for a final defense. You sense that their will to protect the ideals of freedom is still strong. All of you hope for reinforcement, but none is coming. Death and the end of your nation seems perilously close.

"You and your men fix bayonets. You aim your fire into the blackness of the forest in front of you. You see nothing and you hear nothing. You lie motionless in foxholes, waiting for the enemy to strike. Prayers are recited in the quiet stillness and darkness of the night. Beads of sweat form on your face as you think through all the possible scenarios. You listen for whispers of the foe's voice in the forest or the breaking of a twig on the ground, signalling a sneaky approach. Everyone holds their breath in expectation of the final assault.

"Then, in the deafening silence of it all, you hear a rumble. It's only a slight rumble at first. It picks up slowly but gets louder with every second. You lie in your hole as the sound becomes stronger than even the beat of your heart. The ground underneath you begins to shake. Although you wish it not so, you realize tanks are coming your way. The steel of your bayonet and the fire from your gun will not repel the iron horses of the enemy. The lives of the few men left to you depend on your decisions.

"You rise from the ground and look across the empty space behind you. Under the moon's glow, a flat grassy field invites you to cross it. Another tree-filled forest lies on the other side. It certainly appears safer than the soil you're defending at present. All your men stare at you, awaiting your decision. The metal treads of the enemy tanks clamor closer.

"The field seems to be the only way out. If you stay in your holes, you will die in them. You will be over-run by the enemy, and the freedom of your children at home will cease to be. If your men can reach the forest on the far side, the struggle for liberty can continue.

"But there is a problem..... The grassy meadow contains land mines. Explosive killer mines you, yourself, have invisibly laid."

CIA Director Mitrano stared intensely at Julius. The look on his face was of a man torn by the weight of his decisions. It was obvious in his stare that the freedom of the world depended on his next move.

"Julius, that dream was recounted to me by your father less than two years ago. He said it was a recurring nightmare, one of many he had. It was his way of saying, 'Beware of your actions and their unintended consequences.' He must have passed this germ to me because it's now become my continual torment.

"That day to your father, I said I believed America still had time to weather the storm. I'll never forget his response.

"He looked at me with his big sad eyes and said, 'Joe, even rocks weather slowly with time.'

"Your father was always ahead of the curve, Julius. He seemed to know what was coming before everyone else. He had an unusual appreciation for reality. Although he was a romantic spiritual idealist, he never once took his eye off the facts. I always joked with him by saying that with one eye, he saw much more than anyone else with two.

"While he had a great hope and belief in the eternal nature of the 'good' soul, your father had a fatalistic view on the future of the world. Even so, he never quit trying to improve the world's luck. He was the most consummate warrior for freedom I've ever met.

"He was also personally fearless in his approaches to battle. As a young man, he had a reputation for risk-taking with his life. During his first years in Naval Intelligence, he volunteered for several risky missions. He was involved in actions all over the world. He fought the Cubans in Grenada and Angola, the Russians in Afghanistan, communist rebels in El Salvador and Nicaragua, Islamists in Lebanon, and both Iraqis and Iranians in the Persian Gulf.

"Many years ago, I once asked him why he took such chances with his life. He laughed and said, 'At the end, everyone dies, Joe. Life is more difficult than death.' Mind you, he was madly in love with your mother. Not even Olivia's splendor and devotion could keep him from duties to his country. He was the ultimate in service to America. I've never known anyone like Julian Stansfield.

"Your father also taught me another great lesson in life. He believed there were very few one-sided arguments in this world. Points could usually be made for both sides of a major conflict. Before involving herself deeply in the world's quarrels, America needed to study and understand the different points of view. We should only concentrate our efforts in situations directly impacting the future welfare of our nation. This philosophy has helped me greatly during my tenure at the CIA."

Julius Stansfield sat in his chair, somewhat bewildered. He was patiently waiting for Mitrano's punch line. The director was carefully weaving a story for him. The tale was building to a climax.

"America finds herself in quite a pickle, Julius. A great social schism has formed in our nation. She's being pulled apart by extreme elements on both the 'Left' and the 'Right'. Socialist elements are trying to change her dramatically from a traditional past. Ultra-conservatives are fighting for the moral and ethical high-ground. More and more, the people are taking sides in the argument.

Perhaps, both sides have their meritorious points to make, but our jobs as patriotic Americans is to keep a lasting peace in our nation and live up to the standards of our constitution. You and I, Julius, must be fair-minded in our approach to America's freedom. Above all, however, we must insure that America continues to thrive as a republic and persists in spreading her seeds of liberty throughout the world. If America dies, the world dies, Julius.

"I understand you have been placed in charge of naval intelligence for the Mediterranean and Black Sea regions. This area has always been a very important one for us, Julius. Nearly every European conflict in history has involved these bodies of water. I don't believe that will change into the future. They will always be critical regions of operations for the US Navy.

"What do you know about *Operation Europa*?" asked Mitrano.

"I understand it's a joint CIA/Navy mission up the Danube River to intercept dangerous contraband. That is all I know. The operation's plan is classified TOP-SECRET and not available to my eyes," stated Stansfield.

"Are you at all familiar with *Global Directive 93*?" asked Director Mitrano.

"No..... Am I supposed to be?" questioned Stansfield.

"No..... I don't believe you are. But I'm going to tell you anyway," said the CIA Director. "Everything I am about to tell you is highly classified. Your knowledge of these facts entail tremendous responsibilities to keep the information secret. You go to your grave with the material I am about to divulge. It's not to be discussed with anyone outside this room. Do you understand, Julius?"

"Yes, Sir," responded Julius Stansfield.

"GD-93 was a civilian US government-ordered Pentagon plan put into effect in 1993, shortly after the fall of the USSR. It was directed by your father, Admiral Julian Stansfield. He headed a commission of seven top US commanders who were responsible for its military implementation. Everything that has happened in the world since that time is in some way related to GD-93.

"After the abrupt collapse of the Soviet Union in 1991, it was well understood around the world that the planet had changed. The world public-at-large believed the power of the United States was supreme and unchallenged. People thought a 'Pax Americana' would sweep world peace into the twenty-first century and beyond. There would be no more wars. A new 'Golden American Age' would dominate and progress science and technology into a bright future on Earth. The economics of the world could be concentrated on improving living conditions for everyone on our planet. Hunger would be eliminated through the cultivation of genetically-engineered super-crops. The seeds of modern agriculture would bring super-foods to Africa and Asia. Man would go to Mars and explore the far reaches of our universe. There were hopes of mankind eventually becoming true extra-solar explorers of the cosmos. New pharmaceuticals would cure cancer and better treat the chronic diseases of increasing affluence. Infections by micro-organisms could be wiped out. People would live more healthily, and life spans would be routinely extended beyond a hundred years. The world understood these things to be a certainty. We at the Pentagon knew better.

"We expected the rise of radical Islamism. We knew Chinese Communism would empower itself to contest us.

We believed extreme nationalism would overtake Russia eventually and force her to reinvigorate. Russian militarism would spread its wings in a return to a world power position. A new 'Great Game' would be thrust upon us all for the energy riches of our planet. We realized immediately the great dangers created by the fall of the USSR. The world had become much more unstable and unpredictable than ever before.

"*Global Directive 93* was a coordinated effort by the Pentagon, CIA, the US State Department, and 'Corporate Wall Street' to Americanize the order of world commerce and government. A 'Globalization' would take place under American tutelage. We would protect and enforce a 'New World Order' with a unified commercial and political doctrine. 'Peace on Earth' could be ensured with an orderly system of justice and liberty for all.

"All religions and traditional cultures would be preserved. Nation states would have the freedom to invest their potential in constructive enterprises for their people and not on national defense.

"We truly believed that for mankind to exist into the distant future, all of our planet's inhabitants would need to think and act like 'Earthlings'. Tribal, religious, racial, and national biases and prejudices would have to be eradicated as major sources of international conflict. If not, mankind's future was hopeless. Modern technology and modern weapons of war would ensure our extinction in the not-too-distant future. Our hopes were that the dreams of world peace could be achieved before the end of the twenty-first century.

"World events, although not unexpected, were unkind to our plans. The European Union became quickly dominated by German involvement. The Germans were not interested in an American-directed world. They saw it very differently. They attempted to hijack the workings of government in Europe. Britain and America contested them. France began obstructing their advances. The Germans rebelled economically. It's become a tug-of-war between the US and the European Union. The future of Europe has become clouded.

"Rising Russian nationalism does not wish for an American-directed world order. Russia desires a return to imperialism. They want their old lands back, although those lands never belonged to them in the first place. We have not received the cooperation from Russia that we expected initially. At the beginning, they seemed interested in the global idea. Their great natural resources could be sold more efficiently around the world without obstruction from old enemies. Russia could have become extremely prosperous. The quality of Russian life would have improved tremendously. It has not worked out that way. National pride has lessened their great potential.

"Radical Islam became a major impediment to world progress. The Muslim lands have great cultures to share with the world. They can provide valuable insights in literature, music, and science. They are a great people and could take their rightful place in the global structure. However, radical thought and the constant struggles between the Shia and Sunni prohibit their advance into modernity. A reformation of their ideology would be required before their acceptance into the new world order.

"Chinese Communist State Capitalism refuses to allow for an American-directed global structure. Their expansionist ideas and attempts to control the energy riches of the East China Sea and the South China Sea led to the global conflict with the United States. They are suffering great hardship now as a result of their inflexibility. A civil war in a land of 1.4 billion people is a complicated problem for the world. They should have cooperated from the beginning. They negated a potentially prosperous future for themselves. The culture of the Chinese people will suffer for a very long time.

"*GD-93* is still early in its process. Our goals remain the same. The future survival of mankind depends on a peaceful, integrated, and unified system of world commerce and government. The auspices of the United States are essential to the future success of this system. We are the only ones capable of providing the security necessary for its success. Whether the people of the world realize it or not, a complex unified world order is of existential importance to life on Earth. Mankind will not inhabit a future planet devastated by a nuclear winter. GD-93 incorporates all our efforts in achieving a more perfect union on this planet.

"*Operation Europa* is a combined mission between the United States and certain European nations to prevent a major terrorist attack on the American homeland. As you must surmise by now, my explanation of the operation's details will involve you thoroughly in its implementation. You will now become a working member of the mission, and an active knowing participant in *Global Directive 93*. Do you understand the implications, Julius?"

"Yes, Director, I understand..... I suspect there are those who may think *Global Directive 93* is un-American. That it may remove the 'American identity' from the face of the Earth. I don't believe it will. If anything, it may impart the greatness of our country on the rest of the world. The American ideals of freedom will be better promoted to those unfortunate ones presently unable to live free. It raises our Constitution and Declaration of Independence to a more universal level. Our 'Stars and Stripes' will not disappear. It will be raised higher for all the world to see. As an American, I would be proud in sharing our expertise in the 'Liberty Experiment'. I too see it as the world's only hope for the future. Either we all survive freely and peacefully, or all eventually perish in a cloud of radiation."

Director Joseph Mitrano gave an intricate description of *Operation Europa*. He gave Stansfield information on the terrorist groups involved. He explained in detail the terrorists' plan to drive a wedge between the US, and the French and German governments. He also described the contraband involved and its potential to kill millions of Americans on US soil. Without mentioning names, Mitrano described the men on the CIA ship on the Danube and their extraordinary skills. He expressed his confidence the mission would be successful for the United States and that the contraband ship would be sunk into the Rhine River for important geopolitical effect.

The director continued, "Now, let us be specific of the reason for your presence here today. The CIA discussed the operation with several high level officials in the French and Polish intelligence services. Full details were not revealed. However, we did purposely leak to their service directors that the lead US agent in the operation would be in the Crimea to study the contraband ship and its crew before their departure for Romania and the Danube Delta. This agent was intercepted by the enemy outside of Balaclava in the southern Crimea. As I had expected, the superior skills of our agent allowed him to dispose of the enemy without problems and continue on his mission as scheduled.

"I suspect there is a high-level European intelligence official involved in this terror plot. Although I can not say with certainty at this time, I am confident of the identity. In addition, I believe there may be ministers of European governments also involved.

"The latest intelligence reports indicate the lost contraband shipment will be loaded onto the *Katarina* somewhere in Bavaria. Our agents in Europe followed the AZEV trail from the Ukraine into Poland and the Czech Republic, and finally into southern Germany. We expect to find our European government officials at this rendezvous point in Bavaria. Along with the CIA ship on the Danube, we have over 600 agents on land tracking down the lost shipment and preparing to take down enemy agents when the time arrives. We will have a clean sweep of all the bad guys at the end of the day, I assure you.

"Admiral Culligan and I need you to lead a team of CIA field agents to Munich, Germany, and await further orders there. Five very capable and experienced men have been assigned to you. Their specialty is in the removal of high ranking officials of foreign governments who conspire to damage the interests of the United States through activities which endanger the lives of our citizens."

Stansfield looked perplexed and asked Mitrano, "Why do you want me to lead this mission? I'm a submarine commander. I'm neither an intelligence field operative nor espionage expert. I have no experience in this type of operation....."

"We need a coordinator of your quality, Julius, to secure the result of our mission. Your abilities in leading a large group of men in a desperate struggle, full of danger and risk, make you particularly qualified for this mission. The operation demands keeping a cool head under extreme duress to achieve the desired outcome. The job requirements are uniquely suited to your skills. We don't need you to kill anyone at point blank range. I have many assets capable of performing that duty. I need you to coordinate the men in a plan of attack and then confirm for the United States that the enemy has been eliminated from the field of action. I want you to check for a pulse and make sure the target's pupils are dilated, Captain. Then you may walk away, but only then. Do you understand, Stansfield?"

"Yes, Sir..... I understand completely, Director Mitrano," confirmed Captain Stansfield with slight apprehension.

"You will leave for Switzerland on the morning of June 13," added Mitrano. "Contacts there will take you by boat across Lake Constance to Bavaria where you will board a train to Munich. On arrival in Munich, you'll be taken to the Kaiser Hotel where you will wait for your team members to arrive that same evening. Your driver in Munich will provide you with information on the members of your team as you are taken from the train station to the hotel. Familiarize yourself with their particular skills. The team members will meet with you in your hotel room on the afternoon of June 17 to go over your plans. You and your team will remain in Munich until further orders are given.

"Always 'expect the unexpected', as your father would often say. There may be enemy agents on your trail. You will be given information only on a 'need to know' basis. We can not risk you falling into enemy hands and having critical information extracted from you under torture. Previous experience with this enemy has shown us that they practice very effective torture extraction techniques. I recommend you avoid falling into their hands at any cost.

"Just as you would be on an American submarine, you are free to defend yourself in a moment of need. Your skills are to be used as you see fit. I do not tie my agents' hands.

"When the time arrives, I need your team to move quickly, silently, and efficiently - not unlike the *USS Oregon*. If presented with an emergent situation, engage the enemy only as a last resort. We do not want to advertise your presence in Germany. The CIA ship on the Danube has also been instructed to not engage the enemy unless it's absolutely necessary.

"Secrecy is paramount. We wish to quietly draw out the enemy operatives along the route of the contraband ship. Hopefully, their entire organization can be exposed along the secret route, making it easier for us to track and destroy as many of them as possible. The final objective of our plan is to completely disassemble this movement in Europe before they take control of the national governments in Russia and Germany.

"Do you have any questions, Stansfield?" asked Mitrano.

"No, Sir, I don't."

Mitrano concluded by saying, "It's been a great pleasure to see you again, Julius. It is an honor to be in the presence of another of Admiral Stansfield's courageous sons. As an official of the United States, I would like to express my deepest gratitude for your valiant service to your country."

Director Mitrano shook Captain Stansfield's hand and wished him good fortune. Admiral Culligan walked Julius to the door.

Stansfield exited Culligan's office. He immediately realized his brother, Michael, had been the agent deliberately placed in danger in the Crimea. Mitrano had thrown Michael to the wolves in order to reveal the sinister officials involved in the terror plot. Only Mitrano's best agent could have been used as bait without high risk of losing him. Stansfield also realized Mitrano had intended he know this. The director needed Julius to know his brother was a lead agent on the CIA ship on the Danube. Mitrano wanted the Stansfield brothers together on this mission. It was ironic he would be on land and Michael in water this time.

Julius spent the remainder of the day with his wife, Sandra, and his two girls. He would fly to South Florida the next morning and see Nasrin before departing on the mission. It would have been his father's wish. He needed to assure her that Michael was alive and well.

Stansfield boarded a military transport plane at Andrews Air Base the next day and flew to Homestead, Florida. Shortly after take-off, Julius thought back to the first time he ever heard his father tell him, "Expect the unexpected."

Julius was 18 years old. He prepared on the morning of June 6, 1998, at Radford University Baseball Stadium for the AAA Virginia High School State Baseball Championship Game, scheduled later that evening. The admiral accompanied his son to the field early on the morning of game-day.

Julius' high school team had gone a miraculous 33-0 his senior season. The young Stansfield had led the state in batting average, home runs, and runs batted in.

A tall muscular shortstop, he batted cleanup and played defense flawlessly. Julius had been heavily recruited by the college baseball powerhouses. Major League team scouts fervently attended all of his senior season games. Pittsburgh, Detroit, Los Angeles, Boston, and Chicago informed the Stansfield family their boy would be a first-round pick in the upcoming MLB Amateur Draft.

Julius had always dreamed of playing Major League Baseball. Since he was five years old, he envisioned running the bases at Fenway Park and hitting the ball over the ivy at Wrigley Field. He practiced making double-plays in the World Series with the game on the line, and imagined his name being called for the start of an All-Star Classic. After his stellar senior season, it appeared he would be given an opportunity to continue the quest toward his dreams.

It was a cool 57 degrees on that Saturday morning in the Virginia Blue Ridge Mountains. Julius stood in the batter's cage on the field and took batting practice with his high school hitting coach. Although it was before 8 AM, several college and professional scouts sat in the stands and observed the quick and elegant left handed swings of the state's best ballplayer.

Hard hit line-drives skipped off the moist, perfectly manicured, green outfield grass and ricocheted off the wooden outfield wall with an audible thump. Every three or four swings, the ball flew out of the park like a rocket and landed on the far side of the soccer field behind the stadium. After 25 minutes of batting balls to all fields, Julius took ground balls at shortstop and showed his strong right arm with accurate zip-line throws to first base.

He was an oddity for a shortstop. While he threw right handed, he batted left handed. His swing and large size for a middle-infielder projected favorably to the Major League level. Enthusiastic scouts believed Julius was a natural and had extreme God-given talents.

The young boy certainly looked like a professional ball-player. He was made for a baseball card. His firm 6'2" 200 pound frame, with tree-trunk strong legs and lower body, allowed him to turn on most pitches with superior power. He wore his baseball cap low over his short-cropped blond hair, and his brown eyes seemed to stare at you from beneath the bill. His batting gloves showed from his back pockets while he fielded balls at shortstop and would often fall out as he sped between bases during games. His uniform was always soiled at the end of play with red clay and green grass.

After enjoying morning practice, the admiral sat alone in the first row behind the third base dugout. He watched his son take questions from scouts around home plate.

Julius leaned on his bat and kept his cap on throughout the interview session. He would occasionally look back at his admiring father and smile. Julius sensed he was "living the life" that he had wished for as a child. He had finally arrived at the "big times".

When the last scout finished his questions, Julius grabbed his glove and bat and ran over to his father. The admiral looked at his son as he sat down next to him in the stands, and simply grinned.

"You're a veritable Mickey Mantle, Boy!" laughed the admiral. "Enjoy the good times but remember, it's a long slide down from the top of the world. It's easier to get to the top than to stay there.

"Who's the pitcher going against you tonight, Julius?"

"Dad, it doesn't really matter who's throwing tonight. I don't think anybody can beat me the way I'm feeling!" shouted Julius, swinging his bat through the air.

"You don't think the pitcher feels the same way? That he can't be beaten?" asked the admiral with his usual ironic twist.

"If your opponent's pitcher has gotten this far, I don't think he's going to be trembling on the mound when you come to bat. He may respect you, Julius, but he won't fear you. Now tell me about the pitcher, Julius," demanded the admiral.

"He's big and strong at 6'5" and 240 pounds," said Julius. "His name is Jimmy Stobbs. He's All-State with a nasty fastball that comes up at you, sailing 95 miles per hour. He has a habit of throwing a 12' to 6' curveball when he has two strikes on left-handed batters. The scouting report says he's a tough competitor but predictable with his pitch selection. He won't beat me, Dad," commented Julius as he gripped his bat tightly with both hands.

"Well, I'm sure he's saying the same thing to his father right now," added the admiral. "Remember my words, Son..... If you come to bat late in the game in a critical situation and fall to two strikes, don't expect the curve-ball..... Expect the unexpected..... He will throw you his fastball. He will want to beat you with his best stuff, man to man..... Clear your mind and load up for the fastball. Be the game-changer you've always been," said the admiral, before walking with his son to the locker rooms.

After a warmer spring afternoon in the Virginia mountains, it had again cooled into the evening. The State Baseball Championship Game began between the two best teams left in the tournament. Julius' opponents from Virginia Beach took a two to nothing lead in the top of the third inning on three successive doubles. Julius had saved another run by fielding a ball far to his right and turning a double play to end the inning. His teammates scored a run in the bottom of the fifth inning on a single followed by a walk and a two-base error.

The game remained 2-1 into the bottom of the eighth inning. With two outs, the batter in front of Julius walked. Julius stood in the on-deck circle, swinging his two heavy bats. The opponent's manager walked to the mound to speak with Stobbs. Stobbs had pitched a superb game.

Over seven thousand fans screamed as the stadium vibrated with energy and expectation. Over eighty college and professional scouts sat at the edge of their seats along the first base sideline. Admiral Stansfield, Olivia, and Julius' brothers and sister sat in the first row behind the third base dugout.

Julius threw down his weighted bats and grabbed his 34 inch long, 31 ounce, naturally colored ash bat. He swung it three times through the cool air. He placed the bat between his legs and tightened his batting gloves. Julius then removed his batting helmet and wiped the sweat away from his forehead before replacing it.

While the manager slowly walked off the field and back to the steps of his dugout - Stobbs stood with his large 6'5" frame on the far side of the mound, facing centerfield and the 'Stars and Stripes' above the scoreboard. The wind was blowing strongly to left field. The flag stretched out and exposed all her stars. Cameras flashed as young Stansfield stepped to the batter's box and placed his left foot near its back edge.

Stobbs now stood even taller on the mound as he prepared to throw his first pitch. The pitcher's eyes stared down at Stansfield like those of an ace fighter pilot in a chase. Julius placed his right foot into the box and crouched into his characteristic stance.

Julius took the first pitch fastball at 96 mph over the outside corner of the plate for a called strike. The next three pitches were balls inside. He fouled off the following pitch into the stands behind home plate. The count was now three balls and two strikes, with two outs and a man standing on first base. In the most important game of Julius' life, his team was down 2-1 in the bottom of the eighth inning.

Young Julius asked for a time-out. He stepped out of the batter's box, removed his helmet, and dried sweat off his face with his shirt sleeve. He then adjusted his batting gloves again and stared at his father, sitting along the third base dugout. Julius stepped back into the batter's box and awaited the next pitch from Stobbs.

Stobbs' right-handed curveball would appear as a white dot with a red periphery as it spun towards a left-handed hitter. When one-third of the way to the plate, Stansfield could define the V-stitching of the baseball coming at him at a 45 degree angle. Stobbs' fastball would simply come in low as a white dot and rise late as it reached the plate.

Julius remembered what his father had told him earlier that morning. He focused his mind and loaded up for the fastball. Stobbs wound up and came home with his next pitch.

In a fraction of a second, a loud audible crack reverberated throughout the stadium. It sounded like a cannon shot. Everyone in the stands stood to appreciate the moment. The ball flew out of the park in a line over the right field wall.

Olivia and Julian stayed standing, applauding their son as he circled the bases for the last time in his life. In an ultimate test of champions, a duel of heart and mind and soul, their son had been victorious. The feat was deserving of a long ovation.

After being mobbed by his teammates at home plate, Julius slowly walked back towards the third base dugout with a clearly visible smile of satisfaction on his face. As Julius neared the dugout steps, he looked at his father with a twinkle in his eyes. He nodded his head as if to say, "Thank you, Dad."

Stobbs' team did not score in the top of the ninth inning. Julius returned home as State Champion and Most Valuable Player in his final game.

On June 9, Julius Stansfield was Pittsburgh's top pick in the MLB Amateur Draft. Later that evening, when the admiral arrived home from the Pentagon to celebrate his son's achievement with the rest of the family, Julius presented to his parents his decision to attend Annapolis and not enter professional baseball. He hugged his father, and then looking directly into his face said, "Expect the unexpected."

CHAPTER 8

Freedom House

In the maelstrom that is time and space, we often get lost in the insignificant aspects of life. We concern ourselves with the objective measurements of our presence on earth, wasting valuable time counting possessions and achievements. Little by little, we get sucked into the vortex of the irrelevant. Bodily existence slowly turns to spiritual extinction. We end our lives without ever having lived.

The only genuine natural measure of the quality of a life is its content of love. The more you truly love, the more you truly have lived. If there is an eternity, it will depend only on this truth.

Nasrin couldn't sleep. She had lain in bed awake for more than two hours in contemplation. She was lost in a mystical space of deep awareness, ungoverned by laws of nature. In this world, numbers and science were doomed. Phantasm of illusion shrouded reality. Fear of losing Michael tightly filled the space like magma in the earth. There was no room to breathe or move in the solicitude. Nasrin tried to calm her spirit with hope, but it was to no avail. Painful imagination intruded on her, just as a rampaging fire sweeps through timber. She couldn't escape the inferno's surreal power. Her faith was consumed in the violent storm of doubt, obscuring the view to a future with the love of her life. A desperate sense of abandonment shattered her old peaceful paradise of the mind. Nasrin was alone.

Julius had passed the afternoon with her and Alexander. He had assured her that Michael was well. But she realized the mission was of acute importance for Michael to leave so suddenly. Especially since he had already requested transfer to an analyst position in London. In the CIA, important missions were dangerous missions. And this one was emergent enough for Michael to change his planned future.

Besides, Nasrin thought, Julius had come all the way from Washington to soothe her. He wouldn't have done that if the operation was routine.

Since Michael's departure two weeks before, Nasrin worried for his welfare. She had seen him go to war with the Iranian freedom fighters in Chalus. Michael was not one to shy away from danger. He always accomplished his mission, regardless of the risks. This truth only increased Nasrin's concerns.

After feeding Alexander, Nasrin prepared a cup of tea and entered the study on the ground floor of the Sierra-Stansfield home. The room was large and open. It had a twenty foot high plate glass window facing the orchid house and the Atlantic Ocean.

A bright full moon illuminated the pool area and the orchids in their enclosure. The vivid colors of the flowers were discernible among the green stems and leaves. The orchids were awake and lively. In the basking steady light of the moon, they sang their story in chorus to her. It was a hymn for the glory of innocence, devoted sacrifice, and faith in the human spirit's almighty power.

Nasrin opened the door to the terrace and listened to the music of humanity in the cosmos. She stood for a while watching the sea. Its surf foamed and roared at the shore. A warm wind rustled her hair. Nasrin closed her eyes and breathed in the smells of life. She could taste the salt on the back of her tongue. The brine moistened her face and lips. She slowly opened her eyes again and stared out at the dark Atlantic's surface. It reflected the moon's glow back into the sky from where it came, scattering the shine into low lying white clouds. There was a trace of blue in the white. Hypnotized in a trance, Nasrin sensed the Earth's rotation. Everything was moving to her. In the lateness of hour, the world was still alive and free. The energy of the universe was everywhere, if one took the time to perceive it.

Nasrin left the door open and stepped back into the study. A mellow tropical breeze followed her in. She played Rebecca's recording of Beethoven's "Moonlight Sonata" from her concert at the San Francisco Conservatory of Music. The melody suited Nasrin on this night.

She turned on the Tiffany lamp by the dark leather couch. While Rebecca played, Nasrin slowly walked along the walls of the room. They were filled with four generations of photographs and portrait paintings.

Black and white images of Robert and Ann Stansfield in joyous times with their young sons, Julian and Bobby, sailing on Lake Michigan. A forceful wind and heavy waves challenged them to be strong.

A photograph of Raul Sierra with Olivia, fishing with Ernest Hemingway on the *Pilar*. Another image of Raul and Hemingway arm wrestling at a cafe in Varadero Beach while the rest of the Sierra family laughed in the background. In a grainy picture, a very young Olivia swam in a pond in the Escambray Mountains of Cuba.

Annapolis graduation photographs of Julian Stansfield and his three sons - Julius, Michael, and Mark – were isolated in honor on one wall. All of them at the same age, captured in time forever.

Several images of Rebecca taken in concert from venues in Boston, London, and Buenos Aires. Her stunning elegant beauty at the piano heightened the experience for the enthralled audience.

Photographs of young Olivia and Julian on their sailboat in Biscayne Bay. Her attractive face, graceful form, and style overtook a viewer in an instant. Her magnetic charms were unique.

Finally, a large oil-on-canvas portrait painting of Olivia's father, Jorge Sierra, standing as a boy with his father - Raul - on their ranch outside of Trinidad, Cuba. Both father and son living happy free lives under the warm tropical sun, surrounded by the verdant majesty of Cuba's mountains.

Several decades of memories were represented on the walls of the study. Lives lived well but lost from the continuum of time. Special moments shared between loved ones but unable to be relived. There was both great felicity and somber melancholy in the images. Regardless of the path one chose to take through the emotions and passions, and inconsiderate of your state of mind beforehand - after viewing the pictures awhile, they made you heartsick.

The pendulum of time had no mercy. It did not bother itself with the attachments of love and need. It did not listen to the cries of pleading children. It did not care about the oneness of spiritual soulmates. The pendulum did not stop in the presence of honor or righteous justice. With its swing, the flesh and bone of humankind was indiscriminately flung away. The joys of friendship and family were modified without consent. This was the way of the world, and nothing could be done to change it. No force could stop the pendulum and the march of time.

But where did the energy of love go when people died? It couldn't simply disappear from the ether of existence, thought Nasrin..... 'Heartache' must be the burning energy of those you loved and lost, inside of you. Their eternal flame burns forever to remind you of every kiss, every whisper, and every smile that once made you content. The heartache is not seen with the eyes. It is not touched. It is seen only in the mind of the beholder and felt only in the soul of the carrier of the flame. It is the bliss you miss that burns your heart forever. There lies the energy of love.

In the laws of the physical world, energy is always conserved. Energy may change forms, but it is never destroyed. Is the energy force of love any different? It must be passed on to those left behind, reflected Nasrin, and preserved for an eternity. Like DNA, it is transferred down the generations, continuously adding to the complexities of life and people's souls. It is a gift from Heaven, as Admiral Julian Stansfield told her and Michael after dinner, the night before he passed from this world.

The images in the study were snapshots of warm and tender emotions while they were lived. The moments were frozen in time for the appreciating viewer to sense their greatness. They were there to make one think of the purity of love and to stir our spirit to remember its special essence of the heart. We needed to capture for all time its mysterious longing quality. We wished to recall the deep visceral passion we can have for one another. The energy of love was preserved. It was eternal.

Rebecca's sounds provided a magnificent background for the memories held in the study's photographs and paintings. Beethoven's "Moonlight Sonata" was played by Rebecca with her eyes closed and her mind's imagery open, just as Beethoven had intended.

Nasrin sat at the mahogany desk in the center of the room. On the desk, between brass bookends, were Raul Sierra's four books on orchids.

The first one, published in 1953, was a scientific exploration of the orchid family. The thousands of species were described in detail with their taxonomy, physical characteristics, flowering patterns, fruit and seed cycles, and complex mechanisms of pollination. The book also contained long narratives on the ecology and evolution of orchids over the past 80 million years. Each of the following books was progressively less scientific, and more metaphorical and philosophical.

Raul's last book - *My Life in Orchids* - was written in 1980, three years before his death. It was a philosophical treatise on freedom and democracy, and the costs required to maintain them. Immediately sensing the spiritual depth of the book, Nasrin moved to the couch and continued to read.

Raul, a graduate of MIT with a degree in chemical engineering, had an unparalleled intellect. He could think objectively in numbers and scientific notation, but he could also feel spiritually and emotionally. His computational mind was deep but his passions were deeper. Hemingway always said Raul's soul had been directly reincarnated from Jesus Christ.

Nasrin quickly realized Raul's story was full of inferences and expressions on love, peace, and liberty of the mind. She fell into it fully, attracted to its deep sentiments.

As a young country boy growing up in the early 1920s outside the old Spanish colonial town of Trinidad, Cuba, I would finish classes at our schoolhouse in the early afternoons and escape with my friends into the Escambray Mountains. Like adventurers in the dime store novels of the day, we would run up the steep hills of the region, cross rivers, explore the valleys, and swim in watering holes at the base of beautiful waterfalls.

After swimming, we would lie on large flat topped boulders near the waterfalls and talk about girls, flying on airplanes, or maybe one day going to the moon. We would bake our white skin in the sun and dream.

One early afternoon, exploring the hillsides near Caburni Falls, we came across a clearing in the rainforest with a large spring fed pond. Formed from the opening of a rocky underwater cave, its limestone walls were slippery and moss covered. The clear turquoise blue water of the 50 by 30 foot hole would be lit by the sun at midday as the light radiated down through an opening in the rain forest's high canopy. There was lush tropical vegetation all around the pond. Trees were filled with exotic and colorful birds. They sang their songs for us while we played. Large epiphytic orchids of incredible beauty grew anchored to the trees and shrubs around the swimming hole.

I would often support myself on the edge of the ancient coral pool and just stare at the alluring, intricate, natural splendor of the fragrant and colorful flowers. Different hues of blue, red, yellow, and green created a vibrant landscape, beyond further description in words.

We were young and free, and we identified with the nature around us. It was paradise and we knew it. Our small group of boys kept the secret of the forest pond to ourselves. It became a place to meet in the afternoons and enjoy our friendships.

A few months before leaving for college in the United States, I met the girl who later would become my wife. We would run off after school and escape to the forest clearing amongst the orchids. In the passion of youth, we'd remove our clothes and hope not to be discovered. We would spend hours together sharing our bodies, always with the restless energy of young people in love. We became lost in our own dream.

One Saturday, we lay naked together on the limestone, looking up at the green canopy over us. Rays of sunshine filtered through the trees and warmed our skins. We felt free to love with all our strength. My girl and I watched a bright blue and green hummingbird feed from the cup of a giant pink tropical flower. It was amazing to see nature so closely.

I turned to her and looked into her emerald eyes. I passed my fingers through her auburn hair. I kissed her lips and said, 'I love you.' Then I placed a white and yellow orchid flower behind her ear. We made love.

Later, she asked me what a 'full life' meant to me. I answered, 'An earthly existence is worth only the content of your heart, mind, and soul. It can not be measured in time, but solely in quality. And that quality depends only on how much you've loved. If you have loved deeply, then you have lived deeply. How long you live is important only in that a long life allows you to love a long time. A 'full life' was loved fully.

My girl kissed me. I felt her warm breath on my face. I tasted her on my tongue. A ray of light from above shined on her green eyes. I could see my reflection in them. Our souls became one on that day. We both felt the great 'singularity' of love on an afternoon by the coral pond in the rainforest of the Escambray.

Years later, my son, Jorge, and later his daughter, Olivia, learned to swim in those same clear blue-green waters. With time, the swimming hole of Escambray became a place for my family to unite and enjoy ourselves together. To me, it came to symbolize freedom of the spirit and nourishment of the soul.

After the Cuban Revolution, I lost my country and my swimming hole in the Escambray Mountains. I lost the freedom of my youth and the gift to live my life as I chose. Most painful of all, I lost my son. He had been the product of all the love that I had felt in my life.

Orchids will always symbolize freedom for me. They bring me back to the innocence of my youth, to my country of birth, and most of all, back to my son. I miss them all very much. I so very much wish they would return to me.

Nasrin closed Raul's book and gently placed it back on the desk. The morning sun was rising over the Atlantic

Ocean. It shined into the study through the large window. The rays of light gave the yellow painted walls a deep golden tone.

As Nasrin stepped away from the desk, her foot touched a large leather trunk on the floor behind the chair. She leaned over and opened the trunk.

A large Cuban flag was carefully folded into a red triangle, defined by a central white star. Beneath the flag was a briefcase..... Inside the case, Nasrin found a hand written note addressed to Don Raul Sierra from Fidel Castro.

"My dear poor Raul: Enclosed are the ragged pants of your son, Jorge. Soiled and bloodied, they were stripped from his dead body after his execution by my order. Let them stand as an example of what happens to men who defy my revolution. Pathetic people like you and your son stand between me and greatness. Your actions against my revolution, as your son's, will be in vain. We have a new Cuba now. I will be its master and commander. I hope you weep at the delivery of my gift. My wish is for the pain to never cease."

Nasrin, choked in tears, returned the note and torn blood-caked pants to their sacred case. With kind deference, she placed the Cuban flag on top of the briefcase and entombed them in the trunk.

A short time later, Nasrin walked to the orchid house. She found Tomas diligently working on Mr. Sierra's flowers. He looked up and smiled at her.

"Early this morning, I saw you reading Mr. Sierra's books in the study," said Tomas. "Now, you must understand why Mr. Sierra loved and cherished his orchids."

"Oh yes, I understand completely," Nasrin whispered, as she cared for the flowers.

Tomas stared across at Raul's time-keeper. The pendulum was still. He said in a quiet voice, "The gods know what they do."

Nasrin cried silently while she pruned the beautiful orchids of the "Freedom House". She prayed for Michael's well-being and safety, and for the souls of Raul and his beloved son, Jorge.

CHAPTER 9

Witch's Brew

The dark side of the Moon is the far lunar hemisphere, never visible from the surface of the Earth. To most humans on our planet, it is a mysterious place. Its features were only first photographed by the Russian *Luna 3* probe in 1959. Never before then had human eyes seen its topography.

In dark mysteries always lie fears. The fear of the unknown can be stifling. The truth is like light, it illuminates a path of clarity for proper action.

In espionage, the field of battle is always dark. Mysteries abound everywhere. Nothing can be taken for face value. What you see is usually an inverted image of reality. Think black when you see white, and think white when you see black.

It was early evening on June 14. Michael Stansfield sat in the fly-bridge of his ship and watched the sun set behind the rocky cliffs of Golubac, Serbia. Built into the mountainside along the Danube River's right bank was *Golubac Fortress*, a medieval fortification from the early 14th century. The castle's impressive towers and eight foot thick walls had been constructed by the Serbs at a narrow point in the river to help form a final line of defense against the Ottoman Turks. It had also economically controlled river traffic for taxation purposes. In the Middle Ages, a strong iron chain from the fortress to the far side of the river would prevent passage of ships that did not pay their toll. *Golubac Fortress* was built over an old Roman settlement, and had been the site of many battles between the Turks, Hungarians, Serbs, and Austrians. Throughout the history of Europe, every feature of the Danube had been challenged by one army or another.

Earlier in the morning, the CIA ship had passed by the cities of Drobeta, Romania, on the Danube's left bank, and Kladovo, Serbia, on the opposite side of the river. Stansfield saw the remnants of *Trajan's Bridge*, finished by the Romans in 105 AD to facilitate the movement of their army beyond the Danube River in their war against the Dacians in present day Romania. Finished in less than two years, the bridge had spanned over 3500 feet. It remained the longest arch bridge ever built for over a thousand years. The weather beaten *Tabula Traina* - a large Latin inscribed Roman memorial plaque on the Serbian bank - commemorated the completion of the military segmented arch bridge.

Conqueror of Worlds had moved from the Lower Danube to the Middle Danube at the Iron Gate Gorge.

The 83 mile long narrow passage was characterized by strong upstream currents, and formed part of the boundary between Romania and Serbia. The 1500 foot cliffs along the gorge separated the southern Carpathian Mountains from the foothills of the Balkan Mountains to the south. At the "Great Kazan" - the gorge narrowed to 450 feet wide, and the river deepened to 175 feet. The *Golubac Fortress* sat at the upstream end of the Iron Gate Gorge, as it began opening into the approaches to Belgrade.

Michael Stansfield and his team had traveled nearly 800 miles on the Danube River by the end of their fifth day. They would stop in Belgrade for fuel and provisions, and meet a CIA contact at a coffee house in Kalemegdan Park.

The CIA considered the remainder of the mission to be in hostile territory. Although Romania and the Lower Danube were under tight control of a government sympathetic to the United States, the Middle and Upper Danube were not. Serbia, Hungary, Austria, and Bavaria were heavily infiltrated by ultra-nationalists, and their governments had come under the influence of the Fascists over the past two years. The radical extremists in these countries, with help from the FNNP and GPNR, were actively engaged to eliminate US influence over Central and Eastern Europe.

Stansfield glanced at the GPS tracker. He saw the *Katarina* was only three miles upstream from their position.

Dr. Egan sat next to Stansfield and handed him a beer. "It's Happy Hour, Stansfield..... One beer won't break CIA policy!" he laughed.

"I'm taking advantage of this European vacation cruise, Stansfield. We have beautiful women and beer, a cool Italian sports yacht, and riverside historical attractions.

What more can I ask of the CIA?" said the *Conqueror*'s resident chef.

"This sure beats cutting through bamboo forests with a machete in equatorial heat, or trudging through snow up mountains!" blasted the doctor.

Dr. Thomas Egan's meek exterior betrayed his tough spirit. Short in stature, pale, and light-framed, the micro-biologist was an adventurer by nature. He had worked for the CIA in a number of rugged locations over the previous three years.

Besides his expedition to the Likouala Swamps of the Congo in April, the bald and bespectacled virologist had been to Borneo, Nepal, and Antarctica. He had an affa-ble personality and didn't seem much concerned with danger.

"When I sit here on the famous Danube, enjoying a beer in the breeze, shooting the shit with you, Stansfield, I feel like a lucky man after winning the lotto. My last gig was a frickin' nightmare!

"I'm not built for the tropical jungle, Stansfield. Just because I study little bugs, doesn't mean I enjoy them biting my ass when I squat down to take a crap in the rainforest!

"I saw mosquitos bigger than blue jays in the Congo. They'd drain you dry while you slept. I have sensitive skin, goddam it!

"I'm not into the snakes either. They're everywhere.

"Even the little monkeys were aggressive. They loved to throw their shit at us as we worked through the forest. On one occasion, while chopping through the bush, I got monkey crap in my eyes and mouth. I saw the ugly bas-tard in the tree above me, aiming down like a baseball pitcher ready to pluck me again. He wound up and threw another ball of his shit into my face. I tried to kill the little fucker with my machete, but he moved out of the way at the last second. They're quick and smart too!

"No! I must tell the guys back at Langley that I'm more cut out for these European expeditions!" laughed Egan.

"I wouldn't have figured you out to be a 'stay at home' agent," grinned Stansfield. "Calhoun said you were a tough bastard, who liked to get his hands dirty and his feet wet."

"I'm a great pretender, Stansfield!" smiled the doctor.

"Aren't we all, Egan?"

"I guess you're right. We're all great pretenders....."

"Working at the CIA is the toughest acting job in the world. Our performances, Egan, are Academy Award material. We're called upon to be different things for different people at different times. We disguise our voice and looks, speak in strange languages, and act out situations that only insane people would consider. It's hard being brave 24/7. Usually we're only pretending to be. We do it so often that we begin believing in our own sense of bravery. You and I, and everyone else in this business, are great pretenders....."

The men drank their beers..... The night cooled after sunset. The doctor put on a jacket emblazoned with 'USA' and the 'Stars and Stripes'.

"Are you fucking stupid, Egan?"

"Listen, Stansfield, everyone around here may hate America but they all 'do' Americana. They wear blue jeans, drink diet colas and eat burgers, watch American films, and worship 'Made in USA' labels. This jacket's part of my disguise."

"You're a fucking crazy mad scientist!

"Just don't leave the ship wearing that jacket," smiled Michael.

"You know, Stansfield, I can't figure out these Russians. After more than seventy years farting around the world as Communists, they come out of the closet as fucking Fascists. For God's sake, the Russians fought a war against the Nazis not too long ago. The Krauts killed millions of them. They suddenly give up their classless, moneyless, stateless, internationalist worker's social order for the radical, hero he-man, racist Nazi, nationalist warrior spirit? Am I confused on this? Or are the Russians confused?"

"They came out of the miserable economic and social stagnation of Communism, and tried their luck with democracy. It didn't work for them. The Russians were hit by a long financial decline and the realization that 'American Energy' was out-exporting them. There was no prosperity, only more poverty. They went radical and changed their approach. It's as simple as that, Egan."

"Well, they definitely changed their approach, Michael..... Now, they call us Communists!" laughed the doctor.

"We'll be in Belgrade in about four hours, Doc.

"We have two hours to take fuel and supplies, and make an information contact. They want you to come along with Calhoun and I for that contact," added Stansfield.

"Do you think Basha will let your friend, Hickory, leave her for that much time?" blurted Egan sarcastically. "It seems they have become close friends on this trip. Closer than what appears wise."

"What's your inference, Egan?" asked Stansfield bluntly.

"I have nothing against fucking beautiful girls if the opportunities develop. Even on a mission, I reckon, if the girl is as hot as this Polish chick. But your friend has taken this to another level, Mikey," said the brainy doctor.

"My bunk-room shares a wall with your friend's. He's banging her all night, every night. She's quite a moaner. The wall shakes with every climax. It's hard to sleep when the wall is knocking you in the head all night long.

"That Polish girl has a lot of energy! When Hick starts slowing down, she races him back up with her sex talk. Her words turn him into a bull at Pamplona. She's multiorgasmic and lets me know about it. What a mouth that girl has!" laughed Egan.

"So, what I'm saying, Mikey, is that your buddy should cool it down a bit. Maybe tell his pecker to wait until after the mission is complete. A cool head and an overheated prick don't work well together. And on a mission of this complexity, cool heads are more in demand. Don't you agree?"

Stansfield nodded his head but tried to appear uninterested in what Egan had to say. Yet, he was concerned about what he perceived to be an evolving relationship between Calhoun and the female Polish agent. Repeated sexual relations between agents active on a mission were certainly against Agency policy, and even more importantly, against common sense. But who was he to pontificate on the situation, when he had met his wife, Nasrin, on a mission and fallen in love while trying to conduct operations for America in Iran during the last war.

Stansfield believed Ludwik had instigated sexual contact with Calhoun. On the surface, she appeared to be the aggressor in the relationship. Michael's paranoid survival instincts were warning him to the possibility that his interception by enemy agents in Balaclava could have been caused by a leak of information from Calhoun to Ludwik. The Polish agent could be doubling for the other side.

Stansfield decided to wait another couple of days before approaching Calhoun on the issue. He was hoping Hickory would freeze out the relationship before then. Nonetheless, he'd watch Ludwik for any evidence of doubling activity. Time would tell, thought Michael.

"How close are you and Calhoun?" asked Egan.

"We're old friends," answered Stansfield.

"Are you concerned about your friend's relationship with the Polish girl?"

"That's not any of my business, Egan, and it shouldn't be any of yours either," said Stansfield forcefully.

"Well, I think it should be, Stansfield, especially considering that our lives depend on a clean operation without emotional involvement between the men and the women. We can't have your friend fucking this girl all night long and expect him to be sharp the next day?"

"Why not? Was that the only beer you've had today, Doc? Should I be watching you just in case you go extreme on me?

"We're all adults, Egan. Protocol states clearly that you can't fuck a fellow agent on a mission. It also says you can't drink alcohol when on an active case. So both of you guys are fucking up. We all do occasionally. It's only human, Doc. But yeah, I'll watch the situation between Hick and Basha. And I'll watch that you don't drink too much. Now let's leave it at that if it's okay with you, Doctor?"

"You're the quarterback, Stansfield. It's your game to call....."

"Well then, I'm calling an audible at the line of scrimmage. Let's change the subject.

"Calhoun briefed me on the enemy's cargo, Egan. But I didn't receive any scientific details. Tell me what you know about this witch's brew on the *Katarina*."

Egan put his empty beer bottle down on the counter. He settled back into his chair and stared at Stansfield with sharp eyes.

"You're an underground war fighter, Mike. You go up against your enemy feeling confident of your chances. You beat him with your mind, fists, and heavy metal. The enemy goes up against you with the same weaponry. The fights are fair at the start and materially equal on both sides. Up to now, you've been successful at concluding your engagements. You're alive, Mike, and sitting here with me.

"I'm a biological war fighter. My expertise is in the military applications of nature's tiniest toxic critters. I generally don't battle with my fists, knives, or guns, but I do use my mind in the fight. In the laboratory, we take these bugs and engineer them to be even more deadly. We play with their genetic material and juice them up. It's an ugly business, but someone's got to do it.

"I'm accustomed to the study of bio-terror. My colleagues and I view it through the prism of national security. If the enemy creates biological soldiers, we must also. It's a game of deterrence. But this mission involves an unimaginable evil weapon. It's a potion from Lucifer himself. And I'm sacred as hell of it.

"A pestilent 'witch's brew' is a good descriptive term for the contraband on that ship. It's the deadliest biological material to ever exist on our planet. It's capable of killing millions before it can be contained. Your war fighting talents are useless against this enemy. If unleashed, this fight won't be fair, Mike.

"Climate change has made the long and hot humid summer of the American Southeast a perfect substrate for an aggressive Ebola virus. An AZEV epidemic on our homeland would destroy large population centers in a matter of weeks. Cities like Washington, Charleston, Raleigh, Atlanta, Birmingham, New Orleans, Tampa, and Miami would be wiped out. The bug could even thrive as far north as New York. The death and destruction would throw our government into a panic situation and disrupt US military operations throughout the world. I believe the chaos and anarchy created by it could lead to the downfall of our nation. Our present government is not strong enough to keep the show together. The social fabric of our nation is weak at present. There is widespread lack of trust in authority. There would be a revolt, I'm certain.

"This is serious material, Stansfield. It's much more terrorizing to the public than a nuclear attack. A nuclear detonation kills instantly. Sure, there are those who die from the radiation effects over weeks and months' time, but the physical and emotional shock trauma effect is mostly immediate.

"An AZEV bio-terror attack kills your family members slowly over a period of days. Parents will helplessly watch their children suffocate on their own blood. Small children will be left alone in their gradual death, after they see their parents die off. The process is horrific to witness. It's agonizing and utterly demoralizing," emphasized Egan.

"Tell me the specifics of the science, Doc. I want to understand the bug's magic. What happens inside the human body?"

"It's a mysterious organism, Mike. Scientists are afraid of working with it. It's dangerous. Any misstep in the research process can cost lives. We need to learn more about its life cycle.

"There are five Ebola virus subtypes. Since 1976, there have been several significant natural outbreaks of Ebola Viral Hemorrhagic Syndrome in the sub-Saharan Central African nations of Sudan, Uganda, Gabon, and the Democratic Republic of Congo (formerly Zaire).

"It's an RNA Filovirus. It may use insectivorous fruit bats in the wild as a reservoir, passing the infection to non-human primates and humans accidentally through direct contact with body fluids. The virus genome codes for four structural proteins and three membrane associated proteins, of which the envelope glycoprotein (GP) is the most important.

"The glycoprotein has two forms, the secretory GP (sGP) and the trans-membrane GP (tGP). The sGP binds to white blood cells and inhibits the patient's early neutrophil activation, producing a profound lymphopenia, and preventing an effective host immune response. The tGP binds to vascular endothelial cells and destroys them, leading to disseminated intravascular coagulation (DIC), platelet consumption, and diffuse hemorrhaging throughout the patient's body.

"Clinical infection leads to rapid and extensive viral replication in all tissues. There is subsequent necrosis of internal organs, particularly the liver. After a one week incubation, patients begin exhibiting the signs and symptoms of infection.

"Early in the disease, the patient will have fever, headaches, sore throat, skin rash, conjunctivitis, joint and muscle pains, loss of appetite, abdominal pain, and nausea/vomiting. It appears as a severe flu-like syndrome.

"After four or five days, the patients will begin bleeding from all their mucosal surfaces. They develop heart failure with pulmonary edema, low blood pressure, and finally, shock and coma.

"The most lethal naturally occurring Ebola species is the Zaire Ebola Virus (ZEV). Infection with this variant has a mortality rate of 90%. It will affect men, women, and children of all ages. It is highly contagious through contact with mucous membranes and body fluids.

"The Russian scientists at the VECTOR Institute have apparently bio-engineered the viral envelope glycoprotein to be more robust and less inclined to desiccation in the air. The new AZEV is more able to spread through respiratory secretions, and thus move more quickly from one person to another. Although slightly less virulent, it will pass to many more people in a shorter amount of time. It will still generate a very high 75-80% case fatality rate in an epidemic.

"The death at Ibutu was complete. There were no survivors. I walked through the village in a hazmat suit, chilled to the spine. It was a horrible spectacle. There were bloated victims everywhere. Blood and body fluids had oozed from every orifice. There were flies all over the village. Maggots and scavengers picked at the sickly specimens.

"I have never been so afraid in my life. Taking tissue samples with a scalpel, I steadied my hands the best I could. Any violation of my suit would have been the end of me. I don't think I could work with this material every day in a lab. I don't have the balls for it, and I'm a virologist. God help us all if that shit is released on America.

"We have some experimental treatments in evolution, but there are no specific, definitive, effective therapies available to prevent death. We can only provide support-ive care with oxygen, intravenous fluids, and comfort.

"The dead need to be quickly buried in mass graves. There is no time for personal burials. Those doing the bur-ying will soon be filling adjacent holes themselves. The entire scene would be horrifying.

"If AZEV finds its way into an American city - with its multitude of public gathering sites, transportation cent-ers, shopping malls, sports venues, schools, hospitals, and government buildings - it would spread so quickly before outward signs are noted that millions would die in the first weeks of an epidemic. It would be a complete catastro-phe," concluded Egan in a frightful tone.

Michael Stansfield slowly nodded his head in agree-ment. "It sounds pretty goddam awful, Egan. We obviously didn't have our people infiltrated into the VECTOR Institute. Why not? Didn't the US know the bastards were creating this stuff? We should have been inside, sabotaging the Russian program. We fucked up big time. The poison juice should have been cut off at its origins. If the AZEV gets into America, our intelligence services will have to take respon-sibility. We fumbled the ball inside the 10-yard line."

"I agree," said Egan. "I didn't even know AZEV existed. It's not simple laboratory science. Very complicated genetic engineering is required. And it's scary work. I cer-tainly don't envy the poor fuckers who handle the stuff....."

Abruptly, a baffled look came over the doctor. He appeared hesitant to express his thoughts.

"What's wrong, Egan? You have a puzzled look on your face. Stop ruminating and spill the beans."

"I'm sure it's nothing of importance, Michael."

"Let me be the judge of that, Doc."

"My men and I found something unusual near Ibutu. Because it was so unexpected, it's perplexed me ever since.

"The night before moving on the village, we camped in the Congo rainforest. We came across a thatch-roofed structure in the middle of the jungle. It was raining, and we huddled inside of it for cover. At first, we believed it was Pygmy. Soon after, we realized it wasn't.

"Scattered on the ground were dozens of empty US-issued MRE packages. They still smelled fresh. It was very strange. Calhoun said the enemy often uses American food rations. They can acquire them easily in the black market. I believed him. Why not? It was better than the crap they normally ate. I wouldn't have thought more about it, but something else happened later that caught my curiosity.

"As I lay down in the dark to get some sleep, something pricked my back. I turned and used my flashlight to look at the ground beneath my blanket. Half-buried in the soil was a large metallic black pin of an emperor scorpion. It looked like the squad insignia pins that troopers wear on their uniforms. I suspected it had perhaps fallen off one of the previous users of the hut.

"I woke up Calhoun and showed him the pin. At first, he seemed alarmed. Then he blew me off. Your buddy told me not to worry about it and go back to sleep. He kept the pin and never mentioned it again. I just found the whole frickin thing unusual. It gave me the creeps. I reasoned, maybe, you should know about the incident.

"It was probably unimportant. Perhaps an American unit had been through the area on another unrelated mission. God knows all the other shit that's going down in this world. I'm sure these bastards on the *Katarina* aren't the only SOBs trying to fuck America. Right, Mike?

"Well, enough said, Quarterback! You make the call.

"By the way, don't drink any more beers, Michael! We don't want another fumble inside the 10-yard line. Do we?

"I'll be watching you too," grinned Egan.

The doctor left Stansfield alone.....

Michael was familiar with the "Black Scorpion". Not many people were. Egan didn't seem completely cognizant of its significance. To Stansfield, the metallic insignia pin was an ominous finding. It implied immediately a higher sense of insecurity for him and his team. It added a further element of confusion. Why hadn't Mitrano informed him of the Black Scorpions' presence? Stansfield now had more unanswered questions.

Why were American black-ops on the case without his knowledge? What did Mitrano know about them? Were they under his command? And if they weren't, whose command were they under?

Stansfield had encountered the Black Scorpions many times in his travels across enemy lands. They were very tough dudes, specially trained to kill in excess and drive fear into the enemy. These combined US Army/Navy/Air Force raiders were border-line psychotic in their actions. The members of the unit were selectively picked to be violent and reactionary. They didn't have many friends anywhere. Other American units avoided crossing them on the field of battle.

In Stansfield's stint in Aleppo, Syria, he had seen them in action several times. He had watched in person what they did in the Al-Sakhour neighborhood. Their retribution there was legendary. The Black Scorpion offensive into Al-Sakhour drove the Iranians completely out of Aleppo.

After five days of fighting the Iranians for control of the area, a company of Scorpions had lost twelve of their comrades in battle. Over three hundred Iranian Special Forces had been killed. Another hundred Iranian troops had been captured.

From a nearby roof-top, Stansfield saw the Black Scorpion commander order a contingent of Syrian Rebel Army fighters to behead each and every one of the Iranian prisoners, except for two. They threw the heads into two large wheelbarrows and forced the two remaining prisoners to return with their collections to the Iranian lines. Four hours later, the Iranians evacuated Aleppo.

Michael understood the function of the Black Scorpions, but he felt uneasy with them possibly involved in *Operation Europa*. He'd rather have them perform their jobs at a distance. Their kind of work and his kind of work didn't mix well. Besides, their mental stabilities were too labile for espionage. They brought more danger than safety to the mission.

The *Conqueror* docked along the Danube in Belgrade late in the evening. A car waited with two men at the docks to take Stansfield, Calhoun, and Egan to a small restaurant at Kalemegdan Park. All five CIA men were armed with folding 9 mm sub-machine guns.

The cafe stood near the *Belgrade Fortress* on a 400 foot cliff-like ridge, overlooking the junction of the Sava and Danube rivers. It was owned and operated by a Serbian husband and wife who had worked for the CIA since the Kosovo War in 1998.

Kalemegdan Park was a picturesque area along Belgrade's riverfront. It had winding walking paths, fountains, and statues.

Atop the park's highest point was the ancient *Belgrade Fortress*, which had participated in over 2000 years of sieges, battles, and occupations. The fortress mirrored the history of Belgrade, originally founded as a city in the 3rd century BC by a Celtic tribe. Its ancient foundations had seen occupations by Romans, Goths, and Huns. Atilla was believed to be buried beneath the stones of the fortress.

The Byzantines rebuilt the castle in 535 AD. They held it until it fell to the emerging Serbian state in the late 12th century. It was later occupied by the Hungarians for a short period.

Belgrade was conquered by the Ottoman Turks in 1521 during their incursion into Central Europe. The region stayed under Muslim rule for hundreds of years, except for a twenty year period of Habsburg Austrian control in the early 1700s.

Serbia - with allies, Greece, Bulgaria, and Montenegro - regained her autonomy with victories over the Turks in the First Balkan War of 1913, and over the Austrian-Hungarian Empire in 1918. These victories were commemorated by the statue - the *Victor*. Erected near the fortress in 1928, it overlooks the beauty of the riverfront. The warrior statue holds a falcon in one hand as a sentry for new threats on the horizon, and a sword in the other hand to confront these threats.

Serbia suffered over one million casualties in World War One while fighting with the Allies against the Central Axis powers of Germany and Austria-Hungary. Led by Serbia, the Slavic state of Yugoslavia was born from the breakup of the Habsburg Dynasty.

The German Nazi invasion of Yugoslavia in 1941, and the subsequent civil war, killed over 500,000 Serbians. The Russian-supported Communist, Josip Broz "Tito", bravely fought the Nazis and emerged as the undisputed leader of Yugoslavia after World War Two.

Tito managed to keep the ethnically divergent provinces of Yugoslavia together until his death in 1980. The subsequent dissolution of the Soviet Union, beginning with the election of Mikhail Gorbachev as General Secretary by the Soviet Politburo on March 11, 1985, and ending in its final breakup by 1991, allowed for religious and cultural rivalries to flourish in Yugoslavia.

Provincial separatist movements inside Yugoslavia led to its break-up in 1989. Characterized by religious hatred between Christians and Muslims, Serbia fought wars with Slovenia, Croatia, and Bosnia in the early 1990s. Fighting continued with the southern Muslim Albanian communities of Kosovo in 1998.

Ethnic cleansing programs by opposing sides, particularly the Serbians, resulted in over 150,000 dead and over 50,000 rapes. An intense NATO bombing campaign of Serbian positions in early 1999 finally resulted in a ceasefire and a stoppage to the rampant killing.

Since 2000, Serbia had become progressively more influenced by the fascist movements sweeping Central and Eastern Europe. There was much hatred for America in Serbia.

Javor and Jasna Andric were a middle-aged Serbian couple who had worked with the CIA since 1998. Javor had served as a Serbian infantryman during the wars in Bosnia and Kosovo, and personally witnessed the massacres of innocent Muslim civilians by the Serbian military. Likewise, he also saw the murders of innocent Christian Serbs by Muslim militiamen. He understood the complexities of religious wars, and how no one could be completely and truly innocent.

Over the previous ten years, Javor's country had become more anti-democratic. A powerful fascist movement had taken hold. The ultra-nationalists were dominating national politics. Serbia's longtime alliance with Russia had become more radical, and she developed a close working relationship with Fascists in Germany, Hungary, Austria, and the Ukraine.

Michael Stansfield, Hickory Calhoun, Thomas Egan, and two additional local CIA operatives took the short drive from the Danube's docks to Kalemegdan Park. It was after midnight when the men arrived at the coffee house near the *Belgrade Fortress*. Waiting for them in the parking area were Javor and Jasna Andric.

Javor quickly introduced himself. He asked Stansfield and his men to walk with him. While Michael Stansfield and Javor Andric walked side by side, the other team members fanned out in front and behind them in a protective fashion.

It was a clear and cool late spring evening. The operatives walked along a high promenade overlooking the Sava and Danube rivers. The lights of Belgrade lit the sky at a short distance.

Javor opened the discussions. "American, Belgrade is a magnificent city. I hope you can appreciate its gentle side. Believe it or not, my city does have a gentle side," smiled the Serbian as he looked out over the twinkling capital.

"It is beautiful but always troubled. Through the ages, we have been destroyed and rebuilt a thousand times. The Romans, the northern barbarian tribes, the Ottomans, the Austria-Hungarians, the Nazis, the Communists, and now the Fascists again, have all helped write our history. It makes your head spin.

"We have been at the center of religious wars for hundreds of years. We sit in this region between East and West where global powers need to control the crossroads. Our ethnic mix has been like dynamite. Hatred between our mixed cultures has not allowed our nation to prosper. Empires throughout the history of Europe have taken advantage of our people.

"Serbia today seems to have aligned itself with the Fascists of Central and Eastern Europe in a struggle with the United States for control of the continent. People in Serbia, like those in Germany, Austria, and Hungary, believe America sabotaged the European Union to remain economically pre-eminent. America reasoned that a well-organized European Union - under the auspices of German banks, industries, and science - allied with Russian energy resources, would have been a formidable adversary in the future.

"Like the Russians from the old collapsed Soviet Empire, my people also want pay-back for the US-directed bombings of our cities years ago. They do not forget this.

"They feel dominated by American interests and appear to have decided that a fascist bloc of European nations is the best way to rid the region of American influence. I don't agree with this philosophy.

"I believe free democracies, led by the United States, are the only hope for world peace in the future. Freedom and democracy are essential for all peoples to choose an ethical and moral path in their lives. True liberty provides for a justice system that does not discriminate on the basis of religion and culture. No more genocides. No more global wars. The world needs a leader in this process, and I believe it must be the United States."

The agents walked towards the *Victor* statue. They passed a young man and woman making love on the grass of the park.

Andric added, "Last year, Germany appeared to have assisted the United States and NATO in the invasion of Iran. The truth is they fought poorly and were even involved in several bizarre incidents of 'friendly fire' on American and Canadian troops. Four months later in October, Germany withdrew from NATO and signed an alliance of 'friendship' with Russia. Russia has given the Germans partial control of Russian pipelines carrying oil and natural gas into Europe.

"The governments in Russia and Germany are becoming more radically nationalist and anti-American with each passing day. Some of the countries that lie between these behemoths have lined up with them in this anti-American alliance. Poland, Romania, and Bulgaria have stayed with the Americans.

"The United States victory last year over China, North Korea, and Iran has only hardened the anti-American sentiment in Central and Eastern Europe. That is why you and I are here tonight, meeting in this park overlooking my beautiful city of Belgrade."

Stansfield and Andric sat on a bench at the base of the *Victor* statue. The other CIA members established an inconspicuous defensive perimeter around them.

"American, this is what we know. The 'lost' second shipment of AZEV was transported through the Ukraine and into Poland. It recently entered Germany on its way to the city of Bamberg in Bavaria. A big meeting will take place in Bamberg, where the CIA believes high ranking officials from the Russian and German governments - who are conspiring in this terrorist mission - will convene to discuss their plans.

"We know high ranking officers in the Russian Army and Navy are involved. We also know the German foreign minister and possibly the director of Polish intelligence are conspirators.

"The CIA expects the 'lost' shipment of AZEV will be loaded onto the *Katarina* in Bamberg. American agents will be in Bavaria to take down the government officials involved. This 'take-down' will occur at a conference site in Bamberg, after the terrorist ship has left port. We do not want the men on the *Katarina* to realize we have them in our cross-hairs before our attack. The CIA man on the *Katarina* has informed us that the terrorists are oblivious to our operations so far.

"You and your team, American, will later attack and sink the *Katarina* at a specified location in the Rhine. America wants the ship sunk inside of Germany to make a definitive point to the German government. We still believe the majority of the German and Russian people would be appalled at the details of this terrorist mission. Most of them are democratic thinking and don't want to re-live the totalitarian histories of their past. They likely want freedom and democracy for their countries as much as I do for mine.

"As your ship enters Austria and Germany, you can expect much more potential risk. We suspect there may be several thousand enemy agents involved in the mission in this area. If they find your pursuit of the *Katarina*, they will attack you. We will provide as much assistance as possible along the route. We are expecting our agents on land and water to be in constant aggressive action throughout the remainder of the mission. We will do everything we can to take suspicions off of you and your ship.

"The CIA and US Navy Intelligence are on their own. We can not expect significant and reliable help from the governments in Hungary, Austria, and Germany. We don't know who to trust in these governments at the present time. We can rely only on ourselves.

"There is one curiosity, American..... For the past three mornings, two young white males have visited my restaurant for breakfast. I have personally served them twice. They have spoken German to me. I defend myself well in the language. Polite and respectful, they would not have alerted my senses. However, one of them has a small 'USMC' tattooed in red-white-and-blue on the back of his neck. It was mostly hidden by his collar, but I caught a glimpse of it once. I have excellent vision and am certain of the fact. I thought it would be of interest to you."

As Andric passed a large envelope to Stansfield, automatic gunfire erupted all around them. Finding protection behind the pedestal of the *Victor* statue, Stansfield could see muzzle flashes coming from a thicket of trees across the plaza, 400 feet away.

Calhoun and Egan took cover behind a concrete embankment to the left of Stansfield. They fired their submachine guns at the trees across the way. Jasna Andric had been struck in the throat in the initial assault and exsanguinated on the plaza near the base of the statue. Stansfield's driver also died nearby without firing his gun.

Stansfield motioned for Calhoun and Egan to go around and approach the trees from the north, while he circled from the south along a ridgeline. Michael Stansfield sprinted as fast as he could to the south, dodging bullets behind a low brick wall. Shortly, he came up to the thicket of trees from behind. Arriving almost simultaneously with Calhoun on the opposite side, both men emptied their guns on the group of four enemy agents in the thicket. In less than ten seconds of close fire, the enemy agents lay dead.

A bullet grazed Calhoun's left rib cage, and another round passed through the flesh of his lower right leg. Hickory's injured calf muscle bled heavily until Michael applied a tourniquet above the knee. Egan and Stansfield carried Calhoun back to the plaza where they found a sobbing Javor kneeling next to his wife, Jasna.

Stansfield ordered Egan to bring their car closer, and take Javor and his wife's body back to their restaurant. He commanded the remaining local CIA agent to stay with the Andrics until help arrived.

A few moments later, the doctor returned in the car to pick up Michael and the hobbled Hickory. The men sped back to the *Conqueror* at the docks.

Stansfield glared brutally at Calhoun and shouted, "Listen mother-fucker! First Balaclava and now Belgrade! What have you told Ludwik?"

Calhoun, looking puzzled, angrily retorted, "Ludwik? You son-of-a-bitch! What have you spilled to Boroshkova?"

CHAPTER 10

Dialogue with Socrates

In the conduct of human affairs, it is always better to travel the moral high road. It may be a more difficult path, with more obstacles and impediments, with fewer rest stops along the way, but it is the honorable course. It is the better lit passage, illuminated by the shining true examples of historical and spiritual justice which came before you. Let the heart and mind be free, and live the virtuous life. Find a successful approach through the portal of righteousness. There is glory at the end of the track.

Johann Strauss' "The Blue Danube Waltz" played over the *Katarina's* resonant speaker system. The morning was cool and cloudy. There was little wind. A thick white fog hung low over the river like a bed of corpulent cotton-balls, obscuring visibility on the brown waters to less than a hundred feet. The ship moved slowly, blowing its fog-horn every few minutes to declare its position. It had traveled over 1100 miles up the Danube River and was now near Budapest, Hungary.

Enveloped by veiled whiteness, Aleksei Batkin's men performed their morning exercises along the deck's port-side. Captain Konrad Wagner's Germans stood along the opposite starboard side doing calisthenics. Neither side could see the other well through the fog.

The lanky Feodor Dashkov sat in a pullout lawn chair on the after-deck, reading a Russian newspaper he had bought in Belgrade two days before. His sunken eyes, grotesquely bony facial features, and nefarious stare made him look like a monstrous character in a throwback 'Hollywood Horror' film from the 1940s.

Ivan Petrenko also sat on the after-deck, a few feet away from Dashkov. He watched the Russians and Germans try to outdo each other during their muscle-building displays. He would occasionally glance over at the crazy Dashkov, lost in his own world, and shake his head. Petrenko was living a parody. The absurdity of the events around him were hysterical. The Ukrainian laughed to himself while witnessing the lunacy.

Wagner narcissistically exhibited his muscular frame. He shouted orders to his men as he contorted his body, bulging his muscles. The Germans sang old Wehrmacht marches.

Batkin's purple left facial scar darkened while he did pull-ups from an overhanging steel beam. His Russians shouted profanities at the Germans across the way.

Richard Wagner's "Tannhauser Overture" began to play. The Germans jogged laps around the ship's periphery in two separate groups. The Russians impeded their movement by not clearing the way. Several fistfights broke out.

What a foolish spectacle, thought Petrenko. He again shook his head in disbelief, before turning to read Plato's *The Republic*.

Plato's classic philosophical work on good governance and political theory, written in 380 BC, was an interpretive analysis of his mentor Socrates' dialogues on the definition of justice, the just city-state, and the just man. Socrates did not believe that justice existed naturally in the human soul. He thought it was the result of a "well-ordered" soul. Socrates' disciples were taught that the immortality of man's soul was dependent on living a just life.

Divided in three parts, *The Republic* began with a discussion of "utopia" - the ideal community. It later defined the ideal ruler - the "philosopher-king" -who used truth, wisdom, and reason to rule perfectly. The philosopher-king ruled for the good of the city-state, not his personal enrichment. He never exhibited nepotism and did not own private goods. He followed a completely altruistic course of rule under law. Not believing a utopia was truly achievable in human civilization, *The Republic* ended with a deep discussion of the more practical forms of government.

Plato's "Five Regimes" was a cautionary description of Socrates' progressively degrading continuum of governance, from the incorruptible, utopic, virtuous ideal of philosopher-king rule to the progressively more corruptible forms of timocracy, oligarchy, democracy, and tyranny. As corruption increased, so did injustice for the people.

Timocracy was characterized by courageous authoritarian rule. Noble and proud rulers loved honor, and were selected by the state according to degree of honor they held in society. Although respectful of the free citizens, the timocratic leader would decay and eventually value personal enrichment over virtue. Plato believed that Sparta was representative of this form of government.

Given time, timocracy would degenerate into an oligarchy of rich and powerful people who respected only personal wealth. True measures of a virtuous man – honor, courage, intelligence, wisdom, morality, and faithful social responsibility – would lose importance. Society would divide along the greedy rich and the hungry poor, terminating ultimately in class struggle. Human nature would crave money over virtue, and oligarchs would live only to financially enrich themselves.

Given more time, democracy would be born from the tensions between rich and poor. The poor would overthrow the rich oligarchs and grant themselves progressively more liberal freedoms through democratic vote. With the power of the vote came the appropriation of ever increasing amounts of money to themselves. Social and intellectual laziness followed. Unhealthy vices and abuses propagated.

Socrates believed democracy was undesirable and unreliable, and susceptible to being manipulated by unfit, visually appealing, sectarian demagogues who "protected" the interests of the poor and envious lower class majority. Eventually, the people would become uncontrollably euphoric with increasing "freedom", amplifying the risks of tyranny under the "supportive" demagogue who must maintain civil order.

If not controlled by a strong system of legislative checks and balances, democracy would degrade into anarchy. The chaos would be promoted by the "dark sinister hand" of the future tyrant. The unfit ruler would blame the rich upper classes and their greed for the dissolution of society. A "seizure" of power would be required to maintain order. Characterized by lawless and unjust behavior, the demagogic ruler and his entourage of close supporters would subjugate the people with tyrannical overrule for their own "benefit".

Plato's *The Republic* concluded that justice was better than injustice. Tyranny needed to be defended against at all costs. Wise, knowledgeable, and lawful leadership, free of corruption and immorality, was essential to the success of a republic.

Pavlo Mitnick sat next to Ivan Petrenko on the afterdeck. He handed his friend a cold beer. The fog of morning had cleared, and a warm breeze settled on the men as sunshine broke through the clouds.

"It's warming up, Ivan. I dislike the cold. My aging body feels better in the sunshine."

"The rays of the sun are always better than cold darkness, Pavlo. Where there is light, there is life."

"How is it in the cold dark cave in which you live, Ivan? Is it as lifeless as I imagine?"

"What do you insinuate by that?"

"Must I spell it out for you, Ivan?"

"I want clarification of your statement, Pavlo. We are old friends. I expect your honesty."

"Open your mind, Ivan. Remove the cloudy cataracts from your eyes. See and smell the reality. Don't close out your soul from humanity. Allow the obvious to become apparent. Walking blind in this world is not advisable....."

"We are living a farce, Ivan. Better yet, this is a Greek tragedy describing the downfall of a great man.

"I don't enjoy watching tragedies, particularly when they involve people I respect and love. A heavy heart makes me ill. I'm too old for tragedies."

"Perhaps you should have stayed home, Pavlo, and left the fighting to the young men."

"No..... I don't think so..... I reasoned you may need an old worldly wiseman around to keep you honest and true to your principles. I may know you more than you know yourself, my friend.

"Besides, I want the best for my country and my people, Ivan. I am entitled to be here."

"It sounds like you've lost faith in me, Pavlo. Do you not agree with my choices for action?"

"Ah! The light has gone from your eyes, Ivan..... Have you forgotten everything I've taught you? Where is the boy with all the dreams? Is he so lost inside the cold darkness of his cave that the light of reason has vanished? Where is the illumination? Where is the hope and glory, Ivan?"

Petrenko did not answer. A long silence ensued.....

The *Katarina* passed the Hungarian Parliament Building. Hungary's government had been managed by ultra-nationalists for the past year, and it was closely allied with the fascist movements in Russia and Germany.

The middle-aged Mitnick had been a professor of political theory at the University of Odessa. He had been Petrenko's teacher fifteen years before. Both men shared a deep interest in just governance and rule-of-law. They respected each other's thoughts and opinions greatly.

"You realize that Socrates was the first Communist, don't you?" asked Mitnick. "His ideas of a utopic society ruled by wise men must be familiar to you, Petrenko.

You can not honestly believe democracy is a less practical and just form of government than a timocracy or oligarchy. With 'rule of law' and 'checks and balances', democracy is really the only form of acceptable government, Petrenko."

Petrenko looked quizzically at Mitnick as he drank his beer. "Rule of law is difficult to maintain in a modern society, Pavlo. Even America is presently in a struggle between two political camps, both moving away from democracy.

"One movement is pushing America into an oligarchal form of government, while the other is sliding towards tyranny. Corruption and lack of 'rule of law' led them, and the rest of the 'Free-World', into economic calamity and world war. How can you say democracy is the best form of government, Mitnick, I want to move the Ukraine into a timocracy from our present pseudo-democracy," said Petrenko.

"You may want timocracy for Ukraine, Ivan, but we are squeezed between two giants, Germany and Russia. Both of them are moving to tyranny. You remember what happened to our nation the last time we were in this predicament. Hitler and Stalin's tyranny led to the death of seven million of our countrymen.

"Do you really think our country can maintain 'rule of law' with a tyrannical fascist Central and Eastern Europe all around us? I doubt it. In the end, we will have to deal with our ego-maniacal neighbors. Your suppression of that reality amazes me.

"Indeed, America lost her grip on an orderly system of democratic rule. But I believe she will find her way back with appropriate leadership. It was a small stumble in her relatively young history.

"It shocks me to discover the Ukraine failed in her democratic capitalist experiment so quickly. Except for a few years last decade, our government has been lawless and socioeconomically bankrupt since the fall of the Soviet Union. I believe we can learn from our mistakes and make another attempt for lawful orderly democracy. 'Rule of law' and a strong system of checks and balances must be our national priority. That is our only chance for freedom, Petrenko. You can not have true freedom without true democracy. Socrates was wrong.

"To maintain a free constitutional republic is difficult. You need fair markets for trade, where all parties involved feel a socioeconomic benefit. You must have a strong middle class with some financial security. A robust education system for the young is essential, stressing science and mathematics. The children must be taught traditional conservative values of family and civic responsibility. Liberal thought and philosophy must be measured with economic and moral common sense. Above all, we must instill in our youth - pride in living a just life.

"Planning for freedom is simpler than governing it, Petrenko. The Americans showed us that. Powerful and patient backbones are required to show the people the path to enlightenment. It's a long road to liberty. Our political leadership must have a conscience to stay the course and govern properly. Without a moral conscience in our leaders, all is lost," stated Mitnick.

Tchaikovsky's "1812 Overture" began to play. Composed to commemorate Russia's defeat of the invading Napoleonic French Army, the music is a classic expression of freedom and the removal of oppression.

Over the horns, Mitnick continued. "Germany and Russia will be our future oppressors, Ivan, just as they have been in the past. We will need America's help in removing our yoke of tyranny and finding our freedom.

"There is a fault line dividing the opposing forces of the government continuum. These forces grind along the fault line in opposite directions. One towards tyranny, the other towards orderly democracy with 'rule of law'. This grinding leads to 'earthquakes' or wars waged, always between one side fighting for freedom and the other intent on taking freedom away. We simply need to decide which side of the fault line we truly want to stand on. If we miscalculate again, Ivan, it will lead to our enemy's glory and our own misery."

Petrenko stared at Mitnick as Henryk Gorecki's "3rd Symphony, 1st Movement" began to play. The musical composition expressed the laments of mother for child, and of child for mother, in the despair of war.

CHAPTER 11

Appeasement and Redemption

When you appease evil, you can only expect more evil. Putting aside inevitable conflict in hopes of avoiding it altogether is not a successful practice when confronting villainy and iniquity. Pernicious and wicked design must be suffocated at its birth. If you allow the monster to mature, there will be no atonement for your disgrace. There will be no redemption for the calamity you will have caused. In silver armor and on white horse combat the wrongs of the world.

"*L'horreur!*" shouted the young Frenchman in his sleep. Alexis Coffigny awoke in his Munich hotel room, startled from a nightmarish dream. He sat upright in bed, caught his breath, and tried to slow his racing heart. The dark room was cool with early autumn Bavarian night air. Although he had slept with his windows open, Coffigny's pillows and bed sheets were drenched with his sweat.

The Frenchman slowly stepped out of bed to the bathroom. He wiped away perspiration from his naked body. Coffigny wet a towel with cold water and draped it over his neck. He splashed more cold water on his face. Alexis needed to awaken further and distance himself from the dream. He did not turn on lights. He felt more secure in the blackness.

Coffigny returned to the bedroom and glanced at the clock on the night table. A thin sliver of electric light from the plaza lamp posts outside fell directly on the clock's face. It was after 3 AM. He had been asleep for only two hours.

The Frenchman stood in the dark in front of the large windows facing Munich's famous Konigsplatz Square. He lit a cigarette and tried to settle himself down. Coffigny looked out over the square at the perpetual Nazi SS Honor Guard standing at the *Ehrentempel* monument across the way.

The sacred Nazi site held the sixteen cast iron sarcophagi of Hitler's comrades killed in his 1923 Munich Beer Hall Putsch attempt to overthrow the Bavarian government. It had been a prelude to the eventual take-down of Germany's Weimar Republican government.

Coffigny thought of how the rebellion had been Hitler's last failure. Ten years after his putsch and subsequent short imprisonment, Adolf Hitler became Chancellor of Germany. And now by late 1938, he was the unrivaled dictator of the most powerful nation on the continent.

In March of 1936, Hitler had ordered his army to re-militarize the Rhineland, violating the Locarno Treaties signed in Switzerland after World War I. He had supported Benito Mussolini's Italian invasion and conquest of Ethiopia. On March 12, 1938, Hitler's armies had occupied and annexed Austria into the German Reich. Now in late September of 1938, Nazi Germany was preparing to invade and occupy the Sudetenland region of Czechoslovakia. Hitler was also threatening to take land in Poland and Hungary, where large numbers of ethnic Germans lived.

Czechoslovakia had been created in 1919, after the signing of the Treaty of Versailles and the dismemberment of the Austria-Hungarian Empire by the victorious Allies. The Czech borderlands with Germany had over three million Germans clamoring to join Hitler's Reich. In early 1938, Adolf Hitler urged and assisted the Sudetenland German Party leader - Konrad Henlein - in his developing protests to the Czech government and Czech president - Edvard Benes. A series of "abuse" incidents by the Czech government against the Sudeten people had been headlined in Hitler speeches, and the Germans had united behind Hitler in his attempts to coerce France and Great Britain to allow his annexation of the Sudetenland. In early September of 1938, Hitler gave a final ultimatum to the Czech government while he prepared for a military takeover of the Sudetenland. War between Germany and Czechoslovakia's allies, Britain and France, seemed inevitable.

British Prime Minister Neville Chamberlain flew to Munich in the early morning of September 15. He took a train to Hitler's mountain retreat at Berchtesgaden for a three hour emergency meeting. Hitler demanded the immediate annexation of the Sudetenland while Chamberlain obtained assurances that the remainder of Czechoslovakia and Eastern Europe would remain safe. The French and Czech governments agreed reluctantly to the arrangement.

Because the situation remained tense, a second meeting between Chamberlain and Hitler took place in Bad Godesberg near Bonn, Germany, on September 22, 1938. At the Rheinhotel Dreesen along the Rhine River, Hitler made further demands on German territorial claims in Poland and Hungary.

Italian dictator Benito Mussolini organized a third meeting in Munich for September 29. Neville Chamberlain and French Prime Minister Edouard Daladier would meet with Mussolini and Hitler. The British and the French hoped to arrive at a final agreement.

France and Czechoslovakia had a mutual assistance pact, obligating France to come to the aid of the Czech government in the event of war with Germany. Although Britain had no such pact, they had informally given their support to France in the case of war with Hitler. Neither Chamberlain nor Daladier wanted war. Both of their countries had suffered greatly during World War I, and public sentiment was staunchly in support of peace.

Edouard Daladier, prime minister since April 10, had been a French Army company commander during the Great War. He was traumatized by the bloodbath. Unlike Chamberlain, Daladier had no misconceptions about Hitler's true intentions for Czechoslovakia and the rest of Eastern Europe. He fully understood the Nazis wanted the Sudetenland today and would want Hungary, Poland, and Romania tomorrow. He reasoned Hitler would first try to secure the oil and wheat he needed for his war machine, and then turn his aggression west towards France and Great Britain. Daladier felt England and France needed to closely unite their governments to safeguard the independence of Czechoslovakia. If the Sudetenland was surrendered, it would eventually precipitate the war with Germany that they were so desperately trying to avoid.

Drowned out by the discouraged and defeatist attitudes of the leading members of the French government, Daladier disapprovingly allowed Chamberlain to have his way and proceed with the appeasement of Adolf Hitler. His weakness allowed Neville Chamberlain to direct the Allies' negotiations in Munich. Misjudgement had set the stage for the most horrific war in the history of mankind.

The cold night air had finally settled Alexis Coffigny's spirit. As Daladier's chief adjutant-aide, he had flown to Munich on the morning of September 28 to help prepare France's side in the negotiations scheduled to begin the next day at the Fuhrerbau Building on the Konigsplatz. His team of twelve diplomats would organize the meeting schedule for Daladier before his arrival on the morning of September 29.

Coffigny's father had served as a junior officer in Daladier's company during the Great War. A favorite confidant of Daladier, he was killed two months before the armistice.

After finishing doctorates in political science and sociology, the sharp aristocratic Alexis was recruited by the French prime minister in May 1938. The 36 year-old diplomat spoke multiple languages and had a keen intuitive sense for politics and negotiations.

Coffigny stepped in the dark to the table in the corner of his room. He struck a wooden matchstick and lit the large square candle next to the record player. A soft flickering yellow golden light allowed the Frenchman to search through the small collection of music he had brought with him. He chose Gabriel Faure's "Requiem".

The young Coffigny sat and finished his cigarette. He listened to Faure's choral masterpiece, while staring across the plaza at the Nazi shrine. The Frenchman's shadow was cast on the wall by the candlelight.

How could his country allow this travesty to happen, he thought. In only two decades, his nation had lost her spine. They had not prepared mindfully for this possibility. The decent civilized world had permitted Hitler to create a powerful army, navy, and air force without punishment. With the growth of his armed forces, the gangster Hitler only gained confidence.

The proud French government was being pushed over the edge by a little lunatic corporal with designs to master the globe. Who would stand up to the powerful German war machine if England and France did not? When would someone say no to Hitler?

In his dream, Alexis found himself alone on a long march. Dressed in a French Army uniform, which had been soiled and scorched by battle, he had approached his farm in southern France along a familiar country road. The French countryside all around him had been decimated by war. Burned down farmhouses and dead livestock lined the road back home. He could see no signs of life. Weak and exhausted, he finally arrived at his country village on a hill. He ran the last hundred meters to his home and entered it with the emotional sense that all had been lost. Inside, he found his wife and children dead.

The dream reflected Alexis Coffigny's belief that soon the world would be at war again. This time, he reasoned, it would be more vengeful and destructive than ever before. Many more millions would die to satisfy another egomaniac's lust for power.

Coffigny could not see a way out for France. If they stood up to Hitler, the war would come now. If they appeased him, the war would come later. Either way, pain and suffering would be experienced again on a grander scale than anyone could imagine. Modern weapons were more destructive than in the last 'Great War'.

The voices of the choirboys from Faure's seventh and final movement, "In Paradisum", echoed out over Hitler's sacred plaza. Alexis Coffigny was certain the Nazi Honor Guards could hear the boy trebles. Perhaps even Adolf Hitler could hear the cries of the children. Coffigny hoped so..... As the boys' voices faded away, a strong gust of wind blew out the last light of the Frenchman's candle.

Alexis, resigned to the planet's hopeless future, lit another cigarette and sat naked in the chair until the sun rose on the Konigsplatz. It would be a sad day for France and the people of the world.....

The Fuhrerbau was a rectangular three-level building of modern classical Reich architecture. It housed Nazi Party offices in Munich. Adolf Hitler's private office sat above the south entrance. A large balcony faced the Konigsplatz and provided Hitler with an excellent view of the square. A big bronze German Eagle sat bolted to the building facade above Hitler's office. On the morning of

September 29, 1938, Nazi and Italian flags were hung from the south entrance facade. British and French flags were draped from the north entrance facade.

Alexis Coffigny and the French team arrived early in the morning. They entered the Fuhrerbau through the north entrance. Long hallways ran to both sides of the building on the ground floor. A "Great Hall", where Hitler entertained, had been prepared for lunch. From a central portico with open skylights, marble staircases led to the upper floors with columned balconies. Blood red banners with black swastikas hung in rows from the balconies. Coffigny and his team were led to their preparation room where they set up communications to Paris.

Hermann Goering, Heinrich Himmler, Rudolph Hess, and Wilhelm Keitel soon arrived in succession. The German Foreign Minister Joachim von Ribbentrop was followed by Adolf Hitler. Mussolini and Daladier arrived minutes apart, shortly before Neville Chamberlain. Italian Foreign Minister Galeazzo Ciano received his father-in-law, Benito Mussolini. British Foreign Minister Lord Halifax and French Foreign Minister Georges Bonnet received their respective leaders.

Hitler, Mussolini, Daladier, and Chamberlain congregated with their translators in the assembly room to begin their discussions. Daladier's adjutant-aide, Alexis Coffigny, stood in the corner of the room and observed the machinations of world diplomacy.

Adolf Hitler declared he was ready to invade Czechoslovakia by October 1. He sat in his favorite chair, wearing a firmly pressed Nazi uniform with swastika armband. Hitler visually scanned the room without blinking once. He was prepared to verbally attack anyone who would challenge his statement. His crazed blue eyes projected defiance with confidence.

In total silence, Mussolini stood and rapidly presented his proposal in Italian. The German Foreign Ministry in Berlin had formulated the paper the previous day. As the British and French delegations reviewed the translated written proposal, a growing rumble of discontent was heard in the room. The leaders debated the Nazi demands, but only meekly on the Allied side.

Coffigny stared at Hitler. Although he had seen him in action on prior occasions, Coffigny was startled by the despot's powerful presence on this day. Hitler seemed to overwhelm both Chamberlain and Daladier with his intensity.

Chamberlain then asked about compensation for the Czech government and citizens. Hitler simply ignored the question and refused to consider it. Coffigny could sense Chamberlain's weakness. It was palpable by everyone in the room. Daladier, who had allowed Chamberlain to direct the Allies' efforts, also appeared powerless.

By lunchtime, everyone realized the futility of negotiations with Hitler. The Allies' fear of war with the Germans drowned out all other concerns, including the appearance of impotence and humiliation. Selling one's soul for peace seemed agreeable to the Allies. Alexis Coffigny was shocked by France and Britain's obvious diplomatic capitulation, loss of honor, and national disgrace.

The young Frenchman entered the "Great Hall" alone. He didn't have much of an appetite but needed the short lunch break to recover his senses. Dozens of junior diplomats and military officers, friend and foe, assembled for fine food and refreshment.

Under a large chandelier in the corner of the hall, Coffigny found a grand piano. He calmly sat underneath the thousand Venetian crystals and began to play Erik Satie's "Gymnopedie No. 1".

The din of men's voices in the hall, informally arguing the points of the Munich Conference, quieted. A somber silence provided a background for Coffigny's fingers on the keys. Alexis was unaware the room was now his.

As the Frenchman played, the men of war began personally reflecting on the future of the globe. All their faces saddened. Goblets and plates were put down. Discussions stopped in mid-sentence. Attention was directed to the man under the Venetian crystal, playing his heart out for the world.

Coffigny released his frustration into the music. He sounded every note with the passion of someone saying goodbye to the richness of the earth. His love of humanity became apparent to all in the hall. He lost himself in his thoughts, and so did his listeners.

When finished, Alexis Coffigny's audience – French and German, British and Italian – applauded. The Frenchman stood and bowed.

A German captain now sat at the piano. He played Bach's "Air on the G String". He also received the crowd's profound notice. The German officer displayed equal passion as the Frenchman. On reaching the end of the masterpiece, the hall rang up in ovation.

After a few more minutes of meditation, the world went back to its ways. The men of war returned to their drink and alimentation, debate and quarrel, and insanity.

The German captain approached Alexis Coffigny. The men stood face to face.

"I am Captain Carl Simhauser. Good day to you, Sir."

"Good day, Captain. I am Alexis Coffigny, adjutant-aide to the Prime Minister of France."

"I suspect we're having the same dreams, you and I, Coffigny. I hear it in your piano. Like the eyes, music is a window to the soul. Perhaps the world will be kinder because of our playing."

"Yes indeed. We can only hope, Captain.

"If only all duels could be decided by the playing of music, the world would be thankful. But I suppose that feat would be difficult to accomplish."

"I suppose so, Coffigny..... But dreamers can continue to wish their desires. Maybe one day, the world will come around to our wishes."

"Dueling pianos, Simhauser..... Let them decide the fate of humanity....."

The German captain smiled and shook Coffigny's hand. Each slowly returned to his national entourage.

After lunch, the leaders were joined by their advisors. They began a long discussion on each clause of the Italian draft. Later that evening, the British and French delegations returned to their hotels while the Germans and Italians feasted in the Great Hall Room at the Fuhrerbau. The Munich Conference resumed at 10 PM. By 1:30 AM, the pact was ready for signing in Adolf Hitler's private office on the second level. All of the Fuhrer's demands had been granted.

Coffigny entered Hitler's quarters with his prime minister. Both men realized they were allowing a travesty to be committed on Europe which would end in ruin. They stepped together to the desk in front of a large fireplace. Daladier placed his signature on the concluding documents of appeasement. Above the fireplace hung a portrait of Otto von Bismarck by Lenbach. Coffigny stared at the portrait as Daladier slowly walked away. The Munich Pact was complete. The door to Europe had been opened for Hitler and his new Germany. Millions would pay with their lives, and the world would never be the same again.

Without the consent of the Czech government, Britain and France ceded the Sudetenland region of Czechoslovakia to Hitler and allowed his troops to occupy it with impunity. The British and French people were joyous that war with Germany had been averted. The Czech government in Prague objected to the decision but agreed to its terms. The next day, Czech President Benes resigned in disgrace.

In the late morning of September 30, Chamberlain requested a meeting with Hitler at the Fuhrer's apartment in Munich. He pleaded that Hitler not bomb Prague if the Czechs revolted. He asked Hitler to sign an "Anglo-German Agreement", symbolizing their peoples' desire to never go to war with each other again. Hitler gladly signed the paper, not giving it any importance. The Fuhrer later told his generals that their enemies were "little worms". In contrast, Chamberlain returned to his hotel for lunch and in front of his aides patted his breast pocket. The smiling British prime minister said, "I've got it."

On returning to London later in the afternoon, Chamberlain declared that the paper secured "peace for our time". Ironically the next day, the German Army rolled into Czechoslovakia.

Winston Churchill spoke in Parliament on October 3. He forcefully emphasized, "England has been offered a choice between war and shame. She has chosen shame, and will get war."

Hitler annexed the remainder of Czechoslovakia in March 1939. On September 1, 1939, his armies invaded Poland and began World War II. The Munich Pact had been like a free pass to the Nazi war machine, allowing Hitler to begin his enslavement of Europe.

Neville Chamberlain resigned as prime minister in May 1940. He died six months later of cancer.

Daladier resigned his post in March 1940. After the German occupation of France three months later, he was tried for treason by the Vichy government and imprisoned. In 1943, he was transferred to German concentration camps until the end of the war. Daladier lived in shame and obscurity until his death in Paris in 1970.

Alexis Coffigny was also imprisoned by the Germans. He died at Buchenwald Concentration Camp in August 1944, during an inadvertent American bombing raid directed at a nearby armament factory.

The Frenchman wrote secret memoirs while at Buchenwald. American soldiers discovered the personal commentaries beneath a floorboard in Coffigny's prison blockhouse after the war. The papers were safely passed to his family.

Coffigny's last entry was made only moments before his death. His final words should be read by all who have interest in freedom, and a tendency to procrastinate the duty to defend it. If one allows evil to grow, and great suffering results from your weakness, the shroud of shame will be your burial garment. A heavy shadow of guilt will block all light in life and in the afterlife. There is no liberty ever to be had in the mind and spirit of the damned.

I have returned to my dreary stone building after another long night and morning at the munitions factory. Like the thousand prior nights, I was forced to labor for my enemy. I help create products of war which kill the very stock of people I betrayed. I can't extricate myself from the trappings of my own doing. I am weak. The Nazis hold my family hostage. If I don't toil for my captors, my wife and children join me in this hell.....

I can not sleep, so I write. I write of the happenings I see and feel. I try to capture and reflect the hopelessness of it all. The injustice of the cruelty shatters my spirits. I want people to know of this inferno and never forget the mistakes that created it. Please spare all the future generations of children this misery. They have done nothing to deserve our malicious and irresponsible adult natures.

I live in the barracks for 'celebrity' prisoners. Most of us are diplomats, priests, and discredited 'Aryan' German businessmen, bankers, doctors, and lawyers. We also have several ousted corrupt Nazi officials. We work in the factories and quarries around the camp. Regularly, guards come for someone to shoot. It helps keep discipline in the camp, they say.

Next to us are the cellhouses for Allied prisoners of war. The American, French, and British soldiers are treated equally bad.

The Soviet soldiers are worked to death in less than two weeks. They are rarely fed and often beaten. Many are executed every morning. None will survive the ordeal.

The camp has thousands of Jewish captives. They are treated worse than the Soviets. The women and girls are the first to be eliminated. The men and boys are fed just enough to keep them working for a few weeks. When they wither away, the crematorium awaits them as well.

We all have emaciated faces and crumpled bodies. Infectious diseases run through the camp, killing thousands every month. The physical and mental abuse is impossible to understand.

Although few of us will ever leave this camp, many still hope to see loved ones at home one day. We may not know if home still exists, but the dream keeps some alive.

I have been ill. Fever and cough are constant now. I am producing a bloody sputum. I have pain in my chest when I breathe. I am only skin and bones. My last vestiges of strength and faith have faded. I realize my wife and children will never see me again.

I have not finished my cabbage-worm soup and small piece of black rye-sawdust bread. My appetite for food is gone. It is as ragged as the clothes I wear.

I only wish to sleep now, for a very long time. I want to dream of the goodness that could have been. I hope to see my wife Natasha in my eternal sleep. I desire to kiss her lips and hold her close to me. I want to feel the soft skin of my babies against my face. I would like to sense their love in me forever. I pray they have not suffered the insufferable.

I am sorry for my mistakes. In Munich, I should have shouted out, 'No!' I saw the beginning of a new sad chapter in the history of mankind, and I did nothing! I sensed the evil in Hitler and stayed silent. History has been my judge and executioner. Do not forgive my trespasses.

I hear a distant rumble..... Sitting by my window in my stone prison, looking to the northwest, I see the white contrails of American bombers in the blue sky. The B17s seem *like proud eagles coming in defense of freedom. German flak guns are filling the blue with puffs of black smoke. I see Nazi fighters rising to meet my eagles. The Americans will be victorious, I am certain.*

The big birds of war have begun to drop their bombs. One or two loud eruptions have turned into a continuous explosion. Giant fires have started beyond the barbed wire fence. I see the armament factories and SS housing in flames.

A great wave of liberating destruction rolls my way. I am sentient of it. The fiery bursts on the ground are near. I feel their concussions inside of me. I welcome them. The power of the fire is my deliverance. My tide of mercy has come for me at last. The fate of my physical being and the destiny of my soul have arrived.....

Frederic Coffigny - Alexis' grandson - was born and raised in Switzerland. All his life, he had remained outside the microscope of the French media. He had quietly served as mayor of Aborn, Switzerland, for the past three years. Two years ago, he was recruited by the CIA to help them fight the developing fascist movements in Central and Eastern Europe.

The little town of Aborn - on the southwestern shores of Lake Constance, across the waters from Bavaria to the east - was the next stop for Julius Stansfield. The American arrived in the afternoon of June 14, after driving from Zurich. Stansfield was here to meet the next contact on his mission to Munich, Germany.

CHAPTER 12

Sleep With
One Eye Open

Feel the ground with your hands. Dig your fingers deep into the rich soil. Sense the vibrations of your enemy's approach. Thunder of foot and hoof, the earth shakes with the violent awakening of impending battle.

With open eyes, stare into the valley. Search for the reflected light off bayonet, spear, and sword. Watch for the shine of steel armor. Look for the war horses and carriages of combat, they are near.

Listen to the whispers of the wind. They carry the songs and cries of clash as they come closer. Let them blow away with your fears, disappointments, and disillusionments.

Welcome a new age of hope and peace. Be ready to receive a stronger domain of love and honor. It is time to finally bestow on the world a sense of compassion and benevolence.

Unfurl the colors of a righteous universal army and lead the way to a better tomorrow. Save the billions of sacred years of life's evolution. We are all deserving of it.

Julius drove close to the lakefront and easily found the two-story blue pastel-colored home with a dark green shingled roof. It stood one hundred feet from the shore of Lake Constance, a large beautiful mountain lake on the Rhine River at the base of the Alps between Switzerland, Austria, and Germany. A dry cold wind from the northeast swept across the lake, creating whitecaps on its blue waters. The German-speaking picturesque town of Aborn, Switzerland, founded over two thousand years ago, was a resort for leisure since Roman times.

After parking his car underneath the house, Stansfield climbed a short incline to a sundeck. It overlooked the lake and coastline of Bavaria. The mountains of Germany were little more than ten miles to the east. The deck allowed a majestic view of the Alps in all directions. Stansfield zipped up his jacket and stared out over the frothy waters, taking in all the beauty around him.

"Good afternoon, Captain," stated Frederic Coffigny as he came out from his home to greet his guest.

"You're very punctual. My experience with Americans is that they enjoy being late to their appointments. We Swiss are timely people. Even our trains are measured to the second. Perhaps your submarine training requires obsessive exactitude. Whatever the case, I think it's a good character trait to have in this business of ours. Don't you think, Captain?"

"I suppose it usually is," said Stansfield. "As long as your enemy isn't waiting for your arrival. We certainly wouldn't want to make their job any easier. Would we?"

"You could say that," answered the tall, affable, and portly fifty-seven year-old Coffigny.

"If they're expecting you, punctuality could be a negative survival characteristic. Maybe it is best to keep the lions in the bush guessing as much as you can," laughed the Swiss.

"Welcome to my little town, Stansfield," said Coffigny while extending his hand. "Aborn is a magical place. Like an attractive woman, she has a mighty first impression."

"Yes," responded Stansfield, looking out over the blue lake and sky. "I've lived near water all my life. But the mountains add a certain grandeur. Your town is truly a special place, Coffigny."

The mayor smiled and offered Julius a chair. The men sat at the edge of the deck underneath a bright yellow parasol.

"I wish you had more time to enjoy my hamlet, Captain. But it seems your country needs you in Munich as soon as possible. My orders are to get you there in one piece, regardless of risks to me or my family. Let me assure you, the risks are plentiful. Our region is full of fascist agents from several countries that would love to see America stumble and fall. We can not allow that to happen, Captain Stansfield. Without a stable United States, this world would go to hell in a hand-basket.

"*Merde!* That's what the world has become, Stansfield. No matter what angle you look at it from, our planet has become shit. It's not the first time, and it certainly won't be the last. However, it's difficult for my conscience to accept failure without a fight. I need to participate in the reconstruction of peace. It's become an essential moral objective for me.

"Since the fall of the Soviet Union, we've seen a historically unprecedented disruption of the world's social fabric. Economies and governments all over the Earth have risen and fallen with breath-taking speed. Civil war and revolution have become the norm. Lady Liberty has been attacked from the Left and the Right, outside and inside your country, Stansfield.

"Old and new enemies of the United States have strenuously confronted America's plans for a peaceful world order. Even within the US itself, groups have vied to implement their own concepts of world order. The traditional conservatives want deeper American oversight and influence. The champagne drinking, limp-wristed liberals and socialists want to share oversight with their communist friends in Russia and China.

"With the break-up of China, the New World Order Socialist ideas have unraveled and fallen to the side. At least for now, Stansfield, you and your conservative colleagues appear to be winning the contest for the planet. Yet, the battle's final outcome remains undecided. The balance of the world is a fluid situation. Your position as an American patriot is under constant attack. Recently and misguidedly, there were even high government officials in your own country who worked diligently for 'Change'. Who could have ever imagined changing the greatest nation on Earth?

"Not too long ago, there was a significant purge of patriotic American military leaders in your country.

I understand they were against the poorly managed nuclear negotiations with Iran. They also believed China had not been confronted early enough. Appeasement did not lead to peace, Stansfield. Poor diplomacy led to a short but bloody world war. The planet's chaos cost millions of lives.

"Today, we have another dangerous situation evolving in the world. The Munich Conference of 1938 reminds us of the deadly consequences of weak diplomacy. Recent history reminds us as well. Appeasement of evil always leads to more evil.

"America is standing strong this time. She desires to snuff out the early brushfire before it becomes a conflagration. That's why you and I are sitting under this bright yellow parasol, discussing the reasons for your presence here.

"Do you see the Bavarian coastline across the lake, Stansfield?" asked Coffigny as he pointed to the east.

"There lies the village of Lindau. Early tomorrow morning, I will get you there by boat. You will travel with a Spanish alias, Mr. Antonio Sevilla, a businessman from Bilbao with a passion for German culture and pretty women. Not a bad alias, if you ask me," laughed Coffigny.

"In Lindau, you will board the Allgau Railway to Munich, arriving two hours later. You will be picked up by a taxi-driver who will stand at the exit of the depot with your name, 'Sevilla', on a placard. He will take you to the Kaiser Hotel, where further orders will be slipped under your room door that afternoon. You are not to leave your room at the Kaiser until you have received those instructions.

"Munich, the birthplace and spiritual capital of the Nazi movement long ago, is now the center of the Fuhrer's Nest

Party. Like with the rays of the sun, the resurgence of fascist ideology radiates from this crucible to the rest of the world. The city is a fortress of political zealots and fanatical militants.

"Munich is a very dangerous place, Captain. I suggest you sleep with one eye open while you are there. These modern 'Fourth Reich' agents are more ruthless than their tyrannical ancestors. I am told their interrogation techniques are quite unpleasant and usually leave you decapitated in a Munich alley. They are more 'Aryan' and anti-Semitic than their grandfathers, and believe just as strongly in aggressive totalitarian militarism.

"The near-term goals of the Boche Fascists are to weaken America in Europe, expel her, and aggressively re-expand German national boundaries. They also want a nuclear fighting force. A repeat of history, except they hope for a better ending this time. Let's do our part to stop them, Captain Stansfield."

Frederic Coffigny's wife, Ingrid, opened the glass door leading from the home onto the sundeck. She requested Frederic walk their German Shepherd dog, "Texas". The dog immediately came and sat next to Stansfield.

"We all have a spymaster, Captain. My wife, Ingrid, is mine," laughed Coffigny.

"If she says, 'Walk the dog,' I walk the dog. I've learned not to question commands in the last few years. Besides, 'Texas' is my best friend. And I'd like to keep it that way. In our business, friends of the 'human' variety are not nearly as faithful."

"Texas", a handsome black and red shepherd, buried his head in Julius' lap.

"He seems to like you, Stansfield. He's usually weary of strangers."

"I have a way with dogs, Mayor. As a boy, I had a shepherd just like him. 'Zeus' was his name."

"How does a dog in America get a name like that?"

"How does a German Shepherd in the Alps get named 'Texas'?" asked Stansfield rhetorically.

Frederic grinned and said loudly, "I love American cowboy movies!

"Let's take 'Texas' to the lakefront for a walk, Captain."

The men crossed the street to the boardwalk along Lake Constance and sat at a park bench. The disciplined dog ran in a grassy area in front of them. The lake was full of windsurfers taking advantage of the 30 knot winds blowing from Germany. Their colorful sails dotted the horizon while they maneuvered their boards to challenge the high waves.

Coffigny pointed out to the lake and asked Stansfield, "Do you see the board with the magenta sail?"

"Yeah, the one with the beautiful blonde! She's hard to miss."

"She's my daughter, Claudia, a true risk-taker," proudly stated the mayor.

Stansfield watched as Claudia sailed high into the air and performed acrobatic forward and backward loops. She never once fell off the board, using her amazing hips to balance herself.

"She is quite an athlete," said Stansfield. "She must be very strong and coordinated to master the board like she does."

"Oh, she is, my friend..... She is certainly strong and agile, Captain. She is a determined athlete in every sense of the word. God broke the mold after he made her, Stansfield," laughed the mayor.

Claudia saw her father at the shore and began to sail towards him. As she got closer, Julius began to better appreciate the physical magnitude of this woman.

"My daughter is very adventurous, Captain. She doesn't seem to bother herself much with impediments. Obstacles are simply challenges for her. She enjoys climbing every single mountain placed in her way. Unfortunately for her ex-husband, her adventurous nature got the best of him.

"She is a gorgeous twenty-seven year-old woman addicted to adrenaline. That's dynamite in a very tight package. Her physical energy and volatility are chemo-attractants. She's got powerful pheromones, Stansfield. Wherever she goes, men are attracted to her side. They can't stay away from her. What husband can tolerate that for any length of time?" added the mayor, answering his own question.

"By the way, Stansfield, Claudia will escort you for the remainder of your mission," declared Coffigny before walking to the shore to greet his daughter.

Julius stayed on the bench at the top of the pebbly beach. He carefully watched Claudia come out of the cold water in a black wetsuit. She left her board at the shore and ran towards her father. The tight suit outlined her tall attractive figure. Her muscular thighs and shapely breasts were marked through the suit. She had her wet blonde hair pulled back into a ponytail.

Claudia embraced and kissed her father. She used one hand to lean on him while stripping off her wetsuit.

Stansfield's jaw dropped while Claudia exposed in stages her voluptuous body in a tiny white string Bikini. Her flesh was magnificent. He could not take his eyes off of her. She was like a Nordic goddess coming out of a spring forest bath.

As Claudia pulled the wetsuit off her right leg, her left breast sat fully exposed to Julius' eyes. The skin was white like fresh snow, and stretched by the healthy natural fullness of the breast. The areola was dark because of the cool wind, and the nipple darker and harder. The contrasting shades and contours were sensuous, and they aroused Stansfield.

The young woman threw her head back and squeezed the water out of her ponytail. Her posture maximized every curve and valley on her body. Little was left to the imagination. It was a perfect mixture of hard and soft pleasure. She had muscular definition in all the spots you wished it so. And she had soft healthy fullness everywhere in between. Her form was an erotic wonderland.

Claudia's swimsuit was so small and tight that a tuft of curly blonde pubic hair exploded out of it. She noticed the American's interest and smiled at him. Julius smiled back. The mayor's daughter was quite a woman. Her sensuality was overwhelming.

Now only in her small bathing suit, Claudia grabbed her board and quickly said hello to Julius as she ran barefooted by him in the cold air. Stansfield stared in astonishment while she crossed the street to her home. Mayor Coffigny walked up to Julius and beamed.

"She is a wild and amorous woman by nature, Captain. No man has been able to handle her for any length of time. She's a handful in more ways than one.

"Claudia was recruited by the CIA six years ago while studying international relations at the University of

Geneva. They say she has many natural gifts for spy-work. She is also fluent in several European languages. Over the past five years, she has had many missions in Central and Eastern Europe. She seduces with brain and beauty. The CIA believes she is infallible.

"Claudia will be one of your German girlfriends on the trip to Bavaria, Captain. You'll likely not want any others. I recommend you hold on tightly. It will be a turbulent ride, I assure you.....

"Now, let's go have a warm brandy inside by the fireplace."

The afternoon had become unseasonably cold as the men returned to the Coffigny home. A fire comfortably warmed the living room, accented by a large picture window facing Lake Constance and the Bavarian Alps. Frederic and Julius sat to drink French brandy and smoke Cuban cigars.

"I understand you have Cuban roots, Captain Stansfield," said the mayor.

"Yes, I do. My mother was born in Cuba and came to America as a child. She returned once, near the end of her life, to see Cuba finally free."

"I can not fully understand how Europeans have idolized Fidel Castro as a cultural icon," said Coffigny. "The man created a sociological disaster on his island. Although he boasted of his educational and health reforms, my two trips to Communist Cuba proved to me otherwise. The populace was uneducated and lived in unspeakable squalor.

"Bank accounts here in Switzerland are full of money stolen by old regime Cuban government officials. It truly was a pathetic society," added Coffigny.

"The Europeans idolized Fidel Castro and his partner in crime, Che Guevara, as an expression of anti-Americanism," stated Stansfield. "No one who believes in the natural rights of man could consciously embrace Castro's revolution. He murdered thousands of people who simply wanted freedom for their families. Like Hitler and Stalin, Castro was a power-hungry opportunistic egomaniac, who enjoyed dictating to others on how they should live. He enriched himself on the labor and blood of his people. What a pitiful chapter in the history of a proud people," concluded Stansfield.

Frederic Coffigny handed Julius an album full of hundreds of loose yellowed papers, and a thick hard-covered book titled, *Disgrace at Munich*. The mayor threw more wood into the fire.

Stansfield began leafing through the album. Coffigny poured himself another warm brandy and returned to his chair by the fireplace.

"Appeasement of immoral action is never good practice for a government, Captain. It was not good for the country of my ancestors decades ago, and it was not good for your country a while back with Syria and Iran.

"I'll never understand how the United States allowed a terror regime in Iran get so close to mastering a nuclear weapons program. Red lines were drawn and red lines were passed with impunity. Negotiations were conducted by your nation, knowing fully well the Islamist aspirations and expansionist plans of Iran. The US gave their enemy more time to prepare for an inevitable war. The extension of time also allowed the development of stronger alliances with other enemies of the United States. A limited regional war was turned into a global conflict involving North

Korea and China. America was fortunate that Russia saw the light and exited the 'Evil Axis'. Nevertheless, the world war cost thousands of Allied lives. It could have been mini-mized by earlier action.

"The issue of appeasing wrong behavior by renegade nations always comes back to bite you in the ass. The matter is very close to my heart. My blood family was deeply affected by such behavior. Many lives were bro-ken because of misjudgement.

"That book was written on the political life of my grand-father, Alexis Coffigny, from notes in that album, written in his hand while interred at the Buchenwald Concentration Camp in Germany during World War Two. My grandfather was French Prime Minister Daladier's chief adjutant-aide at the infamous Munich Conference in 1938. He person-ally saw his country open the door to German militarism and help sow the seeds for the biggest calamity in human history.

"Alexis was imprisoned after the invasion of France by Hitler in 1940. He died a slave in the Buchenwald Camp in 1944. Those papers were found at Buchenwald in 1945. They were delivered to my family after the end of the war.

"In those handwritten notes, my grandfather outlined the mistakes of his government in their dealings with Adolf Hitler. He explained the diplomatic errors of France and England in detail, and how they led to the Second World War. He understood his disgrace had been France's disgrace. Because of that shame, Alexis Coffigny's son - my father - was forced to leave France with his mother and move to Switzerland in 1948. Our family has lived here ever since.

"I suspect my work with the CIA is a personal attempt to help prevent another fascist program from infecting

Europe. I need to do what I can to return some dignity to the Coffigny name," said Frederic Coffigny.

"I understand your point, Mayor," stated Julius Stansfield. "The circumstances of appeasement are never easy to accept. Sometimes we believe time will correct the thinking of our enemy, or that internal strife will develop to undermine our enemy's government. But these things rarely occur, and negotiations with the devil usually end in an uglier war. The US military, I included, was not in favor of appeasing Iran. We later rectified the missteps, but it was costly.

"The havoc in Europe will be attended to properly. America and her allies will not allow Fascism to disrupt the world order. Tyrants and despots will not flourish and project power on this planet. We have the might to stop and extinguish the wrong and the immoral, one way or another. Along with Communism and Islamism, Fascism will be tossed into the garbage heap of history."

Claudia Coffigny entered the room. Still bare-footed, Claudia looked spectacular in thin white exercise shorts and a flowered blouse. Her long, straight, blonde hair fell to the middle of her back. Her face had fine features with high cheekbones and deep blue eyes. She sat on the couch across from Julius in a crossed leg fashion, exposing her thick muscular thighs and calves. Her shorts were barely noticeable. Even the curves of her feet were the most sensuous Stansfield had ever seen.

"Papa, please bring me a brandy. Let me enjoy the company of the captain with you. He seems nice and polite. He's handsome too."

"French or Spanish, Claudia?"

"It doesn't matter. They're both romantic. Either one is fine with me.

"On second thought, because the captain has Cuban blood, bring me the warm Spanish brandy. I prefer the one with the woody taste, Papa."

"Only a little, Claudia. I don't want you dancing with the captain before you've gotten to know him."

"Yesss, Papa..... No dancing until I get to know him," laughed the Swiss bombshell.

"Don't be unnerved, Stansfield. My daughter has a unique tendency to destabilize a room in conversation. Topics being discussed are forgotten, ideas are misplaced, appetites are lost. It's a supernatural mystery stranger than the Bermuda Triangle.

"So just keep your bearings straight and don't get lost into oblivion," warned the mayor.

"How did I look out there, Captain Stansfield?" asked Claudia with a sly smile.

"Phenomenal," smiled back Julius.

"Good! I always like to look phenomenal," said Claudia in French-tinged English.

Julius could not take his eyes off of Claudia's puckered, pouty, pink lips. Her physical energy was completely suffocating. As a man, it kept you at the edge of your seat. The urge to pounce was immense.

Her attractive forces were so sharp they made a man feel uneasy trying to restrain his sexuality. Her restless energy was infectious to any man in the same room. Your only wish was to mix with her and satisfy her insatiable desire for sexual pleasure. Her body was in constant arousal, and it tantalized your carnality.

Frederic Coffigny returned with Claudia's brandy. He looked at his daughter and said wisely, "Behave yourself."

"May I call you Julius, Captain?" asked Claudia.

"Certainly."

"Julius is a strong name. I instantly conjure up an image of a powerful warrior in battle. Are you like Caesar in Gaul?"

"I'm US Navy, Claudia. I'm a submarine commander, somehow misplaced on land."

"So you're the bravest of the brave, Julius. Fighting underwater is no easy task on the mind. Death underwater is immediate. You have no margin of error. Courage must flow in your veins."

"It's the job I was trained to perform in defense of my country. I don't consider it hero's work."

"But I do, Captain. And in our budding relationship, my respect for your character is of supreme importance to me. I like to know the man I'm with has bigger *cojones* than I have. That realization turns me on. It gives me energy. It makes it more of an experience. It's *caliente*, Julius," smiled Claudia.

Stansfield could understand how a man married to this woman would need to be constantly on guard to fight off all the male attractants around her. Her estrogens were powerful. Her magnetism was astounding. It would be a full-time job, requiring tremendous amounts of energy to keep up with her. Even more energy would be required to satisfy Claudia's sexual requirements.

But she was more than just a femme fatale. She had depth of character and passion. Her face was intelligent, and her mind was incisive. She was the 'total package'.

Julius Stansfield wanted Claudia Coffigny. He wanted her like a man wants water in the desert. His first intelligence mission was going to be a memorable one in all aspects.

Before dawn the next morning, Frederic motored a small boat with Claudia and Julius across Lake Constance to Lindau, Bavaria. They entered the medieval German port town's harbor, passed the tall lighthouse and Bavarian lion sculpture, and docked near the customs office.

"Wait in the boat. I'll be back in a moment with a good friend," said the mayor.

A few minutes later, an older German man came out with Coffigny. He seemed to be a close confidant of the mayor.

"Hello, Claudia," said the German. "Your father wants me to assure safe travel for you and your companion. I can help bypass all these new lengthy regulatory border checks. They can be a nuisance. Your father's friendship goes back a long time. It's the least I can do for the beautiful daughter of an old friend."

"He will personally stamp your papers and get you on the train to Munich," said Frederic Coffigny. "You can trust him, Julius. He's with us. Go with him now. Remember, sleep with one eye open," reminded Coffigny.

Within the hour, Julius and Claudia were having breakfast on the fast train to Munich. The capital of Bavaria was one hundred and fifty miles to the east on the Isar River, north of the Alps. Claudia requested champagne and chocolate covered strawberries with her meal.

She made eating breakfast an erotic experience. She softly licked the chocolate on the strawberries with only the tip of her tongue, before fully biting down on the fruit's flesh with her perfect white teeth and flirtatious smile.

"Do you snow-ski, Julius?"

"I enjoy it very much."

"Have you ever tried helicopter skiing in the Austrian Alps?" asked the Swiss beauty.

"No, I haven't. I don't fly in contraptions unless I'm commanded to do so."

"How about nude-skiing, Captain?" laughed Claudia.

"No..... I can't say that I have," smiled Julius.

"Every winter I go nude-skiing in St. Moritz. You go from the slopes to the hot tub without changing. It's beautiful and sexy, Julius!

"Your body gets numb from the cold. By the time you arrive at the hot tub, you can't feel a thing. As your body begins to warm, all the sensations go into over-drive. You begin to itch inside all the deepest places. It's an irresistible itch which requires immediate attention. I just lay back and let my companion scratch as hard as he can," laughed Claudia.

Later, while the train passed the town of Furstenfeldbruck - twenty miles west of Munich, Claudia left her seat to go to the ladies room in the rear car. Julius noticed a man seated nearby get up and follow Claudia to the back of the train. Uncomfortable, Julius also followed.

The man walked between the last two cars with Julius in silent pursuit. Fast and out of nowhere, Claudia pushed the man against the wall of the steel platform between the last two cars. She held a long stiletto knife to his neck.

"Don't interfere, Julius," Claudia said quietly. "Stay back, Captain. This is my problem to handle. This little man was after me. It's my business to find out why."

Claudia slashed the man's forehead. Blood began to pour over his eyes.

"Hush your tongue if you want to live. One sound from you and you'll have taken your last breath," whispered Claudia.

"Now, softly tell us why you're following me. Do you like my ass and want to fuck me, or is it something else?"

"I'm not speaking," he said. "In less than a minute, we'll be arriving in Munich. Passengers will begin to disembark. You'll look awkward, holding a knife to my neck," grinned the man.

"I suspect you're correct," smiled back, the girl dynamo.

Claudia stuck the six inch blade in his neck, cutting the jugular vein and carotid artery. Blood spurted in her face. She turned and kicked the German in the mid-chest off the train traveling 60 mph.

In little time, Claudia had single-handedly interrogated and eliminated an enemy agent without even perspiring. She stared coldly at Stansfield, frozen by the door of the train. After a short pause of eye contact, she continued into the restroom to wipe away blood splatter from her hands and face, and to remove her blood stained jacket. Stansfield remained silently standing outside the door to the last car.

The train began to slow. The Munich station was just ahead. Stansfield returned to his seat as other passengers stood and prepared to leave the train.

A moment later, Claudia passed the astonished Julius and took her seat across from him. She had removed her jacket. Her silk white shirt was spotless. She had it unbuttoned to her mid-chest. Her face was clean. Claudia fixed her hair as if nothing had happened. She pulled out her bright red lip-stick and carefully applied it. Her demeanor was composed.

"He had been observing us for the past half-hour," Claudia said angrily. "The old man at customs in Lindau is working for the other side. Those fuckers are onto my father. I'll alert Papa when we arrive in Munich."

Claudia brushed her hair back and clipped it into a bun. She smiled at Julius and winked her eye.

"I'm hungry. We'll have lunch at the hotel. I'll make you the best martini you've ever had in your life, Julius."

Stansfield did not know what to think. He still had not regained his own composure, and this woman was hungry for lunch and martinis. In a flash of action like he had never seen, she had nearly decapitated a man with a knife and thrown him off a train. But here she was in front of him, sitting pretty as ever. Unflustered and unburdened by conscience, this woman was a tiger in more ways than one. Julius felt awed by her cold technical reaction.

"So this is the CIA," he whispered to himself.

CHAPTER 13

Kill Them All

In the dark shadows of sin, lie the small fiery embers of goodness. Deep in the probity of the incorruptible, lie the twisted depraved shoots of vileness. The wisdom of fate's great adjudicator allows for the identification and separation of man's natures. In the end, light will shine always on the good - wherever it lies, while blackness devours the bad - wherever it hides.

Julius Stansfield sat at a table on the balcony of his Kaiser Hotel suite. The third story apartment overlooked Munich's old town central square, the Marienplatz, and its famous *Rathaus-Glockenspiel*. Stansfield watched the clock's chiming spectacle, performed every morning at 11 AM. Hundreds of people enjoyed the tradition from the thousand year-old plaza below.

He looked across at the towering red brick, late Gothic, Roman Catholic Cathedral of Munich, the *Frauenkirche*, a block west of his hotel. Stansfield wondered at the beauty of the ancient Bavarian city, and thought of the history that had played out on its many streets and plazas. Much triumph and turmoil had been lived here.

Claudia came out in a short yellow summer dress and joined him at the table. Under the natural light, her almond shaped eyes were a brilliant sapphire blue. They were full of life and shined like her aura. Her lips were pink and full with perfect curves. Her powdery white skin was flawless like a Valais valley after fresh snowfall. Her golden hair matched the yellow of the sun and her dress.

Observing this goddess, it was impossible to see her contradictions. Claudia's darkness and lightness were blended into one another like the twilight of dawn. Night and day were mixed beyond discernment. She was obscure and inscrutable, like the enigma of the origins of the universe or the composition of the human soul. One didn't know whether she was real or a mirage.

Julius was intrigued by Claudia. He was mystified by her. His interest was both physical and mental. He wanted to taste her body but also delve into her mind. The secrets of her being awaited revelation.

"Here's the martini I promised you, Captain. It even has a speared olive.

"The suite has a full bar. We're stocked for the weekend.

"I mix the perfect cocktail, Julius. It has the right balance of taste and zing, I think. Consider it an energy drink if you don't normally have these things!"

"Don't you think it's a little too early for alcohol, Claudia?"

"Is there some decree that states specific times for enjoyment?

"Are there set times for drinking and fucking, Julius?

"Noooo.....

"There's no law in the spy manual saying you can't mix pleasure with work. In this business, Julius, you may be dead tomorrow. You better have fun today before it's too late.

"To your question, Captain, it's never too early for one of my dry vodka martinis," said the coquettish Claudia.

"Be happy! That's why you Americans call them 'spirits'. Drink it and get spirited, Julius. There's no reason to start the party on the wrong foot."

Claudia softly passed the olive along her lips. She tongued it off the spear and bit down.

"Nice and salty just as I like it," she smiled.

Under the table, Claudia rubbed Julius' left leg with the soft curve of her bare right foot. She buried and curled her toes into his flesh. The sexy Swiss winked an eye at Julius. She quickly downed her martini and leaned across the table, bringing her lips up against his.

"Wow," she whispered into his mouth.

"Taste how good it is, Captain....."

Claudia gently pressed her tongue against his. After a long kiss, she withdrew from him and sat back down.

"What do you think, Julius? Is it as good as you thought? Or should I have shaken it more?"

"You make a fine martini, Claudia," he slowly answered.

"Now I see why you consider it an energy drink. It has a good kick to it. Perhaps you have perfected the ratio of vodka to vermouth, or maybe it's the lemon twist. Regardless, it's just about perfect, I'd say," smiled Julius.

"If you like it, why not drink the one I made you, Captain? Loosen up a little. You look like you could be a bad boy with a bit of help.

"I like bad boys. Make me happy, Julius."

Claudia returned to the bar for more. Stansfield shook his head. The mayor's daughter was quite a package indeed. She had all the tools to make one forget the real reasons why you were even there.

On a submarine, it was all work. Battle under the sea did not have the fringe benefits of spy work on land. Your executive officer on an American man-of-war did not look like Claudia Coffigny. There were no French accents and champagne, no chocolate-covered strawberries for breakfast or martinis for brunch. In the past, pleasantry and fun had never been part of the mission.

This girl was changing the whole game plan for Julius. He shook his head again and tried to restrain himself. He left his martini untouched.

Claudia returned with two more. She appeared ready for action.

"What are you waiting for, Big Boy? Do you want me to bottle feed you, or you'd rather have me drink all three of these?

"There are no good boys around me, Julius. I give you permission to be 'bad'. Don't hold back. Show me your manhood," urged the irrepressible Claudia.

She set the drinks down on the table and walked over to Julius. She swung her left leg over his lap and straddled him on the chair. She pressed the toes of both her bare feet against the concrete floor. Their eyes came face to face. They kissed on the open balcony under a warm spring Bavarian sun.

Claudia took one of Julius' hands and placed it on the wetness between her thighs. She put his other hand on her backside.

"Explore me, Captain. Feel for all the warm moist spots. I'm certain you can find at least two. That's why I never wear underwear. It's for moments like these, Julius. Now pleasure me in return for the martini I made you. If you're good, we'll drink the others in bed. That's an order, Captain....."

Claudia had won. She was too irresistible to keep away. The urge to plunge into her was too great. She naturally brought the beast out of the man.

With Claudia wrapped around him, Julius carried her inside. They spent the afternoon sharing each other. Several hours passed.

"Are you married, Captain?" asked Claudia, laying on her naked belly. She pressed her hard body against Julius.

"Not that it would hold me back if you were, Julius. I like you and I'd probably like her as well. There's no harm done. She's free to join in if she wishes."

"You could say I'm married," responded Julius.

"What does that mean, Captain?"

"It means on paper, I'm still married. Her name is Sandra. We've been on the rocks for a year. Ever since I returned from the war, things between us have been bad. I did my best to work it out, but I guess my best wasn't good enough. We both were carrying on a charade.

"The night before I left America for this mission, Sandra asked me for a divorce. It seems she fell in love with someone else. He's an Army colonel. They met at a Pentagon function last year while I was away busting my ass against the Chinese. I suppose I was gone too long. She got lonely and made up for it."

"What do you feel about that?"

"What do I feel, Claudia?

"Shit, at first, I was at a loss for words. I didn't know what to say. I felt betrayed and disillusioned. I felt bad for our two young daughters. Sandra made me question many of my feelings.

"A day later, my mind had cleared. I realized we had lost the spark in our marriage a long time ago. Somehow, passionate love had just dissolved away. Our relationship had become cold and uncaring. We both needed to move on. My disillusionment began to dissipate."

"Do you still love her, Captain?"

"I don't know what that word means anymore. I need time to think about it. I need to reconcile my emotions. Much has happened to me over the past two years. I'll let time tell me if I still love her."

"Did your wife ever fuck you, like I fucked you?"

Julius laughed out loud. Claudia did as well.

"I don't believe anyone is capable of that! You're an Olympic gymnast, Claudia. You spin, and grind, and rock yourself to pleasure. A multi-orgasmic force of nature is really the only way to describe you. The guy is only along for the ride. I mean, what you do, Claudia, is extra-terrestrial!

"I'd rather stay away from comparisons, if you don't mind? Let me soak this in for a while.

"But, yes! You do very well. Let's just say you are incomparable. We'll just leave it at that!"

Julius playfully slapped Claudia's ass. She wrestled herself over him. The pleasure continued.

In the evening, Julius and Claudia walked to the *Hofbrauhaus* beer hall - three blocks from the Kaiser Hotel. Instructions had ordered them to be at the hall by 7 PM.

The buildings around the Marienplatz were covered with red and dark gray FNNP banners and Nazi Eagle flags. The reversed swastika was everywhere. Recently placed posters of Leopold Fuchs, the Munich born German foreign minister and apparent political leader of the FNNP, were on all the storefront windows. The minister's involvement in the FNNP was now publicly exposed. It was no longer a mystery. Things were heating up in Bavaria.

The streets were full of Nest troopers in their dark gray uniforms with red caps. Heavily armed security units would occasionally stop people at random to inspect their identification papers. The atmosphere was edgy and surreal. To an American with any sense of history, the scene was alarming.

The *Hofbrauhaus*, located at Platzl 9, had been established in 1598. It was heavily damaged by Allied aerial bombing during World War Two. Everything but the ground floor was rebuilt in 1958. The beer hall was a national historic site. Here, on the evening of February 24, 1920, Adolf Hitler outlined the Nazi Party program to the German people. He gave many more memorable speeches from the locale before taking the chancellorship of Germany in 1933.

Julius felt like he had been passed through a time machine to an earlier era. The general ugliness was fear provoking.

Julius and Claudia walked past a giant freshly cast bronze bust of Adolf Hitler at the entrance to the beer hall. They made their way to an open table near the back.

Bavarian patriotic music played loudly while Nest troopers sang and drank beer from heavy mugs.

To Stansfield, the whole panorama resembled an old Joseph Goebbels propaganda movie set for a film on Nazi Germany and the robust German people. The young and strong Bavarians enjoyed and honored their potential power. They celebrated their past as if it was their future. However, Hitler and Goebbels had been dead for more than seventy years.

A few minutes after arriving, an older gentleman with silvery hair approached Julius and Claudia. He was wearing a fine dark green tweed shooting jacket. The man made eye contact with Stansfield and sat across from him at the table.

"*Guten Abend,*" said the old man, smiling at Claudia.

"*Ist es in ordnung wenn ich rauche?*" he asked in German, waiting for permission to light up his Calabrian briar wood pipe.

Claudia nodded and answered, "*Ja.*"

Stansfield ordered beer for all of them. The noise in the hall made it difficult for Stansfield to understand the old man's German. Changing to Spanish, Julius said, "*La musica es demasiado ruidosa!*"

The German grinned. "Don Antonio Sevilla, you need not worry. We can speak in English. Many Americans and Englanders have moved recently to Munich. Many Spaniards have also come. They all want to participate in Germany's 'Rebirth'. No one here will suspect anything. You and your attractive 'Aryan' girlfriend are well accepted, believe me.

"Smile and enjoy your beer as we talk. Act naturally and occasionally laugh out loud to mix in with the local ruckus.

"*Fraulein*, grab your man and appear joyous like those around you. Women here make their men feel like the center of their world.

"Don't concern yourselves. This is the last place on earth they would expect to find you. So relax and blend in."

The gentleman smoked his pipe and raised his beer mug into the air. He sang along with all the others in the hall.

After two marches, the music died down. People went back to their conversations and their dinners.

"What a town!" laughed the old man. "What a people!"

He set his mug on the table and reached into his jacket. He pulled out his cell phone.

"Place your arm around the beautiful girl, Don Antonio."

The German took a photograph. He passed his phone to Stansfield.

"You are attractive people," he said.

"Both of you are very photogenic! It is good to be young and in love! It is very exciting to live out one's dreams. It shows in the photograph."

Julius wasn't catching on to the old German's machinations. He waited for the punch line.

"Listen to me carefully," he urged while Claudia and Julius looked at themselves in the photo image.

"Continue to celebrate the picture. Act it out. Smile and kiss each other."

The gentleman asked a waitress to bring them more beer. He then leaned forward and kindly caressed Claudia's face with his right hand. She did not move away.

"You are a beautiful girl..... You remind me of my mother when she was young. You have a striking resemblance to her."

He pulled a worn black and white photograph from his wallet, and passed it to Claudia. It was of a young couple in love. The girl had an angelic face with bright eyes. The young man was handsome in his wartime German Army uniform. They held each other closely in the photo.

"Those are my parents in 1941. They were in love in the midst of a horrible war."

"They were both beautiful," said Claudia, slowly handing back the picture.

"Yes they were. All people are beautiful when young and in love," said the old man quietly.

The singing waitress returned with three large steins of beer. The music and revelry became loud again.

The German leaned forward towards Stansfield and said, "The FNNP is onto you. They know you're in Munich, so you must take my instructions and proceed rapidly with your mission.

"Don Antonio, look at the next image on the phone and then pass it to your woman.

"Tomorrow morning at 10 AM, you will meet with Dr. Gustaf Herrmann of the Max Planck Institute of Psychiatry in the *Haus der Deutschen Kunst* Art Gallery's Main Hall. That is him in the photo. Memorize his image.

"Now hand me back the phone."

The old man erased the images and placed the phone back into his pocket. The hall broke out into more march songs.

Speaking louder, he continued. "You will walk out with Herrmann into the *Englischer Garten* and receive the information he has for you. I believe the data is critical to understanding your main target on this mission.

"The following day, five more action team members will arrive at your hotel room between noon and 2 PM. They will instruct you further on the details of your operation.

"By the way, Claudia's parents were evacuated from Aborn after the CIA intercepted a hit team in Lindau. Her father and mother were marked by the FNNP for assassination. They are safe and sound now. Do not worry, we take good care of our own.

"Our man at the Kaiser Hotel has changed your names on the hotel registry to a Mr. and Mrs. Otto Stickler from Dusseldorf. I suspect you have a clear 48 hours to finish your business in Munich. This is a big city of one and a half million people. Get lost in it.....

"The whole matter is quite mysterious to me. Few of my people are like these bastards. There are many more kind and decent Germans in this country than there are bad.

"I was born in Berlin in 1942. My father was a medical officer in the Wehrmacht. He was not a Nazi. He was a good, hard-working physician who was drafted into the German Army. He had the great misfortune of being sent to Stalingrad. My father died in that frozen hell. He never had the opportunity to see his son grow old. My mother and I survived the deprivations of World War Two without him.

"I have also lived on the wrong side of the 'Iron Curtain'. The Russians took whatever little we had left after the war. They took away our home, our food, and the remainder of our spirit.

"On several occasions in the early occupation, my darling mother was abused by Russian soldiers. They would strip me from her arms and have their way with her.

I only faintly remember the horrors. I have been told of her suffering.

"She pushed herself to survive for me. We had no one else except each other.

"It was a terrible time to be a German. There was great hardship for everyone.

"For all the good Germans in my homeland, I do not want to see a repeat of history. I want freedom and justice for my country, not enslavement.

"I will work to my last breath so that all German children have a father to guide them in this world. I can do no less in honor of the memory of my loving parents.

"Remember my words, Don Antonio. Most Germans, like most Americans, are good."

The gentleman stood and said, "*Auf Wiedersehen und viel gluck.*" He smiled at Claudia after wishing them luck. He took a last drink of his beer, placed the pipe in his mouth, and walked out of the beer hall.

Moments later, Julius and Claudia sped out a side exit and inconspicuously returned to their hotel apartment. From now, they would be on the run.

The next morning, Stansfield and Coffigny arrived at the *Haus der Deutschen Kunst* and waited in the colonnaded neo-classical "Third Reich" style building's crowded atrium for their contact. They had jogged the six blocks in running clothes.

Soon, a tall well-dressed man appeared from the throng of museum visitors in front of Stansfield and extended his hand.

"Hello, I am Dr. Gustaf Herrmann of the Max Planck Institute of Psychiatry. You must be Mr. and Mrs. Otto Stickler. You were not difficult to find. They instructed me to look for the most beautiful woman in the building," said the smiling Herrmann in German.

Stansfield's German was adequate to communicate in simple terms but insufficient to discuss complicated matters. Herrmann noted this.

"Let us walk out to the *Englischer Garten*," stated Herrmann in broken English. The doctor led the couple out of the museum and into Munich's largest public park.

"I am a clinical psychiatrist at the Planck Institute. My expertise is in bipolar affective disorders. In layman's terms, we can call them manic-depressive illnesses.

"I am the German foreign minister's brother-in-law. Leopold Fuchs and I married twin sisters on the same day at the *Frauenkirche*, here in Munich eighteen years ago. I was Leopold's friend since adolescence. I have also known his brothers, Manfred and Andreas, for many years. Manfred is a Bundestag member and Andreas is a virologist.

"The aristocratic Fuchs family of Munich has been highly respected in Bavaria for over 400 years. In World War Two, Leopold's grandfather was awarded Germany's highest decoration for bravery in battle, the Knight's Cross with Golden Oak Leaves, Swords, and Diamonds."

Stansfield instantly realized the peculiarity of the German doctor. The uncomfortable Julius walked with Claudia and Dr. Herrmann near the man-made waterfalls of the English Garden. A nearby green grassy knoll sloped down to the River Isar. In the late morning, this area was full of nude sunbathers.

The men sat on an isolated bench in the shade by the waterfalls. Claudia walked towards the river and stripped off all her clothes. She lay on the grass at the brightly sun-lit water's edge. Her majestic body stopped all conversations on the grassy knoll. The sudden silence was interrupted only by the sounds of falling water and the occasional songbird.

"Fifteen years ago, I noted a change in Leopold Fuchs' personality," said Herrmann. "He began having periods of manic activity with obsessive-compulsive tendencies. He became progressively more intolerant and aggressive. His behavior was characterized by delusional fantasies of power and omnipotence. He began to overestimate himself. Bouts of hyper-sexuality outside his marriage created problems with his wife.

"After his secretive involvement in the Fuhrer's Nest Nationalist Party, he began exhibiting even stronger megaloegomania. His racist and anti-Semitic tendencies became more pronounced. Fuchs became obsessed with developing a 'Fourth Reich'.

"A few years ago, German cultural attitudes became more extreme. Leopold, Manfred, and several other clandestine party members were elected to the Bundestag.

"Last year, Leopold Fuchs was named Germany's foreign minister. He has progressively drawn our country closer to Russia.

"Leopold has been disconnected from me for the past four years. However, I know factually that his intentions are for our country to return to its nationalist past. He desires to force the United States out of Europe.

"The nature of Fuchs' mental condition will lead to more paranoia with time. He will become more desperate in his intentions and more wicked, in his actions.

"Germany's recent alliance with the equally ultra-nationalist Russia is for purposes of creating a radical and belligerent unified bloc against American involvement in European affairs. Fuchs is getting the German people's support for his policies. Even my wife has begun to side with this man. Germany, as a nation, wants America out of her backyard," stated Dr. Herrmann while he glanced over at the naked Claudia.

She was lying on her belly, getting sun on her backside. No man alive could refrain from fixating on her posterior mounds and crevices.

Julius Stansfield did not like his first impressions of the German doctor. He felt uneasy in his company. He found his manner arrogant and unabashed. He was also angered by the doctor peering over at Claudia.

Herrmann looked again at Stansfield and continued his discussion. "Please understand me, Stickler; I don't disagree with all of Hitler's ideology. I happen to concur with many of the policies instituted in Germany after 1933. However, I believe this neo-Nazi movement in Germany today is very dangerous for our country. I do not want Germany to return to her old ways. Eight million Germans died in World War Two. I do not want a repeat of history. Leopold Fuchs' megalomania, and his leadership roles in the FNNP and Germany's national government, can only lead us to ruin.

"Had Hitler been stopped after his 'Putsch' attempt in 1923, perhaps we would have been spared the misery of the subsequent global war. Leopold Fuchs and his clan must be denied the opportunity to create havoc in the world," stated Herrmann as he stood up from the bench.

At that moment, a short distance away, Claudia stood up on the grassy knoll and pressed her golden hair into a bun with a clip. Her tremendous bare figure stunned everyone in her presence.

Herrmann shook Stansfield's hand to bid farewell and again stared in the direction of the River Isar where Claudia stretched her body in exercise. All of her God-given physical attributes were exposed to the sun.

Herrmann laughed and said to Stansfield, "That woman is a credit to her race."

Stansfield agreed with the doctor's opinion of the statuesque Claudia, but he viscerally rejected Herrmann's poorly camouflaged underlying tone of German cultural and racial superiority. Julius strongly disliked this strange man.

In the early afternoon of June 17, Stansfield and Coffigny met with the five other members of the action team assigned to the mission. The CIA Special Operations squad was led by Peter Tucker, an ex-Delta Force operative with over twenty years of experience in attacking high value targets.

The window shades of the Kaiser Hotel apartment were drawn closed. The agents sat at the dining table with open maps of the Bavarian town of Bamberg and its surrounding countryside. Bamberg stood where the Main River met the Europa Canal, connecting with the Danube River to the south at Kelheim, Germany.

The *Katarina* would arrive at Bamberg on the morning of June 20, after sailing north up the Danube from Passau, Germany, to Kelheim and into the Europa Canal on June 19. The "lost shipment" of AZEV would be loaded onto the *Katarina* in Bamberg. From there, it would be taken into the Main and Rhine rivers on its way to Rotterdam and the North Sea.

After personally overseeing the loading of the AZEV, Leopold and Manfred Fuchs were scheduled to meet with several high level members of the FNNP and the GPNR in a castle villa outside of Bamberg. The double-crossing and sinister director of the Polish intelligence service would be there also.

Peter Tucker read aloud their orders from Langley and the Department of Naval Intelligence at the Pentagon: *"Your team will isolate the enemy agents inside the villa's grounds. You will proceed to terminate each and every member. If Leopold Fuchs can be captured alive and questioned, do so, before eliminating him. Kill them all."*

CHAPTER 14

Freedom Tower

In life, there is only one secret for happiness. All other truths are simple accompaniment. You need neither ear nor eye to hear or see it. It can't be felt with your tactile senses. It has no fragrance or taste. It is only with the sixth sense that the power of the secret can be perceived. No material wealth can purchase it. If fortunate to be gifted with it, the secret opens the entire universe for you. Once inside of you, its intuitive energy force burns naturally and eternally. It allows your heart, mind, and soul to reach their highest plane. You can only wish to be annointed with Love, and hope that you are worthy.

In the entrance vestibule of the Sierra-Stansfield home on Key Biscayne, Nasrin arranged a bouquet of red globe amaranth flowers in a white porcelain vase. A tall oak wooden pedestal elevated the flowers to eye level. On the wall next to the flowers hung a large framed photograph of her with Michael and their baby, Alexander, taken on Memorial Day almost three weeks earlier.

It had been eighteen days since Michael left. She did not know where he was or his condition. Nasrin understood the dangers of his duties but she could not stand the thought of losing the love of her life. She had cried herself to sleep every night, hoping that Michael would return to her unharmed. No amount of time could settle her worries for him. It was not an emotion Nasrin could adapt to.

She finished adjusting the beautiful deep red bouquet which symbolized her everlasting love for her husband. She leaned over and gently kissed his photograph.

Nasrin sat in the study near the large window facing the Atlantic Ocean. The setting late afternoon sun gave the cloudless blue sky an orange tinge. White seabirds perched themselves along the edge of the orchid house, pairing up in many love sets of two.

She searched through Admiral Julian Stansfield's large collection of operatic arias and chose Maria Callas' performance of "Un Bel di Vedremo" from Puccini's *Madame Butterfly*. Nasrin sat alone on the couch, listening to Maria Callas sing of the hopeful return of her love from a faraway place.

With the passion of Maria Callas filling the room, Manuela brought Nasrin a cup of tea. The old woman could sense Nasrin's loneliness.

"I thought you would enjoy something warm to drink, Nasrin. It will help settle your spirit."

"Thank you, Manuela. You are very kind."

Manuela set the cup down on the table. She looked into Nasrin's green eyes. She understood the fear in them.

"You mustn't worry, young angel. Many prayers have been said for Michael. He will be safe, I am certain. Don't stir your insides with doubt, it will sicken you. You must be healthy when he returns."

Nasrin reached out and held her hand. The old woman smiled.

"Young hearts in love need to be together. Separation is not the natural process, Nasrin. You speak with Michael when he returns and express this truth. Don't allow the chaos of the world to take him from you again. He has done enough for his country. All of the Stansfields have. Force Michael to manifest his gentler natures. His soft soul should decide the future. Repress his war spirits. Your love must show him the way."

"Please don't go, Manuela. Sit and stay with me awhile. Have some tea."

Manuela had come from Cuba with her husband, Tomas, in 1978. They had immediately gone to work at the house for Raul Sierra. After Raul's death in 1983, Olivia asked them to stay and help her maintain the Sierra estate while the Stansfields were away in Washington. Through the years, they became part of the Stansfield family. Their dedication to the children during the summers spent on Key Biscayne was warm and loving.

Now in her mid-sixties, Manuela was debilitated by Multiple Sclerosis. The degenerative neurological disease had slowed her ability to walk. It had also affected her swallowing and speech. Manuela would often choke when eating, and her dysarthria would worsen when fatigued.

The brainstem lesions gave her slurred and nasal sounding speech, often creating long pauses within sentences.

Nevertheless, Manuela and Tomas refused to retire and leave the Stansfield children. She continued to provide all the domestic chores in the large house and kept it spotless. She had deeply loved Olivia and Julian, and cared for Julius, Michael, Mark, and Rebecca as much as for her own son, Gabriel, who now was a medical doctor in Orlando, Florida.

"Drink your tea slowly, Manuela. There is no rush. Take a rest with me."

"Rest, Senora? I will rest when you do, Nasrin. We will both rest when Michael comes home.

"Besides, today I am stronger than usual. My voice is clearer. I must take advantage of this energy before it leaves me."

"How was Michael as a child, Manuela?"

Sitting in a chair across from the leather couch, Manuela leaned back and closed her eyes. A joyous look came on her face.

"He was an intelligent, precocious child. He was full of mischief. He was not easy to discipline. His energy and warm, loving personality made him very endearing, Senora.

"He loved his pacifier. His mother and I could not get him to give it up. Even at three or four years of age, Michael would roam the halls of the house with a pacifier in his mouth. He had many of them hidden away, scattered in secret locations. We'd stop him and ask for it. He'd give it to us without crying. But he'd pout. A few minutes later, he'd be on the couch watching television with another pacifier twirling in his mouth. We found many of his secret hiding places, but Olivia could never throw any of them away. She would laugh and I would laugh, but neither of us had the heart to throw away his pacifiers. One day, he walked out to the garden and simply threw them all out. His mother picked them up and put them in a box. Let me show you."

Manuela slowly made her way to the kitchen. She returned with a large plastic container full of baby pacifiers. The two women laughed their hearts out.

"So these are Michael's pacifiers, the keys to his heart," quietly said Nasrin, smiling broadly.

"What a boy!" shouted Manuela blissfully. "What a boy," she whispered, shaking her head.

"Yeah. What a boy," also whispered Nasrin.

Nasrin closed the box and set it on the table in front of her. Manuela sat down and rested. Both women remained silent for a few minutes, thinking deeply of their boy.

"The family would spend much of the summer here," said Manuela. "As Michael grew, he became a very handsome young man. He has his mother's dark eyes through which his joy and happiness would always shine. You could not help but love that boy. Life has not changed him, Senora. He is still that same enchanting boy. I love him very much," sighed Manuela.

"I understand and appreciate that," gently smiled Nasrin.

"How did you and Tomas come to America?" asked Nasrin.

"It seems like a long time ago, Senora Stansfield. Memories sometimes change with time, particularly so when they are painful. We wish to forget the pain but it seems to never leave us.

"There was severe repression in Cuba in 1978. Everyday life was very hard. There was little food and much discontent.

"Two years earlier, the Cuban government had launched a large scale military intervention in support of leftist guerillas in Angola against South African occupying forces. The Cubans did not want to fight in Africa for people they could not identify with. They felt the Africans should fight their own war of liberation.

"While Cuban casualties mounted, dissidents in Cuba began to publicly express their displeasure with Castro's adventure. My husband's older brother, Arturo, was one of those dissidents. In December of 1977, Arturo was arrested and rapidly tried for sedition against the government. The next day, he was executed by firing squad in the same place where Mr. Raul Sierra's son, Jorge, had been killed in 1961.

"Soon we heard that the government would come for Tomas as well. Although not involved with his brother's activities, Tomas would be seen in the same places with him in our small town of Remedios in the north of Las Villas province. I suspect Castro's secret police decided that Tomas was equally dangerous to the system and marked him for elimination.

"In the late evening of December 31, 1977, Tomas told me he was listed to be picked up the next morning by the secret police. A friend of his in the local government had informed him of the details.

"Crying, he told me he was going to attempt an escape by boat out of the country that evening. Tomas had been told that the police would leave me and our one year-old baby alone, but he did not believe them. He feared for our safety. He wished to take me and Gabriel with him. He told me it would be a very dangerous escape. He said the odds of success were poor. Chances were greater that we would die. Tomas asked me what I wanted to do.

"I told him I would never leave his side. I would die with him in Cuba or try to escape to freedom. If we all died in our escape, better that our spirits die free than enslaved."

Manuela wiped tears from her eyes with a napkin. As she spoke, her voice had become weaker.

"That evening, after saying goodbye to our parents, Tomas and I with our baby drove my father's old Chevrolet thirty miles north to the Caribbean coast. There was a small marine patrol station there which was manned by only four men. Tomas had expected them to be drunk on New Year's Eve and hopefully away from their station.

"My husband armed himself with an old hunting knife but preferred not to kill anyone. He is a peaceful man who only wished to be free with his family.

"We arrived after 2 AM and parked our car less than a mile away in the bushes along the dark coastline. We walked through the mangrove forest the rest of the way. When we got close to the station, we saw only one man had been left guarding the large powerful Cuban Coast Guard motorboat. The other three men had gone to sleep inside their station house. The lone man in front of the boat drank rum out of the bottle. He seemed only half awake, leaning his head and back against a piling on the dock.

"My husband ordered me to stay in the mangroves with Gabriel. He took off his shoes and crept along the 200 foot long dock towards the lone guard. As he neared the sailor, Tomas broke an old wooden plank under his bare feet. The drunken guardsman saw Tomas and stumbled to stand. My husband rushed him and both of them fell into the water. My heart raced as I heard the thrashing of the water. I then heard a groan followed by silence. I prayed to God that Tomas would come out from the sea alive.

"Seconds later, Tomas rose on the dock and waved for me to come. He had silenced the guard by slitting his throat. Tomas helped me onto the boat and we raced off into the moonless dark night. The other guards, now awakened, shot their rifles at us aimlessly.

"We were young but very brave, Senora. We could not accept that our love would be extinguished because of one crazy dictator's misdirected mind. We would be free or we would die together.

"The commandeering of the boat by my husband secured our lives together for an eternity. My love for him exploded that evening, and it has been the source of our happiness ever since," declared Manuela.

Nasrin could personally identify with this story. She had lived similar experiences with Michael. She survived that same suffocating fear before the bliss.

While Nasrin and Manuela spoke, thousands of miles away, Michael Stansfield and his team sailed up the Danube River into Lower Bavaria. In the darkness of early morning on June 19, they were near the ancient German town of Passau where the Danube was joined by the Liz River from the north and the Inn from the south.

Renown during the Renaissance period for its manufacturing of swords and bladed weapons with their famous "Passau Wolf" trademark, the town had been the home of a young Adolf Hitler in the late 1800s. The local Bavarian government was now managed by the radical FNNP. Nest troopers had taken control of all police work. It had become a very dangerous place for non-Germans.

The crew of the *Conqueror* was prepared to defend the ship at all costs but hoped to stay unrecognized.

Michael Stansfield sat alone in the kitchen galley having a late dinner. Hickory Calhoun entered and pulled a soft drink out of the refrigerator. After the attack in Belgrade, the two men had developed greater suspicions of each other. It gnawed at their friendship. Calhoun was consciously staying away from Basha Ludwik because of pressure from Stansfield.

The assaults at Balaclava and Belgrade had made Stansfield paranoid. Perhaps Calhoun had inadvertently told a double-crossing Ludwik about their secret plans. Stansfield felt unsure of Ludwik's allegiances, and he had told Calhoun about his misgivings. He was beginning to have distrust of Hickory as well.

Similarly, Hickory had expressed to Stansfield his insecurity with Veronika Boroshkova. She was an unexpected addition to their team. She had been with Stansfield in Balaclava. Maybe she was the double-crossing contact responsible for the attacks on them at Balaclava and Belgrade.

At present, the two men were not very happy with each other. They were confused about the secrecy of the mission. They both thought the operation had been compromised. Both of them sensed a lack of specific detail necessary for a successful outcome. Information was being kept from them.

"Let's call a truce, Michael," said the limping Calhoun as he sat at the galley table across from Stansfield.

Michael looked up at Hickory and said in a low voice, "Hick, our lives are at stake here. I wasn't fucking Boroshkova. I'm certain I didn't expose myself or the mission. You, on the other hand, were fucking Ludwik. Someone you don't know for more than a few days, in the beginning stages of a secret mission to save our country from a devastating attack that would plunge it into another catastrophic war. I mean, Hick, that's crazy. What came over you? That's not the man I know. You've never had a weakness for pussy-chasing. How can you develop a weakness now? Our lives are at stake, Hick. I can't accept that."

Calhoun extended his hand across the table. "Shake my hand, Michael. I swear to you I haven't touched that woman. She may want it from me, but I've been clean. I won't say I haven't been tempted, she's a fine looking girl. But I've stuck to the rules.

"Besides, I love my wife. Vitoria is my girl. I have no interest in fucking Basha or anyone else. My only interests are completing my mission, having my team survive, and getting back home to Carolina and Vitoria.

"Do you think I'm stupid, Michael. You know me better than that. I took a sacred oath to protect my country. I wouldn't compromise the safety or success of the mission for sex.

"I don't believe that you would either. I'd rather just leave it at that for now, Michael."

Stansfield didn't know what to think. He was used to acting alone on his missions. He had been dropped into enemy territory with other agents, at times, but usually he'd separate from them in 'lone wolf' operations. *Operation Europa* was only the third squad project he'd been on. There were always more problems with squads. He preferred to be alone. Michael didn't like having doubts about members on his team, particularly friends.

"We'll watch each other's backs and keep an eye on both of the women, Michael. I promise to keep my distance from Basha. The other option is to leave them off here in Bavaria. Hand them over to our contacts in Kelheim and let them deal with it. What do you want, Michael?"

"Let's observe them for now," said Stansfield. "Our options are limited. If need be, we'll lock them up below and go over them for information. Let Langley continue to study the situation and direct our actions. They have not ordered us to terminate their presence. Langley knows the big picture, we don't. My intuitions tell me they're safe. This is likely a misunderstanding of the facts by us. Both of these women are likely on our side. We may need their help on this mission. It's likely going to get very rough around here and we may need the extra shooters."

One of the Navy SEALs, Peter Reynolds, stuck his head into the kitchen. "Mikey, Hick, we've got company up top. A Bavarian FNNP river patrol boat is behind us with its blue lights on."

As the CIA ship passed the *Veste Oberhaus* medieval fortress, situated high atop a mountain crest between the Danube and the Liz Rivers, the patrol boat turned on its siren and requested the *Conqueror* to stop.

Stansfield ordered Reynolds and Garfield to man the light machine guns, and hide from the patrol boat's search light. The moonless night was very dark and provided good cover for the men.

Stansfield told French agent Bruno Bonnet and Polish intelligence officer Jakub Krol to place silencers on their pistols. Calhoun and Stansfield did the same. Boroshkova and Ludwik stayed below.

At this time of night, the Danube was relatively quiet with little river traffic. This area of the river was blanketed in blackness and provided good cover for action, if need be.

The FNNP patrol boat came along side and threw a rope onto the *Conqueror*. Both ships came to a stop.

Back in South Florida, Manuela and Nasrin poured themselves another cup of hot tea.

"Please continue your story, Manuela," pleaded Nasrin.

"The coast guard boat we had taken was magnificent. It had three strong motors and plenty of fuel. We were able to speed into American waters within a short time.

"The US Coast Guard stopped us just northeast of Key West. We were quickly transported to an immigration center in Homestead, where we stayed for three days. We were very well treated.

"In the morning of the fourth day, we were transported to the *Freedom Tower* in downtown Miami. We sat alone in a large assembly hall for three hours. Just before noon, several men in dark suits entered the room. They were all Cuban and made us feel relaxed as they sat at a table across from us. Raul Sierra entered the hall minutes later with two tall Americans.

"Don Raul wore a dark blue three-piece suit. He looked very elegant and distinguished as he shook my husband's hand and introduced himself. 'I am Raul Sierra. I was governor of Las Villas at the time of the revolution. I fought at the Bay of Pigs. Unfortunately, I was captured and detained by Castro's men two days after our landing and our unsuccessful attempt to free our homeland. My son was also captured at the invasion beaches. I regret to say that he was executed, and I was left to survive and keep the fight for freedom alive. I wish it would have been him to continue the fight, but that was our fate.'

"Don Raul sat down next to us. 'I understand that your husband commandeered a patrol boat along the north coast of Las Villas and safely brought his family to America.'

"Raul Sierra looked directly at me. His expressive deep blue eyes became watery as he grabbed my hand. I could feel his rapid pulse in his fingers while he squeezed my hand tightly.

"He continued to speak to us. 'I also understand that he killed a militia man in the process of his fight for freedom. The Cuban government has asked the United States to turn your husband over to them as soon as possible for the crime of murder. I will not allow that. All of you will stay in America for as long as you wish. You and your baby are free. You will not return to Castro's inferno. You have earned the right to live without his oppression. I don't care if it costs me millions of dollars, I promise all of you that your liberty is secure. These men with me will make all of the arrangements for you to stay in America. This building that you are in, our *Freedom Tower*, is our symbol to the world that the Cuban people will not go quietly into the night. We will continue to fight for freedom as long as we have breath. Our struggle will continue until we have a resolution to the aberrant, cruel, and despotic government present today in our homeland. I will never retire from my duty to rid my country of the madman, Fidel Castro.'

"Raul Sierra stood and shook my husband's hand. He began to walk out of the room. Mid-stride, he stopped and turned around to face us again. He looked at my husband and asked, 'What made you take this risk, Tomas?'

"My husband also stood from his chair and said, 'Freedom, Senor Sierra. Freedom. Without it, we were suffocating. We wanted to be free. That is all.'

"Raul Sierra nodded his head and smiled. He told us, 'That is all I need to hear. All my services are at your disposal, Tomas. Take care of your family as you have. You are welcome in my home at any time. If you need work, I can provide it. Always remember this *Freedom Tower*, Tomas. You have helped to build it.'

"Mr. Sierra was a gentleman. He kept his word. My husband and I owe our lives to him. We loved him. We also loved Olivia and Julian Stansfield. We will always love their children. I suppose that Tomas and I will die here. This has become our home, our 'Freedom House'," softly cried Manuela.

"Raul Sierra died only a few years later," said Nasrin. "What happened to him, Manuela?"

Manuela dried the tears from her face. She closed her eyes and took a deep breath.

Still with her eyes shut, she said, "Don Raul lived a very celebrated life. He had education, power, and money. He was respected by all. He had a calling for freedom, and he spent much of his life and fortune fighting for it. The Cubans loved him dearly, and the Americans loved him just as deeply. He lived by his code of honor. He would never trespass outside of his circle of virtues.

"He never gave up on his country of birth, Cuba, nor on his adopted homeland, America. He had a deep faith and love for both of them. He also worked tirelessly for both of them all his life.

"But his greatest love was his family. His wife and children, and later Olivia, all occupied a very special place in his heart and mind. They were the focus of his moral strength and inexhaustible energy. He truly lived for them."

Manuela opened her eyes and stared at Nasrin. "The loss of his son, Jorge, was devastating to Don Raul. He blamed himself for Jorge's death. He felt responsible for the failures of the Bay of Pigs. He felt he hadn't secured the promise of an effective air cover for the invasion. He thought, perhaps with a little more political pull, he could have securitized the success of the invasion. His lack of proper planning, he thought, had cost him his country, and more painfully, the life of his cherished son. He was never able to come to terms with these ideas in his mind. The pain of his perceived failures only grew with time. The pain in his spirit slowly destroyed him.

"After the illness of his wife and her death, his depression worsened. His health deteriorated further after being diagnosed with cancer. He stopped eating and sleeping. But his intelligent and thoughtful mind never declined. His ideas and emotions remained very crisp," sighed Manuela.

"Perhaps it is best that Don Raul explain himself to you directly," said Manuela.

The old woman slowly got up from the chair and walked over to the study's bookshelf. She brought back a white porcelain box and handed it to Nasrin. Nasrin carefully opened it and pulled out a hand-written letter from Raul to Olivia.

My dear Olivia:

I have so loved you. You have been precious to me all your life. I have always hoped for your happiness and well-being. I am grateful to God that you found love with Julian. He is a special man. Your father would have been happy for both of you.

I am sorry for not speaking of your father, my son, more frequently with you. I think it has deprived you of better knowing how great a man he was. This has been an injustice for you, I think. Unfortunately, I allowed my weakness for my son to damage your own creation of his image as a father. This is not right. It was never right. And I am sorry for it.

Your father was strong and brave. He believed deeply in love. He was true to it in all its forms, particularly his love for you. Ideals were important to him. He lived his life always trying to achieve peace and serenity for those he loved and for himself. He was never afraid of consequences if they were required to reach his lofty aspirations. He was a 'great man'. But before he was that, he was my boy.

As a child, your father was also special. He was raised on a farm in the country. In early life, he ran the fields and surrounding hills barefooted. He breathed in the cool clean air of our mountains. He swam in the clear blue waters of our rivers and ponds. He chased butterflies and frogs. He milked the cows and fed the chickens. He talked to the stars and moon. I know all this because I was always with him at his side.

When he was young, he frequently told me of his wishes for his children in the future. He hoped to give them everything he had as a child. He hoped for them all those natural freedoms, so essential to a good life. He wanted them to grow up on a farm just like he had. He wished for them to experience the wonders of nature in evolution. Your father was a uniquely fine boy. And he was a great son.

But above it all, he loved you. In your short life with him, he gave you his heart and soul. You were the most important thing in his existence. He died with your name on his lips.

He was the greatest father a girl could hope for. And he was the greatest son a father could hope for. What more can I say?

I must admit his loss has been catastrophic for me. His absence for you and I is painful in so many ways. Many people can get through these pains successfully. I have not.

My only wish now is for you to have a happy full life with Julian. Raise your family closely and give your children all the love you can. Protect their futures so they can continue to live their lives freely without oppression. Their lives are priceless, always deserving of our deepest sacrifices.

I love you, Olivia, as your father loved you. My last thoughts will be of you, and of him.

Manuela saw that Nasrin had finished reading the letter. She waited for her reaction.

"So what became of him?" asked Nasrin in a hushed voice.

"One summer morning, I awoke earlier than usual," said Manuela. "Dawn was just breaking. From the kitchen, I could see Don Raul in the study. I saw him place the porcelain box on the bookshelf.

"I watched him go out through the garden and walk into his orchid house. I found it unusual that he was wearing his bathing suit so early in the morning.

"After a few minutes, he closed the door of the orchid house and walked out to the beach. I watched him go into the surf and swim out to the south, in the direction of Cuba. I never saw him again. No one ever saw him again."

Manuela bowed her head silently and excused herself. She left Nasrin alone to her thoughts.

Nasrin played Maria Callas' singing of the "Ave Maria". She rested her head on a pillow, shut her eyes, and wept quietly.

Half a world away, Michael Stansfield and his men went into action. In a perfectly coordinated and arranged movement, Stansfield and Calhoun fired their pistols simultaneously at the two men boarding their vessel. Garfield fired a short burst from his machine gun, taking out the other two Nest troopers still on board the Bavarian patrol boat. All four of the enemy were instantly killed.

The dark night was again still as Stansfield released the rope ties from the *Conqueror* and set the German patrol boat adrift. Their mission would continue according to plan. America would not be vanquished.

CHAPTER 15

Dream With My Father

In our dreams, we seek to better understand the mysteries of our lives. All the questions we should have asked but didn't. All the things we hoped to do but didn't. All the words we wished to say but didn't. One never finds all the answers to all the questions we have in life, but in our dreams – we get close.

Michael Stansfield remained on his ship's top deck. The *Conqueror* continued up the Danube toward Kelheim and the Europa Canal, still a hundred miles away. They would arrive at Kelheim in the late morning and enter the first of the Europa Canal's sixteen locks on their way to Bamberg. Stansfield was scheduled to meet a CIA contact in Bamberg on June 20 to receive further orders.

The night air was cool as Stansfield stretched on the bow's deck, looking up at the infinite number of stars in the sky. Although faint, the haze of the Milky Way was visible. The streak of white seemed close enough to touch. The wisp of gas contained a countless number of bright pin-point lights, each a star energizing the universe.

What a mysterious expanse this all was, thought Michael. Human beings lived their daily lives under this wonder, but they didn't think about it much. Why contemplate something you couldn't fully comprehend? How could anyone really understand all this?

The only sound in the night was the low growl of the *Conqueror's* engines while the ship motored up the lonely Danube. Stansfield put on his earphones and listened to one of his sister's piano sonatas. He stared at the heavens and began to count.

Michael had counted stars to relieve stress and anxiety since his childhood. His father, Julian, taught him this ritual when he was a small boy. Any time he fought with his older brother, Julius, their father would send them out to the backyard to count stars. Both brothers would sit on the cold grass in different corners of the small backyard at their Virginia home and begin to count. Within a short time, they would begin to speak with each other again, dissipating their anger. By the time their father would step outside to call the boys in, the brothers would be sitting together as friends.

Only an hour before, Michael Stansfield had taken the life of a young man. In performing his duties for his country in the past, he had killed many men. But this time it felt different. It had always felt shocking and disturbing, but tonight he felt profoundly sorrowful.

Michael had looked into the eyes of the young handsome Nest trooper, standing only ten feet away as he fired his pistol. He had seen the fear in the boy's blue eyes. They had expressed knowledge of his fate. Like in slow motion, Stansfield saw his bullet strike the boy in the forehead and propel him backward into the Danube. The boy's body sunk into the black waters and disappeared from view.

The German boy had seemed very young. He had no facial hair. Stansfield had killed someone's boy. Somewhere in Germany, a father and a mother would grieve tonight. A girl would soon cry over losing her boyfriend or fiancé. He would likely be missed by many, thought Stansfield.

Michael thought of Nasrin and their baby, Alexander. He could not imagine his boy being gunned down at close range by a trained killer. The thought was too painful for him to consider.

The taking of a life still unlived seemed sinful to Stansfield. All the hopes and dreams vanished. The aspirations for true love gone. A young man never to have a son. An unfinished life with unfinished potential never to see a sunrise again.

It had happened so quickly and so simply. How could this be? He thought. How was taking a life so easy?

Being a father himself now had changed his view of the world and his place in it. Was all this cruelty necessary? How could there be so much evil in this world? Was he now becoming evil himself? He thought. Stansfield listened to Rebecca's music and continued to count stars. He tried to ease his mind. He attempted to replace the ugliness with beauty.

The Danube River was empty of traffic on this night. The darkness and silence seemed surreal to Stansfield, considering four men had died in a gunfight just moments before. What a crazy world this was, thought Michael.

Calhoun sat down next to Stansfield. He elbowed his friend in the side. Michael removed his earphones and stopped the music.

"The bad guys will likely find that Nest patrol boat in the next hour or two," said Hickory.

"They'll find three dead troopers on her deck and begin to search for their killers. They'll send more patrol boats up and down the Danube looking for us," added Calhoun.

Stansfield glanced at Hickory out of the corner of his eye and calmly said, "Relax. Do you realize how many countries have agents in this region of the world, Hick?

"America alone has over six hundred agents. Britain has another three hundred. France is working more than two hundred. Poland an additional two hundred, and that doesn't count all the double-crossing German, Russian, and Ukrainian agents in Central Europe. Everybody is trying to kill each other up and down the Danube. We're just one more target along this river. Besides, our agents along the Danube have been ordered to protect us at all costs. Additionally, many of the 'enemy agents' have been turned and are now on the CIA payroll. They've been instructed to confuse their colleagues and defend our movements up the Danube.

"I think the loyal FNNP militia has their hands full, Hick. They're not any more likely to find us after this incident than they were before it. Remember that they still have to remain cautious and keep their terror plans secret from the German people. They won't publicize this incident any more than any other one they consider counter-productive. If the citizens of this country realized what these bastards are up to, they would hang them from trees. I suspect the people don't want another major war in Europe."

Deep down inside, Stansfield knew the risks. These risks would increase exponentially throughout the remainder of their cruise. He was as uncomfortable about it as Calhoun, but he didn't wish to express it. Worry bred doubt, and doubt bred failure.

"I'm going to get some sleep, Hick. It'll be a long day tomorrow. You should do the same."

Michael felt that Hickory was unusually jumpy. He appeared more anxious than ever before. Maybe sleep would readjust his sensitivities.

Stansfield understood that the locks of the Europa Canal would be danger points for their ship. They could expect blow-back from the enemy. Michael needed rest and his mind sharp for what was coming their way over the next twenty-four hours. He was uneasy about the mission going deeper into Germany. Fear was beginning to encroach on his senses. He needed to accomplish his duties and get back to his family. Nasrin and Alexander deserved his safe return. Michael could not allow fear to cloud his judgement and jeopardize the success of the mission. America came first.

Stansfield slipped down to the bunk-room he shared with Bruno Bonnet. The Frenchman was sound asleep as Michael lay down on his side and closed his eyes.

He again thought of his father and how much he loved and missed him. The admiral had deeply loved his children, and they had all returned that love to him. Both of his parents had taught him about the moral righteousness of honor and courage, love and hope, freedom and justice. These virtues were the foundation for

"American Amaranth". These qualities of the mind had been expressed to the Stansfield children as soon as they were old enough to understand. The creed had become their way of life. Michael thanked his parents for this gift and faded away into sleep.

"I fell into a dream. It was a dark dream - the kind one usually doesn't wish for. There was no sound. There was no color. Everything was in black and white. I sensed water all around me. It was stunningly cold. So cold I couldn't move. I felt alone and lost in a state of suspended animation between only dense darkness below me, and bright light above me. I felt I was dying. I tried to swim out of the pitch black, but my body would not follow commands. I tried to breathe, but my lungs were still. I began to slowly sink into the darkness. The light above faded as it became more distant. My life was ebbing away.....
Suddenly, a tight embrace began moving me slowly toward the light. A blue sky and bright yellow sun awaited me when I reached the surface. Color had returned. I took a deep breath of warm life-giving air. Our sailboat sat floating in front of me on a beautiful breezy sea. My father, young and strong, tanned from the sun with his hair blond and both his eyes green, extended his hand and pulled me onto the boat. 'Thank you, Father,' I said. He told me he had been waiting for me. He placed a warm blanket around me and gently added, 'Don't fear.' My father turned the sails toward the Cape's lighthouse. He smiled and tenderly said, 'Welcome home, Michael. We didn't have much of a chance to speak before I left you last. I've missed you, Michael. I'm so very happy you're healthy and joyous in your life. You have found Nasrin. She's a wonderful woman and she loves you. I know this.

That makes all the difference. You also have a handsome son. You can't ask for anything more. Love comes rarely in this life. Nurture it, keep it close, and never let it slip away from you'..... The wind began to blow stronger as our boat sailed towards Key Biscayne. Whitecaps began to fill the sea in front of us. Sea-spray wet our faces. Dark clouds hid the sun. Behind the wheel, my father looked at me and with love shining through both his eyes said, 'Life is usually a long journey, Michael. At times, it may get difficult and even almost hopeless. Don't ever lose faith in yourself and those you love. They are truly the only ones that you can depend on. Hold on to their memories. Always keep them in your heart. Follow your instincts and intuitions. They won't betray you. Continue to chase your chosen duties for a greater good. It's not always easy, but you can do it. Don't fear and don't ever panic. Always remember our family creed: Honor, courage, love, hope, freedom, and justice. As your mother would say, these virtues stand the test of time. Live by them and you will have the strength to overcome'..... Sitting next to him, I said in low voice, 'I killed a boy, Father. He was a young boy. Somehow, I could sense his innocence. It happened so quickly, Father. I wish I could have the moment back. Perhaps he didn't need to die. Maybe I could have saved him. I don't want to take lives, Father.' My father looked at me with kindness. The softness of his eyes entered me and pacified my restless spirit. He didn't say a word. He didn't need to..... 'What does it feel like to die, Father?' I asked. My father's look again penetrated my soul. He put his arms around me. He stared for a long moment into my eyes and said, 'Not any different than being born. Only you don't decide how you come into this world, Michael, but you do decide how you leave it. When the time comes, leave this world strongly. Leave it better than when you found it. While you are still on this earth, make your soul tranquil with as much love as possible. Find the love inside your own heart. Love your life and live the joy'..... My father kissed my forehead, gazed even more deeply into my eyes, and whispered, 'Let's take American Amaranth back home where she belongs'..... I looked towards the Cape and understood the wonder and beauty of my father."

CHAPTER 16

Meeting in Bamberg

The secret garden of youth. Where the color and scent of flower are eternal. Where the leaf of tree and the blade of grass are ever green. Where the sun's ray is strong and always shines, and the sky is always blue. Where the ocean air is pure. Where the hope of spring and summer is everlasting. Where the songbird never sleeps. Where the butterfly is immortal and never flies away. Where Love is for all of time.

In the morning of June 19, the *Conqueror* passed through the sleepy Bavarian town of Kelheim. Above the town on a hilltop, at the confluence of the Danube River and the Europa Canal, stood the *Befreiungshalle* - a more than ten-story tall classical Christian style architectural monument on Mount Michelsberg. The Pantheon like structure provided a panoramic view of the surrounding countryside. It had been ordered constructed by King Ludwig I of Bavaria in 1842 to commemorate the German victories against Napoleon's armies in the Wars of Liberation (1813-1815). These wars, highlighted by the Battle of Leipzig in October 1813, were conducted on Napoleon as he retreated from Russia. They led to the destruction of the French Army east of the Rhine River.

Michael Stansfield sat in the pilothouse of his ship. He looked up at the *Befreiungshalle* with his binoculars and waited for the message. A rapid sequence of flashing dots and dashes of Morse code came from a carbon arc signal lamp atop the monument: **EUROPA CANAL CLEAR; PROTECTIVE PERIMETER SECURE; PROCEED WITH CAUTION**. Stansfield reviewed in his mind the plan of action for the next twenty-four hours.

The *Conqueror's* giant gas turbine engines pushed the heavy gleaming white cruiser towards the first lock in the Europa Canal. The floating arsenal, with its concealed weapons systems of torpedoes and 30 mm guns, was prepared for any action. The Javelin missile launchers and M60 machine guns could be retrieved by the crew in seconds from the ship's hidden storehouse beneath the galley.

The ship's papers with aliases showed that its "French Canadian" owner, Jim Calhoun, and his "wife" Basha were entertaining fellow "Frenchman", Thomas Egan, and his "wife" Veronika Boroshkova on a river cruise through Eastern and Central Europe. The ship's captain, Michael Stansfield, and the remaining crew of Bonnet, Krol, Garfield, and Reynolds, all had aliases with different European nationalities.

The Europa Canal ran 106 miles from Kelheim northwest through the Bavarian countryside via Nuremberg to Bamberg. It rose two hundred feet through five locks in its southern part to Hipoltstein at 1332 feet above sea level. After crossing the European continental watershed divide, it dropped six hundred feet in elevation through eleven locks in its northern part to Bamberg. The Europa Canal connected the Danube River to the Rhine via the Main River. Finished in 1992, the canal helped create a continuous 2200 mile waterway from the Rhine Delta at Rotterdam on the North Sea to the Danube Delta in eastern Romania on the Black Sea. Each of its sixteen locks were 625 feet long, 40 feet wide, and 100 feet deep. While in these locks, the *Conqueror* would be a sitting duck for enemy attack.

Although the Bavarian government was controlled by the FNNP and its paramilitary Nest militia, the German federal government was not. The FNNP had significant influence in Berlin but had not yet developed control of the Bundestag. Both the German military and Federal Intelligence Service were each divided between FNNP and anti-FNNP factions. An undeclared war had developed within Germany for control of the country's direction. The chaotic political situation had grown into an espionage war inside Bavaria. Agents of the FNNP, the Russian GPNR, and the Ukrainian Fascist Party were united against a coalition composed of German federal agents and American, British, French and Polish intelligence. The *Conqueror's* trip through the Europa Canal was to be guarded by the coalition. Still, Stansfield and his crew were ready to defend themselves if necessary.

By late morning, the *Conqueror* arrived at the canal's third lock at Dietfurt. Stansfield slowly guided his ship into the enclosure while maintaining situational awareness of everything around him. It would take thirty minutes to rise 53 feet to the next level.

Basha and Veronika lay in their bathing suits on the bow's deck getting sun. Calhoun and Egan sat on deck chairs having early "Bloody Mary" cocktails.

Stansfield saw three Nest troopers in their gray uniforms come and stand on an overhang above the lock. The troopers were smoking cigarettes as they looked down on the slowly rising ship. They began pointing to its stern, apparently interested in the hump concealing the ship's 30 mm gun.

Boroshkova also saw the troopers. She made discreet eye contact with Stansfield, acknowledging his concern. She stood from her prone position on deck and applied sun tan lotion over her body. She wore a small black bathing suit which maximized her great form. Her thick long red hair was pulled back into a ponytail. Although 42 years old, the tall and athletically built Veronika was a tantalizing knockout of a woman, even for men half her age.

In front of the young men, she spread the lotion on her inner thighs and exposed backside. She then pulled off her bathing suit top and slowly massaged the white cream on her bare breasts. As she did this, she started a conversation in German with the Nest troopers above her.

"Are you boys enjoying the view?" she shouted.

"Please be more discreet in your interest!" she laughed, pinching both her nipples.

The young troopers quickly forgot about the ship as they each tried to control the conversation with the sexy, nearly nude Boroshkova. One of them shouted, "You women are amazing! You're both sinfully beautiful."

"Let us escort you the rest of the way!" screamed another trooper. "You girls are in need of younger men! Those old mules can't possibly satisfy your needs. We can! Let us show you!"

The equally attractive Basha, wearing sunglasses and not much else, sat open-legged on deck. She deliberately exposed her most intimate parts. She drank beer from a glass bottle and casually touched herself at the same time. Although refraining from the conversation, she did everything in her power to seduce the bug-eyed troopers. It was a masterful display of remote-sex espionage.

Stansfield watched the scene and enjoyed the beautifully choreographed production. He couldn't restrain himself from laughing at the troopers' youthful inexperience.

When the water in the lock reached its top, the front gate opened and the *Conqueror* was allowed to proceed on its way. Boroshkova blew kisses at the troopers as they stood above the passing ship. She turned toward Stansfield and winked her left eye, accepting his approval of the performance.

Michael Stansfield steered his ship through the Europa Canal's apex at Hilpoltstein. He then began descending to Nuremberg, another twenty miles north.

Nuremberg, Bavaria's second largest city, was established in 1050. It was the unofficial capital of the Holy Roman Empire in ancient times and the center of the German Renaissance in the 15th and 16th centuries.

Situated in northern Bavaria, 110 miles north of Munich, Nuremberg was also the site of Hitler's Nazi Party conventions and rallies until 1938. At the 1935 rally, Adolf Hitler ordered the infamous Nuremberg Laws which revoked German citizenship for all Jews. The city was severely damaged by Allied strategic bombing during World War Two, requiring the reconstruction of most of its medieval buildings. The Nuremberg Trials for Nazi war crimes were conducted here in 1945-1946.

The city of contradictions certainly had an infamous history. Nuremberg was again a center for radical nationalist ideology and sentiment. Stansfield would avoid stopping here at all costs.

Five miles northwest of Nuremberg, near the town of Furth, the *Conqueror* went off the main canal. It traveled down a small tributary into the Furth Forest. Stansfield docked his ship next to a large country villa thirty minutes later. Hidden deep in a wooded area, the heavily fortified estate was manned by dozens of American and coalition agents. The villa was a staging ground for coalition attacks against the FNNP in Bavaria.

The *Conqueror* took on a shipment of four "Serpent" shoulder launched multipurpose assault weapons to supplement the supply of Javelin missile launchers already on board. The "Serpents" fired 83 mm high explosive anti-armor rockets which could penetrate two feet of steel at a range of 1500 feet. The heavier infrared heat-seeking Javelins had a longer range of 7500 feet. Together, they would allow Stansfield to attack the *Katarina* at a variety of distances, opening up more assault options. After taking on her cargo, the *Conqueror* continued north to Bamberg, thirty-five miles away.

Bamberg sat at the junction of the Europa canal and the Main River, an eastern tributary of the Rhine. Established in 973 AD, the city of 70,000 people had become the

"New Nuremberg" for the FNNP movement in Germany. The authentic medieval town extended over seven hills, each crowned by a beautiful church. The city was not damaged in World War Two, and its classic Romanesque architecture seemed untouched by history. Here in 1926, Adolf Hitler convened his famous Bamberg Conference to foster unity in the young Nazi Party.

Bamberg was a Nest trooper haven. The old Warner Barracks nearby, where US troops had been stationed until recently, was now garrisoned by two brigades of Nest troopers. They provided protection for the FNNP in northern Bavaria. The ratio of paramilitary troopers to civilians in Bamberg was very high. The town's streets were covered with the gray uniformed, red-capped troopers.

Bamberg was also crawling with coalition agents, performing dangerous acts of sabotage and espionage. Michael Stansfield would dock his ship near the town's center and connect with a CIA contact for an important meeting.

The *Conqueror* reached Bamberg in the late morning of June 20. Traveling in separate taxis as ordered, Stansfield, Bonnet, and Garfield arrived at the *Neue Residenz* before noon. The palace on Cathedral Square had been the home of the Prince Bishops in the 17th and 18th centuries. It now housed the State Library and the National Art Gallery of Bamberg.

Michael Stansfield walked into the "Rose Garden" adjacent to the palace. It was a cool day with bright blue skies and sunshine. The dark green hills around Bamberg were dotted with red, purple, and yellow mountain wild flowers.

A classical music festival was being performed in the garden. While Johann Strauss II's "Tales from the Vienna

Woods Waltz" played, Stansfield sat at a bench overlooking the cityscape of Bamberg and the Jura Mountains. Bonnet and Garfield stood nearby, next to the rows of red, white, and pink roses in full bloom.

The garden held a small crowd of elegant people. The men wore suits and ties. The women were fashioned in long dresses, and carried colorful parasols to protect them from the sun. The guests paraded in pairs silently up and down the aisles, listening to the fine music. They sipped German white wine and French champagne.

Michael closed his eyes and thought of Nasrin. Strauss' violins were stirring. The sweet fragrance of rose permeated the air. He breathed in deeply the floral perfume. For a few seconds, he lost himself in a paradise of peace. He felt lucky to be alive and in love. Circumstances could be better, he thought, but for an instant he'd enjoy the sound and scent of beauty.

In his passing trance, Michael felt a nudge on his left shoulder. He opened his eyes and found Julius standing in front of him. Julius grinned and sat down next to his brother.

"What are you doing here, Big Brother?" asked Michael in disbelief.

Both men had controlled their initial emotions. They avoided an embrace to not attract attention of Nest troopers nearby.

Incredulous of his eyes, Michael asked again, "What are you doing here?"

"I'm here trying to save my little brother's ass," smiled Julius.

The two men remained quiet for a short moment. Michael regained his usual professional composure.

"This mission, Michael, is a combined CIA and Navy operation. I'm here with a separate team to perform some peripheral duties. I was instructed to meet you and pass on information regarding your orders. What better place to meet than this rose garden, blanketed in beautiful music. The CIA guys sure know how to coordinate their drop-offs," said Julius, shaking his head.

"You are to proceed into the Main River at a safe distance behind the *Katarina*. As we speak, they are loading the 'lost shipment' of AZEV into her cargo bay in Bamberg. They will be fully loaded. You will continue to follow her past Wiesbaden and into the Middle Rhine. South of Koblenz, you will proceed to attack and sink the *Katarina* at Lorely Rock, the narrowest and deepest point on the Rhine River. You will continue down the Rhine to Koblenz, where you and your team will be extracted.

"Are you comfortable with the mission so far, Michael? Is there anything I can do for you?"

"No, I'm not comfortable, Julius. There's something wrong, but I can't figure out exactly what. We're not being given all the information we need by Langley. I'm concerned about the secrecy of our operation. We may have been infiltrated. The team and I are unsettled by the unusual circumstances. Nerves are frayed. I hold some doubts about members in my squad. They may hold doubts about me. It's a little crazy now, but I'll get it worked out."

"Were you hit at Balaclava, Michael?"

Michael was shocked that Julius would know about the incident in the Crimea. The *Conqueror*'s mission details were classified TOP-SECRET. No one except a handful of people knew about Balaclava.

"Yeah, Julius. I almost lost my life at Balaclava. But how the fuck would you know about that?"

"Mitrano told me his best agent had survived an ambush at Balaclava. I reckoned it was you. I think the director wanted me to know it was you. I guess he figured by my knowing, I would take on the challenge of the mission he had for me. He wanted both of us in the operation.

"Director Mitrano intentionally leaked your presence in the Crimea. He allowed the French and Polish directors of intelligence to know the information. There are people in those offices working for the enemy. That's all I know, Michael.

"This is a complicated case. There are countless working parts to this mission. There are many countries involved, and many intelligence services. I suspect neither of us know shit about the deepest secrets Mitrano's holding in his vest pocket. We're just the tip of the spear, Brother. I think it's a good idea to have some doubts about the others on board your ship, Michael. It may save your life."

The two brothers again remained quiet for a moment. They both took in the smells, sounds, and sights of the garden.

"This place is sure pretty, Michael. It's the flowers that makes it so. I'd still rather be in Mom's garden back home in South Florida. These roses are nice, but the tropical flowers are nicer. There's just no place like home, I guess."

"I am with you on that, Brother. There isn't any place like home, Julius. Let's get through this mess so we can have a glass of Dad's sherry together by Mom's sunflowers and passion vines. I prefer the tropical flowers as well."

"Please be safe, Michael. Remember Dad's words, 'Follow your instincts and intuitions.' Those words have served you true all your life. Continue to believe in them," added Julius.

'Big Brother' gently touched Michael's right knee. He stood and walked away.

Michael watched his brother leave the garden. He finally lost him at a distance, behind the white roses. Strauss' waltz finished playing.

Michael got up from the bench, surrounded by thousands of fragrant flowers of every color. He leaned down into a thicket of pink roses and took in their sweet scent. He turned and secretly signaled his men to move. They all slowly walked out of the garden.

He had seen his brother amongst the flowers for less than five minutes. Michael had not expected it. It had felt good to connect with family. He had appreciated every second of the encounter.

But what were Julius' peripheral duties? Why would Mitrano team up brothers on a mission? Michael had never known the director to do this. It wasn't his way.

Was any of this related to Hick's edginess and anxiety? Hickory was a 'hard' man. Why was he suddenly getting 'soft'? Much about this mission felt askew to Michael.

By nature, Michael was wary of surprises. And this mission was turning out to be full of surprises. He felt there was plenty about *Operation Europa* he didn't know. Perhaps too much. Being an agent on a mission without all the facts was unnerving. The less he knew, the more danger.

Danger may have been interesting to Michael in the past. But now, it was more than an inconvenience. It was threatening. There was something about this operation that felt deeply wrong. The more days passed, the more he realized it.

CHAPTER 17

Death's Head

One does not negotiate with Evil. You do not sit at a table and listen to the lies and threats of the Devil, even if he wears a smile and soft eyes. You do not break bread with him. You do not offer a toast to peace with him. You do not shake hands with the Devil and pretend there is still bargaining room for a successful end. If you do, the only end will be your own.

A dry warm blast of air swept through the Franconian Forest, twenty-five miles northeast of Bamberg. Like teeth of a saw, the tops of fir and spruce along the woody hill slopes leaned in the direction of the currents. Leaves of beech trees, shed before their time, danced in the sky to the canorous sound of rushing wind.

A fast flowing river meandered through the forest like a snake. It dropped along a steep rocky hillside into a series of shallow clear blue pools, before finally cascading more than a hundred feet further down into a big valley.

The sounds of streaming and splashing water on stone mixed with the whistle of blowing air. Together, they composed a symphony of nature's music in the silence. It was a concert of creation at its best, all superbly conducted by the master force of the universe.

Islands of heath and bog sat interspersed among the thickets of tall evergreen trees. Elevated clearings with red, pink, yellow, and purple wildflowers, lit by the sun, accented the land in all directions. Small villages dotted the regions between the hills.

"This forest is wonderful!" shouted Claudia. Her voice was energized by the splendor around her.

"I'd like to come back one day and hike through it, end to end. Would you like to come with me, Julius?"

Claudia and Julius were lying on their backs, next to each other, in a field of yellow daisies. A light misty spray from the waterfall nearby settled on them. They looked at the blue sky and felt the warm sun on their faces.

"Didn't you hear me, Julius?"

"Yeah, I heard you.

"I was just thinking if I would want to come back with you," laughed Julius.

"You bastard! How could you not?" said Claudia in French-tinged English, before putting a yellow flower behind Julius' ear.

Julius turned and kissed her lips. He smiled close to her face and said, "I guess I couldn't pass that up. I mean, who would not want to run naked through these fields with the sexiest woman on the planet?"

"Forget the sexiest woman part, fucker!" Claudia exhorted. "Wouldn't you just want to be with me here, in such a beautiful place, alone?"

Julius stared up into the blue. A long silent pause ensued.

"Is it that hard to answer me?"

"No. It's not that hard, Claudia. It's just that the last few days have been like a whirlwind for me. That's all. It's a little confusing."

"What's confusing about it?"

"Well to start, I found out that my wife was fucking some other guy. Then, I get sent to Europe as a spy, when I don't know two shits about how to be one. There, I meet the sexiest woman on Earth and find out that she'll be my partner in more ways than one. I learn she's faster with a knife than a Japanese steak house cook, and fucks harder than a broodmare in heat. And even more amazing is she can exhibit her great gifts at the same time, only stopping in between for martinis and lunch.

"Yeah, I'm confused. Who wouldn't be? Freud and Jung would be scratching their heads.

"I've never seen someone kill with a knife. You did it so efficiently and so coldly. And on a moving train full of people, no less. A few hours later, after brunch and martinis, the same girl is wrapped around my body like a boa constrictor, giving me the best sex of my life.

"Since, I've learned she recites romantic English poetry and loves French impressionistic music like my mother did. She sculpts and paints as well.

"So yes! My head is spinning a bit. I'm lucky it's still attached to my body.

"Have you always been this way, Claudia?"

Claudia yanked the daisy from Julius' ear. She pounded the ground next to her with clenched fist.

"What do you mean?" she asked.

"Have you always been a tempest in a bottle?" asked Julius.

Claudia sat up among the flowers and closed her eyes. She pouted like a baby. Her succulent pink lips darkened.

"Is that what I am to you, a tempest in a bottle? That implies restrained energy. There's nothing about me that's restrained, Julius. Open your eyes. What you see is what you get, fucker! I am 'me' for as long as I can remember.

"Growing up, I was always a great athlete. I could out-run and out-swim any boy, and I was stronger than all of them.

"In school, I was the ideal student. I was exceptional in my classes and orderly in my dress and manner. The natural and physical sciences intrigued me. I was gifted in the creative arts, music and dance, literature, sculpting, and painting.

"I've always had a strong desire to live. I like to test things in order to appreciate their value. If there's something that I want, I go out and get it. I'm animated, that's all.

"I also have the ability to compartmentalize my emotions. I don't allow feelings to get in the way of doing my job. Perhaps I'm bipolar. Who cares? You should just enjoy me as I am and throw the rest of your hang-ups to the wind, Julius.

"I want you to give us a chance. I like you more every day, and I think you are sensing the same for me. This is a crazy world. It's okay to act a little crazy in it."

Claudia jumped on top of Julius. She brought her face close to his. They embraced and kissed, surrounded by the magic of the colorful Franconian Forest.

"If anybody is a tempest in a bottle, it's you, Julius. Maybe your submarine was your bottle. Possibly, you left your emotions back in a tin can. Your body may have gotten off your ship, but your spirit stayed. Don't do that to yourself or to me.

"You're the one who's restrained and holding back all the time. Be free! At the very least be free with me. I'm safe. I'll let you do with me as you wish.

"Ravage me! Turn me inside out. Use all of me for your pleasure. Smell my body, feel my body, taste my body. Fill me everywhere and never get out of me!

"Do it all. I like it all. Release all of yourself into me, mind, body, and soul.

"But always remember one thing, Julius. If you desire to love me, love me for who I am.

"Now fuck me like the warrior you are!"

An hour later, Julius Stansfield sat in a harness near the top of an eighty-foot-tall European Spruce tree. He looked out across a green meadow at Totenkopf Castle, three quarters of a mile away.

Distracted, the navy captain pulled his eyes from the binoculars and glanced interestingly at a mother Black Stork in her sturdy nest. The dark plumaged bird was only thirty feet away in an adjacent spruce. He watched the mother regurgitate her stomach contents and feed four hungry hatchlings. The wary stork would occasionally stare at Stansfield, protrude her long red beak, outstretch her five foot wingspan, and make a raspy call to warn off his unwanted presence.

Like the bird, Stansfield was also dressed in black. His black commando jumpsuit, wool cap, and dark camouflage face paint were all anti-thermal to help disguise him in the shades of the forest and the upcoming night's darkness. He and his team would be invisible to night vision detection systems while they made their final preparations to storm the Totenkopf and permanently eliminate the political leadership of the neo-fascist movement in Europe.

Julius Stansfield, Claudia Coffigny, Peter Tucker, and four more CIA operatives were supported by forty-three members of the Bundesnachrichtendienst (BND), the German Federal Intelligence Service. Earlier in the day, after seeing Michael at the Neue Residenz Rose Garden, Julius met with four commanders of the BND and finalized the plans of attack on the Totenkopf Castle.

Four squads of elite BND commandos would scale the forest-side castle wall after nightfall and enter the grounds of the Totenkopf. They would quietly kill posted FNNP guards and proceed towards the three annex buildings attached to the castle. They would wait there to storm the main palace building upon orders from Stansfield.

The CIA team would simultaneously climb to the top of the castle tower, eliminate two FNNP troopers, and establish sniper firing positions from the tower platform. A chimney outlet on the platform serviced a large fireplace in the banquet hall, four stories down on the tower's ground floor. A dinner reception would take place in the banquet hall that night, congregating the political attendees until late in the evening.

At exactly 9 PM, Stansfield would pass a long, transparent, large caliber, heat resistant tube down the chimney to its opening in the dining hall. Thirty minutes later, Stansfield would begin to release Kolokol-1 into the reception area.

An odorless derivative of the potent opioid narcotic, fentanyl, dissolved in halothane general anesthetic as an organic solvent, Kolokol-1 took effect within one to three seconds after inhalation. In small doses, it could render targets unconscious for up to six hours. The large volume of aerosol planned for the attack was certain to produce extreme hypo-ventilation, leading to the complete cessation of breathing and death of their targets within minutes.

Leopold Fuchs was to be quickly given Naloxone (Narcan), an opiate reversal drug. Ventilatory assistance would be provided until he regained consciousness.

Fuchs was marked for interrogation by Julius Stansfield. Information regarding the scope of the FNNP involvement in the German government, and the operations of the FNNP paramilitary in Europe and America, was of vital interest to the CIA. Names of collaborators in Eastern and Central European governments were needed to shut down the Fascists as quickly as possible. Contacts to Islamic terrorist organizations in North America were also of critical value to the United States.

Through his binoculars, Stansfield saw the castle's massive valley-side four-story tower with its large decorated death's head coat of arms sculpted into the stone. The early 17th century palace was built by Stefan Fuchs, the Prince-Bishop of Bamberg, and was passed down the family through the generations to the present day Fuchs brothers - Leopold, Manfred, and Andreas. Around the "skull and crossbones" motif were numerous ancient firing slits for artillery and riflemen. Stansfield identified cannon and bullet pockmarks on the tower's face from battle in the Thirty Years War, four centuries earlier. High walls extended from the tower in both directions along the valley and into the adjacent forest. Over 100 acres of land were contained within the moated castle's stone walls. In its early days, it was an impregnable fortress.

On this day, the Totenkopf Castle would host the political leaders of fascist nationalist movements in Russia, and Eastern and Central Europe. For one evening only, the entire think tank of European Fascism would be concentrated in one location. Stansfield's mission was to disrupt this meeting and terminate the attendees.

The Totenkopf Castle was a relic of the Holy Roman (German) Empire. The thousand year reign had begun on Christmas Day in 800 AD with the crowning of Charlemagne, King of the Franks, as emperor of the new realm by Pope Leo III in Rome. The empire had lasted until 1806, when Napoleon conquered and dismantled it into separate German confederations and the Habsburg family's Austria-Hungary territory.

After the Middle Ages (circa 1250), the Holy Roman Emperor's power gradually weakened. The empire decentralized and separated into hundreds of individual entities governed by local kings, dukes, counts, and bishops - collectively known as "princes". The Reformation and religious wars in the early 16th century divided the empire's Protestant north from its Catholic south. The Thirty Years War in the early 17th century (1618-1648) further devastated the dominion.

The Holy Roman Empire was a continuation of the ancient Roman Empire. It was centered on the Kingdom of Germany. It was comprised of the modern day states of Germany, Austria, the Czech Republic, Switzerland,

Liechtenstein, the Netherlands, Belgium, Luxembourg, eastern France, northern Italy, and western Poland.

Stefan Fuchs, the Prince-Bishop of Bamberg in the early 17th century, built Totenkopf Castle as a palace retreat for his family. The Fuchs family retained ownership of the estate for over 400 years. It became forever linked to the rise of the Nazis in the 1920s, when it was used as a para-military garrison center by the Fascists.

A communist uprising in Bavaria after World War One, led by Ernst Toller and Eugen Levine, overthrew the prov-ince's central government in Munich in April 1919. Thirty thousand troops of the German Freikorps, a right-wing volunteer army, entered Munich and defeated the Communists within a month. The Freikorps later formed the vanguard of the Nazi movement. Subsequently, Totenkopf Castle was used as a center of operations by Adolf Hitler and the young Nazi party in their ongoing struggle against the Communists in Bavaria.

On the morning of June 20, Leopold and Manfred Fuchs were present dockside in Bamberg to supervise the loading of the second shipment of AZEV onto the *Katarina*. After meeting with the ship's leaders, Batkin and Wagner, the two Fuchs brothers drove with their security detail to the Totenkopf. By late morning, they began receiving other political leaders of the Fuhrer's Nest Nationalist Party (FNNP), the Russian Galichina Party for National Revival (GPNR), and the Fascist Ukrainian Party (FUP).

The Totenkopf Castle, moated and walled, stood on a hill in the Franconian Forest. The entrance to the grounds was on its eastern edge, facing a valley below. The estate's western backside wall faced the green meadow from where Stansfield's team was preparing to launch their attack.

The fascist leaders entering the grounds from the east passed through a security checkpoint at the base of the eight hundred-foot hill before driving through the castle's iron entrance gates at the summit. More than two hundred Nest troopers patrolled the hundred acres of land within the compound's walls. They were all armed with automatic weapons and hand grenades.

As the leaders neared the castle, they passed several acres of clipped hedge yew gardens with a topiary. South of the topiary were twelve acres of fruit tree orchards. On the north side, there were terraced flower gardens highlighted by a three acre rose garden with sandstone sculptures of gods and hunting animals. The gardens were provided shade by hundreds of Black Pines, Lombardy Black Poplars, and various fir, spruce, and beech trees. A large waterworks fountain and water basin acted as a rotunda in the driveway of the main castle building. Three annex structures, including a 17th century stone chapel building, adjoined the castle. The chapel contained late-Gothic masterpieces and wooden statues of the twelve Apostles.

The ground floor of the castle palace was designed in a neo-classical style. Valuable furniture, tapestries, paintings, Venetian art, and priceless porcelain collections filled the entry rooms. The palace treasury room and vestment chamber contained European Baroque era life-sized portrait paintings of the Holy Roman Emperors. A grand staircase led up to the opulent reception rooms and the "Great Hall of Mirrors", where the leaders were scheduled to formally begin their meeting at 1 PM.

At the precisely scheduled time, Leopold Fuchs entered the "Great Hall of Mirrors" in the Totenkopf Castle and commenced the conference. He sat at a large, round, oak wooden table in front of two larger than life portraits. To the left of Fuchs was Frederick the Great, the famous Prussian king and prince-elector of the Holy Roman Empire in the 18th century. To Fuchs' right was Adolf Hitler.

Seated near Fuchs at the table were his brother, Manfred - the leader of the FNNP in the German Bundestag, Russian Foreign Minister Igor Brish - representing the GPNR, Clement Janko - representing the FUP, the Director of the Polish Intelligence Service Bernard Pawlak, the Director of the Turkish Intelligence Service Abdullah Tilki, and several other high ranking FNNP Bundestag members.

The 44 year old German foreign minister brought the meeting to order. He then stood and turned towards Hitler's portrait. He remained motionless, staring at it for a while.

Leopold Fuchs was a tall man of medium build. He had a full head of blond hair. His coarse facial features and small dark eyes gave him a demonic look in times of anger. He had a very charismatic oratory style and was a master negotiator. He was violently scornful of anyone who disagreed with his radical political beliefs. His aggressive voice intonations and use of his body when speaking reminded many of Adolf Hitler.

Over the past year, Leopold Fuchs had become the undisputed leader of the fascist movement in Europe. All policy decisions had to go through him before implementation. The Russian GPNR leaders, including the Russian prime minister, foreign minister, and several high ranking military officers had recently warmed up to his leadership.

The FNNP was rapidly becoming a force in the Bundestag, and there was talk of Leopold Fuchs becoming the next chancellor of Germany. The paramilitary division of the FNNP had agents manipulating government decisions in Poland, Hungary, the Czech Republic, Slovakia, Serbia, and the Ukraine. Leopold Fuchs had become an unpredictable force of nature.

With his back to the table, Fuchs continued to admire Hitler's large portrait. He then silently gave his "hero" a Nazi salute and turned towards the conference members.

"We have all gathered here today to discuss the current state of our programs in Europe and settle upon our immediate plans to eliminate the mongrel Americans from our countries. The recent 'Friendship Alliance' between my country and Russia will bring together German ingenuity and technology with Russian natural energy resources and abundant military manpower.

"Other countries in Eastern and Central Europe will be made to see things our way. They will be absorbed into a new fascist empire. Unwanted, impure, and intellectually inferior blood will eventually be removed from this part of the world.

"With German leadership, this new empire will outcompete the Americans everywhere. The people of Russia and Eastern Europe will gain in their standard of living. With time, France and Britain will be absorbed as well.

"Our Turkish friends will help us gain influence in the Muslim lands, which will never again deal with American oppression. Defeated, disorganized, and divided China can also be influenced by us to turn away forever from American control. This is our time, gentlemen; we can not lose this opportunity to lessen America's influence in the world.

"Our organization has a plan in place to create a major terror attack inside the United States. Using a newly devised bio-terror weapon, several American cities will be brought to their knees. Our agents are presently involved in transporting this biological material to the United States, where they will work with already established Islamic terror networks to disperse the material in coordinated fashion into several large urban centers. The high infectivity and mortality rates of this bio-terror weapon will lead to the death of millions of Americans.

"A complicated electronic paper trail back to a radical anti-American anarchist group based in France and western Germany has been fabricated by our cyber intelligence agents. This anarchist group will be blamed for the attack. America will believe that the intelligence services in France and Germany allowed this act to happen without giving them forewarning.

"Relations between the countries will deteriorate and dissolve. This will unite Germany and France, and push them into the 'Russian sphere of influence'. The nationalist FNNP will gain power in the German federal government, and I will become the next leader of my country. This will solidify the fascist movements throughout Europe into a radical anti-American bloc.

"The United States will find their position on our continent untenable without going to major war. This, they will not do. America will need to withdraw from their bases in Europe. Their influence throughout the world will suffer. We will finally accomplish what Hitler and Stalin never could."

Fuchs walked slowly around the table. He stopped and looked at Igor Brish, the Russian foreign minister.

"Is your prime minister still with me, Igor?"

Brish answered affirmatively.

"Is your military with me, Igor?"

Again, Brish answered, "Yes."

Fuchs stepped a few paces towards Clement Janko, the Fascist Ukrainian Party representative. The German megalomaniac placed his hands on Janko's shoulders.

"Is the Ukraine resisting America's recent overtures to form an alliance with them against Russia?"

Janko answered affirmatively.

"Can your people resist the temptation for America's love, Janko?" asked Fuchs incredulously.

"Yes, Sir, they can! We are with you, Fuchs!" declared Janko.

Fuchs patted his right hand on Bernard Pawlak's chest. He then pointed at Hitler's portrait.

"I want Poland as an ally, Bernard. I don't want to be forced to crush your nation as he did in 1939. I need you loyal to me.

"Do you still have the confidence of CIA Director Mitrano, Bernard?"

The Polish intelligence director nodded and said, "Mitrano has personally told me how valuable my allegiance is to the United States. Little does he know that my closest people and I are with you, Fuchs."

The German foreign minister proceeded around the table to Abdullah Tilki, the Turkish intelligence director.

"Is the Turkish military with us, Abdullah?" asked Fuchs. "Are they ready to move against the Caucasus and the

Israeli-Cypriot pipelines? Or will they continue to take their orders from the dogs in Jerusalem?

"It is time Turkey regains the glory of her past and cuts all ties to America. I need you at the table of great nations again. I will not discount you like Washington has."

Tilki looked Fuchs in the eyes and shouted, "We are with you as black is with night, Commander! We are prepared to cut off the Azerbaijani-Georgian and Zionist lines on your orders. But we need Israel permanently eliminated."

Fuchs screamed, "Israel will be dust shortly after America swallows her poison! Our Arab and Russian friends will see to that!"

Tilki added, "Although victorious in Iran, America's military is still involved in regional fighting with guerrilla groups. We are secretly providing weapons to these groups to slowly bleed the Americans dry. The US-installed Iranian government is heavily infiltrated by our agents. Turkey can not allow a permanent American presence in Iran, Iraq, and Syria."

"That will not happen, Tilki," stated Fuchs. "Our people are seeing to that. Arrangements have been made. America will soon be out of Europe and the Middle East. Rest comfortably with this thought, Tilki."

"The Turkish Army soldiers are your legions, Sir! We are with you, Commander!" shouted Tilki.

"Are your agents in full control of the Islamic networks still active inside America?" asked Fuchs.

Tilki nodded his head affirmatively.

Leopold Fuchs finally arrived by his last guest at the table. From behind, he patted the man's back and grinned like a hyena. Fuchs whispered loud enough to be heard, "Is your country ready to be delivered to our movement?"

The man answered, "We are ready."

Fuchs returned to his place at the table. Before sitting, he slammed his closed right hand on the oak.

"Then America is finished! They will soon drop out from their self-crowned role of 'Protector' of the world. They will be driven from Europe and the Middle East. The world will be rightfully ours, as it should have been decades ago."

The German foreign minister smiled slyly and sat down. "Now let's talk about logistical details. They are the keys to our success."

The conference at Totenkopf Castle continued until 7 PM, when the leaders broke from their meeting and began to retreat down the staircase to the Banquet Dining Hall on the ground floor of the castle tower. The large sumptuous hall was designed in a classic Renaissance style. A magnificent 17th century Italian fresco on its ceiling depicted the five known continents of the time, with Christ in the middle holding his arms outstretched. The hall's walls were covered with paintings showing scenes from Wagner's operas, *Tannhauser* and *Lohengrin*. Classical music played while the men drank champagne before dinner. Formally dressed waiters and servers catered to their every need. As night fell, the leaders took their seats at the long banquet table and began their several course meal.

At half past eight, Stansfield signaled his team on the ground. It was time to implement their plan. He used his encrypted phone to communicate with the BND teams in the forest, north of the castle. He ordered them to scale the wall at 8:45 PM.

Julius released his harness and quickly slid to the leaf-littered ground beneath his tree. Claudia waited for him at the bottom and handed him his M4 carbine.

He kissed her and said, "At least I have you protecting my ass."

She smiled back.

Within fifteen minutes, Stansfield's team had made their way to the moat near the base of the castle tower. Two CIA snipers with silenced rifles rapidly eliminated three guards walking along the wall. Seconds later, the two Nest troopers atop the tower's platform were also picked off.

Claudia fired a gas propelled hook and rope onto the tower platform. She tugged on the rope to ensure the hook had lodged safely and began to scale the wall to the top. She wore two large gas cylinders on her back.

Tucker and Stansfield followed as did the two snipers. The two remaining members of the team stayed at the base of the tower and watched for more Nest guards.

By 9 PM, Stansfield and his team were in position atop the tower platform. The BND had arrived at their positions near the annex buildings adjacent to the castle.

Claudia and Julius dropped their tubing down the chimney to the unused fireplace opening in the dining hall. At exactly 9:30 PM, Stansfield opened the valve on the tank containing the Kolokol-1 and began passing the heated, odorless aerosol into the banquet room.

With Johann Sebastian Bach's "Komm Susser Tod" ("Come Sweet Death") playing in the dining area, the incapacitating agent began to put the enemy to sleep. Men slumped in their chairs as they ate. Many fell to the ground in convulsions.

Leopold Fuchs, who had been sitting at the center of the table, fell out of his chair with his arms outstretched like the Christ figure on the ceiling above him. Bach's music continued to play.

Outside, the BND attacked the annex buildings with heavy machine guns and assault rifles. Stansfield's snipers picked off troopers running out of the castle to assist their comrades. The enemy had been taken completely by surprise.

Within 90 seconds, the castle became quiet. Stansfield's team ran down the tower stairs to the ground floor. They put on gas masks and entered the hall.

While Tucker and his men fired pistol shots into the heads of the asphyxiating enemy leaders, Stansfield and Coffigny searched for Leopold Fuchs. They found him at the center of the room.

Claudia stripped off the German's jacket and shirt, and injected Narcan into his left antecubital vein. Stansfield placed an ambu bag over Fuchs' nose and mouth, and provided positive pressure ventilation. Within minutes, Leopold Fuchs started to revive.

A short time later, Fuchs opened his eyes in a daze and asked his captors, "What happened?"

Julius Stansfield got close to his face and said in a low voice, "America has just kicked your ass."

CHAPTER 18

The Interrogation

After a geo-political and sociological calamity, always look back along the historical timeline for precedent events which may have contributed to the calamity. Horrible events in history just don't happen spontaneously without birth seeds. Be aware and understand timelines. They will hold the truths to the calamity event. Knowledge and wisdom are our best tools to prevent social catastrophes in the future. To paraphrase Sir Isaac Newton's 'Third Law of Motion' - for every reaction, there was a prior equal action to induce it. Every move a nation-state makes has consequences. The more risky the move, the more risky the consequences.

Julius Stansfield had stared down death many times as the captain of the Virginia class nuclear attack submarine,

USS Oregon, in America's military campaign against China in the South China Sea a year earlier. However dangerous, he and his ship had engaged the enemy only at long distances without ever seeing the whites of their eyes. He had likely killed many hundreds of men with his torpedoes and missiles, while watching the action on video screens in the *Oregon*'s control room. Killing from a distance was impersonal. At times, even almost imaginary.

Fire-engulfed sinking ships and dead sailors floating on the ocean surface had been seen only on live video. Stansfield's sub had not surfaced and recovered bodies or taken prisoners. He had left injured survivors of his attacks struggling on the heavy seas without hope of being recovered. He had left them to die with little regret, but always at a distance. The fast and furious pace of submarine warfare provided little time for reflection or redemption.

Captain Stansfield had not seen the blood and gore of close encounter battle before the raid on Totenkopf Castle. He had never stared into his enemy's eyes and seen their hatred.

The dining hall in the castle was full of dead and dying enemy agents. More than a dozen Nest trooper guards, with their sub-machine guns still harnessed over their shoulders, laid breathless from asphyxiation near the dark mahogany entry doors. More than thirty political leaders had fallen around the banquet table in a similar state. They all had single gunshot wounds to the head to ensure death.

Stansfield walked around the hall, photographing dead ministers and intelligence agents. The information was passed back to Langley for proper identification and confirmation. Occasionally, his boots would slide in blood and brain matter splashed on the marble floor.

After spraying a chemical absorber into the hall to eliminate the incapacitating gases more quickly, Stansfield's team safely removed their masks. The smell of blood iron was thick in the air.

"Inform me immediately, Tucker, when we get the IDs back from Langley. I want to know the names and positions of each of these men," said Stansfield.

Leopold Fuchs recovered after being injected with Narcan. He was moved to the castle's library where he sat strapped to a chair under CIA and BND guard. Tight bindings secured his hands and feet to the chair, physically immobilizing him for interrogation.

The castle library's floor and walls were paneled with German Brown Oak. The rich finely-textured wood gave the room a golden brown butternut color. A rare collection of German medieval weapons hung on the walls. Double-bladed axes, battle flails with spiked iron balls, war clubs and hammers, crossbows and swords gave the room a macabre feel. The ceiling was painted with symbols of Norse mythology. Golden shields of Valhalla, and the Valkyries carrying chosen dead German warriors to the Hall of Odin, sat above Fuchs while he waited for Stansfield to enter the room.

Shortly after 1 AM, Julius Stansfield stepped into the library with Claudia. Peter Tucker stood by a bronze sculpture of a Teutonic Knight in battle during the Christianization of Prussia in the 13th century. Stansfield glanced at the crusader figure, wearing a large black cross on the front of his surcoat and wielding a heavy sword. Two BND guards sat in the corner of the room, opposite the large windows facing the front courtyard of the castle.

Stansfield pulled a chair to sit in front of Fuchs. Through the windows, the captain saw BND agents packing dead Nest troopers into the back of a closed truck in the courtyard. Claudia and Tucker remained standing near the library's entry doors.

Stansfield opened the interrogation. "Mr. Fuchs, I represent the American government. I have been sent here to ask you some important questions regarding your organization and its attempts to destabilize the governments of Europe and the United States.

"We know of your plot to attack our country and inflict millions of casualties on our people with bio-terror weapons. We also know of the FNNP's plans to ally with fascist groups in Russia and the Ukraine and eventually establish an anti-American fascist bloc of nations in Central and Eastern Europe.

"I have been instructed to use any means necessary to extract further information from you regarding these matters and to uncover the level of penetration of your fascist organization into the federal governments of Europe."

Leopold Fuchs interrupted Stansfield with a yell. He jutted his head forward towards him. The German's small dark eyes, and uniquely primitive facial structure in a harsh grimace, made him appear more animal than human. Stansfield could almost envision small horns sprouting from the top of his head. He was an embodiment of the devil.

With red face, Fuchs stared at Stansfield and asked, "Is my brother, Manfred, dead?"

Stansfield stared back and shouted, "Yes! He and all the other sons of bitches are dead! Every single person on these grounds who was plotting to destroy the United States of America is dead. Except, of course, you. You have been spared for now, but that can quickly change on my order."

Fuchs retracted his head back to the chair's headrest and snarled.

Stansfield continued. "Are you the unrivaled leader of the neo-fascist movement in Europe, Fuchs?

"Did you have the ear of the Russian prime minister and foreign minister?

"Did you control a significant percentage of the German Bundestag and the Ukrainian federal government?

"Did you control the intelligence services of Poland and Turkey, and were directing them to undermine their central government's support for the United States?"

"Yes! These statements are true, America!" yelled Fuchs at Stansfield.

"I have accomplished these things, and many more skillful feats which will remain silent to you and your country. This movement is grander than myself alone. There are millions who think like me and want the same things. Even some in your own country, America," grinned the German.

"We want the United States and the Globalist bankers out of our affairs!" shouted Fuchs. "If we are prevented from striking at you today, we will eventually succeed tomorrow.

"America can not steal the riches of the world and pretend they were yours to take. The oil and minerals of the Earth are not stamped with 'Made for America'.

"Quite simply, the people of Europe want you out. The Muslims want you and the Zionists out.

"A new fascist revolution will change the way the world functions. It is inevitable. You can not police the world as if it was your personal backyard. It is too big. In the end, we will win."

"What are your ties to the Russian prime minister, Fuchs?" asked Stansfield sternly. "How much control does the GPNR have over the Russian government and military? How deeply integrated is the FNNP into the workings of the Bundestag and the German armed forces?"

Leopold Fuchs maliciously smiled and said, "I am no longer talking. You might as well kill me now. Free my hands or I will silence my tongue."

Stansfield nodded towards the BND guards. They released Fuchs' hand restraints.

The German minister held his right hand out in front of him and Stansfield. With his palm facing up, he repetitively closed and opened his hand several times.

"Have you ever seen a live beating human heart, American?"

No, nodded Stansfield without speaking.

"It's a miraculous muscle. It beats independently of one's thoughts," said the German, opening and closing his fist.

"You can not order it to stop. It is that powerful. It is a wonder organ, American.

"The heart sends vital oxygenated blood to all the organs. The brain is able to think, compute, and measure because of the heart's function. The eyes see and the ears listen because of it. The lungs, kidneys, liver, and intestines perform their critical functions. There can be no life without the heart. It is essential.

"America could have been the heart of the world. They won the world war last century. They defeated the Soviet communist pigs in the Cold War. They controlled the oil and energy reserves of the planet. They ran the world's finances from their big and corrupt banks. They were the sole superpower.

"Yet, the United States allowed itself to be over-run by the leftist socialist movement. Over the past fifty years, the Communists slowly took over the American media, the universities, and finally the government. The big corporations and banks were turned over to them. Laws were passed to enhance their effectiveness in the destruction of the old American democracy. The people's freedoms were slowly and silently stolen from them. The 'Progressives' - as you Americans call them - drove your economy into the ground, leading to a world-wide depression. The European Union fell apart. The Muslim lands were thrown into upheaval. Trade and resource wars ensued, culminating in another global war. At the end – not even America has remained intact. Nothing today is as before. The American people are no longer able to choose their destiny. Their fate has been chosen for them.

"America, herself, helped create the Neo-Fascist Revolution in Europe. The actions of your nation, American, and her communist turns helped produce me and my movement. I am simply a reaction to America's poor choice. The people of my country, and the rest of the world, lost faith and trust in the authority of the United States. You are as much to blame as I am for the fear you have of Fascism. It's too late, American. Your people will fall as all the others will," grinned Fuchs.

"Are you going to answer my questions, Fuchs?" asked Stansfield with unease.

"To hell with you, American. To hell with your rotten nation!"

Stansfield got up from his chair. As he walked out of the room, he made eye contact with Claudia.

Claudia Coffigny was handed a black medical bag by the BND. She went to a table next to Fuchs and began emptying the bag's contents. The German's hands were again tied.

Claudia checked Fuchs' pulse and drew 4 milliliters of lidocaine 4% into a syringe. She turned and stared at the German maniac while preparing her secret inducer. They exchanged smiles. Claudia seemed comfortable, Fuchs was not.

"The BND and I want you dead, Fuchs. America wants you alive," said Claudia. "I suspect that alive with one eye is just as acceptable to America."

The two BND guards restrained Fuchs' head while Claudia injected the lidocaine behind his right eye. Within seconds, the German's right upper eyelid drooped closed. He sat in the chair screaming and cursing.

Claudia lifted the paralyzed upper eyelid with her thumb and asked, "Can you see out of the eye, Fuchs?"

Fuchs shouted in anger, "You bastards have blinded me!"

Claudia laughed. "You're only blind in one eye, Mr. Minister. Now answer Captain Stansfield's questions or we will blind the other eye."

The interrogation had been conducted under new German intelligence ground rules. Medical torture was in the game plan. The lidocaine anesthetic had only temporarily halted the electrical transmissions down the right eye's optic nerve to the brain. The eye would resume normal function within a few hours, if Fuchs was allowed to remain alive that long. Fuchs yelled more profanity as Stansfield re-entered the room.

The captain sat back in his chair and asked, "Are you ready to cooperate, Fuchs, or do we blind the other eye?"

Fuchs nodded his head, yes.

"I don't want to hear any more of your political babble, Fuchs. I already know the sad state of the world. I don't need to be instructed on its sick history or machinations.

"Now tell me! Is the prime minister of Russia in agreement with the terror plans on America?" asked Stansfield.

Fuchs sweated profusely. He again nodded his head affirmatively.

"Is the Russian military behind their prime minister on these plans?"

Fuchs again nodded, yes.

The German foreign minister added, "The FNNP's plan is to establish a new Holy European Empire, a 'Fourth Reich'. We wish to exterminate America's Globalist ideology. It has been a thorn in our side too long. It is time for a fascist pan-Europeanism to rule the world.

"German technology and brains combined with Russian energy and manpower will be the central core of this empire. We will control the economic workings of empire from Berlin without US interference.

"The Ukraine, Austria, Serbia, Slovakia, and Hungary are with us. We have influence in Portugal, Spain, Italy, and Poland through their intelligence services. There are still some significant holdouts in these governments, but they will eventually fall to us.

"Turkey's military and intelligence services are with us as well. With their cooperation, we will take over your role in the Middle East.

"Your Zionist partner, Israel, will be extinguished. The Jewish Kingdom will be nuked by our Arab friends, while the Americans die in the millions. The Russians are coordinating this from Saudi Arabia. A nuclear retaliation from the 'Land of David' can not burn all of our allies. The Zionists do not have enough bombs to kill us all. We are willing to lose a few millions to David's spears, as long as he ceases to breathe and is eaten by the worms.

"We are also unworried of an American retaliation. We have a 'snake' in your bed, Captain. The viper will strike when the time is right.

"Within a short period of time, the European Empire will stretch from Portugal in the west to the Pacific coast of Russia, and southeast to the Arabian Sea. We will rule the world."

"Too much babble for my ears, Fuchs!

"What are your networks inside the United States?"

The minister remained silent. Stansfield ordered Claudia to prepare another retrobulbar ophthalmic injection.

"Give me the networks, Fuchs!" shouted Stansfield while Claudia drew the lidocaine into another syringe.

"Our networks inside America are controlled by our spymaster. He knows everything. You know nothing!" cried Fuchs.

"Are you tied to Muslim extremist networks inside the US?" asked Stansfield.

"Yes! Of course we are, you idiot! We are tied to everyone. The whole world is against America!" yelled Fuchs.

"Give me specifics!" shouted Stansfield.

"You want specifics, American, on things which you can not understand. Facts which you refuse to accept. The world is against you, and it's too late to change the world's conception. My voice is irrelevant to the realities that face the 'divided' United States. My tongue will remain silent. Your heart will soon be silent as well."

Julius Stansfield stood from his chair and again nodded at the BND. He waved off Claudia.

"One last question, Fuchs," said Stansfield. "How deep is your organization inside of Germany?"

Fuchs stared at Stansfield with his only open eye and stated, "We are millions. How deep are the brains of millions of united Germans? Very deep, American. Very, very deep.

"The FNNP can survive without me. We will be victorious in the end." Leopold Fuchs finished speaking.

A German BND agent placed a 9 mm pistol to Fuchs' left temple. He fired one round. The brains of the foreign minister splattered the window behind him. He slumped dead in his chair.

Stansfield had known about the BND's final plans for Fuchs. They wanted him dead and not imprisoned. They could not allow him to serve as a continuous nidus of infection for the German people. If Adolf Hitler had been killed after the Munich "Beer Hall" Putsch to overthrow the Bavarian government in November 1923, perhaps history would have been recorded differently with a better result for Germany. The BND was not going to allow an imprisoned Fuchs to write another *Mein Kampf* and further crystallize the neo-fascist revolution. Leopold Fuchs was a dead man since his capture.

Julius Stansfield walked down the Totenkopf Castle's long central corridor to the front entrance. He thought about how much he disliked this killing business.

How had he gone from being a high school kid playing baseball in Virginia to commanding one of the US Navy's stealthiest killers, the *USS Oregon*, in the war against China? How had he killed hundreds, if not thousands, of Chinese in the South China Sea and the Taiwan Strait?

Stansfield thought about the horror of just seeing a man's brains blown out at close range. A bit of brain splatter had landed above Julius' right brow. Claudia had gently wiped it off with her black silk head scarf.

Keeping America safe was not an easy clean business. There wasn't any chivalry involved in destroying an enemy intent on making your country extinct. As much as it disagreed with his emotional make-up, Julius Stansfield would continue to perform the required duties necessary to defend his beloved country from destruction. He would protect the virtues upon which America was founded. 'American Amaranth' would survive, even if he did not.

In the entrance courtyard of the castle, Julius and Claudia got into a German BND staff car and drove off to the next leg of their mission. They would follow by land the *Katarina's* move into the Main River. They had been ordered to coordinate attacks on possible ground attempts by the FNNP to assist the *Katarina* along her route to the Rhine.

The CIA speculated the FNNP may now try to unload and redirect their AZEV cargo by land to the German North Sea coast. Langley wanted to rout out all the major FNNP operatives remaining inside of Germany. They would allow the *Katarina* to survive as long as possible in order to draw out their colleagues.

The men on the *Katarina* would quickly hear of the demise of their political leadership at Totenkopf Castle. Like a wounded animal when cornered, they were expected to strike out violently at their enemies and request assistance from their comrades. America would have an opportunity to bag the entire organization.

Stansfield failed in getting significant information from Leopold Fuchs. Nearly all of what the German spoke was already known to the CIA and Mitrano. Julius felt ill over the fact. The failure had many possible consequences. And they were all bad for America.

As their car passed through the castle's iron gates, Claudia held Julius' hand tightly. Both of them realized *Operation Europa* had become greatly more dangerous.

Stansfield received a call from Peter Tucker on the encrypted phone. He was expecting it.

"Captain, we have IDs on the KIAs. Everyone we expected to be there, was there. Langley is satisfied with the result of the mission. But there was one thing I found unusual."

"What's that, Tucker?" asked Stansfield.

"There was one UD, and he was red-tagged," said Tucker, with his voice fading.

"What the fuck does that mean, Tucker?"

"There was an 'Undisclosable' in the group. By the CIA's red-tagging, it implies that the dude's identity is of the highest security clearance. Only the director and a close circle of aides have access to the dude's ID. Whoever he is, even dead, he's a threat to the United States. That's very scary shit, Stansfield."

"Yeah. That's very scary shit," whispered back, Stansfield.

CHAPTER 19

Thinking Minds

When making important choices for social welfare, or considering a plan of critical action for humanity, select what is logical and rationally correct. Develop and use sound reasoning, justice, and empathy to arrive at sensible conclusions. Form these skills in yourself by training your mind to be insightful.

Don't rely on your leaders to have this discerning ability. They rarely do. It is an uncommon gift. Wisdom requires two extraordinary qualities, an intelligently thinking mind and an intuitive, keen sense of compassion. It is uncommon to find both these qualities in a human being. They are seldom seen. Usually, if ever present in the first place, these qualities have been polluted by greed and corruption.

If a situation is illogical, it will likely not survive into the future. Voice out your carefully considered opinion. Use your thinking mind to persuade others of reality. If one chooses unwisely or decides to remain silent in the face of wrong, perhaps you won't survive into the future either.

The *Katarina* churned through the waters of the Main River on its way to Scweinfurt, only 12 miles away. As previously coordinated, the ship would pick up two smaller escort boats in Schweinfurt to help protect her on the remainder of the journey from southern Germany to Rotterdam. Having been informed of the raid on Totenkopf Castle, Batkin had made provisional changes in the plans for the rest of the trip.

The Main River forms in the Franconian Forest and the Jura Mountain range. It then runs a circuitous course of 300 miles from Bamberg to its confluence with the Rhine at Mainz-Kostheim. Along its route, marking the border between Protestant northern Germany and the southern ultra-conservative Catholic regions, are the cities of Schweinfurt, Wurzburg, Frankfurt, and Wiesbaden. Because of delays in the Main's 34 locks, the *Katarina* was not scheduled to arrive at the Rhine until the late evening of June 23.

Batkin ordered the *Katarina's* leaders to congregate in the mess hall shortly before 2 AM on June 21. A half-dressed and only mildly sober Batkin entered the hall and sat at his usual chair.

The Russian slammed the table with both fists. His face was red and purple.

"Gentlemen, nearly our entire political leadership has been wiped out! I was just informed by my military contacts at the Kremlin that a combined CIA and German intelligence special operations squad raided the Totenkopf Castle in the German forest northeast of Bamberg last night. The enemy murdered everyone at the political conference being conducted there. No one survived!"

Aleksei Batkin glanced at Andreas Fuchs and said, "Both of your brothers are dead. So are Russian Foreign Minister Igor Brish, Polish Intelligence Director Pawlak, and the Turkish Intelligence Director Tilki."

Batkin then looked at Ivan Petrenko and added, "Your friend and representative Clement Janko is among the dead.

"This now puts our clandestine Kremlin and Russian military in charge of the whole operation, both politically and militarily. Our secret partners in the Russian government are demanding total control from here forward.

"Our friends are also actively engaged in the process of taking command of all decision-making at the Kremlin. They are meeting some US-supported resistance in this process. There are still numerous high-ranking Russian officials, including our president, who are defiantly against us and refuse to allow our rise to power. We will eventually overcome this stubborn resistance. The end of the Americans is near.

"The German FNNP will follow our lead into the future. We don't feel that the FNNP's decapitated leadership without Leopold Fuchs is fit to make further final decisions regarding our mission.

"The incompetence of the FNNP militia guards at the castle allowed this disaster to happen. Your people, Wagner, could not do their job. They have betrayed us and the direction of our cause."

Captain Konrad Wagner, the FNNP militia leader on the *Katarina*, stood by the galley's coffee maker smoking a cigarette. He looked at Batkin and said, "Leopold Fuchs may be dead but the FNNP is not. I'm still here alive and don't intend to allow Russian control of this operation."

The tall, physically fit German poured himself a cup of coffee and sat at the other end of the table. Staring at Batkin, Wagner added, "Because Leopold was in control of the political aspects of the movement, I agreed to allow you and the GPNR to command this military mission. Now with Leopold dead, the political direction of the movement falls to me. I won't accept Cossack rule of the neo-fascist revolution in Europe. The movement began in my homeland and there it will stay. Until the FNNP chooses another official political leader, I will carry that mantle. I refuse to allow you to dictate to me the future course of the revolution."

Wagner drank his coffee, holding the cup with his left hand. He slowly unclasped the security straps on his double shoulder harnessed 9 mm pistols with his right hand.

Ukrainian secret CIA operative, Pavlo Mitnick, could not allow this opportunity to pass. He was under orders to create as much conflict as possible between FNNP and GPNR leaders. He leaned towards Petrenko and whispered into his ear. Petrenko nodded and stood up at the table.

Looking at Batkin and the strange and mysterious Feodor Dashkov, Petrenko asked, "Why should we believe the CIA was behind this raid, and not the Kremlin and the GPNR? Even at the cost of your foreign minister, your prime minister and military would stand to gain greatly with a decapitated FNNP. We all know that Leopold Fuchs was the charismatic leader of this movement. Without him in control, the Russians could dictate the movement from the Kremlin. They could conceivably manipulate the situation in their favor. Perhaps, we should all doubt these 'facts' as a ruse, contrived by your leaders to subjugate the German Fascists and press them into following your lead. This all sounds unusual to me. Totenkopf Castle was being guarded by the finest of the FNNP militia. It could easily have been an inside job by the GPNR. I motion that we discuss the situation and not leave this hall until we have arrived at a decision concerning the future leadership of this mission." Petrenko sat back down.

Batkin jumped from his chair. He pointed his finger around the table and with angry foam in his mouth screamed, "The disaster at Totenkopf Castle may have an effect on our political leadership, but it does not change command of this ship or mission! I am in control of the decisions on the *Katarina,* and I am ultimately responsible to get this cargo to Rotterdam. You can not vote to change this command structure near the end of our operation. I will not be threatened with mutiny! If I have to kill all of you, I will!"

Wagner, still with his pistol holsters unstrapped, laughed at Batkin and barked back, "You must be delusional! No man threatens me, Batkin! I have died a thousand times in my life. Death does not intimidate me. But I will agree to continue the mission with you in command of the *Katarina,* only because that is how we began.

"I will assume the political leadership of the FNNP until the politicians in Munich can arrive at a final conclusion. I will abide by their decisions. I will not agree, however, to take political orders from the Kremlin. We are presently in my country and we will continue to receive orders directly from the FNNP office in Munich. They have a better overall understanding of the political situation. They may consult with the GPNR in Russia if they wish. But you, Batkin, will continue to follow the general orders of the FNNP until the mission has been completed."

Wagner lit another cigarette and took two long drags. He looked with his blue eyes around the table and spoke again.

"I was informed of the assassinations at Totenkopf two hours ago. Munich instructed me to give our condolences to Andreas Fuchs for the death of his two German patriot brothers. They also informed me of a CIA ship which has been trailing us since we entered the Danube, nearly two weeks ago.

"Southern Germany is crawling with American agents. All our FNNP assets have been assigned to intercept the CIA ship and hit the American coalition agents on land wherever they can be found. We are essentially at war with these people.

"We are to proceed to Frankfurt where we will unload half of the AZEV cargo. This portion will be transported north over land by truck to Bremerhaven on the German North Sea coast. A safe corridor will be provided on the autobahn all the way to the sea. By dividing the cargo again, we stand a better chance of having it reach its final destination. It will be taken to an old Nazi U-boat base where it will be loaded onto a Greek flagged transport for transfer to America.

"Our mission remains the same. The *Katarina* will continue onto Rotterdam with the rest of the AZEV cargo. There it will be transferred to a Spanish flagged freighter for delivery to Charleston, South Carolina.

"Our job on the *Katarina* is to defend it from attack by the CIA and the German Federal Intelligence Service, which still has not come over to our side. The rest of the way will be difficult. We can succeed only if we remain united on this ship.

"Does everyone here agree with this plan?" asked Wagner.

Tiny Andreas Fuchs, looking through his myopic spectacles, glanced at Wagner and saluted him. He said in a high pitched voice, "I agree to proceed with the present command structure and the new plans."

Petrenko and Mitnick nodded in agreement. Dashkov also agreed. Batkin, now completely sober, also nodded affirmatively. The mission of the *Katarina* would continue, albeit under much more perilous conditions.

While the men filed out of the galley to get some rest before dawn, Petrenko and Mitnick poured themselves a cup of coffee and returned to sit at the table. Mitnick stared at Petrenko with big eyes and sighed.

"What's wrong, Pavlo?" asked Petrenko.

"Ivan, you have been my friend for many years. You are an intellectual and a deep thinker. At the university, you were my best student. You are educated in the ways of the world. You have keen senses of computation and rational thought. But, I think you are blinding yourself to the realities of our situation.

"Your grandfather was in the Galichina SS Division and died fighting the Russians in 1944. Your father, Viktor, was the founder of the GPNR in Moscow. He was assassinated by the Russians.

"Can you really believe and work with these Russians? Do you trust them?

"I don't!

"Their political history is replete with only repression and conflict with their neighbors. I can not imagine any scenario where they will act in the benefit of the Ukrainian or any other people.

"Similarly, are you going to put faith in the German FNNP after our country's experience with Fascists in World War Two? Do you really believe they will allow us our freedom if we assist them in their plans to push the Americans out of Europe?

"I can not believe this!

"They, with the Russians, will likely dismember us and subject our people to political and economic enslavement. Just as they have done to us and others in the past.

"They will also subjugate the peoples of Poland, Bulgaria, Romania, and the rest of the Balkans. In time, they will spread like cancer throughout all of Europe. Their 'Fourth Reich' will be our prison.

"The Ukraine wants to be free. Freedom is the natural state of all mankind. True humanity demands it.

"Man has been striving for that equilibrium since he came down from trees and became a tribal animal four million years ago. The need for freedom is not learned. It is an instinct, like mother-love, social cooperation, curiosity, compassion, competitiveness, and inventiveness. It is ancient and embedded in the human DNA.

"We don't need the Americans to achieve that natural state, but we should certainly refrain from damaging them deliberately. They have done no harm to us.

"We also especially don't need the Russians or Germans. Neither of them have our interests in their plans.

"We, the people of Ukraine, are the only ones that should control the destiny of our nation. Many millions of us have already died at the hands of these people. Why should we cooperate with them now?

"It makes no sense to me!

"You know, Petrenko, freedom is an ethereal concept. It is more a spiritual state of mind than a physical state of being. Why are people willing to die for it?

"Throughout the ages, on all habitable places on this Earth, men and women have sacrificed their lives attempting to gain it. Human beings in their desperate struggle for liberty even lose touch with the self-preservation instincts of their nature. They throw caution to the wind. Oppressive governments take advantage of this forgotten caution and slaughter them in the streets. Yet, they keep fighting and dying. Such is the passion to live free.

"Don't throw caution to the wind, Petrenko!

"Why is freedom so essential to the human spirit? Why not acquiesce to your oppressor and live to see another day? Why not do as you're told and follow the law issued by your dictator or occupier? Why not allow your mind to be manipulated to serve the 'greater good' as set forth by your ruler?

"Well, the answers to these questions should be obvious to us. They have been shown many times in history.

"Quite simply, it is because an enslaved existence is not worth living. We would all have lives not worth living if we continue on this path you have selected, Petrenko.

"The 'thinking mind' can not be ruled. There is no force powerful enough to control it. It yearns to be free in order to create. Only a free spirit can see the joy in life. Great discovery is born from this freedom to explore with the mind.

"The 'thinking mind' can only follow the rule of law as set forth by other 'thinking minds'. Great societies have been built on this premise, and great societies have crumbled when that premise was lost. Freedom is indispensable to the continual progress of man, but so are 'thinking minds'.

"We will not have freedom in our future if we continue on this passage you have selected.

"So yes, Petrenko. Human beings will continue to fight for their freedom. But we must be honest with ourselves in deciding our trajectory to liberty. Freedom will remain ethereal if we don't choose wisely.

"We need our 'thinking minds' to arrive at true liberty. Advancements in human civilization will continue to be made only by 'free men with thinking minds'.

"If our trail is not well chosen, fathers and mothers will continue to die in vain attempting to give their children a better life. It's been the story of mankind, an epic of the grandest proportions."

CHAPTER 20

Venus in the Garden

In the arc of life - you are born like an exploding star, you live like a comet, and one day, you cease to be in dark matter. As in the many colors of a rainbow arching across the sky, life's curving line of development is full of separate and different emotions. To have a full life, you must feel all of them.

However, what fuels the brilliant flaming tail of the comet, the radiant light of the 'shooting star', and the boundless and endless energy of your trajectory across the cosmos is the emotion of 'Love'. Without it, you are empty space and time. With 'Love', your soul is immortal, and your spirit will shine forever.

Nasrin had finally fallen asleep. In the late hour, she lay in bed dreaming. Her dream-scape was vivid with detail. A story of immense intensity was unfolding. She had become an active participant in the drama. She fell deeper and deeper into it, swept into its vortex of surreality.

Nasrin heard mournful cries coming from downstairs. The sorrows seemed to be calling for her. She slipped out of bed and stepped towards them.

A fiery morning sun was rising over the Atlantic Ocean. Its calm warm light filled the sun-room. Nasrin could feel the kind warmth on her skin as she walked through the room. The radiance of our star fell on her green eyes. Its life intensified all her sensations. Like the dance of the Earth around its brilliant sun, she gravitated further into life's dream.

Nasrin passed the piano and softly touched its keys. Their sounds echoed gently into the universe, losing themselves in the solace. Time slowed down.

She flowed towards the garden courtyard. As she approached, Nasrin could see the eminent focus of her dream through the large glass window. The apparition of the Holy Spirit stopped time absolutely. The clock on the wall lost its tick.

A young and beautiful Olivia sat in melancholy. She softly leaned against a marble statue of the *Birth of Venus*. With her spirit in sadness, Olivia buried her face in her hands. She lamented the loss of her children with tears.

The garden was exposed to the east where the blue Atlantic Ocean waited. Filled with red bougainvillea, orange heliconias, and pink and yellow hibiscus, the garden reflected the life of the world.

A few feet behind *Venus*, on the southern edge of the garden, stood a limestone wall covered with "Maypop" passion vines. The lavender and white flowers blanketed the wall to the sky.

Around *Venus* were the early lemon yellow blossoms of a Bahama Cassia tree. The sandy ground of the open east end of the courtyard was covered with beach sunflowers. They created a dense yellow flower carpet over the sand dune and onto the beach beyond.

The door from the sun-room was open. Nasrin passed into the courtyard. Beautiful bright red flowered trumpet vines twined and climbed a coral rock trellis next to the door.

Nasrin stepped closer to Olivia as sunshine began to brighten the colors of the garden. She sat next to Olivia, and everything became more alive.

A green jewel-colored Malachite butterfly fluttered onto Nasrin's right shoulder and stayed for a while. The emerald green of the Malachite matched Nasrin's eyes.

Nasrin placed her hand on Olivia's knee and asked, "Why do you weep?"

Young Olivia raised her tear streaked face and smiled. Olivia's face was dominated by her dark profound eyes and gentle attractive smile. Her grace immediately captured you. Her charm and soul were as captivating as her external beauty. She was ravishing in every sense of the word.

"I have lost my sons to war," said Olivia. "I will never see them again. They are beyond my reach. I miss them. My family was my life, and I long for all of them."

Olivia continued looking into Nasrin's eyes. Her face illuminated with beams of love and her smile widened.

"You are Nasrin, Michael's wife. You are as beautiful as I was told. I sense in your eyes you love my son as deeply as I do. Eyes do not lie.

"I am content in that. It's all a mother can hope for. I wish for your happiness, Nasrin.

"Being in love is the greatest gift a human being can have. You and Michael are fortunate to have found each other.

"How is my son, Nasrin?" asked Olivia.

Now Nasrin began to weep.

Olivia edged up closer to Nasrin and embraced her. Their love grew.

"It's alright, Nasrin. Don't fear. Michael chose to defend his country when he was just a boy. He's strong in the mind. He is a survivor and he has much to come home for. He would never leave you behind. He loves you too much. He'll soon come home and never leave you again."

A colorfully striped butterfly floated into the garden. It passed Nasrin and Olivia, softly landing on a passion vines' lavender flower behind them. God's beauty gently rocked its wings dry in the morning sunshine while it drew nectar.

The wet white marble of the *Venus* glistened, reflecting light from the sun. The Roman goddess of fertility and military victory was most associated with the concept of "Love". Both of the women in the garden knew love in its purest form.

"I have a grandson named Alexander," said Olivia. "I would like to see him."

Nasrin smiled and dried the tears from her face.

"I'll bring him to you," said Nasrin before she stepped back into the house.

Nasrin returned moments later with Alexander in her arms. She placed him on Olivia's lap.

Olivia cradled her grandson closely in her arms against her heart. She sang softly into his ear.

"He's a fine boy," said Olivia.

"I'm very happy for you all. Treasure your family, Nasrin. They will always be the light of your life. Be with them all you can and never place anything above them. Nurture the children for the rest of your life," urged Olivia.

A ruby-throated hummingbird flew into the garden and onto a bright red flower on the trumpet vine across from Nasrin and Olivia. The small bird, with a red iridescent throat and metallic green back, passed its long bill into the flower and began to drink sugary nectar. The Atlantic Ocean's surf roared in the distance.

Olivia, still holding Alexander close to her heart, spoke again. "I love this garden. I have seen great joy here."

She took a deep breath and closed her eyes. She raised her face to the sun. She absorbed its life with the passion of a saint.

"My children would play here. I'd sit and watch them chase butterflies. Observing nature, they learned of the wonders of the world. I saw their metamorphosis into thinking and caring human beings. We shared our souls in the splendor of the moments spent here.

"Julian and I spent great moments here also. We would sit together and listen to Rebecca play the piano. Her music was inspiring. She had a way about her. Her sounds moved you to a spiritual realm where one was free to feel. Rebecca liberated your passions to their extremes. What a wonderful girl. What a magnificent gift.

"Oh! I have many sweet memories of this garden," said Olivia.

Olivia opened her eyes and looked away from the sun. She kissed the sleeping Alexander on the cheek and returned him to Nasrin.

"I think you should take him to bed. He needs to rest a while longer," said Olivia.

Nasrin looked at Olivia's smile. It radiated serenity and a warm comfort of being. It was peaceful and accepting of life's injustices. It scintillated with love and hope and faith. Olivia's smile reflected a thousand tender emotions, each one too deep to express in words. It was like a mirror for all the loving wishes and dreams of your life. Olivia helped make you whole.

Nasrin did not wish to depart. Olivia leaned over and kissed Nasrin's face.

"Young love," whispered Olivia.

"It's the energy that runs the world," she gently said as Nasrin walked away.

Nasrin returned Alexander to bed. She quickly ran back to the garden. She desperately needed to talk with Olivia.

But Olivia was gone.

A deep feeling of loss entered Nasrin's soul. She suddenly felt emptied of energy. A great opportunity had vanished. She had sensed the spirit of Olivia only for a short moment. It was not enough. She wanted more of the "Amaranth", the central essence of the Stansfield family.

Nasrin sat alone by *Venus* in the light of the sun and quietly wept. The tick of time began again.

Nasrin awoke, crying in bed. Her pillow was wet with tears. Her dream had introduced the tender beauty of Olivia to her.

Nasrin sat up in bed and continued to cry uncontrollably for several minutes. She felt a deep sorrow for not having had the gift of Olivia's company. What a travesty.

After taking a warm bath, Nasrin came down to the sun-room and sat watching the Atlantic. Occasionally, she would glance towards the garden courtyard. She hoped to see Olivia again. But it had been all a dream. Reality could not be so fair.

Rebecca Stansfield was expected at any moment. She had phoned the day before to ask Nasrin if she could stop and spend a few days with her on Key Biscayne before departing for a concert tour in Argentina. Nasrin was delighted to have her company and continue to learn about the Stansfield family.

In the afternoon, Rebecca and Nasrin went for a swim in the Atlantic. They had an early dinner and later sat in the sun-room, having a cup of coffee.

"Have you heard anything about Michael?" asked Rebecca.

"No. Nothing. Not one word. It's exasperating and hurtful," stated Nasrin.

"I'm sure he's fine," calmly said Rebecca.

"He's a big and strong, intelligent boy. The best man America has. I'm sure he'll be home soon," added Rebecca encouragingly.

"I miss him so much," lamented Nasrin.

"He's been gone for three weeks and I don't know anything about his situation. This is mind-bending. I can't tolerate it.

"Remember, Rebecca, I have seen him in action. He's not afraid of anything. He is constantly putting himself in dangerous positions. It's his nature. He can't help it. He's America's best because of his invincible spirit. He is pure 'American Amaranth'.

"I just pray for his good fortune, and that the grace of God allows him to return to me safely. I couldn't live without him," said Nasrin as she began to weep.

Rebecca embraced Nasrin tightly and gently soothed her aching heart.

"Let's have a glass of Spanish sherry," shouted Rebecca, as she sprung from the couch to the nearby bar in an attempt to brighten Nasrin's mood.

"My parents loved sherry after dinner.

"When we were children, they had a collection of hundreds of bottles in a variety of styles. My mother preferred the dry light finos. My father liked the darker, heavier olorosos.

"We'd laugh when they would drink too much and begin dancing to music in this sun-room," smiled Rebecca.

"They were special people. I miss them very much. It's sad how life takes the people you love away. You can never be ready for losing someone you love," added Rebecca, while returning to the couch with two large glasses of sherry and her acoustic guitar.

"You play the guitar?" asked Nasrin as she sipped her sherry.

"I sang and played the guitar better than the piano until after my twentieth birthday," said Rebecca.

"I got heavy into piano after I began at Julliard.

"I went to music school on a combined voice and classical guitar scholarship.

"One day, I was playing the piano for fun with some friends in our concert hall when one of the piano professors walked through and heard my playing.

"The next day, I received a call from that professor. He encouraged me to audition for the staff. I took him up on the offer because I had tired of the guitar.

"A few years later, I was playing in front of the Queen of England at the Royal Albert Hall. Life is funny."

The girls drank their sherry wine and laughed while Rebecca strummed popular rock songs on her acoustic guitar. They spoke of their youth, growing up with their parents at home. They shared special memories of family. They became more intimate in their shared sorrows.

"You were with your father when he died, Rebecca. Can you speak of that?" asked Nasrin.

"Our last moments together were special, as were all my moments with him," answered Rebecca in a hushed voice.

"He was such a warrior, and such a gentle man at the same time. He loved us all very much. He lived for us.

"He had great faith in me. He understood all my ingredients. He tolerated my passionate childishness and allowed me to expand in my own manner. He believed in my gifts to move people with music. 'The power of song,' he'd say, 'use it to bring peace on Earth.'

"In those last minutes of his life, I happened to ask him about the secrets of love. He loved my mother so much that I considered him an expert in the emotion.

"He kindly explained to me how the secrets of love were just that - 'secret'. One could not know them until one could experience them. Only with true love in the heart, would the secrets reveal themselves.

"He didn't belittle me for asking the question. He simply smiled in his characteristic way and told me to wait. That I would one day know the secrets for myself.

"He kissed me and told me he loved me. He told me to be patient and wait for love to come my way.

"His love for my mother was always on his mind. He couldn't live without her.

"After his collapse, I ran to him. I held his head in my hands and cried for him to wake up.

"With his eyes closed and a kind smile, he took a shallow last breath and whispered, 'Olivia.'

"I kissed his cheek and whispered her name also."

The drama of the depiction stilled the room. Both girls paused in silence. A long moment passed.

"How was your mother?" asked Nasrin.

"She was the most incredible woman I have ever known," said Rebecca. "She was drop-dead gorgeous, smart, witty, and spiritually strong.

"But above all, she loved my father. He was her life. They made a perfect couple.

"Naturally, we were important to her also," added Rebecca.

Nasrin just smiled.

"My mother was a strong believer in 'young love'. She felt 'young love' was the energy that ran the world," said Rebecca.

Nasrin just smiled.

"My mother always said falling in love young was the elixir that kept a marriage alive. I believe it, although I have not had the great fortune to have found it like my mother. But I'm still young and looking," laughed Rebecca while strumming her guitar.

"Did your mother enjoy your singing and guitar playing as much as your piano?" asked Nasrin.

"They were different in their own ways. My mother appreciated all of the music," said Rebecca.

"My piano was mainly classical, while my guitar was contemporary. She loved to hear me sing and play the

'Rolling Stones', the 'Beatles', 'U2', 'Coldplay', and all the other great bands."

"What was her favorite contemporary song that you played?" asked Nasrin.

"Oh, that's easy! She loved to hear me sing the 'Snow Patrol' classic, 'Chasing Cars'. She thought it was emblematic of 'young love', and it reminded her of my father when they were young."

"Would you play that song for me?" pleaded Nasrin.

"Sure, I'd love to," responded Rebecca.

Nasrin walked towards the garden courtyard as Rebecca began to play her magnificent and magical guitar. With her angelic voice, Rebecca sang the words of the most beautiful song Nasrin had ever heard.

Nasrin pressed against the window and stared into Olivia's garden. Tears streamed down her face while she rejoiced in the unique glory of the "Amaranth".

CHAPTER 21

Into the Belly
of the Beast

In a hidden recess of my collective unconscious memory sits a holy shrine where the great sacred deeds of my forefathers sleep. Like in a forest at dusk, the achievements lie in shadow, waiting to be called upon. They lie behind stone and tree, across meadow and field of flower, and on the far side of brook and stream. I can not see them, but they are there. They always have been and always will be. The echoes of their courage are sensed in my mind, coming to me at special times when I need it most to carry on.

Before dawn on June 21, both Jimmy Calhoun and Michael Stansfield had come up top to the foredeck of the *Conqueror* to get some fresh air. Neither could sleep. Still dark, the night was cool and the men wore windbreakers. Their ship motored down the Main River towards the Bavarian city of Schweinfurt, an hour and a half away. With a cup of coffee in hand, they sat down and talked.

"Listen, Michael, I'm sorry for having doubted your initial assessment of Boroshkova. I should have accepted your intuitions about her. I'm embarrassed by the whole thing. I've known you long enough to realize you're always on target. I should have had more faith in your opinion."

Earlier in the evening, Langley had informed the *Conqueror* of the attack on Totenkopf Castle and the elimination of Europe's neo-fascist political leadership. CIA headquarters also revealed the source of the inside leak which had endangered Stansfield in Balaclava and the *Conqueror's* crew in Serbia.

Polish Intelligence Director Pawlak had been working with the FNNP and GPNR all along, just as CIA Director Mitrano had suspected. Veronika Boroshkova and Basha Ludwick were in the clear. There were no longer suspicions concerning their allegiances. Both were patriots fighting for freedom and the destruction of Fascism in their countries.

"Hey, stop right there, Hick!" demanded Stansfield.

"I was just as guilty for doubting your opinions about Basha. I thought you were blinded by your interests in her and couldn't see the possibility of her being the leak. I was wrong for not believing in your skills at a critical moment. I was wrong in not seeing Basha's true side. I'm sorry for my weakness in not properly assessing the situation," added a remorseful Stansfield.

The two old friends shook hands and agreed their training had required them to have doubts in such a situation. Covert CIA operations required agents maintain a clear perspective and never allow allegiances of friendship to distort reality. Everyone was to be considered a possible leak in moments when the facts did not make sense. This was CIA protocol.

Michael Stansfield slapped Hickory's broad back and laughed. "I still love ya, Jimmy, you big red-neck! I have since our judo days at the Academy. If I hadn't kicked your ass so many times as a sparring partner, maybe I wouldn't have been college champ!"

"That's right, Mikey! Half of that trophy back home is mine, you bastard," grinned Calhoun.

The men drank their coffee as dawn broke. They took a short respite in the war to share their friendship. They spoke of many things, but especially of family. Both had a deep appreciation and loyalty for the ties that bind the tightest.

"Michael, I've always meant to ask why your father wore that black eye patch.

"I remember the admiral coming to Annapolis to give the fresh incoming plebes a series of talks on freedom and its costs. As a young eighteen year old kid sitting in the Naval Academy Chapel, surrounded by all the marble statues of American heroes, he just blew me away with his emotions for our country.

"I distinctly recall the admiral saying your mother had taught him more about the concept of 'freedom' than anyone else in his life. How she losing her country to Communism had shown her how difficult it was to be free in this world. He cautioned us all about the difficulties in preserving our great republic, and the price Americans had paid in the past to maintain our country safe.

"He was an inspiration for me to be at my best always. His black patch over his left eye commanded respect. He became iconic like the statues surrounding us in the chapel. He encouraged us as he spoke about America and our privilege to help defend her.

"What happened to his eye, Michael?"

"My father went to work for Naval Intelligence as a young lieutenant commander in late 1978. His first assignment was to go to China as a military observer in the PLA's invasion of Vietnam in early 1979. What he learned there catapulted him to develop modern missile technology for the US Navy. He became convinced America would eventually go to war with China. He was right. He was always right as far as I can remember.

"He lost the sight of his left eye shortly after being injured in a land mine blast in Vietnam. He was America's last casualty in Vietnam.

"He was both a tough and kind gentleman of the highest degree. The three true loves of his life were my mother, his family, and the United States of America. He never stopped doing the best he could for all of them. I miss him dearly. My father was a good man," sighed Michael.

"So, it was a battle wound, Mikey. We all figured it was, but were afraid to ask. He was a sacred icon to us, no doubt about it. We all miss him."

"In our years at the Naval Academy, Hick, I heard many times your grandfather had been a hero in the Second World War. There were a lot of stories.

"You never spoke about that while we were there. When people would ask you about your grandfather, you would simply change the subject and not address the issue. Why not, Hick?"

"My grandfather - George William Calhoun - was born in Boone, North Carolina, in 1915 to an unwed mother. He never knew his father. His young mother moved with George to the nearby town of Hickory to get away from all the ugly talk in Boone.

"In Hickory, George became a great high school football and baseball player. After graduating, he went to the University of North Carolina in Chapel Hill and became an aeronautical engineer.

"He learned to fly and barn-stormed the state in a biplane. He won several acrobatic flying competitions as a young man.

"After Pearl Harbor, he joined the Army Air Corps and quickly rose in rank to captain. He was transferred in early 1943 to the US 8th Air Force in England. From there he flew his B-17, *Bastard from Boone*, on eighteen missions over Europe.

"He won several combat medals for bravery, and they say he was as much a terror on the ground in England as he was in the air over Germany. Legend claims he left several English girls with babies, many of the mothers already married to British soldiers serving overseas.

"His last mission was over the city we're about to pass by, in this ship - Schweinfurt. 'Old George', as our family called him, was a bigger than life American hero. He was a character out of a Hollywood action movie. He cast a big shadow which no one in our family was ever able to match, Mikey."

"I know the feeling, Jimmy."

"While a kid growing up in Hickory, North Carolina, I remember hearing stories about my grandfather as if he was 'John Wayne'. I would walk into our town's dime store or movie house and everybody inside would whisper to each other, 'There goes George's grandson.'

"It had been even worse for my father right after the war. He became a pharmacist assistant after finishing high school. He went to work in our local drugstore and spent the rest of his life busting his ass for our community. Until his last days, people asked him why he hadn't joined the military like his hero father. Why he was satisfied filling prescriptions and not fighting for his country in Vietnam. It dogged him his entire life. Not everyone is made for fighting, Mikey," said Hickory sadly.

"When I got to Annapolis, it became quickly evident to me the story of my grandfather was known around campus. I couldn't understand how an Army Air Corp guy from the 1940s was so popular at the US Naval Academy, sixty years later in the twenty-first century. It was mind-boggling. I couldn't get away from it. So, I just didn't acknowledge the fact. I'd be asked about him, and I would change the conversation to something else. Imagine, Mikey, I was embarrassed to be a hero's grandson. I seemed to always be chasing his shadow without ever quite reaching it.

"Now being older and wiser, I accept what my grandfather did for our country as a great achievement. I honor his contribution to our freedom every day. I try to do the best I can for my country, just as he did. I'm comfortable with my family's legacy now. I don't mind chasing his shadow in my attempt to be the best American I can be. I love his memory, just as I love my father's contribution to his community," concluded Jimmy Calhoun.

"What happened to your grandfather at Schweinfurt?" asked Stansfield. "What do you know about his last mission? Can you talk about that?"

"The story was told to me many times, Mikey. Everyone back home knew all the details. 'Old George' was a hero in Carolina. The town of Hickory celebrated his birthday every year with a parade and party at George's high school. His bravery medals were behind glass at the old town hall.

"At dawn on August 17, 1943, a heavy fog had settled over England. Young American fighting men anxiously waited in their B-17 bombers on airfields in the English Midlands and East Anglia for orders to take off on the most dangerous mission yet over German-occupied territory in continental Europe. The double target mission by the US 8th Air Force was sending 376 B-17 bombers against the southern German cities of Regensburg and Schweinfurt. They would be escorted part of the way by hundreds of P-47 and Spitfire fighters based out of southern England.

"The 4th Bombardment Wing's 146 B-17s, led by the famous Colonel Curtis E. LeMay, got into the air shortly before 8 AM. Their orders were to attack the Messerschmidt aircraft factories in Regensburg in an attempt to slow down production of the Bf 109 fighter.

"The 1st Bombardment Wing's 230 B-17s, led by Brigadier General Robert B. Williams, were delayed by fog and did not take off until 11 AM. They were divided into two task forces of 116 and 114 planes, respectively. Each of the group's flights were more than twenty miles long. The 1st's mission was to bomb the ball bearing factories in Schweinfurt, essential in the production of Nazi aircraft and tanks.

"The deep penetrating raid into Germany would only be escorted by Allied fighters as far as Belgium. Beyond that, the unescorted bombers would have to defend themselves. They were flying into the belly of the beast. It was to be the deepest raid yet into dangerous territory. American losses were predicted to be heavy. Of the three and a half hours to be spent over German occupied territory, more than two hours and ten minutes would be without fighter escort. These brave young men were destined to sit in their flying contraptions at subfreezing temperatures and beat off the entire Luftwaffe. It was a daunting task that only the bravest of the brave could be expected to tackle at this stage of the war. They were all very courageous boys.

"My grandfather, Captain George William Calhoun, was psychologically built for this mission. He was a fearless character who enjoyed confrontation. He never backed away from a fight. 'Old George' led the first formation of the 1st Bomb Wing across the Dutch coast at 1:30 PM. Flying at an altitude of 25,000 feet, they encountered several dozen Bf 109s and Fw 190s near Antwerp. An escort of P-47s tangled with the German fighters, allowing my grandfather's plane, *Bastard from Boone*, to enter Germany unscathed."

By sunrise, Calhoun and Stansfield had moved to the pilot house of their ship. They sat on *Conqueror of Worlds* having a cup of coffee. The old friends talked about Calhoun's grandfather and his part in the history of the United States.

The ship passed through the Bavarian city of Schweinfurt, site of the famous US strategic bombing raid in 1943. The *Conqueror* was three hours behind the *Katarina*. They would make up distance along the Main River to Frankfurt.

Stansfield listened with interest to Hickory's description of the events from August 1943. The story of his grandfather's legendary exploits in the B-17 raid on Schweinfurt had been passed down to Jimmy by his father. It had become a form of bond between the Calhoun men. Indeed, great love had been born from the legend for a grandfather Hick never knew.

Schweinfurt, on the north bank of the Main, had been destroyed and reconstructed three times during its 1500-year history. The town joined Martin Luther's Reformation in 1542 and suffered through the subsequent religious wars. Schweinfurt was destroyed a second time during the Napoleonic Wars of 1796-1801, sustaining heavy civilian casualties. The Allied bombings of 1943-1945 leveled the city for a third time.

Michael Stansfield had the *Conqueror* on high alert, after being advised by Langley of the CIA's attack on Totenkopf Castle earlier in the morning. Tom Garfield and Peter Reynolds each manned an M60 machine gun along the sides of the ship's bow. Bruno Bonnet and Jakub Krol were assigned a Serpent missile launcher, as were Thomas Egan and Basha Ludwick. Veronika Boroshkova had been charged with the medical supplies kit and providing first aid if the need arose. Stansfield had activated the twin-fed MK-46 30mm gun at the stern of the ship with armor piercing high explosive rounds, and controlled it remotely from the command console near the ship's pilot house. The *Conqueror's* hidden 12 inch torpedo tubes were charged for action. Both Stansfield and Calhoun carried an M4 carbine with a 100-round capacity magazine. Calhoun also carried two 9mm pistols in a shoulder cross harness. The team was prepared for all-out war.

After pouring a third cup of coffee, Stansfield asked Calhoun to continue his story. Hickory obliged.

"The flight through Germany was rough. The bombers were incessantly attacked by Bf 109s, Fw 190s, and Bf 110 heavy fighters, all the way down into Bavaria. Five miles from Schweinfurt, the German anti-aircraft guns began putting up a curtain of flak into the path of the B-17s. Only 183 of 230 bombers in my grandfather's wing arrived safely over Schweinfurt. They dropped over 400 tons of bombs on the ball bearing plants, producing heavy damage. The raid on Regensburg, although also costly for the Americans, had been even more successful in destroying their targets.

"My grandfather dropped his bombs on target, but the *Bastard from Boone* got caught by flak and crash landed near this river. My grandfather survived the crash but was killed resisting capture.

"Captain Calhoun truly was the 'Bastard from Boone'. He carried two Colt .45s on his waist and a long-nosed .357 Magnum in a shoulder holster as backup. Two surviving crew members, who became POWs, told my father years later that the bastard emptied all his guns on the Nazi 'sons of bitches'. He refused to surrender and yelled profanity at his enemy while they overran his position along the Main riverbank. He personally killed ten Nazis before going down.

"What a character 'Old George' must have been. He was a one-man wrecking crew. He brought steel to his enemy in every way he could. Either with bombs from the air or bullets on the ground, the 'Bastard from Boone' made the enemy pay a heavy price for confrontation. He was never afraid. I would've liked to have known him," said Hickory with a laugh.

Stansfield smiled widely and pulled on Hick's double pistol harness. "He couldn't have been a bigger bastard than you, you big old Carolina mountain man! Look at you! You look like John Dillinger for God's sake. What is this shit with the Calhoun men? They're all cowboy gunslingers waiting for a shootout!" shouted Stansfield.

Hickory sat back in his chair and laughed with Michael for a while. Then both became quiet as they thought of home and family.

"You know, Michael, my grandfather may have been a tough SOB, but I had never done anything really dangerous in my life before my trip into the Congo jungle. Between the wild animals of the Likuola Swamps, the tribesmen of the rainforest, and the rough dudes we were after, I was scared to death. I mean, I was shitting in my pants. I tried to hide the fact from my men. I hope they didn't see through me."

"That's alright, Hick. We're all entitled to shit in our dungarees once in a while," grinned Michael.

"That's easy for you to say, Mikey, because you don't feel the fear. You've been in so many dangerous situations you're desensitized to it."

"Desensitized? What are you talking about, you crazy red-neck hillbilly?

"I've been scared so many times in the past I can't keep count. From my first to my last mission, I've been scared to death. I just work through it, Hick. That's all. You work through it."

"What's the most scared you've ever been, Michael?"

"Aleppo! Aleppo in Syria was the most scared I've ever been, Hick. There was no escaping fear in that goddam place. The things I saw there and the things I did there would make the devil shit in his pants. I lost most of my team in that miserable hellhole.

"You had the loyal Syrian Army dudes, the Hezbollah fighters, and the Iranians on one side, and the Free Syrian Rebel Army of jihadist killers on the other. Everyone looked the same to me. I looked the same to me! You couldn't tell friend from foe. To me, everyone was the enemy.

"We lived in rubble, surrounded by jagged rock and iron bar. The heat was stifling. Snipers from both sides were active all around us, and they often didn't discriminate who they shot. There were booby-trap bombs everywhere. Aleppo was a city of over two million people, where everyone was trying to kill each other.

"The killing on the ground in Syria was bestial. Beheadings, eviscerations, and chemical gassings, all competed on the list of torturous deaths. You could also get stabbed in the back by a woman or a twelve-year-old kid in the dark. If the knives, machetes, swords, bullets, or shrapnel didn't rip you up, then a sarin shell would end your days in a horrible instant of asphyxia. There was also fire from above, with every goddam air force in the world dropping napalm bombs on your ass, day and night.

"The air we breathed was always full of dust and smoke. Packs of hungry and vicious feral dogs roamed the streets, eating dead and live humans. The bug-infested food we had was putrid, and the water was poisoned.

"Aleppo undeniably made me shit in my pants, Hick. Everything else seemed easy after that.

"Fear is part of the game, Jimmy. You have to instill more of it on the enemy than he does on you. It's a battle of nerves out there. The guys who last the longest without having to change their underwear get the prize of victory.

"But you know all this, Jimmy. Why am I wasting my time talking all this crap to you?

"Whether you want to believe it or not, you're a brave SOB just like the 'Bastard from Boone'. Your grandpa has nothing over you, Hick."

The friends settled in their chairs and finished their coffee. They prepared themselves for the day.

River traffic on the Main had picked up around Schweinfurt. Dozens of boats filled the river in both directions in the early morning's daylight. Michael Stansfield closely observed the movement with his binoculars.

"We got two river patrol boats, Hick, about two miles east of us. Both are heading in our direction at a high rate of speed. Power up the *Conqueror* to 30 knots!"

Jimmy Calhoun opened up the steel-reinforced yacht. It sped west beyond the traffic around Schweinfurt's docks.

"I think we have trouble, Hick! These guys are really moving at a fast clip. Their decks' heavy machine guns are manned and all the troopers are wearing combat helmets. They look like they mean it! Open up the 30mm gun and arm it for action!"

The hump at the ship's stern opened like a clam, exposing a metal gray navy gun capable of heavy damage on an enemy. Stansfield rotated the MK-46 into position, facing east.

"Get those M60s back here and prep them for action. I want both Serpents armed!" commanded Stansfield as the patrol boats made their intentions clearer.

The neo-Nazis got within one mile range and prematurely fired their heavy machine guns. The rounds were off target.

"Take it up to 35 knots, Hick!" ordered Stansfield.

Stansfield swung around his binoculars to look ahead on the river. A surge of adrenaline popped his eyes. Another enemy patrol boat was coming their way at the front. This one was closing very fast. Alarm shot through Michael's body.

"Get the Serpents near the bow and immediately fire on that ship! Pronto!" commanded Stansfield.

Both Bruno Bonnet and Egan fired their missiles simultaneously, sending two eighteen pound high explosive armor piercing warheads to target. The rockets caught the patrol boat at a distance of 1000 feet. The direct hits didn't leave much of the ship above water, as the explosions ignited on-board munitions and tore the patrol boat apart.

Stansfield fired the MK-46 at the trailing ships. The high explosive 30mm rounds obliterated the German neo-Nazi deck crews and set both patrol boats ablaze.

Yet, Stansfield was jolted by adrenaline again. A fourth FNNP boat appeared out of nowhere and sprayed heavy machine gun fire across the bow of the *Conqueror* from only a few hundred feet. Several high caliber rounds ricocheted into the pilot house near Calhoun as he shot his M4 at the enemy.

Garfield and Reynolds poured hundreds of rounds into the small FNNP vessel with their M60s, killing three Nest troopers. Stansfield turned the MK-46 gun turret onto the Germans and pumped dozens of 30mm shells into them. The enemy ship exploded into a huge ball of red flame and acrid black smoke. None of the Fascists were left alive.

The river became quiet. Michael Stansfield ran to Hickory where he slumped over the ship's wheel. A bullet had entered Calhoun's belly on the right side and exited his back. He was bleeding profusely.

"How does it look, Mikey?" asked Hickory with a weak voice.

"It ripped you up pretty good, Hick. Stay quiet and let me get you comfortable on the floor."

"Can you see my liver, Michael?"

"Yeah, Hick..... I can see your liver," said Stansfield as he carefully pulled Calhoun onto the floor and applied pressure to stop the bleeding.

Basha Ludwik and Veronika Boroshkova came quickly up the steps to assist Stansfield with Calhoun. Basha screamed in disbelief when she saw the horrific scene.

"Call for help, Basha. Get a medivac helicopter out here as soon as possible!" ordered Michael.

Boroshkova handed medical supplies to Stansfield. Michael gently waved her away.

"Things are getting real cold, Michael..... I can't feel my feet or hands..... I don't know if I'm going to make it."

"Just do the best you can, Hick, until help arrives," pleaded Michael.

"Do you really believe the US Cavalry is going to make it here on time, old friend?" asked Calhoun.

"That look in your eye, Michael, is all I need to see..... It tells me I'm fucked, and there's nothing we can do about it. I've got a massive liver wound, and I'm going to bleed to death here on this boat..... Who would have thought? Two Calhoun men dying along the Main in Germany, separated in time by more than seventy years....."

"It's okay, Hick..... I love you and I'm with you..... Please rest until help arrives."

"I need to tell you something, Michael..... I want you to listen to me clearly. Don't doubt what I have to say. It's the truth..... Listen to me carefully, and promise me you'll put a stop to this.....

"Those two dudes we captured in the Congo - the Russian colonel, Asinus, and the Kraut, Draker - spilled their beans to me in interrogation.....

"These neo-Nazi bastards in Europe are working closely with an American movement. The Americans are government boys, Michael. Their blood is supposedly red, white, and blue like ours. But in reality, they're treasonous mother-fuckers who want to change the leadership and direction of our country..... There's an American 'Fifth Column', Michael, and they're planning on overthrowing the government and Constitution of the United States....."

Hickory's voice faded. His body softened. His breathing became difficult.

"Stay still, Hick. You've lost a lot of blood. Don't worry, I'll get the mission done."

Calhoun's eyes became big. He mustered as much strength as he could.

"The AZEV in the *Katarina* is American-issue, Michael..... These traitors stole it from the medical research labs at Fort Detrick in Maryland. It's got 'US Army' all over it..... They passed this shit to the GPNR Fascists. They want it used on America to destabilize her, so they can implement their sick plan.....

"Only Mitrano and I know this. Now, you know.....

"The director is working like a madman to uncover these SOBs. You must stop the *Katarina* and take back the AZEV..... The world must not discover that Americans are trying to kill Americans..... You do your part, and Mitrano will do his.....

"Promise me, Michael..... You must get these sons of bitches."

"I promise, Hick. I'll stop them and get the AZEV back."

Michael grabbed a seat cushion and placed it behind Jimmy Calhoun's head. He took his handkerchief, soaked it with water, and wiped blood away from Jimmy's face and mouth.

"Are the Black Scorpions involved, Hick?"

"Who the fuck are the Black Scorpions, Mikey?"

"Don't you know, Hick? Didn't Egan show you a pin he found at Ibutu?"

"No, Mikey. I don't know anything about a pin or the Black Scorpions. Egan didn't give me anything at Ibutu."

"Okay, Hick. I believe you and everything you say. Just rest until help arrives."

Hickory smiled like a boy. He squeezed Michael's hand gently. "Please tell Vitoria I love her. Tell her she's been my sun and moon since I laid eyes on her..... Tell Vitoria she was my last thought..... We'll see each other again.....

"I love you, Mikey," he said softly.

"I love you too, Hick."

James "Hickory" Calhoun, an American hero, closed his eyes and drifted off into his dream. His friend, Michael Stansfield, bowed his head and cried.

CHAPTER 22

Together in Battle

In our Promethean struggle for the empire of the mind, the hounds of hell will always be at our heels. Take hold of your brother's hand, and through strength of character, vanquish those who wish to do wrong. Carry the torch of victory together to the promised land, and on your way, light the souls of other brave men to do the same. Let our ceremonious lyric poem open the eyes, ears, and hearts of all those who wish freedom. In good or bad weather, our ode to the dream of joy will ring true and faithful.

"How does this happen, Julius?" asked Claudia.

"What do you mean?"

"How does the world go to hell in such a short period of time?"

"People have been asking that question for thousands of years, Claudia. The greed for power and wealth dominates the human psyche. Human nature takes over, and history repeats itself."

Claudia relaxed behind the steering wheel of their car. Julius rested his head back in the passenger seat next to her. They waited in a dark alley in Frankfurt for their next sign to move.

"Let me capsulize it for you," said Julius as he racked the slide on his .45 pistol and placed it back into his shoulder holster.

"Events in history don't just happen, even when they seem to, Claudia. The history of civilization is like a long movie. It started thousands of years ago, and it just keeps on playing.

"You and I only live a few years. We come in together to the movie house, buy our popcorn, and sit down to watch the show. Two hours later, we leave our seats to another couple. They do the same thing. The movie keeps on running, as long as mankind does.

"The film had a beginning, and it has a plot. The actors change, but the premise stays the same. Wealth and power, Claudia."

"I don't understand it, Julius. After the fall of the Soviet Union, America was at the top of the world. What happened? How did your country lose control?"

"That is a complicated question, Claudia.

"As a child, my father taught me to always look at problem events from the perspective of precedence. Analyze the development of a calamity by studying the precedent causes.

"Observing the world today, you ask why we're in this fucking hell of a mess? To find an answer, you must rewind the film. Take it back and watch events unfold. I guess you could keep rewinding to the dawn of man, because each precedence has one of its own.

"But in a nutshell, I think going back a couple of hundred years explains a lot."

"You mean to tell me, Julius, that you and I are here, sitting in the blackness of night, stalking to kill our enemy, because of what happened hundreds of years ago?"

"No, Claudia! I'm saying that rewinding the film a few hundred years may explain much of the mess we're in. You would probably be forced to rewind thousands of years to understand all of it."

"That's crazy, Julius."

"It may be, but it's the honest truth.

"The French Revolution in 1789 opened up a radical social and political can of worms. It had a fundamental impact worldwide. Frustration with monarchial ineptitude, and continued decadence of aristocracy, led to the people's revolt and a 'Reign of Terror'.

"Napoleon became a 'freedom fighter', and the revolution was embraced all over the Western World. Even Beethoven composed a symphony to honor the general. Soon, people thought, 'freedom' would come to everyone. Naturally, other monarchs of Europe disagreed.

"Bonaparte allowed power to poison his brain. He crowned himself 'Emperor' and attempted to spread the 'ideals of freedom' across Europe. Millions died in the ensuing chaos.

"After their victory over the French, England and Russia became stronger empires. Bismarck eventually united the many German provinces into a powerful nation-state. A European 'Great Game' began between them.

"With time, a new France and Austria-Hungary also played into the contest. They wanted a piece of the action as well.

"Alliances evolved in the complicated diplomacy. The Crimean War and the 'Scramble for Africa' worsened matters between the great European powers.

"Japan was soon urged by the English to spread her wings in Asia, presenting a problem for the Tsar of Russia. Victory in the Spanish-American War allowed the United States to become a colonial power, and also involve themselves in the ruminations of empire.

"Nations were interested in acquiring more wealth and power. Threat of war became a powerful diplomatic tool.

"As Germany rose, other countries took notice. The next great war was planned. Western banks began financing the development of French and British armies to combat the Teutonic threat.

"The First World War directly led to another 'rebellion' of the people against an inept ruler. The Bolshevik Revolution in Russia eventuated in the rise of International Communism and an existential threat to the West.

"Germany, although formidable on the battlefield, died an economic death. Revolt and chaos spread throughout the country after her defeat in the world war. The Communists tried to take over the government. The Nazis under Adolf Hitler fought them off and rose to national prominence. A new 'great menace' had been born for the rest of the democratic world.

"World War Two came shortly. Many more millions died. The United States and the Soviet Union were victorious. They divided the world between them in the 'Cold War'.

"Israel was born from the Holocaust. The Muslims were angered by it, and by the perceived American and British exploitation of the oil lands.

"Communist China also evolved from the Second World War. It became a menace to the interests of the United States in Asia and the Pacific.

"With the years, radical Islamic fundamentalism and terrorism encroached on American interests in the Middle East and Africa. Islamism became a threat to the American 'way of life'. Israel's survival became precarious.

"Chinese Communism morphed into an International State Capitalism with expansionist ideas. It also threatened American power around the globe.

"The world's economic collapse in 2008, with its subsequent decline in American and European power, helped the Chinese rise further. A rush for control of the world's energy ensued. The Muslims teamed up with the Chinese. Another global war came.

"The decline and break-up of the European Union was blamed on the American economic mess. Many in Europe believed it was orchestrated by the American financial houses to weaken a potential economic competitor. Neo-Fascism grew from the European disgust. A new threat appeared for the 'Free-World'.

"So, here we are, Claudia. Because of the vagaries of King Louis XVI and 'Little Bonaparte', you and I are sitting and waiting in a dark alley of Frankfurt, Germany, to kill our enemy before he kills us. It's incredible, I know, but it's reality. It's all part of the film's plot. A movie we're all forced to watch for a while, until the next audience is ready to replace us!" laughed Julius ironically.

"This is pathetic!" blurted Claudia. "I don't enjoy it at all. There are many better things you and I could be doing, Julius."

"It's not supposed to be enjoyable, Claudia. You understand that. You do your job well, yet I know for a fact you'd rather be elsewhere. I would too. But if this fire gets out of control, it'll lead to further chaos and war. Many more millions will die, and the movie's story will just thicken. Let's see if we can turn the film into a romantic comedy. Everyone would enjoy that flick."

"I don't think we can, Julius."

"I don't either."

While Bavaria was under the control of the FNNP militia, the bordering German region of Hesse was in a virtual state of espionage civil war between the clandestine forces of the FNNP and the BND German Intelligence Service. The US Army Europe Command and Battle Center in Wiesbaden, the last remaining American military base in Germany, provided support for the BND in their fight against the Neo-Fascists.

Frankfurt, the largest city in Hesse and fifth largest in Germany, sat at the center of this watershed area. Lying on both sides of the western Main River, southeast of the Taunus Mountain range, Frankfurt's adjoining metropolitan regions contained over five million inhabitants. It was the financial and transportation center of Germany. It was also the seat of the crumbled European Central Bank and now greatly weakened German Federal Bank.

The Main River flowed west through Frankfurt on its way to Wiesbaden and its confluence with the Rhine. Altstadt, the historical and financial district of Frankfurt, sat near the center of the city on the north side of the Main. Having been severely bombed during World War Two, Frankfurt had that modern German mix of tall skyscrapers contrasted with reconstructed medieval buildings.

The St. Bartholomeu Cathedral was the architectural gem of Altstadt. Originally constructed in the 14th century, it had been rebuilt after the Second World War. The emperors of the Holy Roman Empire had been elected there since 1356. They had been crowned at St. Bartholomeu from 1562 to 1792. Its 330-foot-tall tower provided a bird's eye view of the city and its waterfront harbor.

Shortly after 3 AM on June 24, Peter Tucker stood at the top of the Frankfurt Cathedral's tower. He wore full black camouflage and watched the waterfront a short distance away through night vision binoculars. He carefully scanned the area for his targets.

Julius Stansfield and Claudia sat in a sedan nearby, in an alley next to Romerberg Square. Two BND armored vans and an additional CIA attack truck were parked only a hundred feet away. All members of the attack squad were connected by voice encrypted communications equipment.

Romerberg Square had emptied of pedestrians on this early Saturday morning. Motor traffic around the central district still remained significant.

Tucker finally spotted his marks. He watched the riverfront while the *Katarina's* crew unloaded part of her deadly cargo and packed it onto a heavy truck.

At 3:23 AM, Stansfield's phone crackled on his lap. "Julius, they're on the move," said Tucker, with background wind muffling his voice.

"There are three dark-colored SUVs in front of a heavy ten-wheel truck, followed by two light-colored SUVs. The truck has a fully closed metallic cargo bay without slit openings to the exterior. The SUVs have at least three or four men apiece, and all the vehicles appear armored. When do we engage?" asked Tucker.

Stansfield looked at his GPS device, showing the cargo truck traveling towards his position along the main road running parallel to the river's north bank. It was approximately eight blocks away. The AZEV had been tagged by Pavlo Mitnick, as it was loaded onto the truck for transfer to Bremerhaven.

"There are at least 20 heavily armed troopers in that caravan, Tucker," said Stansfield. "The streets are still too crowded with civilians to get into a firefight. We'll follow them north out of town and intercept them when most appropriate. Now get your ass out of that tower and let's roll!"

Within a few minutes, Julius Stansfield's team was in pursuit of the world's deadliest cargo. They followed it north on the German Autobahn motorway system and prepared to initiate combat contact on Stansfield's order.

Julius looked at an Autobahn map of Germany. He saw there was a tunnel along the projected course of the cargo near the town of Giessen, forty minutes north of Frankfurt. He radioed his team.

"I want two BND assault trucks to rendezvous with me at the north end of Tunnel A36 on the highway to Hanover. I need the BND to purposefully slow down traffic around the cargo caravan, in order to isolate the contraband and get it into that tunnel alone. It must be done inconspicuously to not tip them off. Do you understand? I need graceful ballet dancers out there. We're going to lock them up in that 1200 foot long tunnel and shut them down permanently."

Stansfield expected a bloody fight at the end of Tunnel A36. The FNNP was certain to have protective escorts along the way. The CIA and BND would trap as many of them as possible in the tunnel and attack them from both ends. It would have to be coordinated perfectly to not endanger innocent German bystanders. The AZEV cargo would hopefully be captured intact without violating the cargo truck's protective steel container.

Captain Stansfield had commanded submarine wolf-pack attacks on Chinese enemy convoys in the South China Sea and Taiwan Strait. They had been complicated and dangerous, but not any more so than this mission. The attack in Tunnel A36 would have to be finely choreo-graphed for it to be successful.

While Julius loaded a two-drum magazine into his M4, the AZEV caravan passed his car on the highway. The CIA and BND vehicles fought for position around the enemy.

By 3:50 AM, the Autobahn north of Frankfurt was like the stage at Lincoln Center during a New York Ballet pro-duction of a Tchaikovsky score. Cars and trucks maneu-vered for attack. Additional BND units joined the mixture as the caravans neared Giessen.

BND units slowed down bystander traffic adjacent to the AZEV convoy. They carefully fell back behind the enemy and allowed for some separation.

Twenty miles before A36, Stansfield's car pulled ahead of the contraband and darted to the northern end of the tunnel. Two fully equipped BND attack teams had already blockaded the road at the distant end and waited for their arrival.

A fortified roadblock was strategically prepared for the enemy. Captain Stansfield arrived on the scene and began to give orders. "I want the RPGs to the right of me. Claudia and Tucker stay here and prep that 'Serpent'. Set up the M60s to the left. They can't be allowed to break the roadblock. Team members set up for combat!"

The enemy convoy entered the south end of the tunnel without realizing the inferno they were getting into. The German federal agents had succeeded in not allowing any innocent travelers to file into the tunnel behind the enemy. The AZEV cargo had been isolated in Tunnel A36. The Fascists were rolling toward Stansfield's combat preparations and the battle of their lifetimes.

At 4:09 AM, Stansfield ordered Claudia to shoot out the tunnel lights near them. The north end of Tunnel A36 became pitch black. The enemy's headlights appeared from the bend in the road.

Three CIA and BND assault vehicles had followed the fascist caravan into the tunnel. They stopped as the tunnel bended towards the north end. Men got out of their vehicles and prepared to assault the enemy on foot from the south end. Tremendous firepower would be brought onto the Neo-Nazis from two directions.

Twenty seconds later, Stansfield gave the order, "Fire!"

Instantaneously, the first two enemy escort vehicles disintegrated from direct projectile hits. The third careened off the tunnel wall and flipped on its back. Total mayhem ensued.

Automatic gunfire filled the tunnel in both directions around the bend. The few enemy survivors shot back in the dark.

Four men got out of the ten-wheel truck's cabin and fired machine guns toward Stansfield's end of the tunnel.

Claudia used an M110 sniper rifle with a night sight to neutralize all of them within fifteen seconds.

By 4:19 AM, the fight was over. Stansfield and his team approached the AZEV cargo truck at the bend in the road. The cargo's protective steel container had not been penetrated by gunfire. The mission was a complete success.

"Call in the disposal team, Tucker!" commanded Stansfield, after exiting A36. "Get me Mitrano on the line, Claudia!"

"I won't have to, Julius!" shouted Claudia above the noise of a helicopter's engine and rotor blades.

She pointed to the transport copter which had just landed next to the highway. Three men dressed in plain clothes suits had fanned out in front of CIA Director Joe Mitrano. More men followed them out. They all carried machine guns.

The director called over Stansfield with a wave of his hand. He walked away from the loud roar of the helicopter.

"Good job, Julius!" shouted the director.

"Thank you, Sir!"

Mitrano motioned for Stansfield to walk with him into the tunnel opening. The ambient noise lessened.

"I don't want you or your people to approach that truck. It's dangerous," said the director.

A squad of men, dressed in black hazmat suits, raced from a second helicopter which had just landed. Mitrano's guards stood around the truck with their machine guns prepped.

"Director, we had a red-tagged 'Undisclosable' at the castle. I never got follow-up ID on him," said Julius Stansfield.

"You didn't and you won't, Captain," said Mitrano. "Everything and every bit of information in our business is on a 'need to know' basis, Julius. And the only things you need to know are the things I tell you. All other data is irrelevant. Do you understand, Captain?"

"Yes, Sir. I understand."

"I would love to tell you that your mission is complete, Julius, but I can't. At this time, the *Katarina* is motoring down the Rhine towards Koblenz. Your brother, Michael, on the *Conqueror* just passed Wiesbaden a half-hour ago on his way to intercept the *Katarina* at Lorely Rock, forty miles further north.

"My helicopter is going to get your team onto the *Katarina* after it's slowed down by your brother. We're going to try to recover the rest of the AZEV cargo intact if we can. If unable to do so, we will extract you from the ship before sinking her into the Rhine.

"Two German military attack copters will escort you in and provide cover fire while you rope down onto the ship. You will not engage until after Michael initiates contact at dawn. We have a friendly on the *Katarina* who will guide you to the cargo, once on board. Secure the cargo and don't mess with it. Our support teams will take over from there."

Michael Stansfield and his ship, *Conqueror of Worlds*, had stopped briefly in Wiesbaden, twenty-four miles west of Frankfurt. The ancient Roman fort town, established in 6 AD, stood on the right northern bank of the Rhine River below the confluence with the Main.

After Hickory's death, Michael had gently washed his noble friend's body and prepared him for transfer to American authorities in Wiesbaden. He placed Jimmy's US Naval officer insignia on his shirt collar and his Annapolis graduation ring on his right hand. He combed Hickory's red hair in his usual neat manner. Tom Garfield and Peter Reynolds had joined Michael in singing two of Hickory's favorite hymns from his days as a cadet at Annapolis. It had been a very painful and moving experience for the crew of the *Conqueror*, but particularly so for Michael Stansfield.

After saying his final goodbyes to Hickory, Michael quietly ordered Basha and Jakub Krol to summon Dr. Thomas Egan for a meeting in the ship's galley. Michael waited at the kitchen table for the doctor to arrive.

A short time later, Egan entered the galley.

"Get a beer, Doc, and get me one too. I need it. It's been a long night for all of us."

Egan opened the refrigerator and reached with his right hand for the beers. Stansfield watched him closely. Michael saw an interesting tattoo on the doctor's wrist.

"Come and sit with me, Egan. Let's talk for a while."

Thomas Egan smiled nervously and said, "Sure, Michael. It's good for you to vent after what happened to your friend. Let's talk."

"You're a very dedicated man, Egan."

"What do you mean, Mike?"

"A man of your education with a doctorate in science can make a lot of money in the private sector. Universities and pharmaceutical companies pay their doctors very well. And you certainly don't have any of the risks of dying for your country. You work a few years in a lab somewhere, earn your money, and retire into the sunset after making your contributions to science. Making money in a safe and noble cause isn't so bad, Egan. It's a wonderful life.

"It takes a great man of ideals and principles to give all that up, and instead, labor secretly for the CIA in defense of America. I respect your call to duty for your country. It is very noble of you. You have selfless devotion for the United States. I honor your sacrifice, Egan."

"Thank you, Mike. I appreciate your feelings," said a more comfortable Egan, sipping his beer.

"That's an interesting tattoo on your wrist, Doc."

The doctor stretched his right arm to the side and laughed.

"Yeah! After a night of drinking in Borneo, I had some Indonesian girl stitch this into my wrist.

"I had just broken up with a girlfriend back in the States, and I was a little bummed out about it," grinned Egan.

"It's very cute, Doc. Let me see it up close," smiled Stansfield.

Egan extended his arm across the table to Stansfield.

"Oh! How nice..... A red heart with her initials, 'BS', in black," said Michael, trying to remain composed.

"It seems she stole your heart and then broke it. What was the girl's name, Doc?"

"Brittany Smith is her name," responded Egan. "She's from my hometown in Indiana. She certainly screwed me over. The 'BS' could just as well stand for 'Bullshit', I guess," laughed Egan, staring at the tattoo.

"Yeah! I know what you mean, Doc..... We've all been fucked over by a girl at least once in our lives," expressed Stansfield. "It does feel like bullshit, doesn't it, Doc?"

"Yeah, it does, Michael. Bullshit is about all her and I ever spoke about," added Egan.

Under the table, Michael reached down and pulled his .38 revolver from his ankle holster. He brought the snub-nose up, level with Egan's belly. He looked at the doctor across the table and grinned widely.

"What's going on, Michael?" asked Egan, somewhat nervously again.

"What do you mean, Doc?"

"Well, you called for me to come and speak with you. Basha said it was important. And all you seem interested in is my tattoo. I just find it a little weird, that's all."

"I was just thinking, Egan. Perhaps, you're not as noble as it seems. Maybe there's no Brittany Smith. Maybe it truly is all 'bullshit'.

"The 'BS' may stand for something else. Couldn't it, Egan? Like perhaps, 'Black Scorpions'."

Thomas Egan froze in his chair. After a few seconds of mental analysis, he reached for his waist with his right hand.

"I wouldn't do that, Egan, if I were you," calmly said Stansfield. "I'm very good at shooting people's balls off under kitchen tables. My accuracy astounds me. I'll usually take both balls without touching the dick. It's quite a challenge to shoot off balls without at least nicking the dick. Pin-point precision is the key, Egan. Also, practice makes perfect, I think. I certainly have had a lot of practice. I have quite a collection of balls from the four corners of the earth. I have them in black and brown, yellow, red, white, and even blue. I think I've shot off balls on just about every continent, except for Australia and Antarctica. So if you're smart, Egan, save yourself the embarrassment of having yours blown off on the Rhine. Keep your fucking hands flat on the table!"

Egan didn't say a word. He placed both his hands on the kitchen table in front of Stansfield. Both men stared into each other's eyes.

"So you really never found the Black Scorpion pin on the ground in Ibutu, did you, Egan? And you passed that information to me only to see if I knew anything about the Black Scorpions. You wanted to see if I was aware of their involvement in this caper on America.

"You worked previously at the virology labs at Fort Detrick. You were probably involved in transferring the AZEV to the Russians. You got away with it, mother-fucker. Your ruse must have been expertly planned in order to deceive all the smart people at the CIA. You're one smart bitch, Egan.

"You know, Doc, it doesn't surprise me one bit that the crazies in the Black Scorpions are involved in this action against my country. I worked with these maniac secret black-op dudes in Libya, Syria, Pakistan, and Iran. I have no doubt they're bad-asses. I saw them kill many enemy combatants.

"Some of the Scorpions were okay. You could still rea-son with a few. But the sensible ones didn't last very long in the field. They may have been picked off by their own men. The majority were rabid fanatics without command structure. They seemed to enjoy the killing. They were marauders without a code of ethics in battle.

"Half the times, they were scorched out on heroin. In Pakistan, practically all of them were dope addicts. It led to several frenzied actions which hurt our position there.

"I never fucked with those guys. I thought they were all wacko. In my opinion, they could do the ugly things they did because they were out of their minds, most of the times.

"I never figured out how America lost control of these dudes. How did we allow a unit like this to exist? I mean, who had responsibility for these guys?

"I understand better than most how cruel war is and must be, but I couldn't have approved of the things I saw these guys do. I saw entire villages wiped out in retribution. Little children, Egan, with their brains blown out. Women raped and dismembered. Men decapitated and eviscerated. They became morally worse than the enemy. No..... We lost control of these guys. I saw it with my own eyes.....

"It doesn't surprise me the Black Scorpions are fighting for a more radical America, a fascist America. I think my country held on to the Scorpions too long. It makes all the sense in the world that they've turned around to bite us in the ass. I always considered them more foe than friend. I never imagined them on my side in the first place.

"Maybe now, with America's back to the wall, the 'good' Scorpions will take out the 'bad' before it's too late. Perhaps, they can make-up for all the wrongs of the past. I sure hope so.....

"I do have three questions for you, Egan. To start, in Belgrade when we were ambushed, did you set us up?"

Egan laughed out loud. "Come on, Mike! You're not a dumb bastard like all the others. Of course, I set you up. I killed Jasna Andric also. I needed to slow down the operation. It was moving too fast, Mike."

"How about the rocket you fired, Egan, at the FNNP patrol boat on the Main? You took them out in a flash."

Egan smiled and answered coldly, "I needed to look like one of the 'good guys'. Sometimes you have to kill a few of your own to stay in disguise."

"Did you set us up for attack outside of Schweinfurt, Egan?"

"I most certainly did, Stansfield. It was my duty for the 'New American Fascist Movement' to slow down or stop your ship. We want the AZEV to reach America. A catastrophe at home will allow us to take control of the government. We want to re-Americanize our people. Forget this 'Globalist' shit. We want the 'American identity' and our jobs back.

"Fuck Europe and the Middle East, China and Russia too. We don't want our troops scattered all over the goddam world protecting everybody's rights except our own. We're all tired of dying for other people's flags. Screw the world. Let them all figure it out on their own.

"Do I really give a shit if a black African starves? Or if a yellow-belly dies of disease in China? Do we really want our boys to intervene in the 'rag-head' sectarian wars of the Middle East, or the 'spic' civil wars in Latin America? Do we always have to protect Israel's ass?

"And how about America's responsibilities to promote democracy around the world? That's all a bag of shit, Stansfield. Should we really care if dictators in the crap countries of Asia or Africa kill their own people? Or if Russia crumbles economically under the weight of poor government? I don't give a damn about anybody or any country, unless they speak English as their primary language. Fuck everybody, except the true Americans."

"You are one dumb mother-fucker, Egan! You're so small it's almost a waste of ammunition for me to put a .38 round into you. God help our country with people like you alive. You make me sick!"

"So, what are you going to do with me, CIA man?" asked Egan, sarcastically.

"I'm going to kill you. I'm going to first blow your balls off, because I don't think you deserve them. Then, I'm going to place a bullet into your brain. When you're dead, I'll toss your rancid body into the Rhine. You don't deserve to be buried in America. I don't wish for our soil to be poisoned by the stinking presence of your corpse.

"You know, Egan, your ambush at Schweinfurt claimed my good friend's life. But what Jimmy told me before dying, induced me to think a bit about your role on this ship. It all became clear to me. You were a Black Scorpion turned against our country. If allowed, you would have killed all of us.

"In a very real way, Jimmy saved our lives so we could save America and the world. And also, he condemned you to death."

Michael Stansfield fired his gun under the table. Egan fell off his chair in pain. Michael walked over and stood looking down on the doctor. He fired one more round into Egan's brain.

After leaving Wiesbaden, Stansfield opened up the *Conqueror's* engines and sped toward Lorely Rock and his appointment with the *Katarina*. He planned to meet up with the enemy on schedule as light broke at 5:30 AM.

Michael raised a large American flag to halfway up the ship's mast and sat on the *Conqueror's* deck staring up at the stars in the night sky. He put on the earphones to his music player and listened to his father's favorite operatic choral piece, "Vesperae de Dominica K.321 Laudate Dominum", by Wolfgang Amadeus Mozart.

Looking up, Michael found the night sky's brightest star, *Sirius*. With Mozart's music playing in his ears, he remembered back to his youth and an unforgettable incident with his loving father while living in Virginia.

One night after another of his famous fights with his older brother, Julius, the admiral had sent the boys outside to sit quietly and look up at the stars. As usual, both brothers had chosen different corners of the backyard. A few moments later, the admiral had stepped out and sat next to Michael on the cool backyard grass.

"Do you see that bright star up there, Michael?" asked his father. "Look at it closely. That's *Sirius*, always the brightest star in the night sky. It's very far away. Although it's many times bigger than our sun, it looks small because of its great distance.

"Pretend your brother, Julius, was sent to the far side of that star and you couldn't ever see him again. How would you feel, Michael?" asked his father.

The eight year-old Michael began to cry. Admiral Stansfield embraced his son and told him, "Now you've thought of how it would feel to lose your brother. No more fights, Michael, only love."

The admiral kissed his son's forehead and stepped back into the house. A few minutes later, Mozart's beautiful choral piece began to play inside their home. Michael got up and went to lie on the grass next to his brother. They never fought with each other again.

CHAPTER 23

The Costs of Freedom

From the cold soil of my tomb, I see the white cross only bears my name. I do not see mention of my life on the marble. Where are the hopes and dreams I had? Where are the songs I sang, and the poems I read? Where are my laughs and sorrows? Where is my love?

I gave my life for an ideal, a wish of peace and justice for all. I was young and desiring of a long and good presence in this world. I had things I wanted to do, places I anticipated to see, people I yearned to know. What happened?

I am surrounded by my brothers. They all feel the same as I. Remember our lives, not only our names. It is in our living where the sanctity lies.

The romantic Upper Middle Rhine River flows north towards Koblenz, creating a deep gorge through a fertile vineyard-filled green valley. Strategically positioned high above the river along its course, like sentinels on watch, stand more than thirty medieval castles. Although many of the castles are in ruins, they provide an ancient perspective on the rich cultural heritage of this land.

Germany is a country of great contradictions. Many of the world's most magnificent minds have claimed her as their homeland, but so too have some of history's most nefarious characters. Good and evil forces were again at work in this beautiful country, and they would face off here below the sentinels of the Rhine.

Lorely Rock, a 400-foot tall geologic formation, soars above the Rhine River's eastern bank near the town of St. Goarshausen, 25 miles south of Koblenz. Across the rock on the western bank stands the sister town of St. Goar. Lorely Rock marks the narrowest and deepest part of the Rhine. Wickedly strong currents in the 390-foot wide channel, and the occasional apparition of a beautiful seductive mythological feminine water spirit maiden, have historically caused many ship accidents and sinkings along Lorely Rock.

The *Katarina* had taken the bend in the Rhine River, 15 miles west of Wiesbaden, and was now only 23 miles south of the approaches to Lorely Rock. She would pass by the Rhine's most famous natural landmark and proceed another 300 miles to Rotterdam on the North Sea coast of Holland. Her mission was almost complete. Escorted by two smaller clandestine FNNP river boats, all her men were on high alert after being informed of the attack on the AZEV cargo caravan to Bremerhaven.

The pre-dawn morning was cool, and the dark cloud-less sky was full of bright stars. Ivan Petrenko and Pavlo Mitnick smoked cigarettes on the top deck of the *Katarina*. Like the other men on the ship, both of them were fully armed with a high capacity 9 mm pistol and an automatic assault rifle.

"Tell me, Pavlo, do you really feel all the things you told me the other night?" asked Petrenko cautiously. "Do you really believe I've chosen poorly? That my decision to align the Ukraine's future with the FNNP and the GPNR is incorrect? That we should rather side with America and fight for our freedom?

"If you, Pavlo, truly believe these things, and you are still here with me on this ship, it means you are here to prevent the success of this mission. Is that not so?

"It means to me you are working with the Americans, Pavlo. That is the logical conclusion I must draw. Why else would you be here?

"I seem to have many more questions than answers, Pavlo. It reminds me of when I was your student. There was so much I wanted to learn.

"I searched for answers of why cultures prospered or died. I wanted to understand why nations became brutally expansionist and destroyed other nations. Why was war the central theme of man's existence?

"I studied the mass genocides of world history. I researched the destruction of the aboriginal peoples of the Americas by the European settlers, Tsarist Russia's extermination of the Circassians of the Caucasus in the 19th century, the Armenian Genocide by the Ottoman Turks in the early 20th century, the murder of millions of Chinese by Japan's Imperial Forces and the horror of the

Jewish Holocaust by the Nazis in World War Two, Mao's killing of his own people in Communist China, and the more recent genocides in Africa and the Balkans.

"Mass murder as foreign policy has been committed by many nations throughout history. The 20th century was cataclysmic. Years ago, our country suffered greatly at the hands of the Germans and Russians. We, as Ukrainians, understand fully well the terror inflicted on innocents.

"The murderers know who they are. Few of them admit to it, but the evidence speaks for itself.

"I appreciate your concerns, Pavlo. Perhaps, I have chosen poorly. It appears I have not absorbed all of your wisdom."

Pavlo Mitnick did not speak. He continued to smoke his cigarette and stare into the cosmos. Several minutes of silence passed.

"I love you like a younger brother, Ivan," said Mitnick. "You are a brilliant man who has gone off course. I don't understand this, Ivan. How can a man of your intellect believe the Ukraine's future is in better hands with the Germans and Russians? I don't understand this thinking. It is irrational and irresponsible. And you have not been either of those two things in the past.

"You are not a fascist terrorist, Ivan. You are a freedom fighter. You want the best for your country but you don't know how to achieve it, my dear friend. You have been long on knowledge and short on wisdom. You have also been short on courage to recognize your illogical position.

"Circumstances have drawn you into a corner, and you don't know how to free yourself. History is full of great men and women who committed similar mistakes. They are all described as sources of calamity and social injustice. Most of them paid for their errors by dying in their misdirected cause. If you live by the sword, Ivan, then you will die by the sword. Making a pact with the Devil is not the answer," pleaded Mitnick.

Petrenko put his hands on Mitnick's shoulders. He looked into his eyes and said, "You are working with the Americans, Pavlo.....

"I have always looked up to you like the father I never had. I have trusted you with my life since I became a man, Pavlo. You have always been a beacon in the fog of doubt, a light in the dark night.

"Is it too late for me to join you in this fight? Is it too late to change course for the freedom of our people, Pavlo?"

"It is never too late to fight for freedom, my friend. The call of Liberty's bugle always sounds for those who listen," answered Mitnick. "Follow my lead and I will show you the way."

Aleksei Batkin and Captain Konrad Wagner had their men prepared for combat. Heavy machine gun and shoulder fired surface to air missile teams had been scattered across the deck of the *Katarina* in hidden and protected positions. The two smaller escort boats were also on high alert and ready for action. It would take them another day to reach Rotterdam, but they expected to be confronted before then.

FNNP agents on land along the Rhine were instructed to defend the river convoy at all costs. Significant elements of the German Air Force had gone to their side after the killings of Leopold and Manfred Fuchs at Totenkopf Castle. Wagner had been promised air cover over the Rhine to the North Sea.

The German Army and BND still aligned with America. They had surrounded several Luftwaffe bases in the

Rhineland region and were preparing to enter them under force of arms.

US Air Force bases in Holland, Belgium, France, and Italy had gone on high alert. The Pentagon promised the German government control of the air space over Germany if the rebellious Luftwaffe put planes into the sky.

Russia massed several hundred thousand troops along her borders with Estonia, Latvia, Lithuania, and Poland. Six mechanized and three armored divisions entered into western Ukraine in support of two Spetsnaz paratroop spe-cial-op divisions setting up along the borders with Poland, Slovakia, Hungary, and Romania. The Russian Air Force was put on alert. The Russian fleet at Sevastopol prepared to leave port and enter the Mediterranean. The Baltic Fleet at Kaliningrad readied to leave their base in the Russian exclave lying between Poland and Lithuania, and sail into the North Sea.

America raised the ready status of her remaining bases in Eastern and Central Europe. The Pentagon still held confidence that the CIA, German Federal Intelligence Service (BND), and the German government would stop the *Katarina* in the Rhine and put an end to this sad chapter in German post-World War Two history. Taking the FNNP out of the European fascist movement would destabilize it and stop its political growth. The GPNR in Russia would begin to die.

With the *Conqueror of Worlds* prepared for battle as she approached her appointment with destiny at Lorely Rock, Michael Stansfield mentally checked his ready list in the ship's pilot house. Dawn had not broken, and the Rhine River was lit only by starlight.

Veronika Boroshkova came up the stairs and asked permission to sit awhile with Stansfield. She appeared peaceful and serene.

"Your calmness and poise are beautiful to watch, Veronika. You relax me," said Michael from behind the wheel of the ship.

"Believe me, Michael, I feel at peace. I know fate and destiny are on our side. Perhaps, how one sees the world depends on the purity of ideals. When one feels just in a cause, and she has given all her energies to it, the soul rests in an unmatched state of freedom and tranquility. You see simply what I am."

"I am sorry for dragging you along, Veronika. Your mission should have ended in the Crimea. Your job was to guide me at the docks of Sevastopol. It was not to fight the Fascists in Europe on a long dangerous mission. Your service to the CIA will be rewarded."

"As a Ukrainian, I have much to fight for, Michael. The existence of my people is in play. In a raging storm, you can not always choose to run with the wind. At times, you must run against it to survive. Having the privilege and ability to fight is enough reward for me.

"My job was not only to guide you in the Crimea, Michael. It was to assist you in performing your duties in the service of freedom. All my knowledge and energies were to be available at your request. The responsibilities of an agent are open-ended. Circumstances determine our involvement. Degrees of danger and risk were not factors in deciding to help you or not. We both have the same goals. Both you and I wish for more civility in this world. We wish to extract hope from the jaws of doom. We wish to see rainbows after the thunder and lightning, not the destruction of innocent human life.

"No..... You must not apologize for bringing me onto this ship. I am honored for having been invited. I am not scared, Michael. I am fully prepared to die, if I know my actions will aid the cause of justice. I have faith in your leadership, and I am proud to serve with you."

Michael smiled and thanked Veronika for her brave service. He was very appreciative of her help.

"Do you have a wife, Michael?" she asked, returning the smile.

"I have a wife and young son. She is Iranian. She too struggled for freedom in her land of birth. I understand completely the emotions involved for a woman. I praise her strength every day."

"She must be proud of you, Michael, for risking all you have with her. I sense you love her and your son very much. I see it in your smile as you speak of them. You are a great man, and she is a great woman. Your son is fortunate to have such a gift. I will pray for all of you."

Veronika Boroshkova left Michael alone in the pilot house of the *Conqueror*. He looked downstream into the darkness of the Rhine. He thought of Nasrin and Alexander. He had not seen them in nearly a month. His love for his family had only strengthened with their separation. Michael wondered of how unfair it would be to them if he never made it back. The "costs of freedom", he thought.

Michael pulled from his pocket the letter his father had written to his family a year earlier, just hours before the Battle of Taiwan. When the admiral arrived on the *USS Ronald Reagan* after being rescued from two days on a lifeboat in the Philippine Sea, he was dehydrated to the point of delirium. The medical staff on the *Reagan* had stripped his clothes while they emergently attended to him. The doctors found the letter in a water-proof plastic envelope in the admiral's pants pocket. The Captain of the *Reagan*, an old friend of his father, saved the letter for the Stansfield family and passed it on to the Pentagon. It was discovered on the admiral's desk in his office, two days after his untimely death.

Believing he could perish in the expected Chinese air and sea assault on his command and control ship, the *Ocala*, Admiral Julian Stansfield had written a letter to his four children. It was to be read only after his death. It eventually was - six weeks after the Battle of Taiwan.

Michael Stansfield always carried the letter on him. It was still pristine in its plastic water-proof envelope. He slowly read its beautiful prose, expressing the deep love the admiral had for his children and their late mother, Olivia. The letter ended with the following reflection: *"Remember always the costs of freedom. Your mother taught me these costs long ago. Always believe in America. It is truly the best nation the world has given. Let it live on for the betterment of mankind and let us always do the most we can to preserve her in her original beauty."*

Michael Stansfield prepared for battle. He remembered the lessons of Leonidas and *Achilles*. He whispered prayers for his mother and father. He thought of the courage of his brothers, Julius and Mark. He thought of the sacrifice and devotion of Jimmy Calhoun. And he said, "I love you," to Nasrin and Alexander.

Michael looked up to the stars and then pushed the *Conqueror's* throttle speed control to its limit. Dawn broke over the Rhine, and his target was only fifteen minutes away. He would not be late for destiny.

CHAPTER 24

Purity of Purpose

I will be in every heartbeat, and in every breath you take. I will never leave you. I will shine for you for always. Unlike the sun and the moon who abandon you regularly, my light will be in you forevermore, keeping your soul warm with love eternally.

We will never cease to be special, you and I. For where there is such love, the energy never dies. It keeps burning without end. It is a cosmic force unlike any other.

It is extraordinary, yet so simple. Although stronger than the power of the universe, it can be contained in a kiss, an embrace, a gentle thought, a loving whisper or look.

You are my love in this world, and in any other world that awaits us. Of that, I am certain.

Julius Stansfield sat inside a German Army transport helicopter while it flew south along the Rhine toward Lorely Rock. His team was only five minutes away from contact with the *Katarina*. They were escorted by two "Tiger" attack helicopters.

Julius fastened the chin-strap of his combat helmet. He counted the four grenades on his military vest and charged his assault rifle. He prepared mentally for the high risk boarding of the enemy ship.

This was a first for him. He had never stormed a ship on the water from above. Frankly, he didn't know what to expect.

Julius thought of his life. Was he satisfied with it if it all ended on the Rhine in a flash of light and smoke? If he was to die today, had he accomplished all the things he needed to?

Julius thought of his two young daughters and the failure of his marriage. Where had he gone wrong with Sandra? Why had she not been faithful to his love? Could anyone be truly blamed? Had he been gone from home too long? Had duty to country eroded his duty to his wife? How could Sandra have fallen out of love with him? All these questions passed through his mind as the rhythmic sounds of the copter's blades echoed off the slate rock cliff walls of the Rhine River canyon and ricocheted back into the transport cabin.

Julius looked out over the Rhineland countryside. To Stansfield's eyes, the "heroic" Rhine's romantic ancient castles seemed quiet but poised for battle in the shadows of early morning. Their hard masonry appeared as prepared for war as Stansfield's team.

He watched the eastern sunrise awaken the tiny villages and the vast fields of grape. Another day was beginning in the valley. In all of God's beauty, Julius whispered to himself, "Expect the unexpected."

His father would frequently repeat this phrase to him and his brothers. The admiral wanted his sons to be alert at all times. It was always better to be expectant than surprised. Counter-attack was easier when prepared. The philosophy had become part of Julius' sense of being.

Julius remembered the remarkable nature of his parents, and how they had remained in love all their lives. There was an amazing energy between them which only intensified with time. He would not live this experience, he thought.

What a lady, Olivia had been - devoted daughter, loving wife and mother. She had always stressed to her children the concept of "Purity of Purpose". She believed strongly in keeping the intentions of goals virtuous and emotionally pure. Accomplishments would thus have more significance. She felt it was a key component of her family's creed, "American Amaranth".

Growing up, the Stansfield children understood the "Purity of Purpose" in their ancestors. Their great grandfather - Raul Sierra - had fought for the independence of his homeland, Cuba. Both grandfathers - Dr. Robert Stansfield as an American combat surgeon in Italy during World War Two, and Jorge Sierra, executed as a freedom fighter in the Cuban Revolution - had sacrificed deeply for their countries. Indeed, their father had worked his entire adult life to preserve America's freedom. Selfless dedication to liberty ran in all their veins. They were all patriots with "Purity of Purpose".

Olivia fought just as hard to keep America free. She taught and raised her children to be honorable human beings. This had been her greatest gift to them. It was her legacy.

A red light came on inside the cabin of the helicopter. Julius knew visual contact with the enemy had been made. They were now "hot".

Julius looked across at Claudia. She stared back at him. Their eyes locked intensely with each other. All fear seemed to evaporate away in an instant. The presence of the moment took over. The emotional release was familiar to Julius. Dreadful alarm would always build up to the moment of attack. Then, like a mystical reprieve from the gods of war, apprehension would disappear from consciousness. The mind tightly focused on the task at hand. With the sound of his rapidly beating heart in his head, trepidation was drowned out. He was ready for battle.

The Tigers swept low on the Rhine at 175mph and fired their Hellfire missiles at the enemy. The *Katarina* and her escort boats shot back from 2000 feet away. The German choppers continued over their targets, attacking with their 30mm cannons. Red hot metal flew in both directions. Geysers of water from the Rhine erupted from explosions. The serene silence of the early morning had vanished. The Rhineland frenzied with the convulsions of martial fire.

The transport helicopter passed safely behind Lorely Rock, protected from enemy shooting. The Tigers continued to make runs over the enemy ships for several minutes.

On the Rhine, the *Conqueror* maneuvered along the *Katarina*. Michael Stansfield swept the pirate ship with his 30mm cannon. He directed heavy machine gun fire and multiple Javelins at the other two enemy ships. Two small torpedoes from the *Conqueror* destroyed the *Katarina's* propellers at her stern. The enemy was stopped in the water channel at the base of Lorely Rock.

Like a scene from an ancient battle on the sea, red tracers and balls of fiery black smoke filled the space between the fighting ships. Visibility through the medium became obscured.

"Do not stop shooting!" shouted Michael Stansfield to his crew. "Pour it into them! Keep firing until the decks are quiet!"

The Tigers blew out the bridge of the *Katarina*, killing Aleksei Batkin and Feodor Dashkov. Wagner shot two surface-to-air missiles at one of the Tigers but missed both times. Men on the *Katarina* fired RPGs at the *Conqueror*, hitting her bow and killing Basha Ludwik.

From the north, three German Luftwaffe Typhoons flew over the *Conqueror* and fired Iris-T air-to-air missiles at Mach 3 speed. Both Tigers were destroyed in gigantic explosions. Their debris fell into the Rhine a few hundred feet from Michael Stansfield's ship. One of the Typhoons dropped a 500 pound bomb over the *Conqueror* but missed.

"Give me your Stinger, Veronika!" yelled Stansfield.

She passed the rocket launcher to Michael. He steadied himself against the *Conqueror*'s railing and fired a salvo at the trailing Typhoon. He caught the Euro-fighter squarely, disintegrating it.

Flying low from the south, two American F-15 Eagles maneuvered through the Rhine Gorge. They appeared out of nowhere and fired multiple Sidewinder missiles at the remaining Typhoons, destroying both of them. One of the Typhoons exploded on impact after falling into the town of St. Goar. The other crashed into Lorely Rock, sending debris down into the Rhine.

The F-15s made a return pass. They dropped guided munitions on the escort ships, sinking them in a hurry.

The *Conqueror* and the *Katarina* continued to exchange fire across the Rhine. Several men on the deck of the enemy ship were caught by a Javelin missile explosion and were dismembered on the spot. Michael Stansfield's 30mm gun continued to spray rounds onto the deck of the *Katarina*.

The F-15s passed rapidly over the *Katarina* and fired their 20mm six-barreled Gatling guns from bow to stern. Konrad Wagner, exposed on the deck of the ship, was cut in half.

Jakub Krol received a direct hit from a heavy machine gun on the *Katarina* and fell dead into the Rhine. Peter Reynolds was killed by another RPG hit on the *Conqueror's* bow.

Only Michael Stansfield, Veronika Boroshkova, Tom Garfield, and Bruno Bonnet remained alive on the smoking *Conqueror*. Bonnet was flat on his belly behind sandbags. He carefully picked targets through his scope and fired his bolt action sniper rifle across the Rhine. Each pull of the trigger killed an enemy combatant on the *Katarina*. For twenty minutes of hellacious activity, the Frenchman had performed his specialty many times. The deck of the *Katarina* was littered with his accurate results.

The F-15s continued to strafe the *Katarina* until they emptied their Gatling guns of bullets. Two F-16 Fighting Falcons replaced them, firing three Maverick 125-pound penetrating blast-fragmentation warheads into the *Katarina*. The enemy ship sat on the Rhine ablaze but miraculously still afloat. There were no signs of life on its deck. Michael Stansfield held his fire on the *Conqueror*.

The German transport helicopter hovered over the *Katarina* and released two ropes onto its deck. Julius Stansfield, Claudia, Peter Tucker, and the rest of the CIA team quickly dropped down and went into action. No enemy fire was encountered.

Veronika Boroshkova grabbed Michael's binoculars to look at the scene. The gray and black smoke of battle had thinned. She had a clear view of the *Katarina* across the Rhine.

Veronika saw Pavlo Mitnick come up to meet Julius. The planted Ukrainian CIA operative directed the attack squad into the bowels of the enemy ship.

"My husband is your man on the *Katarina*, Michael," she said in a low voice. "He's the CIA contact. I lied to you on the Greek fishing trawler in the Black Sea. I am not divorced, nor childless. That man you saw guiding your people on the *Katarina* is my dear husband, the father of my four children."

Michael Stansfield did not speak. He nodded in respect.

A few moments later, heavy gunfire broke out below decks on the *Katarina*. Shouts could be heard along with the rattle of machine pistols.

"I must go, Michael! There is no time to waste!" yelled Veronika Boroshkova.

"We'll take the jet-skis!" hollered Michael.

They sped across the Rhine to the burning hulk of the enemy ship. Both armed with M4 assault rifles, they used a flashlight to see their way toward the firefight. They found it on the lower deck.

Automatic gunfire was concentrated in the ship's large galley area. Michael and Veronika crawled on their bellies into the smoke-filled room. Bullets whizzed over their heads. Veronika crawled over a dead Peter Tucker. Michael pushed aside the bodies of two more dead CIA men and continued moving deeper into the dark hall.

They found Julius and Claudia behind an overturned table. Mitnick and Petrenko were several feet away behind a stack of wooden food crates. All of them were firing their guns furiously towards the far end of the galley.

Andreas Fuchs and seven of his colleagues returned fire with their machine pistols. They were trapped in a corner of the hall.

The room was dark except for an emergency light on the ceiling above Fuchs' position. The smoke thickened from a fire in an adjacent room.

"Big Brother!" shouted Michael as he pulled up next to Julius.

"You keep on surprising me, Julius, showing up in the strangest goddam places!"

"I'm just following you into this mess, Michael!" retorted Julius.

Michael smiled and patted his brother on the back. "I'm always happy to have you with me, Big Brother."

Michael stared across in the dim light at Claudia and introduced himself. He then turned to his brother again and said, "We're in a helluva situation, Julius."

The gunfire from Fuchs' men was unrelenting as the smoke became heavier around them. The terrorists would need to make a move quickly before they suffocated.

"Our CIA partners over there, Julius, are pinned down behind the crates. They can't follow us out of here if we retreat. Besides, my partner, Veronika, is not going to abandon her husband in this hellhole."

"We don't have much more time, Michael," said Julius. "Smoke and fire inside ships don't lead to anything good. I estimate we have only ten more minutes to stage an end to this thing."

"We've got much less time than that, Julius. The enemy will be storming our position in less than two minutes. The smoke is heavier on their side. They need to get out soon or they'll die from smoke inhalation. The only way out is behind our position. They must get through us to survive. Okay, Big Brother, let's roll on this!

"Veronika and Claudia stay put! Keep your heads down and shoot low! They're coming right down our throats! Wait until they get close and you can see what you're shooting at!" shouted Michael.

Michael silently motioned to Petrenko and Mitnick to stay at their location. He alerted them of the coming strike.

The Stansfield brothers moved silently nearer to the enemy on the right side. They would have a close crossfire to terminate the terrorists before they reached the other CIA positions.

Seconds later, Fuchs and his men made their move. They charged across the hall with their guns blazing. There was a heavy barrage of bullets in all directions.

Julius tossed a stun grenade behind Fuchs. The concussive effect shocked Fuchs' men for an instant.

Petrenko and Mitnick charged forward toward the terrorists. The Stansfields attacked on the right flank. Fuchs and his men returned fire through the smoke, hitting both Petrenko and Mitnick.

Michael and Julius used their pistols to tangle with the remaining enemy at close quarters. The room went quiet fifteen seconds later.

Veronika Boroshkova ran to her husband, Pavlo Mitnick, lying in a pool of blood. Michael found Petrenko dead with a wound to his head.

"My dear Pavlo, you mustn't leave me! I love you too much for you to be taken from me! We don't deserve this!" cried Veronika.

She held her husband closely and whispered in his ear. Tears streamed down Veronika's face and onto Pavlo's cheeks and mouth. Pavlo smiled peacefully. With a trembling right hand, he wiped Veronika's tears from her eyes. Claudia, Julius, and Michael stood around them.

The fire in the adjacent room had died away. The smoke began to clear.

Choking on his own blood, Pavlo said, "My love, my life, you are the same as I first saw you. You are still the young beautiful ballerina skating on the ice in Kontraktova Square on a Christmas evening in our beloved Kiev.

"My eyes caught your ballet under the light of a bright full moon, dancing to the music of Pachelbel's Canon. Your beauty and elegance cleared the ice of people. We all wished to see you alone under the moon and music, such was the greatness of your being.

"Your hair flowed in the wind. The movements of your body were perfection. You were lost in the uniqueness of your moment.

"I sat there with everyone else and enjoyed you. I fell in love with you before even meeting. All the boys present fell in love with you. How could they have not?"

Pavlo Mitnick coughed up blood. He became more short of breath. His voice became weaker.

"What is your name, American?" asked Pavlo.

"Michael Stansfield."

"And you?" Pavlo asked, turning his head slightly towards Julius.

"Julius Stansfield."

"Oh! I see..... You are brothers. Two American brothers with strong names, fighting for freedom together. This is very inspiring to me," said Pavlo, struggling to breathe.

Pavlo Mitnick held his wife's hand and smiled at her. He turned again to Michael.

"Veronika and I have four sons. They are brothers also. We hold them in very high regard, just as your parents must revere both of you.

"Remember, Americans, 'Liberty' is a universal concept. No single people own the idea. It is an idea for all of mankind.

"Thank you both for protecting the love of my life. And thank you also for being so courageous in spirit. The world needs more of it," smiled Pavlo.

Pavlo squeezed Veronika's hand. He took a gasp of air.

"I always hoped to go before you, Veronika. I am not brave enough for you to leave me behind, alone. God has worked it out alright."

Pavlo took another gasp of air. He smiled gently at his wife.

"We did it, my love. We are where we always wished to be. We will see the glory, not the despair. You will live in hope, not in misery. We are free, just as I had promised. What more can I ask.

"Our sons will be free to think and create a better future for our homeland. It has been all worth it as I had dreamed.

"These are the costs of freedom, my love..... My purity of purpose..... Love our sons for both of us..... Remind them always that I will remain in every beat of their hearts and in every breath they take..... To you, I leave my soul. It has belonged to you since the beginning..... Now, please take my last breath away, extinguish my pain, and release me to the stars..... Amongst them, I will shine and wait for you," slowly whispered Pavlo.

A crying Veronika Boroshkova softly kissed her husband's lips. With her love, Pavlo Mitnick took his last breath and departed this world a "free man".

CHAPTER 25

Libertas Americana

I came upon the 'Black Dragon' in the forest. It had left its lair to confront my approach. Its armored dark hide and fanged teeth were ready for battle. Great wings created a perilous wind all around. Fire from its mouth scorched the earth in front of me.

I was to slay this evil beast with only my sword. I had neither armor nor shield. My size was small in comparison.

I maneuvered for position. I closed the distance with my enemy. When prepared to plunge my iron into its sinful heart, the dragon spoke to me.

"I am one of many beasts in this forest wishing to destroy you, 'White Knight'. Even if you kill me, there will be countless more coming to meet you. How will you battle with so many enemies as dangerous as I?"

"Courageously well," I answered.

"Are you not afraid, 'White Knight'?" asked the beast.

"I fear more the dragons inside of me than those I come to slay."

Michael Stansfield peered out a window of the C-17 transport plane bringing him home from Germany. It was a clear and bright early Sunday morning on June 25 in South Florida. The usual storm clouds of summer were absent. It would likely be a day of sunshine and no rain. How timely and appropriate, Michael thought.

He looked along the coastline of Key Biscayne while the plane descended towards Homestead Air Force Base, several miles to the southwest. The old Cape Florida Lighthouse stood tall in the sun. It casted no shadow so early in the morning.

Michael spotted his family home, only a few hundred feet to the north along a white sandy beach. He could see people near the shore behind his home. In his mind, they could be Nasrin and Alexander enjoying a morning together. But it was impossible to tell for sure.

The plane flew low over the expansive Biscayne Bay. The many small islets, rimmed in sand color, were clear to the eye. Dozens of boats created foamy white wake trails as they crisscrossed the deep blue. Near the islands, the shallower bay turned a beautiful shade of turquoise.

To Michael, the bay was warmly familiar. Its natural seascape held many fond memories. He had spent every summer of childhood playing in these waters. He was introduced to the sea on Biscayne Bay. Here, he had grown up to be a man. The sight of blue and green welcomed him home.

A few hours earlier, Michael had said goodbye to his brother at the US airfield in Wiesbaden. Julius and Claudia returned together to Lake Constance in Switzerland. The US Navy captain needed to clear his head for a while. He had much to think about. Windsurfing on Lake Constance with Claudia would help settle his mind.

Nasrin did not know of Michael's arrival this morning. He had kept it a secret. She liked surprises more than he did.

Nearly a month had passed. Michael desperately needed to see her and Alexander. His desire for Nasrin was extreme. He longed for her. He needed to make love to her. Leaving Nasrin again in the future seemed an impossibility. Michael sensed he had become too weak for that.

He had always been fearless, even as a child. But Michael had felt different on this mission. He thought, perhaps, he had lost his "edge". Maybe he wasn't the warrior he had been in the past. He asked himself whether he was still built for the job. Had his skills deteriorated? Could he still protect America as she deserved to be protected? Unusual for Michael, his mind was filled with more questions than answers.

Stansfield stepped off the C-17 at Homestead Air Force Base. He stopped on the tarmac to feel the warm Florida sun on his face. The humid breeze off the Atlantic Ocean felt good on his skin. Michael took in a deep breath of the salty air. He noted a scent of jasmine. The tall palm trees and tropical flowers around him were calming. He was back in America where he belonged. He had survived to see his family. Again, Michael had been one of the lucky ones. He was grateful.

As he walked to the terminal building, a caravan of four black Cadillac SUVs rushed towards him from the far side of the tarmac. It could only be Mitrano, thought Michael.

The third vehicle in line pulled up next to Stansfield and stopped. A man dressed in a dark suit, sitting in the front passenger seat, got off and politely invited Michael into the back of the Cadillac. Stansfield nodded and agreed to the inconvenience.

"It's nice to welcome you home, Michael," said CIA Director Joseph Mitrano. "Do you mind if I drive you to Key Biscayne?"

"Could I really say, no thanks?" questioned Stansfield, somewhat angrily.

"No, I guess you couldn't, Michael."

Mitrano ordered his driver to move. The caravan started towards the key.

Several minutes of silence ensued. Michael stared out his window, not paying much attention to the endless number of shops and strip malls along South Dixie Highway. Both men were lost in thought.

"I'm very sorry for the death of your dear friend, Jimmy Calhoun, Michael. He was a great patriot. He will be greatly missed by all of us.

"We're sorry also for the deaths of Reynolds, Mitnick, Krol, and Ludwik. They were all outstanding agents. They fought bravely for the cause of freedom and will never be forgotten."

The CIA director gently placed his right hand on Michael's shoulder. He ordered his driver to take his time through Coconut Grove.

"I really enjoy Coconut Grove," said Mitrano wistfully, looking out through his window at children roller-blading along Main Street. The sidewalks were full of artists painting on their canvases, and musicians playing their guitars.

Outdoor cafes and flower shops provided color and a warm ambiance.

"The times I visited your parents on the key, we'd always come to dinner here in the Grove. They loved this area very much, I remember. Although it's eclectic, and not for everyone, I certainly enjoyed my times here with Olivia and Julian. This place grows on you. I miss it very much."

Another pause of silence ensued. The men passed a park on the bay. Young people played tag football and soccer. Beyond them, there were countless sailboats on Biscayne Bay. Like an Impressionist painting, the bright-colored sails dotted the brilliant blue water backdrop. The purples, reds, greens, and yellows enlivened the senses.

"You would never know the world was falling apart. Would you, Michael?"

"No, you wouldn't, Sir. Everyone seems free and happy. Boys and girls doing their thing, I guess," softly answered, Michael.

"I reckon it's the way it's supposed to be - people living their lives freely. But there's a cost for all this. Isn't there, Michael?"

"Yes, there is, Sir..... I certainly can attest to that fact."

"I congratulate you for a job well done, Michael," continued Mitrano. "We were able to confiscate the entire AZEV cargo without having to sink it into the Rhine. The FNNP movement in Germany has been shut down. All three Fuchs brothers are dead. Wagner is dead.

"The Polish and Turkish intelligence directors are dead. The fascist movements in their respective countries have been destroyed.

"The GPNR's leaders - Brish, Batkin, and Dashkov are no longer with us. Their movement in Russia has been weakened.

"The Fascist Ukrainian Party's Ivan Petrenko is dead. It's fortunate he saw the light at the end. He fought bravely for us on the *Katarina*. That will never be forgotten. His legacy to his country will be one of freedom, not dishonor. We will make sure of that. Every nation needs its heroes.

"Today, Europe appears more peaceful and hopeful. It will be good for America and the rest of the world.

"Your brother, Julius, seems made for this line of work," added Mitrano. "His skills are sharp and nearly equal to yours when you began in this business. He barely had time to acclimate himself to his new role. He'll be an outstanding agent. I think his leadership qualities, developed in the submarine service, were essential to his success in the operation. We're very proud of him, Michael.

"Julius' interrogation of Leopold Fuchs revealed the Russian prime minister's role in the terror plot. I hadn't expected his involvement.

"We have already sent our condolences to the Kremlin for the recent sudden death of the prime minister from a heart attack. It's a shame. He was so young and energetic before his mishap. It goes to show how one should know their physical limitations before embarking on a jogging program. Always check with your doctor," smiled Mitrano.

"Julius also uncovered the Russian military's role in this plot. Changes have already been made and most of the offending officers have been 'retired'. We have been assured Mother Russia will name the new members of her high command next week," said the director.

"German Ambassador Albrecht Jager was the FNNP's spymaster in America. His recent suicide in Washington was surprising to most people. I never knew he suffered from depression and addiction to pain medications. The newspapers described the ambassador's 'delicate' personal situation. Apparently, his suicide note explained everything," smiled Mitrano.

"Before his 'suicide', the German disclosed to one of our agents the entire Turkish Muslim extremist terror network he coordinated inside the US. This network has now been retired," stated Mitrano.

"I would say *Operation Europa* was a complete success for the United States," the CIA director declared triumphantly. "You and Julius were both outstanding. Your work was critical in achieving all our goals in Europe. America and I commend you."

The SUV drove onto Key Biscayne. Michael Stansfield listened to Joe Mitrano's compliments. They were upsetting him.

Michael's thoughts wandered off to those who had lost their lives in the operation. He remembered Hickory's selfless devotion to America. His friend had a family legacy of courage and honor. The grandson of the old "Bastard from Boone" had given an equal last measure of his devotion to his country.

Michael thought of Veronika and Pavlo. He could physically sense their painful "costs of freedom" and "purity of purpose". His heart had ached with Veronika's as she took Pavlo's last breath away.

Michael thought back to Balaclava, and how he had been taken by surprise while viewing the "Valley of Death". He remembered the ambush in Belgrade and the attack on his team on the Main River near Schweinfurt. He had come close to paying his own "costs of freedom" several times on this mission. Michael believed all the surprise ambushes could have been prevented if only he had known the details of the operation. In retrospect, he had been blind to the most significant aspects of *Operation Europa*. Only his keen situational awareness had saved his life.

Michael returned from his haze and stared angrily at Mitrano. The director had been waiting patiently for the volcanic eruption. He opened himself to it.

"Go ahead, Michael. Feel free to ask the questions you need to find answers for. But remember, there are issues which must remain silent and unanswered. There can not be solutions to all the mysteries of men. In the national security of our great nation, there are things best kept quiet. In my position as Director of the CIA, I am as much a maker of mystery as I am a problem solver. My job demands me to create more questions than answers, at least in the minds of our enemies. Do you understand my role completely, Michael?"

"Yes, I do, Director. However, I feel I have earned your confidence. If I would have known what Jimmy Calhoun knew about the New American Fascist Movement, and that the AZEV was of American origin, perhaps I would have become aware of Egan's infiltration and betrayal sooner. Hick could have been alive here today with us. We were all bait, Director. I don't much appreciate that reality."

"My best agent in the field is never bait, Michael," said Mitrano with emphasis. "We allowed the information of your presence in the Crimea to pass on to Polish

Intelligence Director Pawlak. He was made to think others in our circle knew of your activities in Balaclava. In reality, Pawlak was the only one to know, outside of Calhoun, Admiral Culligan, and myself.

"I had always suspected Pawlak of having sympathies for the Fascists. I was right. When they came down on you in the Crimea, we instantly knew of Pawlak's double-cross. That allowed us to investigate further and uncover the rest of the political network in Europe and the United States. It helped reveal the entire organization. It also led us to discover their plans for a meeting at Totenkopf Castle, outside of Bamberg on the evening of June 20. There, we were able to neutralize their entire political leadership.

"Revealing your presence in the Crimea helped secure our success in the mission, Michael. I could have done that only with you. You are my only agent that could have survived that revelation.

"I could not have prevented the attacks on your team in Belgrade and Schweinfurt. Those were orchestrated by Egan. We did not know of his involvement with the New American Fascists and the Black Scorpions. The doctor outsmarted me. You were the one, Michael, who uncovered his betrayal of America. It is hard for me to believe you could have revealed Egan's activities any sooner. The only clue you had was his mention of the Black Scorpion pin from the Congo. At the time, you surmised the Black Scorpions were working on the mission for America as well. Any of us would have thought the same. To you, it was another unknown variable on a mission full of them.

"Let me back up for a moment and give you some history. What I am about to tell you is classified, TOP SECRET. Your skin is in the game, Michael.

"After the fall of the Soviet Union, America's Cold War ended. The military-industrial complex of the United States and our secret intelligence services suddenly had a great deal of time and money to re-appropriate. We thought of all the opportunities we had to better the world. We actually believed a new Pax Americana had dawned on our planet.

"By 1993, we realized titanic opposition would come our way. Islamic Fundamentalism grew to Global Jihad. The Chinese Communist war machine began to develop its expansionist ideology. There was a resurgence of Russian nationalism. A neo-Fascism was born in Russia and Europe.

"*Global Directive-93* was created by the union of secret think tanks at the White House, the Pentagon, the State Department, the CIA, and Corporate Wall Street. The directive ordered the commencement of a slow and organized 'Americanization' of global commerce and government. Free and fair trade under American tutelage would be conducted around the world. Free and fair government with 'rule of law' would be promoted everywhere. The American military would function as a fair enforcer of the doctrine. Slowly, a true Pax Americana would be born. A global peace with more prosperity for all nations would exist. Global wars would become extinct. The Earth would be for the 'Earthlings' and would not be allowed to divide itself over differences of culture, race, or religion. Eventually, national boundaries would disappear, and 'Peace on Earth' would exist eternally.

"Your father, Admiral Julian Stansfield, was chosen by the President of the United States to coordinate the initial stages of the directive. It was a very big job for a very big man. But he was the right choice.

"It was a well-intentioned plan. It began strongly. But the events of September 11, 2001, hijacked the directive. The military was given progressively more responsibility to carry the directive out. The economic debacle of 2008 led to further world-wide upheaval. Popular uprisings and civil wars propagated themselves in Asia, the Middle East, Africa, and Latin America. Global war ensued. Fascist governments began taking power in Europe. Radical Islamic Sunni terrorism had a resurgence. The world became a mess again.

"In the last few years, groups in America against the pure and ideologically peaceful doctrine of 'American Globalism' gained strength. American Socialists have tried to steer our government to the 'Left'. The 'Right' has slowly become radicalized into a loosely unified Fascist movement. These people do not wish for peaceful globalization.

"The 'Left' urges the rise of the underclasses and anarchy. Let the 'workers' of the world overthrow their corrupt leaders and establish a more 'just' communal system. They want 'Big Government' to control the people of our nation. They want to make all the decisions for us, as if we are too stupid to decide for ourselves. The Socialists buy the vote by granting easy money. They yoke the American populace with an ever increasing debt, unpayable by any standard. Economic imprisonment is what I call it.

"The 'Right' neglects the poor and the feeble. While they advocate personal freedoms and civic responsibility, they promote an 'American Identity' of racial, religious, and cultural superiority. To them, the global process threatens the 'old America'. They want an isolated America, unentangled by the problems of the world. They do not see a 'Unified World' as the only hope for humanity.

"*Global Directive 93* tries to steer in the middle. It has attempted to adopt the healthier aspects of the extreme points of view. It discarded the sicker and unjust ideologies. I believe your father did well in the plan's development. His aura of fair-mindedness and humane spirit was carefully chosen to direct our cause. After his death, the leadership of the directive was passed on to me.

"Over the past years, the directive has been under assault from the left and the right. It's been very difficult to maintain order in America's cause. Many hijacks have been tried. I sense America is more divided today than at any other time since the Civil War. Lincoln would be distraught with our present situation. All this information is important to understand *Operation Europa*, Michael.

"In the Congo, Jimmy Calhoun captured Colonel Asinus of the GPNR, and the German terrorist, Draker. The village of Ibutu was wiped out by AZEV. The CIA was aware of the AZEV recently taken from Fort Detrick in Maryland. My first concern was that the AZEV had been taken by the Russians. Very few of our people knew all these facts. Not even the Deputy Director of the CIA was informed of Ibutu.

"Through interrogation of Asinus and Draker by Calhoun in the Central African Republic, we came to realize the AZEV from Fort Detrick had been stolen by the New American Fascist Movement (NAFM). They had passed it to the Russians for use against American civilian population centers. In the mayhem of a bio-terror attack, the principals of the NAFM would take control of the American government in a coup. A cooperative between the European and American Fascists would be established. The Americans would be allowed domination of Central and South America. The Europeans would control Africa, the Middle East, and parts of Asia.

"While the FBI and CIA investigated the NAFM, I came to realize some members of the secret Black Scorpion Brigade had aligned themselves with the Fascists. I was the only one with that knowledge. Calhoun was unaware of the Black Scorpion involvement.

"Now, I know Egan was a NAFM operative. He was also working with the Black Scorpions in the Congo. A squad of Scorpions was in the jungle outside of Ibutu, waiting to ambush Calhoun's CIA team. They did not want us to make a connection of dots. There was a poor coordination of time by Egan, and the Scorpions left the swamps before Calhoun arrived at Ibutu.

"This guy, Egan, took us all by surprise. Only you figured it out, Michael. This last revelation blew the lid on their entire organization. We discovered two US senators, a congressman, several US generals and admirals, and six other CIA operatives working with Egan in the NAFM. In the last few days, all of them have met their deaths. You took Egan, and your brother eliminated the congressman in Bavaria. All the others had accidents inside the United States. The traitorous Scorpions were taken out by their loyal Scorpion brothers.

"So you see, Michael, I've had my hands full over the past month. This has been a complex mission. There were many unknowns at the beginning of it. But without your service to your country, the results of *Operation Europa* would have been very different. You and I, if still alive, would be doing a post-mortem on America. All of your father's struggles to keep our nation strong would have been lost forever.

"Keeping America alive is not an easy task. Even your father's great efforts and sacrifices met difficulty. Sustaining our country requires good minds and brave souls. Luckily, we have many of those in the CIA.

"Spy-work is a social science, Michael," declared Joe Mitrano, "and you are a scientist. No other human being I know could have gotten out of that jam in Balaclava. None would have seen the importance of the Black Scorpion pin. Only a master spy, a scientist, could have survived these predicaments.

"I had complete faith in your abilities. I never doubted for a moment your success. I have known you since you were born, Michael. You were made for this. You are truly a defender of freedom. You are America's greatest protector."

Michael looked out again through the darkly tinted bullet-proof window of the Cadillac. He stared without focus at the tall palm trees lining the road onto Key Biscayne Bridge. He was lost in his own mind.

As the SUV went onto the bridge over Biscayne Bay, Michael looked down at the reflected sunlight from the blue water below. The brightness of it hurt his eyes.

"Do you mind, Joe, if I open the window a bit? I just need to breathe the salt air," said Michael.

"This is America, Michael. The air is free to breathe here. It belongs to you."

Michael turned and smiled at Joe Mitrano. The two men understood each other very well.

"Did your father ever tell you about his solo sailing trip to New York City and the Statue of Liberty on his sixteenth birthday?" asked Mitrano.

"No, Sir, he didn't. He didn't speak of his youth frequently."

"Your father and I go way back, Michael. We graduated together from Annapolis more than four decades ago. We were close friends at the Academy.

"One day a few years back, while having drinks with your father at my farm in Maryland, Olivia and my wife left us alone in the study. We spent an hour talking of old times.

"I asked him why, as a young cadet, he would take a sloop out alone on the Chesapeake and sail for hours by himself. He looked at me straight in the face and said, 'To survive, Joe, to survive!'

"He went on to explain to me in detail the loss of his brother and father when he was only a young boy. He described the sadness he had felt so young in life.

"For his sixteenth birthday, shortly after the death of his father, Julian Stansfield asked his mother to allow him to sail the Great Lakes from Chicago to New York City. His loving mother allowed this to ease his pain.

"She gave him an envelope and told him not to open it until he arrived at the base of the Statue of Liberty. He followed her instructions.

"A few days later on a beautiful spring morning in New York, Julian arrived at his destination. He sat under the sun in his father's sailboat and opened the envelope. He found an old yellowed letter from his father, written to his widowed mother, from Rome, Italy, in June 1944.

"As you are well aware, your grandfather, Dr. Robert Stansfield, was a combat surgeon in America's Italian campaign against the Germans in World War Two. The letter to the doctor's mother described the hardships of saving lives as a surgeon in wartime. It expressed the despair of the young surgeon in trying to repair the damages inflicted on man by man. It spoke of the injustices of war, and the doctor's attempts to make amends for them.

"Although young himself, your father could sense the pain in the words on those pages. The letter's emotional tone moved your young father to tears.

"He confided in me he had sat for more than an hour on that sailboat, crying his heart out. He so missed his father.

"Julian's father took on heroic proportions after that day. Julian made a promise to his brother and father he would do great things with his life. He pledged he would become a naval officer of the United States, and vowed to protect and defend his country for the rest of his life.

"Afterward, sailing became a therapy for Julian to keep his mind at ease. Irrelevant of the water conditions, he was fearless on the seas. He felt closer to his brother and father when sailing alone. The US Navy became his home.

"Undeniably, a few years later, he met Olivia and his life changed forever. She became the joy of his existence, the reason of his being.

"Both your mother and father were unique people, Michael. I've never met two people who loved each other more. They made you envious of their love. It was a gift, they would say.

"It certainly was a gift they gave all of you. They gave their souls to their children."

Mitrano paused for a moment. He pulled a small, time-weathered, black leather box out of his coat pocket.

"Several years ago when I became CIA Director, your father went to see me at Langley one afternoon. He gave me this."

Joe Mitrano opened the box and pulled out its contents.

"This is a 1783 silver *Libertas Americana Medal*, originally conceived and ordered by Benjamin Franklin. It is the most famous of all American medals. Very few were made. This particular medal belonged to Benjamin Franklin himself. It celebrated America's victory in the Revolutionary War.

"One side of the medal depicts an infant *Hercules* in his cradle, representing a young and growing America. In his hands, he strangles two serpents representing the British armies at Saratoga in 1777, and Yorktown in 1781. Standing next to the infant is *Minerva*, the ancient Roman warrior goddess of poetry and wisdom, fending off the British Lion with its tail between its rear legs symbolizing defeat. *Minerva* is clad in breastplate and plumed helmet. She holds a spear and shield. She is defending and protecting the infant *Hercules*. Above the scene is the Latin inscription from Horace: **'NON SINE DIIS ANIMOSUS INFANS'**, translating into **'The courageous child was aided by the gods'**.

"The other side of the medal has a portrait of *Lady Liberty* with her hair flowing freely in the wind. She holds a pole topped by a pileus, the helmet like emblem of freedom.

"To me, you are the infant *Hercules*, Michael. Your parents, Olivia and Julian, are *Minerva* and the gods. Together, you all protect and defend *Lady Liberty*, America.

"This medal represents your family. I now return its ownership back to you, where it truly belongs."

Joseph Mitrano handed the gift to Michael as the SUV pulled into the driveway of the Sierra-Stansfield home.

The Cadillac came to a stop. A security man opened Michael's door.

The director smiled and said, "I wish you and Nasrin happy long lives together. You certainly deserve it. Teach that boy of yours what it means to be an American, just as your parents did for you. God bless you, Michael."

Michael Stansfield got out of the vehicle and saluted Joseph Mitrano. He held his salute until the SUV disappeared down the road. He then walked into his home.

Rebecca played and sang her favorite Coldplay song, "The Scientist", on her acoustic guitar in the sun-room. Her angelic sounds filled the home.

Michael pulled a red globe amaranth flower out of the bouquet in the hallway. He tip-toed into the sun-room and placed his right index finger over his pursed lips, indicating to Rebecca to not announce his arrival. His sister continued to play and pointed with her eyes towards the garden.

Across the terrace in the orchid house, Tomas tended to his flowers. He nursed a fragile one which had ceased to thrive. Through the glass of the 'Freedom House' and the early light of day, he saw Michael in the sun-room.

Tomas carefully placed the recovering flower back in its hold. He looked at Raul's time-keeper. The clock had remained silent. In front of his eyes, the pendulum began to swing again.

Tomas went over to the holy observer of time. He stared at the moving accountant of perpetuity. He listened to the sweet tick-tock of eternity. Tomas softly shook his head and smiled. "The gods have spoken..... *Muchacho* is home."

Michael walked through the sun-room toward his mother Olivia's favorite place on Earth. He saw Nasrin looking away, sitting among the flowers and butterflies where Michael once played as a child.

Without making his presence known, Michael entered the garden and quietly stepped up behind the sitting Nasrin. He tapped her right shoulder. She turned and faced the love of her life as he tenderly placed the red amaranth in her hair and kissed her lips.

Acknowledgements

The amaranth flower is a symbol for all things we wish eternal. A metaphor suggesting eternal honor and courage, hope, justice, and freedom. Most of all, the amaranth is an expression of everlasting love. The ancient Greeks tossed them onto the graves of their dead warriors to honor them in the afterlife and placed them on the heads of their champions as crowns to praise their victories. Poets and lovers have used the amaranth as a symbol of love throughout the centuries. The amaranth flower never fades and never dies.

I would like to thank my loving wife, Alina, for her assistance throughout the writing of my novel, *Libertas Americana*. Her thoughts, critiques, and spiritual guidance throughout the process have been essential to its development. Her undying love and support allowed me to express my mind to its fullest. She is my companion of the soul. She is my amaranth.

Selected Sources

The novel, *Libertas Americana*, is a work of speculative historical fiction. Any resemblance of characters in the novel to real persons, living or dead, is purely coincidental and not intentional.

Set in the near future, *Libertas Americana* is a cautionary tale. It presumes a further degradation in the economic and political union of Europe and America. It further presumes the development of anarchy and radical nationalistic extremist movements throughout the world, particularly in America, Russia, and Eastern and Central Europe.

The re-emergence of Fascism in Europe is not an incredible concept. The social and economic conditions exist presently to allow this distinct possibility in the future. The repercussions to the "Free-world" would be chilling, and all our "thinking minds" must focus on preventing this scourge on humanity from ever developing again.

As expressed in William Shakespeare's *The Tempest*, "What is past is prologue" seems to consistently drive the writing of history. In order to prevent the horrors of the past from repeating themselves in the future, we need to firmly understand the dynamics of history, social cultures, and human nature.

Human beings, regardless of intellect, seem to be at a peculiar disadvantage in their ability to suppress their own innate tendencies to self-destruct. We are constantly devising new ways to destroy ourselves.

Irrational political ideas seem to poison the extremist mind and often lead to the indiscriminate destruction of innocents. A middle ground in civilized cultural stability must be always sought. Radical thoughts of "change" and extremist political doctrine, whether socialist liberal or ultra-conservative, usually lead to social chaos. Prophylaxis against undesired social change begins with a full understanding of history and all of man's previous errors in the conduct of human behavior.

Like many concepts in sociology and political science, Fascism can only be fully understood by having a firm grasp of the history of Western civilization. A thorough serial review of the following timeline in European history must be performed to feel confident in understanding the potentialities of the future: the development of democracy and ancient classical Greek political philosophy, the rise and fall of the Roman and Holy Roman (German) Empires, the rise of Great Britain and France, the French Revolution and subsequent Napoleonic Wars, the rise of the German Empire in the 19th century, the First World War, Soviet Communism, the Nazi "Third Reich" in Germany, the Second World War, American Euro-protectionism, the Cold War, the fall of Soviet Communism, the formation of the European Union, and finally the "Great Economic Collapse of 2008" and Euro meltdown. Over twenty-five centuries of European history are behind the present struggles. It is a complicated multi-factorial problem.

Along with numerous internet information sites, these selected sources were instrumental in creating the novel, *Libertas Americana*.

- The Republic by Plato
- The Rage of Achilles by Terence Hawkins
- The Iliad by Homer
- The Holy Roman Empire by Friedrich Heer
- Peoples and Empires: a Short History of European Migration, Exploration, and Conquest, from Greece to the Present by Anthony Pagden
- Europe: A History by Norman Davies
- The Making of the West: Peoples and Cultures, a Concise History: Volume 1: To 1740 by Lynn Hunt, Barbara H. Rosenwein and Thomas R. Martin
- The Ottoman Centuries: The Rise and Fall of the Turkish Empire by Lord Kinross
- The Siege of Vienna: The Last Great Trial Between Cross and Crescent by John Stoye
- Napoleon by Emil Ludwig
- Napoleon Bonaparte by J.M. Thompson
- The Thin Red Line: An Eyewitness History of the Crimean War by Julian Spilsbury
- Iron Kingdom: The Rise and Downfall of Prussia, 1600-1947 by Christopher Clark
- The Guns of August by Barbara W. Tuchman
- Mein Kampf by Adolf Hitler
- The Rise and Fall of the Third Reich: A History of Nazi Germany by William L. Shirer
- The Second World War by Winston S. Churchill
- No Simple Victory: World War II in Europe, 1939-1945 by Norman Davies
- Armageddon: The Battle for Germany, 1944-1945 by Max Hastings
- Thunder in the East: The Nazi-Soviet War, 1941-1945 by Evan Mawdsley

- The Unseen War in Europe: Espionage and Conspiracy in the Second World War by John H. Waller
- The Schweinfurt-Regensburg Mission: American Raids on 17 August 1943 by Martin Middlebrook
- Diplomacy by Henry Kissinger
- The Next 100 Years: A Forecast for the 21st Century by George Friedman

www.ingramcontent.com/pod-product-compliance
Lightning Source LLC
Chambersburg PA
CBHW021122260626
47169CB00005B/1399